THE SLOW
MARCH
OF LIGHT

THE SLOW MARCH OF LIGHT

A NOVEL

Inspired by a True Story of Resilience and Hope

HEATHER B. MOORE

SHADOW
MOUNTAIN

Photo on page 311 courtesy of Bob Inama.

© 2021 Heather B. Moore

All rights reserved. No part of this book may be reproduced in any form or by any means without permission in writing from the publisher, Shadow Mountain®, at permissions@ shadowmountain.com. The views expressed herein are the responsibility of the author and do not necessarily represent the position of Shadow Mountain.

This is a work of fiction. Characters and events in this book are products of the author's imagination or are represented fictitiously.

Visit us at shadowmountain.com

Library of Congress Cataloging-in-Publication Data
CIP data on file
ISBN: 978-1-62972-928-2

Printed in the United States of America
Lake Book Manufacturing, Inc., Melrose Park, IL

10 9 8 7 6 5 4 3 2 1

Dedicated to Bob Inama,
a remarkable man who has brought
inspiration to so many

AUTHOR'S NOTE

In early 2020, Chris Schoebinger with Shadow Mountain Publishing contacted me with a story idea about a man named Bob Inama, who had recently shared details with his children about his experiences as a US soldier serving in West Germany in the early 1960s. When Chris sent over a short summary of what Bob had experienced, I knew that this story needed to be shared.

When I grew up in the 1970s and 1980s, it seemed that the animosity between the United States and the USSR had always been part of the news, and the many spy movies produced during those eras were keen to create scenarios that would grip audiences' imaginations. But Bob's story is not an ordinary spy story. It is one of a remarkable man, a humble man, who served his country, looked beyond himself, and changed lives around him.

COVID-19 was a growing force in the United States when my first meeting loomed on the horizon with Bob and his wife, Diane. So I met this extraordinary couple over a video call. Through the video call, I listened as this eighty-five-year-old man told me of his experiences, from first being drafted into the army in 1959, which waylaid all of his plans to attend law school at George Washington University, until the day he received an assignment to go undercover in East Berlin and send nuclear target information back to the US Army.

When I asked questions from my prewritten list, Bob stopped me at one point and said, "There are just some things I had to forget." As such, I have taken a respectful approach to Bob's story and experiences. He endured a lot through his many trials, and he became an inspiration in my personal life as the world around me was ravaged with a devastating pandemic that forever changed everyone's lives. Throughout Bob's life, no matter what he endured, no matter the pain, the fear, or the unknown, he faced it with hope in his heart. He treated everyone around him as if they were a family member— from his army platoon, to the German people, to the East German guards, to the Soviet soldiers and officers who reviled and abused him.

Bob walked a straight line through his life, according to his beliefs in a higher power. His humility and gratitude for his blessings, even on the darkest of days, echo religious leader Joseph B. Wirthlin, who said, "Come what may, and love it." This phrase truly embodies the way that Bob chose to live his life. Whether it was at Fort Sill in Oklahoma or at the army post in Hanau, Germany, Bob was generous and loyal, despite the fact that he was serving in the epicenter of the Cold War, where one wrong move from either side of the heavily guarded West/East German inner border could have resulted in the next devastating world war.

Following WWII, the European continent was suffering from immeasurable economic destruction, in addition to the travesty of millions of lives lost. What followed should have been the rebuilding of nations and peoples, but instead, the contest over power continued. The United States and the Soviet Union came out on top as the superpowers of the world, and they were not friends in the proverbial sandbox.

Germany was sharply divided, the west from the east, and the Allied forces of Britain, France, and the United States had subdivided West Germany. Joseph Stalin and the Soviet Union took over the east, slowly integrating the ideals of Marxism and Leninism into a society that had already been living in fear and control for decades beneath the Nazi regime.

The city of Berlin became a political hotspot even before WWII was over, and none of the Allies would agree to give up their portion. Therefore, inside East Germany sat the quadruple-occupied city of Berlin, with Britain, France, and the United States inhabiting sectors in West Berlin, and the USSR occupying all of East Berlin. In this way, the western portion of the city was like its own "island of democratic administration and market economy in a Communist landscape" (Funder 2002, 160). The western powers focused on establishing "a federated system of states, the division of political, administrative and judicial power, and guarantees of private property. In 1948 they handed over these institutions to the newly created Federal Republic of Germany (West Germany) together with massive injections of funds from the Americans' Marshall Plan" (Funder 2002, 160).

In contrast, the Soviets governed East Germany until they established the German Democratic Republic (GDR) in 1949—which was considered a satellite state of the USSR. This meant that East Germany was under USSR military control, politically and economically. Because of the communist ideals the USSR operated on, East Germany "production was nationalized, factories and property turned over to the state, health care, rent and food were subsidized. One-party rule was established with an all-powerful secret service to back it up. And the Soviets, having refused the offer of American capital, plundered East German production for themselves" (Funder 2002, 161).

In 1961, Soviet premier Nikita Khrushchev authorized the construction of the Berlin Wall. This wall was erected with barbed wire overnight in the early hours of Sunday, August 13. The Berlin Wall officially divided Berlin citizens from their friends, families, and colleagues, as well as from the rest of the world. Over the next months, the wall was fortified by 32,000 East Germans who installed materials that had been collected far in advance. According to Frederick Baker, the first phase was a simple construction of barbed wire, cobblestone, and wooden posts. Sections of concrete were soon added as reinforcements. Homes and buildings that were on the border were bulldozed in order to prevent escapees sneaking through buildings and arriving in West Berlin on the other side (see Baker 1993).

The second phase of the wall consisted of concrete walls, pipe laid on top, and 260 guard towers. Other features such as embedded flares, trip wires, and attack dogs were also implemented. A final prevention measure included five-inch spikes "designed to impale the feet or bodies of any who attempted to jump from the top of the wall" (*The Berlin Wall* 2015, 46).

The year of 1976 brought on the final phase of the wall, in which the concrete barriers were strengthened. And finally, in May 1982, the order to shoot any escapees was officially added to the GDR constitution.

Most Germans weren't happy with the dividing wall in Berlin, and there are many stories of East Germans escaping, but there are also lesser-known stories of the West Germans who put their own lives and well-being on the line to aid those escapees. West German citizens such as Michael Hinze collected passports to smuggle to East Berliners. "We had no trouble getting hold of the papers," wrote one participant. "People were more than willing to help others get out of [East Berlin]" (Funder 2002, 209). Tunneling was another way that facilitated escapes, but "only around 300 people escaped over the course of nearly 30 years through tunnels that took months to dig and were, more often than not, discovered before being employed for their intended purpose" (Aguirre 2014). Tunnels were dug from both sides of the wall, and a group of West German students began to tunnel, "beginning in a derelict bakery in the West and burrowing underneath more than the length of a football field. The passage later became known as Tunnel 57. During the two days it operated, it was the single most successful escape in the history of the Berlin Wall" (Aguirre 2014).

Unfortunately, at least 171 people were killed while trying to escape over or under the Berlin Wall. "From 1961 until the wall came down in 1989, more than 5,000 East Germans (including some 600 border guards) managed to cross the border by jumping out of windows adjacent to the wall, climbing over the barbed wire, flying in hot air balloons, crawling through the sewers and driving through unfortified parts of the wall at high speeds" (History.com editors 2019).

In all, the Cold War persisted for forty-five years, crumbling in 1989 when the Berlin Wall came down on November 9 and finally disintegrating in 1990 when West Germany and East Germany reunified into a single country.

HISTORICAL TIMELINE

May 20, 1935:	Albert (Bob) R. Inama is born in Nampa, Idaho.
December 7, 1941:	Japan bombs Pearl Harbor.
December 8, 1941:	The United States declares war on Japan, officially entering World War II.
December 11–13, 1941:	Nazi Germany and its Axis partners declare war on the United States.
February 4–11, 1945:	The Cold War begins with the Yalta Conference meeting of Roosevelt, Churchill, and Stalin. The Soviet Union is granted control of Eastern Europe.
May 7–9, 1945:	Germany surrenders.
July 17–August 2, 1945:	Potsdam Conference—Germany is officially partitioned into four zones of occupation, and the city of Berlin is also divided into four zones.
August 6, 1945:	The United States drops an atomic bomb on Hiroshima, killing 80,000 instantly.
August 8, 1945:	The Soviet Union declares war on Japan and invades Manchuria.
August 9, 1945:	The United States drops an atomic bomb on Nagasaki, killing 40,000 instantly.
September 2, 1945:	Japan formally surrenders, ending World War II.
March 5, 1946:	Winston Churchill delivers his "Sinews of Peace" speech against the Soviet Union and the Iron Curtain.
April 3, 1948:	The Marshall Plan is signed by President Harry S. Truman, setting a precedent for helping countries combat poverty, disease, and malnutrition.
June 24, 1948:	The Berlin Blockade begins, lasting eleven months.
August 29, 1949:	The Soviet Union tests its first atomic bomb.
January 20, 1950:	Truman approves H-bomb development.

June 24, 1950:   The Korean War begins. Stalin provides weapons to North Korea.

March 17–June 4, 1953:   A series of eleven atomic weapons are tested at the Nevada Test Site.

July 27, 1953:   The Korean War ends.

May 14, 1955:   The Warsaw Pact is formed as a mutual defense treaty between the Soviet Union and satellite nations to counter the NATO alliance.

November 1, 1955:   The Vietnam conflict begins.

1955–1957:   Bob Inama serves a volunteer church mission to the East Central states.

October 29, 1956:   The Suez crisis begins with Israeli attack against Egyptian forces in the Sinai.

September 1957:   Bob Inama returns to Utah State University to pursue a prelaw degree.

November 1958:   Soviet leader Khrushchev demands the withdrawal of troops from Berlin.

January 1959:   Cuba is taken over by Fidel Castro.

December 1959:   Bob Inama receives a draft letter from US President Dwight D. Eisenhower.

February 13, 1960:   France tests its first nuclear bomb.

February 1960:   Bob Inama heads to basic training at Fort Ord in California.

May 1, 1960:   A United States U-2 spy plane is shot down over Soviet territory.

May 1960:   Bob Inama is assigned to the Artillery Fire Direction Center at Fort Sill, near Lawton, Oklahoma.

August 1960:   Bob Inama is assigned to Headquarters Company 75th Field Artillery in Hanau, Germany.

August 13, 1961:   The Berlin inner border is closed, and construction of the Berlin Wall begins.

HISTORICAL TIMELINE

October 16–28, 1962:	Cuban Missile Crisis
October 16, 1964:	China tests its first nuclear bomb.
April 1970:	Richard Nixon extends the Vietnam War to Cambodia.
October 1973:	Egypt and Syria attack Israel; Egypt requests Soviet aid.
April 30, 1975:	The Vietnam War ends.
December 1979:	Soviet forces invade Afghanistan.
March 1985:	Mikhail Gorbachev becomes a leader in the Soviet Union.
October 1987:	President Reagan and Gorbachev resolve to remove all intermediate nuclear missiles from Europe.
November 9, 1989:	The Berlin Wall is demolished.
October 3, 1990:	West Germany and East Germany reunite to become one nation.

CHARACTER CHART

HISTORICAL FIGURES

Adolf (real name unknown)

Dr. Hugh Bennion

Albert C. Inama (Bob's father)

Blanche Inama (Bob's mother)

Bob Inama

David Inama (Bob's cousin)

Diane Inama (Bob's wife)

Giuseppe Inama (Bob's grandfather)

Margaret Inama (Bob's sister)

Marie Inama (Bob's grandmother)

Tom Komori (name has been changed)

Major Nelson (name has been changed)

Professor Schmitt

Johannes Stumm

Susan (name has been changed)

Major Taggett

FICTIONAL CHARACTERS

Adel

Mrs. Beck

Mrs. Belding

Nurse Bevin

Officer Braun

Charlotte

Curt

Erika

Franz Fischer

Sonja Fischer

Dr. Greer

Greta

Mrs. Herrmann

Jonas

David Jones

Josh

Karl

Hans Keller

CHARACTER CHART

Mona Keller

Mrs. Klein

Mrs. Lange

Mr. Leon

Rick Murdock

Mr. and Mrs.
Neumann

Oma

Opa

Mr. Roth

Luisa Voigt

Officer Voigt

Mr. and Mrs. Wagner

Mrs. Weber

Soviet Officer 1

Soviet Officer 2

Dr. Stoddard

Map of Germany with boundaries of the Soviet zone, British zone, French zone, and American zone, as established after World War II. July 28, 1953. US Congress, Archive of Americana.

CHAPTER ONE

"We are all enlisted till the conflict is o'er;
Happy are we! Happy are we!
Soldiers in the army, there's a bright crown in store;
We shall win and wear it by and by.
Haste to the battle, quick to the field;
Truth is our helmet, buckler, and shield.
Stand by our colors; proudly they wave!
We're joyfully, joyfully marching to our home."

—Anonymous (text) and William Bradbury (music),
"We Are All Enlisted," 1866

IDAHO
DECEMBER 1959

The words from the hymn "We Are All Enlisted" echoed in Bob's mind as he drove through the gray afternoon that promised snow. "Haste to the battle," he hummed, possibly off tune, "quick to the field . . ."

The hymn had been sung at a church service Bob had attended with a friend before heading back to Utah State University. He'd never heard the song before, and he didn't know why he couldn't get the lyrics out of his mind now. "Truth is our helmet, buckler, and shield." It wasn't like he'd ever been inclined toward military service since he already had a career path in mind, although he could say he was a proud citizen of his country.

1

Fiddling with the radio, Bob realized he was on a stretch of Idaho road that delivered only garbled static. Silence reigned again, and he reconciled himself to his own thoughts as flakes of snow began to drift from the sky, landing haphazardly on his Ford Fairlane's windshield.

Christmas had come and gone, and he'd enjoyed the break with his family in Twin Falls, Idaho. But now it was time to get back to reality. After changing his major more than once, from civil engineering to accounting and then to a double major of prelaw and economics, Bob felt content about his most recent choice. At twenty-four, he was behind many other college students in the nation, but that was because of the time he spent a few years ago as a missionary for his church.

Bob couldn't help the smile stealing onto his face now. He'd been accepted to some of the most prestigious law schools in the country, including the University of California, Berkeley; the University of Chicago; George Washington University; and Harvard. His life was on the fast track now. One more semester at Utah State would be followed by a summer internship at the US Department of Justice.

"Law school, here I come," he said to the falling snow that fell faster and faster now. Bob switched on the wipers, and the rhythmic swiping created a hollow sound—almost lonely.

He didn't mind the moments of loneliness that sometimes crept over him. It was easy enough to push away with his classes, his papers to be written, his volunteer hours at church, and writing letters to keep in touch with his family.

He had friends too, no one particularly close though. No current sweetheart. Susan was in the past and had been there for quite a while. They'd planned to get married shortly after she finished school, but Bob had committed to volunteer as a missionary, requiring him to head back east . . . Susan hadn't wasted much time before sending a letter and ending things. He had dated off and on since Susan, but nothing had stuck with any other woman. Perhaps it was because Susan had hurt him more than he cared to admit.

Or perhaps he felt that a serious relationship could come later, when he was through with school. Besides, studying law took most of his focus.

Bob drummed his fingers on the steering wheel as he neared the Logan exit. Not too far up the canyon sat the quaint, bricked buildings of Utah State. The temperatures could be fierce in the winter this high up in altitude, but he loved the mountain air.

Continuously falling snow collected on the road, slowing his progress. The setting sun and dropping temperatures put him more on alert. Why the drive through the canyon felt different somehow, he couldn't explain. Perhaps it was because so many changes were on the horizon—the product of years of hard work. He'd finally be on his way to becoming a government lawyer. He hoped to stay in Washington, DC, among the country's history. He wanted to excel, to make a mark in the world, to see how far he could go.

By the time he parked in front of the house where he rented a room, he was already thinking of tomorrow's classes and workload. Christmas break was over, and it was time to get back to work. The snow had lightened to large, lazy flakes, which promised to completely cover the entire university campus by morning.

He made a dash to the house and retrieved the mail that had been left for him. There was already a letter from his older sister, Margaret, which made him smile. She must have written it soon after she'd left their parents' home after Christmas.

She always asked about his progress in school. Margaret and their parents were pleased with the internship he'd secured. His parents were both hard-working and practical. His mother wasn't the affectionate sort, but she was generous and cared for others in her own way.

"You're too thin, Bob," she'd say. "Are you eating enough at your university?"

Probably not. He ate once a day in the cafeteria at school. Yet he wasn't all that slender. His six-foot build rivaled that of any of his college friends. He'd always been a good runner and could have played football and participated in track in high school, but instead, his parents had urged him to work at the 7UP bottling plant.

Bob sorted through the mail as he walked into the quiet kitchen of the home. The family he rented a room from said they would be back the next day, so he had the place to himself for the night. He paused next to the table when he saw an official-looking letter from the US government—the president, more accurately.

Had he received an official congratulations letter about his internship with the Justice Department? Or maybe this was protocol for his acceptance into George Washington University?

Bob settled onto the kitchen chair and carefully opened the letter, assuming it would become a keepsake.

> To: Albert R. Inama
> Salutations,
> Greetings from the President of the United States and
> Friends.

The smile on Bob's face dimmed as the next words leapt off the page. The letter was not the congratulations he'd suspected. No, the letter was an official order. Albert R. Inama had just been drafted into the US Army.

Basic training would start in February at Ford Ord in California.

The letter from his sister forgotten, and all other pieces of mail now inconsequential, Bob read through the draft notice a second time. And then a third. The words were all still there. They hadn't changed. He hadn't awakened from a strange dream.

He didn't need to speak to his parents or a professor to know that turning down the draft wasn't an option. Not if he wanted to retain any moral character throughout the remainder of his life.

But as he stared at the letter, the words began to blur as the realization settled like a stone in his stomach. All of his plans would have to be put on hold. The coveted internship, the acceptance at George Washington University. His breath stalled. The current semester at Utah State.

What about the professors who'd taken him under their wings? What about his tuition, his room rent . . . his family?

The letter from his sister seemed to mock him now. Writing to a brother living one state away to attend college was a far cry from writing to a brother at an army post. Who knew where he'd end up?

Something wrenched hard in his chest, and the disbelief and shock were replaced by doubts. He was almost a law student. He'd hunted as a kid—pheasants with a shotgun when he was fourteen, and deer with a rifle at sixteen. But he was no soldier.

Bob dropped his head into his hands as his future plans slowly splintered out of reach. He knew a couple of guys who'd been drafted, sure. One had failed the physical examination and hadn't been inducted after all. Bob knew that wouldn't be the case with him. He'd pass. And he'd be hundreds of miles away come February.

Two years. He'd be in the service for two years. Minimum.

Slowly, he stood from the table and crossed to the phone at the edge of the kitchen counter. He'd told his mom he'd call to report his safe arrival, although the news would be much different now.

"Hello?" she answered on the third ring.

"I'm back in Logan," he said.

"Oh, that's good to hear." The relief was plain in her voice, although he'd made the drive many, many times. "How was the drive?" she continued. "Did you run into snow?"

The conversation was so ordinary, and he hated to change that. "It's still snowing, but the Fairlane did well."

He could almost hear his mom's smile. She loved that his car was a cheerful yellow and white. Another thing he would miss. Before his mom could ask about his stay with his friend who he'd gone to church with that day, he said, "Can you bring Dad to the phone? I need to tell you both something."

CHAPTER TWO

"I, _____, do solemnly swear (or affirm) that I will support and defend the Constitution of the United States against all enemies, foreign and domestic; that I will bear true faith and allegiance to the same; and that I will obey the orders of the President of the United States and the orders of the officers appointed over me, according to regulations and the Uniform Code of Military Justice. So help me God."

—"Oath of Enlistment," Title 10, US Code

FORT SILL, OKLAHOMA
US ARMY FIELD ARTILLERY CENTER
MAY 1960

Bob opened his eyes to the pale light of dawn slowly pushing aside the deeper gray of the barracks. Morning seemed to come earlier every day, especially since he'd made a habit of setting his alarm for five, an hour before everyone else woke up. He loved the quiet of the early morning and time to spend with his own thoughts before the day consumed him.

This morning, instead of rising and setting about his tasks, Bob slipped out from beneath his pillow a couple of recent letters from his family. One letter was from his sister, and the other, from his parents. He reread them, imagining the events taking place at home—simple things that he hadn't fully appreciated at the time. Family meals. Margaret teasing him. His mother's soft smile.

Bob tucked the letters back into place, then said a quick prayer in his heart for his family that all would be well. Then he gazed up at the rectangle pattern of light coming in through the blinds. The light would shift slowly with the movement of the sun, but for now, it seemed suspended in time. It was hard to believe it was the middle of May, and he'd been a soldier for over three months.

Following eight weeks of basic training at Fort Ord in California, turning his body into a formidable force, Bob had been reassigned to Fort Sill to train in field artillery. He'd stayed open minded, determined to excel wherever he was assigned. He didn't plan on volunteering for anything though. After a conversation back at his university, a couple of the men in the National Guard at his church had told him to never volunteer for anything—to do his duty and only his duty. Bob had stuck to that advice so far.

"Up with the birds again, Inama?"

Bob glanced at the bed next to his. Tom Komori was grinning.

"It's too early to smile," Bob said, but he smiled anyway.

"Well, it's going to be a good day," Komori pronounced, his dark-brown eyes full of amusement.

One of the other soldiers in a nearby bed grumbled, "Keep it down. Some of us are still sleeping."

Komori smirked. In the two short weeks that Bob had been here, he already felt like he and Komori were close friends. Unlike Bob, Komori came from a military family. His father had been a decorated Japanese-American soldier in World War II. There was no need for Komori to be drafted. He had enlisted while attending the University of California. As a third-generation Japanese American, Komori served his country with pride, with a smile on his face.

Various watch alarms went off in the barracks, a cacophony of melodies completely out of harmony. Bob slipped on his military glasses—or at least that's what he called them. He wasn't allowed to wear glasses made out of glass, and these plastic ones were black, horn-rimmed.

By 7:00 a.m. the barracks were spotless—including the latrines and common area—the beds were flawlessly made, and everyone had assembled in formation for head count, where the first sergeant announced the day's training. Firing range, then a demonstration of a 105mm howitzer, and finally Bob would section off to the Fire Direction Center. After breakfast, the unit headed for drill, which consisted of an hour of marching.

Komori sat by Bob on the bus that took them out to the firing range. They passed by the two stately stone buildings named after World War II vets, McNair Hall and Searby Hall.

Leaving the main post, the bus drove past wide expanses of field, passing the artillery trainees practicing using radar to track targets. Soon, the bus reached the firing range. At Fort Ord in California, Bob had become proficient with the M1 rifle, the carbine pistol, and the 50-caliber machine gun, which had a maximum range of 8,100 yards. Perhaps he could thank his youth scouting for giving him his first taste of marksmanship and his growing up in Idaho hunting pheasant and deer.

"Ready?" Komori said as they headed off the bus. "You going to show off again?"

"If hitting the target means showing off, I guess I am." Bob kept a straight face, but Komori laughed.

"Then it will be a good day," Komori said. "And a good night. Don't forget you promised to go into downtown Lawton with me."

Bob nodded. He had promised. It was Friday, and his battery didn't have night training. The downtown area of Lawton was where the soldiers would spend their off-hours. Restaurants, shops, and a movie theater . . . Lawton had it all. He didn't always join a group when he went off-post. He was more likely to catch a bus and do some sightseeing on his own.

After the firing range, where Bob had hit every target dead center, the unit headed out to watch a demonstration of a 105mm howitzer. The bus took them to a field with a wall of trees. Tucked against the trees, the 105mm howitzer was large, even from a distance, its 2.5-ton weight making it an impressive force.

The howitzer was fired in a series of three tests—dawn, day, and night. Bob's unit was observing the daytime test. The bus stopped, and the soldiers unloaded. They stood in formation as they watched the loading of the 105mm. It required a crew of eight to operate.

"There are thousands of these out there, if you can believe it," Komori said. "Dozens of countries own them, since they're accurate and powerful. I hear they have the 280mm in West Germany. You know, what they call the atomic cannon."

"West Germany, huh?" Bob said. The center of the Cold War. Where Germany had been defeated by the Allies in World War II and then divided up by the victors—France, England, the United States, and the Soviet Union. There was not an active war in Germany, but the political tensions there were part of the news every day. It was said that one false move by either a West German or an East German could set off World War III.

A shiver passed through Bob even though the May day was plenty warm. A couple of weeks ago, on May 1, the Soviet Union had shot down an American U-2 spy plane. The pilot, Francis Gary Powers, had disappeared. At first President Eisenhower claimed that it was a weather plane that had gone off course. But then Soviet leader Khrushchev revealed the wreckage of the U-2 as well as a picture of the pilot, who was alive and now a political prisoner of war. On May 11, a chagrined Eisenhower was forced to admit that the United States had indeed sent a spy plane over Soviet territory.

Tensions had only escalated between the two superpower leaders when Eisenhower refused to back down on future plans for spy flights right before the Paris Summit. Khrushchev and his delegation left the summit before talks had even started. And Powers was sentenced to three years in prison and seven more years of hard labor.

In this moment, as Bob stood watching soldiers load the 105mm, he understood both the necessity of such a weapon—since another superpower was intent on dominance—and the measures of protection that his government had taken to ensure peace. The men surrounding him had all dedicated their lives at the risk of losing all else.

Bob stood a little straighter, a little taller, and when the gun fired with its double recoil, he felt more a part of his unit than he ever had before. The soldiers remained absolutely silent. As the sound ricocheted through the air, Bob felt the same ricochet straight to his heart. The men around him had all made the same oath, the same promise, the same sworn allegiance. *I will support and defend the Constitution of the United States against all enemies, foreign and domestic. I will bear true faith and allegiance to the same. I will obey the orders of the President of the United States and the orders of the officers appointed over me, according to regulations and the Uniform Code of Military Justice. So help me God.*

The cannon struck an old army tank, and the explosion burst through the air in a mass of fire and smoke. Bob watched the flames climb into the sky, then recede. He felt sufficiently sobered, and as they loaded onto the bus to head back to the main campus for lunch at the mess hall, he said very little.

Komori seemed to sense his mood and draped his arms over the seatback in front of them and chatted with a couple of other men.

Following lunch and another hour of marching, Bob prepared to spend the rest of the afternoon at the Fire Direction Center, while Komori left with the unit that would return and practice firing 105mm howitzers.

Bob made his way to the deuce-and-a-half-ton covered truck that was set up as an operation center. Inside the truck, desks had been covered with maps containing the location plotting for targets.

"You're late, Inama," Olander said. He was from another unit. Five of them total worked in this small space, radioing the information to their own batteries.

"I'm five minutes early," Bob said, and Olander laughed.

"What's so funny?" another soldier asked as he stepped inside.

And so the conversation went, but Bob was no longer paying attention. His radio came to life, and the coordinates of the weapons were called in. He measured how far the target was from the coordinate. Then he calculated the amount of gunpowder needed to reach that target, according to elevation, after doing a quick check in one of the military books that listed distance versus elevation versus how much gunpowder the howitzer needed.

He'd taken to the plotting easier than he thought he would, and he enjoyed figuring out the calculations. Most of them he did in his head, but he always double-checked them.

When Bob finished his assignment, he found Komori waiting for him at the barracks. "We're skipping dinner."

"We are? Bed check's at 11:00," Bob said, observing that Komori was looking entirely too pleased with himself.

"Don't worry." Komori had already changed into civilian clothing, the red of his shirt offsetting the black of his hair. "We'll be back in time."

The grin on his face made Bob doubt Komori's promise, but he changed quickly, ignoring the protesting of his stomach. His sleep was on the clock, and so were his eating expectations.

As they walked along the road toward Lawton, it was clear that other soldiers from the post had the same idea. Bob recognized quite a few of those walking around, even though he didn't know names yet.

Komori slowed in front of a restaurant window, and Bob joined him to look through the glass. Inside, the place appeared nice, with lace tablecloths and everything.

"Let's go in," Komori said. "Lace tablecloths must mean the food is good."

Bob laughed but walked with Komori to the door. A sign by the hostess stand read: *No Coloreds Allowed*.

Bob wasn't too surprised. As a missionary he'd spent time in Kentucky and Tennessee and had seen those signs there, warning the "coloreds" away from certain establishments. The good news was that Eisenhower had signed another Civil Rights Act into law earlier that year, which was intended to reinforce racial equality. Progress was being made, or so Bob thought.

The hostess stepped away from the stand, and Bob assumed she needed to check on something, but then she didn't return right away. Instead, a man in a button-down white shirt came out of the back serving area. Bob wondered if he was replacing the hostess, although the man's face was flushed a tinny pink.

"What's gotten into your scrawny head, boy?" the man practically yelled, his deep-set blue eyes flashing at Komori. "Your kind's not welcomed here. Can't you read? Or does it have to be in Chinese?"

Bob stared at the man, disbelief settling like greasy meat in his stomach. "Sir, I think you—"

"You with this Chinaman?" The man's vehemence swung from Komori to Bob.

"I'm Japanese American," Komori said.

"Japanese! Chinese!" the man sneered. "I don't care *what* you are. Read the sign! No coloreds allowed, and *you* are a colored."

The twisting in Bob's gut rose to his chest, then clawed up his throat in heated anger. He knew, as a representative of the US Army, he shouldn't slam his fist into the man's jaw. But Bob wasn't entirely capable of standing down either. "Look here," he said in a low voice, moving between Komori and the man. "We're US soldiers from—"

"I don't give a rat's tail who you are," the man hissed. "Get. Out. Of. My. Restaurant."

"Inama," Komori said in a clipped tone from behind Bob. "Let's go."

Bob's breath rushed from his chest, and he turned to look at his friend. Komori's forehead was lined with determination, and his hands were clenched at his sides.

"It's not fair—" Bob began.

"Let's go," Komori repeated. "We're done here."

Bob knew it was probably the safer decision, but he wavered. When Komori opened the door and left the restaurant, Bob's hands throbbed and his pulse raced, but he followed after his friend. He wanted to punch something. Put his hand through the restaurant window. Something. Anything.

He had to hurry to catch up with Komori.

"I'm sorry," Bob said as soon as he was beside Komori. "That man was scum—"

Komori lifted a hand to stop Bob's apology. "There are scum everywhere. Forget about it. I know I will."

Yet Bob doubted. He'd heard the rasp in Komori's voice and noticed his eyes were red with unshed tears.

"I'm never going back to the place again," Bob added.

Komori gave a satisfied nod. And for once, he was the quiet one as they walked back to the post.

It was nearly two days before Komori was back to his smiling, teasing self. But Bob couldn't shake the frustration he still felt. On one level, he knew that there was injustice throughout the entire world, and that extended to the smallest corner in the smallest town. Yet, day after day, Bob watched Tom Komori give his all for the country he loved and revered. A person like that deserved respect—everywhere and always.

Bob knew there was little chance their next assignments would put them in the same location, but he hoped that he and Komori could remain friends.

Weeks later, Bob was preparing to do the target coordinating at the Fire Direction Center for the nighttime artillery shooting when the unit leader told him he was being summoned to the major's office.

Bob hurried to the office, anxious to hear what Major Nelson wanted yet not wanting to miss the night training either. Bob tapped on the door, and when the major asked him to enter, he walked in, saluted, then took a seat.

Major Nelson took up most of the room behind his desk. Bob was pretty sure Nelson's arms were as thick as tree stumps and that he could out bench-press anyone at the post. Bob guessed him to be about thirty years old. For a moment, Bob wondered if this Southern-speaking major with his dark skin had ever had problems like Komori had in town.

"We have your assignment, Inama," Major Nelson said, cutting into Bob's thoughts.

He knew he'd be reassigned soon, but this felt fast and sudden, even though some of the guys in his unit had received their assignments already.

Major Nelson didn't waste another second. "You'll be reporting to Hanau, Germany, to the headquarters of the Co. 75th Field Artillery of the 7th Army."

Germany. *West Germany.* The epicenter of the Cold War. The major continued to give a few details, but Bob's mind was racing. He was going overseas. To a country where he was already familiar with the language. He'd taken German in college for a few years, but it was impossible to get fluent through textbooks and a handful of classes.

He released a careful breath, turning over the idea in his mind. He was nervous, certainly, but excitement whispered through him all the same. He'd never traveled out of the country before. What would it be like? he wondered. Perhaps being in someplace like Germany would be enjoyable enough to make the next couple of years speed by.

Then Major Nelson spoke, pulling Bob back to the present moment. "You might want to call your folks in case they want to come visit you before you leave for Germany."

CHAPTER THREE

"As [Francis Gary] Powers flew over Sverdlovsk (present-day Yekaterinburg, Russia), a Soviet surface-to-air missile exploded near his plane, causing it to drop to a lower altitude. A second missile scored a direct hit, and Powers and his aircraft began to plummet from the sky. The pilot managed to bail out, but when his parachute floated to earth, he was surrounded by Soviet forces. Powers landed in the center of a major diplomatic crisis."

—U-2 Spy Incident, May 1, 1960

FRANKFURT, WEST GERMANY
AUGUST 1960

Luisa Voigt held back a furtive smile as she spotted her father, a police officer in Frankfurt, slip into the back of the room. When others in the room noticed *der Polizist* at the back, a few eyes widened. Her father seemed pleased to be at her graduation, although those near him would never guess that his stern expression—with his blue-gray eyes, dark brows, and thick mustache—was pleasant . . . but it was. For him.

It had taken Luisa longer to graduate, at the age of twenty-three, from the nursing program than most in her class because of her mother's death two years before. Luisa wanted to believe her mother was there in spirit. Luisa touched the pendant necklace that hung beneath her blouse. The oval pendant a white background and painted flowers had been her mother's—and passed onto Luisa on her sixteenth birthday.

Luisa nervously wiped her hands over her pressed navy skirt. She didn't have a new dress for graduation like the other women in her class but instead wore an old skirt of her mother's.

"Luisa Voigt," the university president said. "*Glückwünsche.*"

She nearly sprang out of her seat, and with her heart thumping a rapid rhythm to the clapping, she strode to the president. His smile was genuine, if a bit worn, and she thanked him and shook his hand.

She'd done it. She'd finished. Now that she could work as a nurse, she planned to pay back some of the tuition money to her father. Luisa cast a glance at her father on the way back to her seat. But he was gone. Had he been there when her name was called? A slow weight crept onto her shoulders, but she tried to shrug it off. Her father had come, and that was something she could be pleased with.

"*Herzlichen Glückwünsche,*" the young woman in the seat next to her whispered.

Luisa looked over at Sonja Fischer. Her yellow skirt perfectly complemented her yellow-and-white blouse, which was added to by a gold brooch that gleamed in the overhead lights. "Congratulations to you, too."

Sonja grinned. Her blond hair and round face reminded Luisa of one of those famous cherubs. Pretty, young, and fresh. It was impossible for Luisa to feel melancholy around Sonja. Her lightheartedness was contagious.

Everyone started clapping again, signaling the end of the ceremony. The women around Luisa stood and cheered. Her heart soared at that sound, and excitement buzzed through her. They'd done it. *She'd* done it. Life was about to begin.

"Are you coming to my church social tonight?" Sonja's dark-blue eyes flashed with eagerness.

"Aren't you going to celebrate with your family?" Luisa asked.

Her friend looked heavenward as if she couldn't believe Luisa would ask such a question. When her blue gaze landed on Luisa again, there was laughter in her eyes. "Dinner with my family will be over in twenty minutes. My brothers will argue about politics, my mother will reprimand them, my father will order them to stop, and everyone will forget me as quick as that."

Luisa smiled, but inside, a wistfulness grew. As an only child, she'd never experienced the affectionate chaos that Sonja described. Luisa's gaze cut to the back of the room where her father had been standing. He was probably well on his way to work right now, and Luisa would be facing an empty house all evening.

"I'll come," she told Sonja. From time to time, she went to the socials at Sonja's church, and sometimes even the services.

Her friend grasped her hand and squeezed. "We'll pick you up. My brother will drive us."

"All right," Luisa said, and before she could ask what time, Sonja was surrounded by two other school friends.

Everyone congratulated each other, and then the picture taking started. Luisa was included in one with Sonja and a few friends, but then Luisa slipped out and began the walk to catch a tram home.

The sun had nearly set by the time she reached her neighborhood. Lights had winked on inside of homes, and every few steps she'd catch the aroma of someone's dinner cooking. She was hungry, too, she realized, and she'd likely be eating more leftover stew that she'd made earlier in the week. Luisa wasn't an excellent cook like her mother had been, but she'd made an effort so that her father would feel cared for.

She opened the wooden gate separating the front yard from the street. The stone walkway leading to the house was cracked and stuffed with stubborn weeds. Bypassing the neglected yard, Luisa unlocked the front door and stepped inside the cool interior. Her mother's slippers were next to the door where her father set them every evening. Every morning, he switched them out for her heeled shoes. It had been his routine since the day she'd passed away, and somehow it brought them both comfort. As if her mother were still nearby, present in their lives.

After turning on a light, Luisa made her way into the kitchen. Her mother's influence was preserved in the well-worn kitchen table, the blue dishes in the cupboards, and the yellow pots and pans. Luisa remembered the day her mother found them at a bargain sale.

Luisa used one of the pots to warm up a bit of spaetzle. Then she noticed two cards in the center of the table. Picking them up, she immediately recognized her father's handwriting on one. The other had her grandmother's. Curious, she opened her father's envelope quickly.

> *Luisa,*
>
> *You have accomplished a great deal, and I am proud of you.*
> *Congratulations on your graduation.*
>
> *Father*

Her father was not an expressive man, but his words were sincere. And for him, this was his way of reaching out more than usual. She carefully tucked the note into its envelope, then opened her grandmother's. Luisa smiled as she read, teary eyed. Her oma lived in East Berlin and had refused to move despite repeated attempts by Luisa's mother to convince her. The last time Luisa had seen Oma was at her mother's funeral.

Luisa remembered her father speaking with Oma about moving out of East Berlin. But Oma had declared her husband and her son were both buried in East Berlin, so that's where she would stay.

Luisa knew that Oma had long felt betrayed by Luisa's mother, who had left home at eighteen, then met her husband and never returned to East Berlin. Marriage, the war, and other complications had always been an excuse. But Oma had not been happy about it.

She set down both cards and gave the spaetzle a good stir, then dished it into a bowl. The pasta smelled heavenly. Luisa sat at the table to eat—alone. She was used to eating alone. Used to traveling to school and back alone. She spent most of her nights alone while her father was on shift. It had been the way of things in her life for two years now. She should be used to it, used to her mother's absence and used to the stillness. But in the quietest moments, she felt empty like a washed-out cooking pot.

Tonight at least, she'd be going to a social, and that motivated her to quickly clean up after her meal, then head to her bedroom to decide what to wear. By the time Sonja's brother honked the car horn outside, Luisa had applied her lipstick, combed through her honey-blond curls, and slipped on her shoes. On her way out, she snatched a cardigan that hung between two heavier jackets on a rack by the front door. Moments later, she settled into the back seat of a Volkswagen.

Sonja's brother, Franz, grinned back at her. "I hear congratulations are in order."

"Yes, thank you," she said.

Franz was blond like his sister, with the same rounded features. He had a sweetheart in their church group, and so he never missed a social. Luisa wouldn't be surprised if the two became engaged soon.

Sonja nearly bounced in the front seat as she rattled off the news of who would be at the church social. Luisa always marveled how Sonja kept up with everyone and everything.

" . . . and Beatrice said an American soldier came to church last week, and so he might be at the social, too."

Luisa was used to Sonja's overexcitement about soldiers, especially American ones. But as her friend talked, Luisa trained her gaze on the window and the passing homes. The lighted windows flashed by, and she saw snippets of family dinners. She supposed that someday she might marry, and she hoped to have a family of her own. She wanted more than one child so that child wouldn't grow up alone like her.

"Now you can practice your English on someone else, sister," Franz said, drawing Luisa's attention.

"I'm not as good as Luisa, but I'm getting better," Sonja said. "Listen to this."

When she repeated the phrase in English, Luisa couldn't help but laugh at the "v" sound that she used in the place of "th." "Your words are right," Luisa said. "But you need to practice your accent. The word is 'this,' not 'vis.'"

For the next few moments, Sonja regaled them with various forms of the "th" sound until Franz finally said, "If you don't stop, I'm dropping you off at the next corner."

Sonja scoffed. "Then I'll tell Charlotte that you sleepwalk."

Franz shot his sister a glare. "You wouldn't dare."

Sonja laughed, and the siblings continued to banter the rest of the drive. Luisa smiled at their conversation, but it only made the ache in her chest grow wider. She'd always wished she had a sibling.

When Franz pulled up in front of the church building, he let out a low whistle. "Quite a crowd tonight. I wonder why. Maybe they're serving a full meal?"

"It's the American soldiers that draw the attention," Sonja said.

"Ah, so if I change into one of their uniforms, I'll be surrounded too?" Franz teased.

Sonja huffed a sigh then looked back at Luisa and winked. "Ready to practice our English?"

Luisa smiled and climbed out of the back seat of the car. "I'll leave it to you."

Franz was already ahead of them and had disappeared into the building, probably searching out Charlotte.

"Ah, come on. Surely your father hasn't forbidden you to talk to an American soldier," Sonja said with a pout.

"No, that's true," Luisa conceded. "He speaks about them as if they're dirt under his feet. And I can only guess what else he'd say if I asked him directly. He doesn't think Americans should be in Germany at all."

"That's pretty harsh."

Luisa agreed, but she also understood where her father was coming from.

Sonja remained silent as they neared the building. Music and conversation blended in a cacophony that seeped through the entrance doors. The music meant there must be dancing.

"Well, you have to stay with me," Sonja said. "And you can have your own opinions about Americans, you know. You can be friendly. It's not like you need to date any of them."

Luisa knew her friend was teasing, but a pinch in her chest reminded her that it had been months since she'd been on any dates. Months since she'd broken up with Curt, that was. His personality had become too overbearing. She already had a police officer for a father. It seemed all of their nights out had consisted of Curt talking and Luisa listening. Over the course of their dating, her identity had become smaller and smaller. Thankfully he didn't attend this church, so there was no chance of running into him unexpectedly.

"Come," Sonja said. "Let's go talk to the Americans."

Luisa exhaled. Still, her stomach tensed at the thought of getting to know any American soldier. Her father's rants echoed in her head, and his memory of the war wasn't too far gone. Even after all of the Nazi war crimes had been exposed, her father still thought Germans should be left to run their own country. And it didn't help that several German women had been assigned to work as housekeepers for families of American servicemen.

"We lost the war," her father had said more than once, "but that doesn't mean we should turn over our country to any of the Allies."

Ironically, he spewed negativity about only the Americans, not so much the French and British, who also occupied West Germany. The Soviets were a different matter . . . "At least the Soviets are establishing order—which our country needs desperately," her father would say.

Yes, Frankfurt was occupied by the Americans. The western cities were controlled by France, and the northern part of Germany was controlled by the British. Those three allies played nice together, but the former ally of those countries, the USSR, only butted heads with the others over political policies.

All of East Germany, with the exception of West Berlin, was under the GDR regime—the German Democratic Republic, or *Deutsche Demokratische Republik*. The socialist republic was based on the Soviet Union government.

Luisa wished she could push aside all of the political power struggles and that citizens could live in peace.

Inside the building, they entered the social hall, where chairs lined the walls. Punch and other drinks were available at a table in the corner. About a dozen couples were dancing in the center of the floor, including Franz and Charlotte.

Sonja greeted one person after another, tugging Luisa along. Luisa knew only a couple of people from previous socials. Everyone commented on their graduation until she felt overwhelmed with the attention. She smiled and said "thank you" so much that her cheeks began to ache.

"There they are," Sonja said close to Luisa's ear as they reached the table with the punch.

Luisa didn't need to look around to know that Sonja was referring to the American soldiers. They could be spotted a kilometer away by their green fatigues. But at Sonja's insistence, Luisa looked over at the three men—surrounded by a few young women, likely practicing their English in order to flirt with them.

Two of the soldiers were blond, their hair cropped short, and one was dark haired, a few inches taller than the rest. The blond soldiers seemed to be smiling with ease at their eager admirers. The dark-haired soldier was listening, but there wasn't humor or excitement in his gaze. He seemed to stand apart as an observer, not as a participant.

Yet a soldier's personality or moods were none of her business. She turned back to the punch table and poured herself a glass, along with Sonja.

"What do you think?" Sonja asked after taking a sip of her punch. "Should we worm our way in? Or wait until they aren't as popular?"

Luisa shook her head. "I think they'll be popular all night. There have to be at least five ladies over there."

Sonja downed the rest of her punch as if she were on the verge of dying from thirst. "I'm not worried. Come on."

"I'll wait here," Luisa said. "Truly. Go ahead."

Sonja scrunched her nose. "No one here knows your father."

That might be true, but it might not. Her father was a police officer, and who knew what connections there might be?

Sonja linked arms with her. "We're practicing *English*," she whispered in her ear in very stilted English.

Luisa smiled at the awful pronunciation.

"See, I need your help desperately."

"All right," Luisa agreed. "But only for a moment."

The sea of young women seemed to be never-ending, but leave it to Sonja to work her way in with her bright personality.

"Where are you all from?" Sonja said after asking their names.

One of the blond men, Rick Murdock, said he was from Oklahoma. The second blond, named David Jones, said he was from Kansas.

"Where's Kansas?" Sonja asked.

"The Midwest," David said.

Sonja looked at Luisa with a frown. "What's the Midwest?"

She explained in German how America was divided into regions. When she looked back at the men, she found the gaze of the dark-haired man upon her. He'd said his name was Bob Inama, but nothing more. He was the quiet one out of the group of soldiers, and that only made Luisa more curious about him. Which she shouldn't be.

When Sonja asked him where he was from, he said, "Idaho and Utah."

"I've never heard of I-ha-do." Sonja looked again at Luisa for explanation.

"*Idaho* is next to Utah," Luisa told Sonja in English. "Right?" She looked to Bob for confirmation.

He nodded, his brown eyes watchful. Was he uncomfortable at the social? She wondered how long he'd been on assignment in Germany.

23

Sonja set her hands on her hips. "But how can someone be from two places at once?" she asked in German.

"I grew up in Idaho," Bob said in German, surprising all of the women. "But I go to school in Utah. I'm getting my degree in prelaw and economics. Or I was until . . ." He glanced down at his uniform.

Had he been drafted? Luisa wondered.

"Ah, you speak German!" Sonja declared. "It must be school-learned, though." Then she laughed. "I think I can help you get better."

Bob's smile was slight, but he made no comment or commitment.

"What are you all talking about?" David asked.

"Getting drafted," Bob told him in English.

"I was drafted, too," David announced to the women with some pride. "But Murdock here, he's from a military family, so he's been wearing a uniform since birth."

Murdock shoved David in the shoulder, but he only laughed.

Again, Luisa's eyes connected with Bob's. She was intrigued, when she shouldn't be intrigued at all.

CHAPTER FOUR

"As a commander of a Field Artillery Unit in West Germany, we trained daily on the possibility of the Soviets crossing the border. We went to various locations in West Germany and identified areas where we might have to engage in combat, exercised the tactics that we would use, and spent countless hours at training locations where we could actually fire the artillery that we had. This was in addition to honing our skills with rifles and pistols."

—Patrick Wick, US Army Captain and
Field Artillery Battery Commander, West Germany

FRANKFURT, WEST GERMANY
AUGUST 1960

The buzz of the rapid conversation, switching from German to English then back to German, had Bob's thoughts colliding with each other. He'd let Jones and Murdock talk to the young women who seemed to swarm them like a drove of bees. After basic training at Fort Ord in California, then working at Fort Sill in Oklahoma, he should have been used to these types of socials where the young women flocked to the soldiers and asked so many questions. Then danced. Sometimes sweethearts were produced as a result and promises to write letters and meet at a later time.

Bob wasn't opposed to dancing, but he'd never lead a woman on. Never make promises he couldn't keep. His relationship with Susan had taught him enough about how geographical distance between a couple could send things awry. Besides, he'd been taught by his parents to stay chaste until marriage, and he'd seen enough consequences from friends around him who hadn't, so he'd stuck to it. Respecting the women he met was more important than temporary satisfaction.

Anyway, he wasn't here to find a sweetheart because he knew a future relationship would be impossible. It wasn't like he'd want to remain in Germany after the army, and he would never expect a German woman to follow him to America. So he only smiled and nodded, answered a few questions, and mostly avoided the women who had that eager look in their eyes.

But the woman named Luisa was different. He saw that from the beginning. She was more serious than the others, didn't giggle or flirt. She listened to the conversation, but there was something distant in her gray-blue gaze. He wouldn't mind talking to her—in German—to improve his accent, but the women all seemed determined to speak English.

As the conversations morphed around him, he took a break and fetched a cup of punch. Then he walked into the foyer, which was quiet and abandoned. He'd been in Germany for only a couple of weeks, and he'd barely seen any of the country. On his next day of leave, he hoped to change that. He wanted to try the foods, see the sights, learn about the people. He'd likely be in Germany for eighteen months, and he already felt like he was running out of time.

Bob crossed the foyer and stepped outside. The autumn night had cooled, but the temperature was a nice change from the stuffiness of the social hall. Cars were parked haphazardly around the building, and the traffic on the street was light this time of night. He leaned against the stair rail and looked up at the sky.

The clouds that had been there earlier in the evening had dissipated, leaving a clear view of the stars and the moon. He thought of his family—his sister and his parents. They were a world, and several time zones, away.

He exhaled slowly. He'd been a college student and a missionary and had lived away from home for years, so why did he now feel homesick? Sure, the language made him feel like he was on a different planet altogether, but he'd taken German in college and had a decent grasp of the fundamentals of the language.

The sound of the building's doors whooshing open caught his attention, and he turned to see a young woman walk out. He recognized her as the one who'd said her name was Luisa, and he straightened from where he leaned against the rail.

"Oh, I didn't know anyone was out here," she said in German.

At least that was what he thought she'd said. "You're Luisa, right?"

"Right. And you're Bob?" She paused near the doors, her gaze curious. He couldn't see the color of her eyes in the dimness, but her honey-blond hair seemed more gold in the light of the streetlamp.

He nodded and slipped his hands into his pockets.

"Why aren't you with the other soldiers?" This she asked in English, and it was quite decent. Then her brows lifted. "Oh, are you on a smoke break?"

"I don't smoke," he said, also answering in English.

"Like my friend Sonja. She attends church here and invites me to tag along. Are you religious, then?"

That was one way to think of it, he supposed. "I am."

She walked to the other rail, on the opposite side of the stairs from him. Folding her arms, she leaned against it. "Where did you learn German?"

"I took some courses in college, but I think I read it a lot better than I can speak it." At her smile, he added, "It seems you agree."

"I do."

He thought she might laugh, but her attention was caught by a passing car, then the silence settled between them.

"Did I hear right that you and your friend graduated from nursing school today?"

Her gaze slid to his, and her expression softened. "We did. Now, I need to set up interviews and find a job."

Bob pushed back an unexpected wistful feeling—perhaps he was envious of another person graduating with their degree. He would have been in his first year of law school right now if he hadn't been drafted. But here he was, and he must make the best of it. "Congratulations to you. That's a remarkable achievement, and I'm sure you'll get hired soon."

"*Dankeschön*," she said. "What about you? You said you were in school in Utah. What did you graduate in?"

She'd asked the questions in English, so he replied in English, telling her about changing majors, then settling on prelaw and economics.

"You were drafted then?"

At his nod, she went quiet, studying him for a long moment, her eyes an indistinguishable color. Finally, she said, "That must have been a sacrifice."

"Many people sacrifice for their country. Why should I be any different?" It was a dialogue he'd repeated to himself more than once, but this night, speaking to Luisa, he realized he truly believed it. He was still sacrificing, but he was also serving—his country, the American people, which meant his family and his friends.

"So if you hadn't been drafted, you would have a university diploma?" she said, gentleness in her tone. "And perhaps you'd be married to your sweetheart?"

He smiled at that. "I don't have a sweetheart. The law is a jealous mistress."

Her brows jutted up. "Ah, you are a diligent student it seems." At his shrug, she pressed, "If you could have any career in the world, what would it be?"

The question was easy, and his answer automatic. So why did he hesitate? "A government lawyer in Washington." He told her about the internship at the US Department of Justice and how he'd gone to artillery training in Oklahoma instead. He told her how his parents had been upset that all of his plans had gone awry, but in the end, they were proud that their son was serving their country.

Finally, he told her about the volunteer work he'd done as a missionary for his church and how right before opening his draft letter, the song "We Are All Enlisted" had never left his mind. When he finished talking, he was pretty sure he'd stunned Luisa. He'd stunned himself. He had never been so open around someone he'd just met.

She straightened from where she leaned on the opposite rail and crossed the space between them. She settled against the rail next to him, a few feet away, and her gaze focused on him. "You've led a remarkable life, Bob, and that can mean only one thing."

He was truly curious. "What does it mean?"

"Your life will continue to be remarkable." Her voice was as soft as the night. "Germany will only add more to all of your talents and skills. I know you miss home and your university and all the opportunities that would have been yours, but my country has a lot to offer as well."

His chest warmed, and for some reason he felt like smiling. So he did. "What does Germany have to offer a soldier like me?"

The edges of her mouth quirked, and he saw the amusement in her eyes. "First, the people are wonderful." She spread her hands. "Especially the nurses."

Bob laughed. "I can't disagree there."

She folded her arms, her smile remaining. "And the food. You have to try the schnitzel, or you'll leave Germany in great shame."

With a tilt of his head, Bob said, "Continue."

"The alpine forests are unparalleled," she said. "Every good fairy tale starts in a forest."

Another laugh.

"Germany has some of the best composers in the world," she said. "You'll have to go to at least one opera."

"One opera, noted."

"Oh, and the architecture is beautiful," she said. "Right here in Frankfurt we have the PalmenGarten—a huge greenhouse unlike any you've ever seen.

29

The vestibule on the west side was damaged during the war, but it's now been replaced. The Haus Wertheim, which survived both wars, is the only timber-framed building left. And don't miss the oldest church in Germany—the Justinuskirche—it's over a thousand years old."

"I feel like I should be taking notes," he said. "I don't want to forget any of these places."

Luisa turned fully toward him, her eyes dancing. "Come to the next social," she said. "I'm sure I can get Sonja to invite me, and I can give you the list again if you've forgotten."

He was about to ask her when the next social would be when Murdock and Jones came out of the building.

"Where did you go?" Jones asked.

"We were looking for you—" Murdock stopped talking when he saw Luisa. "Oh, hello. Luisa, right?"

Luisa nodded, looking amused. "Right."

"You have a beautiful country," Murdock continued, his smile directed toward Luisa. "Do you offer tours?"

She laughed, but Bob said, "I'll catch up with you later, Murdock."

"Come on," Jones said, tugging Murdock's arm as he backtracked toward the stairs. "Sorry. We'll, uh, leave you alone."

"We need to leave soon though," Murdock said. "Can't miss curfew."

Bob didn't care for the speculation in Jones's tone or Murdock's friendliness with Luisa. "I'll be there soon."

Jones elbowed Murdock before he could make another comment. "We'll wait for you at the corner," Jones said. They hurried down the stairs and were in the parking lot before Bob could tell them he didn't need alone time with Luisa.

"Sorry about those guys," Bob said, glancing at Luisa.

She looked flushed, even in the dimness of the streetlamps. "It's all right." She tucked a bit of hair behind her ear.

He should say something, explain. Even if they didn't see each other again, and especially if they did. "Luisa, I'm not like the other soldiers. I don't have a sweetheart back home, but I'm also not . . . going to lose focus from my assignment."

She stilled. "I understand. And you don't have to worry. My father would not approve of me speaking to an American soldier in the first place."

Bob frowned. "But you were allowed to come tonight?"

"Yes, and no." She exhaled. "Father lets me come to socials with Sonja. But he doesn't know American soldiers are at this one."

Bob understood perfectly what she was saying, and he was fine with it all. He extended his hand. "Well, nice to meet you, Luisa, and best of luck with your future."

She moved closer and shook his hand, her smaller hand in his rougher, larger one.

"Remember to enjoy Germany, Bob," she said. "Don't forget your list."

He chuckled and released her hand. "I won't. Maybe I'll see you at the next social, but we don't have to talk if you don't think we should."

She smirked and stepped past him. "*Auf Wiedersehen.*"

He echoed her goodbye, "*Auf Wiedersehen,*" then he strode to the two very nosey soldiers gawking at him from the street corner.

CHAPTER FIVE

"Western Germany, which is being remilitarized, and her inclusion in the North Atlantic bloc, . . . increases the danger of a new war and creates a threat to the national security of peace-loving states."

—The Warsaw Pact, May 14, 1955

FRANKFURT, WEST GERMANY
AUGUST 1960

Luisa's step should have been light as she exited the city tram and headed to her interview at the hospital. Instead, she was bothered that her father had stopped her before leaving the house to tell her that their neighbor had informed him that Luisa had come home very late the night before. So she'd told her father exactly where she'd been, and he'd immediately asked if there had been American soldiers there. When she'd confessed, he'd set into a good, long lecture.

She'd had to catch a later tram. She was still on time, but she'd hoped to be early. Once she reached the hospital, she followed the signs to the administration office, then told the receptionist why she was there.

"Take a seat and wait your turn," the forty-something woman with heavy-rimmed eyeglasses said.

Luisa turned to the handful of chairs lining the wall and paused when she saw a familiar blond head bent over a fashion magazine. "Sonja?"

Her head popped up. "Luisa! What are you doing here?"

The other two women who were waiting in chairs glanced up.

Luisa quickly took a seat next to Sonja. "I have an interview."

"Me too." Sonja's brows tugged together. "Do you think it's for the same job?"

Luisa pulled out a mailed notice from her purse.

"Oh," Sonja said, her tone disappointed. "I'm interviewing for the same one. Perhaps they have more than one opening?"

Luisa doubted she'd get the job over someone as outgoing as Sonja. Luisa pushed back her dejection though. "That would be wonderful." She smiled as if none of this was bothersome. "Hospitals always need nurses."

"Of course." Sonja lowered her voice. "You never told me what you talked about with that American soldier for so long last night."

Luisa glanced over at the other waiting women. She didn't know them at all, so there wasn't any way her father would hear of what she'd say.

She told Sonja the basic conversation, and all the while her friend's smile grew.

"But," Luisa said, "my father knows about the American soldiers being at the social, and he told me I can't go to them anymore."

Sonja's mouth opened in surprise. "No. That's not fair."

Luisa only shrugged. She felt the same way, but going against her father wasn't an option. It never was. He was the only family she had, and he knew the pulse of the city better than she.

Sonja's name was called before she could continue protesting.

"Good luck," Luisa whispered.

Sonja smiled then hurried after the receptionist.

Luisa touched the floral pendant she wore. Somehow touching the pendant made her feel closer to her mother. Her mother *would* be proud of this moment.

"Luisa Voigt?" The receptionist had returned.

Luisa stood as another woman appeared from around the corner. She was about a foot shorter than Luisa, and her blond hair too bright to be natural. "I'm Mrs. Klein. Follow me, Ms. Voigt."

Luisa was taken into a tidy office where she sat in a narrow chair across from Mrs. Klein. Her first question was unexpected. "What made you want to go to nursing school, Ms. Voigt?"

But the answer took no thought. "When I was a young girl, my mother and I used to visit my father's aunt. She was elderly, and every few days, we'd bring her a meal. While my mother visited, I'd clean her house and do other tasks that needed to be done. One day, great-aunt Ada told me that I would make an excellent nurse one day. I suppose the idea stuck with me."

Mrs. Klein seemed to consider this. "Thank you. We will be in touch."

Walking out of the hospital, Luisa didn't know what to make of the interview, and her thoughts were soon distracted when she saw Sonja waiting for her.

"What did they say?" Sonja asked, nearly bouncing on her toes with excitement.

"She said she'd contact me later." Luisa studied her friend. "You look like you're about ready to burst. What happened?"

"I got the job," Sonja said. "Although I'm sorry if that means you didn't get the job."

"If we were interviewed by two different people, then maybe they're filling several jobs."

"I hope so," Sonja said. "Come on. We must get lunch together. We'll celebrate."

"We'll celebrate *you*," Luisa said with a laugh.

"Both of us," Sonja insisted. "We've completed our first real-world interviews."

Being with Sonja made Luisa feel lighter and forget about her strict father for a short time. They stopped at a café and ordered schnitzel and *eis*. Which drew her thoughts to the American soldier. Would he take her suggestions seriously? Her breath stalled when two soldiers walked into the café. Their lighter hair told her immediately that neither of them was Bob.

"Oh, let's talk to them," Sonja said immediately. "We can practice our English."

Luisa smiled. "You never give up, do you?"

"Why should I?" She smirked, then rose. "Come on."

The soldiers were heading out of the café by the time Sonja and Luisa reached them. They were friendly and exchanged a few words with Sonja while Luisa remained mostly quiet.

Truthfully, Luisa was glad when the soldiers left, and she and Sonja began walking in the other direction. This area of town was in her father's jurisdiction, and one of his co-officers could easily spot her talking to a soldier.

"Maybe it's your friend," Sonja said suddenly.

Luisa glanced up ahead and saw a US Army truck rumbling toward them.

"I don't think so," Luisa said, although she couldn't help but search the men she could see at the front of the cab. "He's stationed in Hanau."

"Well, I still think you should be able to go to the socials," Sonja said.

Luisa sighed and linked arms with her friend. "Me too." Even though her father had been adamant, Luisa thought it was fine to be friends with a person from another country—even if he was a soldier.

"Call me when you find out about your job interview," Sonja said when they neared the bus stop. "We can go to work every day together if we both get hired."

Luisa smiled. It would be nice to have a friend right when she started working.

She returned to a quiet house, and when the stillness was interrupted by the house phone ringing, she rushed to it so that her father wouldn't awaken.

"Hello?" she answered.

On the other end was Mrs. Klein, offering her the job. Luisa accepted on the spot. Her mind was buzzing so much with the good news that she wasn't sure she'd caught all of the information Mrs. Klein gave her. She found a scrap of paper and began to take notes, writing faster than she could make sense of.

"Tomorrow, then?" Mrs. Klein said.

"Oh, tomorrow?" Luisa repeated. "What time?"

Mrs. Klein made a small tutting noise. "Five o'clock in the morning. Don't be late."

When the woman hung up, Luisa sank onto the kitchen chair. She'd been hired, and she started first thing in the morning. Looking at her scrawled notes, she could barely decipher them. She didn't know what she needed to prepare for. Or what to wear. Had Mrs. Klein told her anything about the uniform?

Luisa hurried to her closet to dig through boxes of her mother's things, looking for the most sturdy and comfortable shoes she could find. She wasn't even sure how long her shift was.

Then, she remembered she'd promised to call Sonja. Her friend answered on the second ring.

"Is that you, Luisa?"

Luisa laughed. "You are presumptuous."

"Not exactly," Sonja said. "I've been dying to hear from you but thought you should call me first. So I know that you have good news. Well, have you?"

"I do." Luisa was grinning. "I got the job I interviewed for, too."

Sonja squealed rather loudly into the phone. "Amazing!" she nearly shouted.

Once Sonja had calmed, they figured out they were on the same shifts—early morning into the afternoon. Sonja would be working in the emergency center, and Luisa in wound care and rehabilitation.

When her father woke, Luisa already had dinner prepared. The aroma of sausage and baking potatoes filled the house. Her father strode into the kitchen, freshly shaven, save for his mustache. He wore a clean, pressed shirt that would be part of his uniform once he put on his jacket. She waited until he was seated and they'd blessed the food before telling him about her new job.

Her father cut up the small potatoes on his plate. "They must be in dire need of help at the hospital," he said in a slow tone. "What is the pay?"

Luisa tried not to flinch at his cold words. Most things to her father were business, and this was another one.

She told him her pay, then said, "My shift starts at five in the morning."

He took a bite of his potatoes, then met her gaze. "I will put in a request to change my shift, or we won't see each other much."

Her father continued eating, but Luisa could only stare at him.

He had never offered to change his shift before. She'd been in school and working, and they crossed paths only once or twice a day. Why was he willing to change now? "I thought you liked working nights."

"I guess you graduating made me realize that time is going by too fast."

Luisa nodded, but she wasn't fully convinced.

Her father sighed. "I worry about you being alone at night all of the time. We've been on the watch for increased Soviet activity in Frankfurt. There's no telling who might be a spy. No level of society is immune."

She thought of the US Army truck she'd seen that morning with the young soldiers inside.

But he continued to talk about the complexity of spies and how the police department was putting everyone through rigorous questioning.

"Even you?" she asked, surprised since her father had been a member of the police force for as long as she could remember.

"Even me," her father confirmed. "The police chief, Johannes Stumm, believes everyone is susceptible to bribery. I have to work extra hard to stay above reproach." He set his fork down and leaned forward, his gaze solely on Luisa. "You must be watchful at every turn, Luisa. Every day more and more East Germans come into the West. The young people your age are rebelling against the GDR and coming to West Germany in droves. It will have to stop, somehow. Our economy can't support them all. Soon, all of our jobs will be in jeopardy."

Luisa nodded at her father's counsel, although she didn't know what she could personally do.

But her father had more instructions. "Stay out of the political rallies. Don't become a target. Don't attract notice from activists. For if you do, it will also reflect on me."

This she could understand and agree with. "I won't," she promised.

CHAPTER SIX

"The truth of the matter is that Europe's requirements for the next three or four years of foreign food and other essential products—principally from America—are so much greater than her present ability to pay that she must have substantial additional help, or face economic, social and political deterioration of a very grave character. The remedy lies in breaking the vicious circle and restoring the confidence of the European people in the economic future of their own countries and of Europe as a whole. The manufacturer and the farmer throughout wide areas must be able and willing to exchange their products for currencies the continuing value of which is not open to question."

—GEORGE C. MARSHALL, THE MARSHALL PLAN, JUNE 5, 1947

HEADQUARTERS COMPANY
75TH FIELD ARTILLERY
HANAU, GERMANY
SEPTEMBER 1960

Bob had been in Germany only a few weeks, but he was already in a routine. The 5:00 a.m. wakeup call had taken some adjusting to since he still liked to wake up before everyone else. Starting the day off with some reflection before the day's activities began—he'd done it at Fort Ord and Fort Sill, and it worked well here too.

But this morning, he didn't need the help of his alarm to wake up, which told him he was fully on schedule. He switched off the alarm before it could disturb anyone else, then he set about doing his chores. By the time he was finished, the other men had roused for the day.

Formation for head count was followed by breakfast, which was a quiet affair, as most of the men in his unit needed coffee to fully wake up.

"Any plans this weekend, Inama?" Murdock said, sitting next to him with his tray of food.

"Not specifically," Bob said. "Might hang around Frankfurt. Go to church on Sunday."

Murdock grinned. "Of course you are. Unless . . ."

Bob ate a few bites of his food, waiting for Murdock to continue. "Unless what?"

Murdock chuckled. "Unless you want to come south with me and Jones. We're putting a trip together with a couple other guys."

Too crowded for Bob. "I'll be fine here."

Murdock shook his head, amusement in his eyes. "Suit yourself. If my plans change, maybe I'll come with you."

Bob nodded and returned to his food while Murdock started talking to Jones, who'd joined them as well. Bob didn't mind Murdock teasing him, not really, as long as the guy was respectful to the women. Bob knew he was fortunate to have friends who weren't obnoxious around the German ladies. By nature, they didn't seem to care for the loud, boisterous male Americans. So it was fine with Bob if Murdock chose to come with him to church, even if he had to set him straight a time or two.

"Ready?" Murdock said a few minutes later.

Bob was ready. Today they'd be training on the 8-inch howitzers, a division-four weapon. Usually he was in the Fire Direction Center, but today, he was with the fourteen-member crew. Bob, Murdock, and Jones would be together in the howitzer, with the other eight in the personnel carrier that would follow behind.

The cooler fall weather demanded an army jacket, and once everyone was assembled, they headed to the artillery range. Since the 8-inch howitzers shot a two-hundred-plus-pound projectile up to nineteen miles, they headed to the long-range fields. Suited up and wearing their hard helmets, Bob knew they were in for a long day of training. But he enjoyed it. He enjoyed the precise methods used in targeting.

He also enjoyed reading the topographical maps—measuring and calculating the distance to the targets had become second nature.

As they reached the target range, Bob directed the driver of the cannon to continue to the top of the next hill. The cannon lumbered on, the ground churning up beneath the power of the tracks. When the cannon came to a stop, Bob climbed out and set to work leveling and stabilizing the cannon according to the elevation of their target.

The crew from the personnel carrier joined Bob and the others. Everyone knew their duties and set to work. Murdock and Jones loaded the two-hundred-pound projectile into the rear of the cannon. Next, the crew packed bags of propellant behind the projectile in order to close the breach. Once the back of the cannon was closed, Murdock inserted the firing pin, then attached the lanyard.

Once Bob had the setting set for the distance, he gave the command to fire.

Murdock yanked the lanyard, and the 8-inch projectile launched. No one moved as they watched the projectile blast into the target. Success.

The day progressed, and when it was lunchtime, everyone searched for a patch of sun. Murdock joined Bob while Jones sat with another group of guys.

"You're outshining the rest of the boys, Inama," Murdock said after taking a bite of the sandwich that was part of his brown-bag lunch.

Bob rested his elbows on his knees. "You aren't so shabby yourself."

Murdock laughed. "That will be the day. I've never been the top man of anything. Middle-of-the-road Murdock, that's me."

Bob looked over at his friend in surprise. "What do you mean? You're an excellent soldier. You've never fallen behind in anything, and you always carry your own weight."

"Nice try." Murdock took a long swallow of water from a portable jug. "You might be an eternal optimist, but I know what I am. There's a reason I didn't have to be drafted into the army. It was my way of proving to my old man that I could become something despite what he thinks."

Bob let that sink in. Murdock was definitely no tenderfoot, and that made Bob wonder what sort of father he had. Sure, Bob's own parents had always expected and demanded a lot, but there was an edge to Murdock's voice. Bob looked over at the soldier who'd become a friend over the past few weeks. Murdock had taken off his helmet, and his dark-blond hair lifted in the wind.

"What's your old man like?" Bob asked.

Murdock finished off his sandwich, then brushed his hands together. "Well, his sole purpose in life is to make his sons as tough as he is."

Bob frowned. "Was he in the army?"

"Yes, sir." Murdock gave a fake salute.

The mocking motion bothered Bob. But he'd never seen Murdock disrespect his superiors. Perhaps that only extended to his father.

"And your brother?"

Murdock's square jaw flexed. "Died in a car accident while on leave." His laugh was short, bitter. "Of all the things for a soldier to face. At least dying in battle is honorable. A car accident—that's tragic. I enlisted the day after his funeral. The grief was too much at home, if you know what I mean."

Bob could only guess, but he sympathized with Murdock. "How old were you?"

"A month after my eighteenth birthday," Murdock said, tugging up a tuft of grass then letting it scatter in the breeze. "Oh, I was bound for the army anyway, I suppose. Coming from a military family. I just knew . . . Well, it doesn't matter now."

"I'm sorry about your brother," Bob said quietly.

Murdock gave a brief nod. "Me too. I never expected to live up to him anyway, and now, it's impossible. He's gone, and I'm here. My father would want it the other way around."

The dejection in Murdock's voice tugged at Bob's heart. "Well, I'm glad you're here, for what it's worth."

Murdock glanced at him. "You're a good man, Bob Inama. I think I'll stick by you."

Bob smiled, but he also felt heartsick for Murdock's loss and his damaged relationship with his father.

"What was your father's job in the army?"

"He was a field artillery man like you and me," Murdock said. "Became a sergeant major. His favorite thing to talk about is that he was able to see the atomic cannon be tested at the Nevada Test Site."

Bob knew a little about the history. The atomic cannon, often called "Atomic Annie," was an M65 280mm motorized heavy gun. It had launched a nuclear warhead only once, at Frenchman's Flat in Nevada, although twenty more atomic cannons were built and deployed overseas. "In 1953?"

"Correct," Murdock said.

A shiver traveled the length of Bob's spine. What a sight, a horrible sight, that would have been to see the double mushroomed cloud of smoke, brighter than the sun, rising from a disintegrated ground, knowing the destruction it could cause to human life. It had been the first and only nuclear shell to be fired from a cannon.

"My father said that the gun could be set up for firing in twelve minutes and then returned to traveling mode in another fifteen minutes."

"And it could shoot twenty miles, right?"

"Right!"

Bob nodded. The cannon was the most deadly one in existence.

"There's a 280mm here in West Germany," Murdock continued. "They move it around a lot."

"That cannon can hit within twenty yards of the intended target," Bob said.

"Impressive," Murdock mused.

"I hope it's never needed again."

"Agreed."

"Well, enough about that," Murdock said. "Have anything cheery to talk about?"

"The weather is fine . . ." Bob started.

Murdock smiled and shook his head. "It sure is."

"The breeze is just right," Bob continued. "Those sandwiches were decent."

"True." Murdock chuckled.

"I don't think it's going to rain, so we won't be getting wet in our uniforms."

Murdock laughed. "All right, you win. It is a fine day, and lunch hit the spot."

Bob grinned.

A burst of laughter erupted from the group Jones was sitting with nearby.

Both men looked over at Jones and the other guys. Jones had a cigarette dangling from the corner of his mouth, as he gestured to the tune of some story he was telling.

"You know," Murdock said in a thoughtful tone. "Jones reminds me of my brother. I think that's why I was drawn to him when I first joined the Hanau unit. Chuck was always surrounded by friends, making them laugh, teasing all the time."

"Sounds like a good brother to have around," Bob commented.

Murdock gathered up the trash and stood. "Time to get back to work."

As they continued the drills throughout the afternoon, Murdock's words about the loss of his brother continued to drive through Bob's thoughts.

After they finished up in the late afternoon, the drive back to post was quieter than the morning journey. Everyone was tired and looking forward to dinner. Bob still had Murdock's story on his mind.

CHAPTER SEVEN

"1. Abolition of property in land and application of all rents of land to public purposes.

2. A heavy progressive or graduated income tax.

3. Abolition of all rights of inheritance.

4. Confiscation of the property of all emigrants and rebels.

5. Centralisation of credit in the hands of the state, by means of a national bank with State capital and an exclusive monopoly.

6. Centralisation of the means of communication and transport in the hands of the State.

7. Extension of factories and instruments of production owned by the State; the bringing into cultivation of waste-lands, and the improvement of the soil generally in accordance with a common plan.

8. Equal liability of all to work. Establishment of industrial armies, especially for agriculture.

9. Combination of agriculture with manufacturing industries; gradual abolition of all the distinction between town and country by a more equable distribution of the populace over the country.

10. Free education for all children in public schools. Abolition of children's factory labour in its present form. Combination of education with industrial production, &c, &c."

—KARL MARX AND FREDERICK ENGELS,
MANIFESTO OF THE COMMUNIST PARTY, FEBRUARY 1848

FRANKFURT, WEST GERMANY
OCTOBER 1960

Luisa accepted Sonja's invitation to go to her church that week, hoping she might see Bob Inama. She slowed her step as she walked past the social hall in the church building, where the English-speaking members met. The building held two separate church services—one in English and one in German. The English services were over, but a few people still lingered. She was curious; that was all. Did Bob come to the services, and had he seen anything of Germany besides the *Kaserne*, or army barracks, in Hanau?

She'd liked talking to him at the social a few weeks back. He was different than most men she'd met and basically had the opposite personality of Curt. Bob really seemed interested in what she had to say. He stayed quiet when she spoke and truly listened. Bob didn't seem to have an agenda or ulterior motive when talking to her but simply seemed to enjoy an engaging conversation. Despite their deficiencies in each other's languages, they'd had an easy time talking and relating to one other.

As she reached the other side of the doorway, her steps paused. A group of young people were standing together, and plainly, some of the men in the group were American soldiers. Their short haircuts and their clothing gave them away. One was blond, the other dark haired, and her gaze shifted to the taller one. *Bob.* It had to be him, although his back was to her.

Before she could turn and go into the chapel, the group broke up, and the American soldiers headed directly toward her. Well, toward the exit, which she was next to. It was too late to turn away and act like she hadn't seen them because Bob was looking right at her. Maybe he wouldn't recognize her?

"Luisa?"

"Hello . . ." she said in English, looking from Bob to the other soldier with him. He was the same man from the social. Murdock?

"We met the other week," Murdock said with a broad smile that softened his square jaw. "Were you at our English service?"

"No." Her gaze moved to Bob's again. His eyes were the brown that she remembered. "I'm meeting with the Germans in the chapel."

"Bob could probably go to the German service and understand every word," Murdock said with a laugh. "There isn't much that Bob can't do."

"I don't know about that," Bob said.

"Come on," Murdock continued, his English almost too fast for her to understand. "You're already outranking everyone in the barracks in just a couple of months." He looked at Luisa and winked. "That's why we stick by him. It's good to have a friend who's smarter than you."

Bob's face seemed to tinge pink. Luisa wondered what they were referring to.

"I'll wait for you outside," Murdock told Bob. "Nice to see you again, Luisa."

It wasn't how Luisa had planned anything, but with Murdock taking off, she was nearly alone with Bob. As alone as someone could be in a building populated with a congregation in the next room.

Bob rubbed the back of his neck. Was he nervous? This was all a bad idea, she decided. Sonja was waiting for her in the chapel, and the prelude music had already started.

"It sounds like you're adjusting to life at the *Kaserne* in Hanau?" she ventured, because no matter what one side of her mind was telling her to do, the other side was curious.

"Murdock is making sure I don't slack off in anything," Bob said with a sheepish smile.

She nodded, figuring he was being very modest. "How were the church services?" She tilted her head toward the social hall.

"Different," he said. "But nice. I've not been to a regular church in a long time. Well, since college."

Luisa folded her arms. "You're doing a lot better than me. Do you always have Sundays off?"

"Not always." He folded his arms too. "I took your advice and had a schnitzel."

"Ach gut. And what did you think?"

"I loved it." His eyes seemed brighter. "I had two. I probably should have stuck with one, though. Next time."

She laughed, but she quickly stifled the sound. She could hear the over-the-pulpit announcements start up in the other room.

"And you were right about the architecture and sites in Frankfurt," Bob said, his brown eyes warm, his smile wider. "I plan to visit a different city every chance I get."

"Wonderful." She was still smiling, and so was he.

"Hey, did you find a job yet?"

Hey was one of those English words she quite liked. "I did. At entry level, of course, but it's still nursing," she said, a bubble of pride in her chest.

His brows rose above his glasses. "Congratulations. I had no doubt."

"Oh, really?" She felt so light right now. Almost giddy.

"You did say that nurses are wonderful people."

"I did." Did he remember everything she'd said? Bob was quite remarkable. "I see you haven't had any trouble remembering the list I gave you."

His gaze shifted past her as a couple walked by. Luisa nodded at the pair. She didn't know them, but they looked familiar.

"There's a concert tomorrow night at the church," he said. "Murdock and Jones will probably come with me. I told them we need some culture."

"Ah," Luisa said. "Sonja took me to one once. It was well done."

"You should come."

She drew in a breath. He'd asked her to meet him at a concert? Why couldn't she think straight?

"Bring Sonja," he said with a shrug. "Either way, it's up to you."

His words were casual, but anticipation hummed through her anyway.

"I'll see if I can make it," she said. "I don't know if . . ." She didn't have to finish because she could see that he understood.

"If not, then maybe I'll see you at another social."

"All right." She wanted to explain, but the opening hymn had started in the chapel, and the singing congregation was her signal that it was time to go.

"Have a good week, Luisa." Bob stepped away. "*Tschüss*."

"*Tschüss*." She shouldn't be watching him leave the building, but his tall form and dark hair made a striking combination. No, she needed to get into the chapel and find Sonja.

She hurried toward the chapel, then slipped into the back. Spotting Sonja's blond hair wasn't hard, and Luisa settled beside her.

"You're blushing," Sonja whispered with a coy smile as if she knew exactly who Luisa had been speaking to.

Luisa touched her cheek, then exhaled as the chorus of the hymn swelled around them. She shouldn't be blushing over an American soldier. Her heart rate began to slow as she forced herself to take steady breaths, then join in on the song. On the last verse, her heart rate finally returned to normal.

When she arrived at home an hour later, her father asked her nothing about church, or about American soldiers. And for that she was grateful.

The following day at the hospital, she was assigned to several patients for wound care. Luisa cleaned and rewrapped the foot of a young man who'd had surgery. She checked a child's stitches from his appendicitis. Between each patient, she drew curtains for privacy. When she reached an older woman's bed, Luisa saw from her chart that Mrs. Weber had had a rotator cuff repair.

"How are you feeling?" Luisa asked the woman.

Mrs. Weber had been gazing out the window, and now she turned her head. Her eyes were a surprising bright green. Luisa guessed her to be in her fifties, although her hair was colored a deep brown.

"That's a pretty necklace," Mrs. Weber said.

Luisa's fingers automatically went to the floral pendant. "It was my mother's."

"Was?"

"My mother passed away."

"I'm very sorry to hear that." She studied Luisa for a moment. "Can you help me?"

Luisa moved closer. "Of course. I'm here to check on your incision and rebandage you."

Mrs. Weber's thin hand grasped Luisa's. She looked down at the woman's grasp. Luisa didn't feel alarmed, but it was a strange thing. Perhaps the patient was upset about something, or the pain medicine was making her react strangely.

"I can get the doctor if you need—"

"No," Mrs. Weber said immediately. "He won't understand. I need someone who understands. You are a daughter, and you understand what it's like to be separated from your mother."

Luisa swallowed over the growing lump in her throat, not sure how she should answer. "What can I do for you?"

Mrs. Weber lifted her head, as if she could see around the drawn curtain. Then she motioned toward the bedside table, where she had a handbag.

"It's in there," she whispered. "The note. It's blue paper because I had nothing else. Can you get it out?"

Luisa hesitated. She didn't want to go through the woman's personal belongings. Perhaps she was delirious and should be reported to the head nurse. But to keep the woman happy, she decided to do as she asked. It took only a moment for her to locate the folded blue paper.

Mrs. Weber seemed greatly relieved once Luisa pulled it out.

"Now," Mrs. Weber said, "I need you to deliver it to my daughter. Don't delay since I don't know how much longer I'll be kept here before I'm transported back home. I don't want to miss her—" The woman's face crumpled as her words cut off.

The address on the outside of the envelope told Luisa that the daughter wasn't too far from the hospital. "Does she not know you are here?"

Mrs. Weber wiped at her tears with a shaky hand. Luisa looked about for a tissue then handed it over. Again, Mrs. Weber looked furtively toward the curtain.

"I'm from East Berlin," she said. "I'm not allowed to cross the border without government permission since my husband . . . Well, he broke the law and was imprisoned last year. So I cannot leave because of his crime. And my daughter is too afraid to cross the border the other way."

Luisa's mind reeled. "But you are here, in a West German hospital?"

"Frankfurt had the doctor who has done this surgery before," she said, her tone still hushed. "So many of our best doctors and nurses have left East Germany. I got a special release, only for a few days though."

Nodding, Luisa looked down at the envelope.

"Will you take her the note?" Mrs. Weber asked in a pleading tone. "I can pay you." She motioned for her handbag again.

"No." Luisa wouldn't take payment for this. A mother missing her daughter should never have to pay. "I will take it on my way home from my shift."

Mrs. Weber's tears started again. "You are a wonderful girl, a dear girl."

Luisa smiled, but her stomach knotted at the gushing praise. When she finished rebandaging Mrs. Weber's wound, Luisa went about her other tasks, her mind continually on the East Berliner.

After her shift, she hurried to the location marked on the blue envelope and soon arrived at a neighborhood of small homes with stucco façades and exposed beams. Opening the gate of a picket fence, she strode to the front stoop and knocked on the wooden door. Almost immediately, the door opened a crack, and a woman said, "What is it?"

Luisa peered at the young woman and guessed her to be in her mid-twenties. She wore a blue scarf over her head, and her brown eyes were nearly as dark as the door. Perhaps her father had brown eyes.

"I have a letter from your mother." She looked down at the envelope. "Are you Greta?"

The woman snatched the letter and said, "Wait there." Then she shut the door.

Luisa blinked. What had just happened? Well, this was the right address, and she'd done the errand she'd promised. She turned and was about to leave when the door opened again behind her.

"Who gave this to you?" The woman was back, her voice as sharp as ever.

Luisa spun to face her. The woman had the door open only a crack, so there wasn't much Luisa could see. "Mrs. Weber. Is she not your mother? If you're not Greta, then—"

The woman raised her hand. "I'm Greta. Who are you?"

Luisa inched back. "I'm a nurse at the hospital, and Mrs. Weber—"

"What's your name?" Greta cut in.

"Luisa. Luisa Voigt."

"What organization are you with?"

Luisa stared at the woman. "I work for the hospital."

"Yes, yes, you said that." Greta's words were rapid. "Which organization do you work for, Luisa Voigt? If you don't tell me, then I have my ways of finding out."

Luisa exhaled very slowly, trying to gather her thoughts. This visit was not what she had expected. Greta was not a humble, grateful daughter . . . Was she afraid of something? What crimes exactly had her father committed? Perhaps—

"Ms. Voigt," Greta said. "I will ask you one more time. If you do not answer, then there will be consequences."

Was Luisa in a dream? "I told you. I work at the hospital. I recently graduated from nursing school and was hired only a few weeks ago. I don't belong to any organization."

Greta held Luisa's gaze for a long, charged moment. Then she gave a brief nod. "Thank you for the letter. And it would do you well to forget this ever happened and especially forget Mrs. Weber."

Before Luisa could recover her wits enough to ask Greta what in heaven she had meant, the door swung shut again.

The way home was long because Luisa was so distracted that she missed getting off at her tram stop. So she had to get off at the next stop and retrace her steps. She walked into an empty house. Her mother's heeled shoes were still by the door, which told Luisa that her father hadn't awakened yet for his night shift. He hadn't been able to change his shift after all. Something about the assistant police chief turning down his request.

They'd make do; they always did, Luisa told herself. She was used to their short stints together. She'd make him dinner, and they'd spend a little time together before he started his shift. He'd read the newspaper, and she'd read a book or review some of her old textbooks.

The incident with Greta had been bizarre, and Luisa didn't know what to make of it. The phone in the kitchen rang, and she hurried to answer it. Maybe it was Sonja, asking if they were going to the concert tonight. Luisa still hadn't decided what her final answer would be.

But the person on the other end of the line was Mrs. Klein from the hospital. "Luisa," she said in an urgent tone. "Do you know anything about Mrs. Weber? You were assigned to rebandage her today. It seems she has left the hospital without being discharged. She's missing."

CHAPTER EIGHT

"So we have before us the prospect of two or three monstrous super-states, each possessed of a weapon by which millions of people can be wiped out in a few seconds, dividing the world between them. It has been rather hastily assumed that this means bigger and bloodier wars, and perhaps an actual end to the machine civilisation. But suppose—and really this is the likeliest development—that the surviving great nations make a tacit agreement never to use the atomic bomb against one another? Suppose they only use it, or the threat of it, against people who are unable to retaliate? In that case we are back where we were before, the only difference being that power is concentrated in still fewer hands and that the outlook for subject peoples and oppressed classes is still more hopeless."

—George Orwell, "You and the Atom Bomb," October 19, 1945

HANAU, WEST GERMANY
OCTOBER 1960

The map stretched as wide as the desk it sat on in the barracks room, and Bob traced the overland route with the tip of his finger from his current location in Hanau to the small village in Sanzeno, Italy. He would need to make more inquiries, but right now it looked like he could take trains as far as Torento, Italy. From there, he hoped there was a bus system the rest of the way.

This was all premature, of course, but he wanted the journey to be well planned out.

First, he needed to write a letter to his grandfather's cousins and find out if he could stay with them. When he was allowed to take a two-week leave in about four months, Bob planned to visit the hometown of his Grandfather Giuseppe Inama. The man had left Italy as a seventeen-year-old and immigrated to America, never to see his parents again. His grandfather had worked job to job across the country until he ended up in the mines of Kemmerer, Wyoming.

Once the Minidoka track had opened for homesteading, he moved his family to Rupert, Idaho. Later, religious differences put a wedge between Bob's father and grandfather. Bob didn't have a close relationship with his grandfather. In fact, every time he'd visited as a boy, his grandfather had spoken only Italian, leaving Bob unable to communicate with him.

Yet a trip to his grandfather's homeland had been on his mind ever since being assigned to Germany. Perhaps if he visited the town of Sanzeno, he'd understand his family heritage more and, in turn, know his grandfather better.

"What, are you daydreaming?" Murdock asked, clapping a hand on Bob's shoulder.

Bob had been so engrossed in the map that he hadn't even heard Murdock come in. "I'm dreaming of Italy."

Murdock laughed. Then he leaned against the desk, his arms folded. "This about your grandfather?"

"Yeah." Bob's gaze once again shifted to the map. "You and Jones should come."

"Nah," Murdock said. "Even if our time off did match up, I'm going to a warm beach somewhere. Not hiking around a small village taking pictures of old buildings. No offense."

Bob chuckled. "None taken."

"Jones is ready," Murdock said. "We'd better leave now if we don't want to be late for the concert."

Bob hadn't forgotten about the concert, not in the least. Especially since Luisa might show up. He was looking forward to a couple of hours of losing himself in music. It had been too long. His mind wandered to Luisa again. She was different than other women he'd been around. Besides her German heritage, she seemed genuine. Open-minded and sincere toward anyone or anything. She had a quiet, calm presence about her, yet she wasn't hesitant to speak up or ask questions.

"I'm ready," Bob said, folding the map quickly, then tucking it into the drawer of the desk. He followed Murdock out of the barracks to the bus stop.

They reached Frankfurt in about thirty minutes, and by that time, both Jones and Murdock had broken down every guy in their unit and ranked them by their marksman skills from the last two days of training. Bob shook his head when they ranked him as a perfect ten. "No one is a perfect ten."

"I'd usually agree with you," Jones said. "But what you did yesterday changed my mind."

"You're going to be our unit leader any day now," Murdock said. "Maybe even get promoted in rank."

Bob was satisfied keeping his head down and doing his job. Some of the fellows wanted accolades and recognition. All that could go to someone else, for all Bob cared. Although he still took satisfaction from a job well done.

A good percentage of the unit had been drafted, and there was a marked difference between the men who'd decided to commit with their whole hearts and minds, and the men who were still pining for life beyond the army. Yes, being drafted had been a tough awakening, but there was a reason for everything. There had to be, and he had to hold firmly to that belief.

Yet sometimes he felt like he was straddling two lives. The one he'd hoped for, and the one he was currently living.

When they arrived at the church, a group of young women stood out front. Sonja was among them, which meant there was a good chance Luisa was there too.

Sure enough, on the other side of Sonja was Luisa.

"There's your girl," Murdock said in a teasing voice.

"She's a *friend*," Bob said.

"Sure, we believe that," Jones added.

As they approached, Bob found he was already smiling before the group of young women had turned around. He barely had a chance to straighten his features before Luisa's gaze locked with his. Her hair was pulled back into some sort of braid, and she nodded the moment she saw him.

Murdock nudged Bob, but he ignored his friend. The two groups fell into a lively conversation, mostly in English, as they walked into the building. Luisa was smiling along with her friends, but Bob noticed that she seemed ill at ease about something. Her gaze would meet his, then quickly flit away.

With all the shuffling and conversation going on, Bob didn't know who he'd end up sitting by, and when it was Luisa, he couldn't deny that he was pleased.

There were still about ten minutes before the first number, but the conversations around them were hushed.

"Is everything all right?" Bob asked Luisa, keeping his voice low.

She looked at him, her blue-gray eyes wide. "What do you mean? Did you hear something?"

Was that panic in her voice? "I've heard nothing. You seem like you have something serious on your mind."

Her gaze fell, and she looked down at her folded hands. "I don't think I can talk about it."

Bob nodded. He couldn't force her to say anything if she didn't want to, but that didn't stop the questions running through his mind. Was it her father? Bob knew the man was a police officer. Or something about her new job at the hospital? Was she well? He peered at her more closely without making it obvious that he was scrutinizing her. The color of her face seemed normal and from what he could guess, she appeared healthy.

"Whatever it is," he said at last, "I hope it will all work out."

"Thank you." She stayed quiet after that, and moments later, the concert began with the small orchestra. The music was classical, and Bob was transfixed as the notes soared through the room, pushing his emotions around with the ebbs of the melody.

When the intermission was announced, Murdock and Jones rose from their seats, as did the other young women in the group.

"Coming?" Murdock asked.

Luisa hadn't moved, so Bob shook his head.

Murdock shrugged and headed out of the social hall to where the refreshment table was set up.

"Do you want anything?" he asked Luisa.

"No, thank you." She released a slow breath, touching the floral pendant on her necklace. "Sorry about earlier. You're right. I am distracted. Today, one of my patients who had recent surgery left the hospital without permission. She disappeared, and it seems that I was the last one to have seen her."

Bob frowned. "Maybe she was discharged, and there was a clerical error?"

Luisa met his gaze; her eyes were troubled. "No. There was no clerical error. She asked me to deliver a letter for her . . . and I think it was a mistake. I think I might have broken some law, but I don't know."

Bob wasn't connecting the different points of her story.

Then she told him the entire scenario of the woman from East Berlin— Mrs. Weber—who had given her an envelope to take to her daughter. But now Luisa wasn't sure if the woman in the house was the patient's daughter at all. "And tomorrow, I'm going to meet with the hospital administrator to talk about what happened. But what if . . . what if I tell them about the letter and I lose my job? My father's a police officer, and if his daughter is caught breaking the law, then that will affect him too."

Bob leaned forward, his mind spinning with unknowns. "If she's from

East Berlin, then maybe Mrs. Weber truly needed help, and what you did made it possible for her to get that help."

Luisa closed her eyes for a moment. When she opened them again, she said, "I can only hope so. But what do I tell the administration? I don't want to get anyone in trouble or arrested. Whatever Mrs. Weber told me or didn't tell me, the desperation in her eyes was real. If she really needed help, then should I feel guilty for helping her?"

The intermission was over, and people started coming back into the room again. Bob was out of time to have any sort of private conversation with her. He'd heard of the many East Germans who were relocating into West Germany. The GDR was making it harder to travel freely between the two portions of the country.

"Don't feel guilty," Bob said. "You didn't understand everything that was going on, and you were only doing what you thought was best. As far as your meeting with the admin tomorrow, follow what your heart tells you to do."

Luisa gave a slow, thoughtful nod. "All right. I guess I have a lot to think about."

Before Bob could say anything else, Murdock and Jones had reached their aisle with the other young women. They were full of chatter, and moments later, the second half of the concert began.

Again, the music soared around him, but he didn't get caught up in it this time. His thoughts were occupied with Luisa's situation. But by the time the concert ended, he didn't have any better answers for her. The conversation buzzed around them, and the building slowly cleared out until it was just their group left. Luisa's friend Sonja kept practicing her English for everyone and had them laughing at her pronunciation.

"At least I'm learning English faster than you're learning German," Sonja told Murdock.

"Not all of us can be Bob," Murdock said with a laugh.

Bob smiled. He was far from fluent, but he was getting better at the language every day.

"Before we know it, Bob will be speaking Italian too," Jones said.

"Right," Murdock agreed. "You should invite Luisa on your trip to Italy."

"Italy?" Sonja said. "You're leaving?"

Bob felt Luisa's curious gaze on him. "When I have leave in a few months, I'm going to visit my grandfather's hometown. He left there when he was seventeen and never returned."

"So your Grandfather Inama is Italian?" Luisa asked.

"Yes, and he still has extended family there."

The others in the group were no longer paying them attention, and their conversation was more private.

"He's still alive?" Luisa asked, her blue-gray eyes curious.

"Yes, and he always spoke Italian around me when I was a kid," Bob said. "Haven't picked up the language yet."

Luisa smiled, and something in Bob's chest eased.

"Have you decided what you'll say tomorrow at the hospital?" he asked.

"I think I'll take your advice and follow my heart." She tilted her head. "Tell me about your grandfather."

Bob considered her question. "He's always been a hard worker, whether in the mines in Wyoming or at his farm in Idaho. When my father began going to other churches, my grandfather, a devout Catholic, wasn't happy. So there hasn't been much of a relationship between my grandfather and my sister and me. No Christmas gifts or anything like that."

Luisa touched his arm. "I'm sorry. Perhaps visiting his hometown will bring you closer? You could show him pictures. Maybe he'll appreciate that?"

It seemed Luisa was of the same mind as Bob. "That's what I'm hoping. I'd love to bring him pictures of my trip."

Luisa smiled, and Bob smiled back.

"You'll be at church this Sunday?" he asked.

"I can be. I think Sonja is going."

"We're heading to the bus stop," Murdock called from the doorway.

Bob turned to see that he and Luisa were the only ones in the social hall.

He hadn't even noticed that the orchestra had packed up and the others had slipped out.

"Coming." Bob turned back to Luisa. "Let me know how your meeting goes."

"All right."

"You coming, Luisa?" Sonja was the next to poke her head into the room.

Luisa laughed. "Goodbye, Bob."

He watched her go, then left with Murdock and Jones, smirks on their faces. His mind wasn't on their ribbing though. Instead he was thinking of what Luisa had said about bringing back pictures to his grandfather. And how she was going to be questioned tomorrow at the hospital. He hoped it would go well and that Luisa would know the right thing to say.

CHAPTER NINE

"It should be clear to everyone that there is no means and no force which can halt this struggle of the peoples for their liberation, for it's a great historic process, one of ever-growing and invincible power. It may be possible to prolong the dominion of one state over another for a year or two, but just as in the past the bourgeois order of things came to replace feudalism and as, now, socialism is replacing capitalism, so colonial slavery is giving place to freedom. Such are the rules of human development, and only adventurers can believe that mountains of corpses and millions of victims will delay the advent of a radiant future."

—Soviet Leader Nikita Khrushchev,
Address to the United Nations, September 23, 1960

FRANKFURT, WEST GERMANY
OCTOBER 1960

Luisa saw the light on inside her house and knew that her father was waiting for her. Her pulse leapt, but then she reminded herself that she'd done nothing wrong. She'd gone to a concert at Sonja's church. She'd talked to others in attendance. That was all.

Yet the guilt still pressed against her stomach because she knew her father had warned her against American soldiers. She'd heard of girls falling in love and marrying American or British soldiers, then leaving their country and families behind when the soldier was reassigned.

She unlocked the door and slipped inside. Walking past her mother's slippers next to the door, Luisa found her father sitting at the kitchen table, his shoulders hunched as he read through a collection of papers. Luisa's mind went to Mrs. Weber again. She wondered if the hospital had contacted her father as well. Who was Mrs. Weber really? Had anything she'd said been true? And was she in pain from her surgery in a place where she couldn't find help?

"How was the concert?" Her father sounded tired, something she was familiar with as of late.

"It was very nice." She didn't offer any more information and wouldn't unless he asked. She joined him at the table, sitting down, because the mood emanating from him warranted it.

Her father nodded, but he seemed distracted.

She waited, not speaking, while her imagination went through many twists and turns.

When his gaze lifted again, she saw only storm clouds in the blue-gray eyes so much like hers. "I'm being transferred."

Luisa blinked. "To another department?"

"To another city."

Luisa exhaled, trying to absorb this information. She'd started her job, and now . . . if her father moved, she'd have to change jobs. Unless the city wasn't too far. "Where?"

"Berlin."

Luisa's breath froze. "What?"

"West Berlin." His tone was resigned, but Luisa wasn't ready to give in. Did he have no say? Could he turn it down?

Not only was Berlin over six hundred kilometers from Frankfurt, but traveling there meant going through Soviet-controlled East Germany. Did she have to go with him? She knew other young women who shared apartments. But as she looked at her father's downcast face, she didn't know if she could choose a job over him. Besides, her oma was not far from the inner border of Berlin, which divided the two halves of the city—east from west.

Her father rubbed a hand over his face. "I know that it will be a sacrifice for you," he said. "You have friends here, and your job only started. But Oma will be happy to have you closer."

"I was just thinking that." She offered a smile. But she was also thinking of what Mrs. Weber had said about the changing conditions in East Germany. Berlin was surrounded by Soviets on all sides, and the city itself was divided among the Allied forces. People were fleeing from East Berlin to West Berlin. Maybe if she and her father were in West Berlin, Oma would be willing to move the short distance and live with them. She would have to apply for government permission, but why would they turn down an elderly woman who wanted to live with her family?

"My new assignment is a promotion," her father said, as if adding an incentive. "I'll be assistant to one of the police chiefs. We'll have paid-for housing, so we can finally get out of debt, and once we sell this house, we can look for a place of our own. You'll be able to find a nursing job easily. There are plenty of openings."

His words hung in the air because they both knew *why* there were plenty of openings. The young professionals were vacating East Berlin to come into the main cities of West Germany, where they could work and live under less volatile conditions.

Her father's expression relaxed, and he gave her a gentle smile, a rare smile. "You'll adjust. You will see. I'll be moving up in the police force, and we'll . . . make a new start. We can visit Oma often, or we can talk her into staying with us."

Perhaps this new start was also him moving on from the painful memories of her mother's death. Losing her was still raw for the both of them, and Luisa knew that no matter how much time passed, living here, in this house that was so much her, was always a reminder.

Luisa could see as plain as day how much this was affecting her father—to leave their home, the home he'd shared with his wife. Even though selling the house would pay off the rest of her mother's medical debts, relocating to West Berlin was such . . . a change. Of everything.

She drew in a breath, then released it. Moving to another part of Germany wasn't the end of the world. She could take holidays and visit Sonja in Frankfurt. Luisa's thoughts skipped to Bob Inama. He was a friend, a new friend; that was all. There wasn't anything to be sorry about there.

So then why did her thoughts feel so heavy?

Her father was waiting. Her patient, quiet, grieving father. She placed a hand over his.

"I agree," she said in a soft tone. "It will be a new start for both of us. Oma is getting older too, and I'd like to spend more time with her."

Her father gave a satisfied nod, and she saw something akin to relief cross his features. "I begin next week, so we will have to pack things up as soon as possible. I'll find an agent who can sell the house, and I'll have to return at some point to sign the selling papers."

Luisa's throat constricted, so all she could do was nod. The real pain would come later, but in front of her father, she'd be strong. For him.

Luisa rose from her chair and set about fixing a sandwich for both of them, cutting open a loaf of bread and adding cheese and meat, then mayonnaise. When Luisa fell into bed later that night, she wondered if her mind would ever shut off. Not only did she have the admin meeting tomorrow, but now she'd be turning in her notice.

Somehow she slept, and somehow in the morning, she didn't feel exhausted. But a numbness settled over her as she walked to the bus stop. The fall day was beautiful, with its crisp air and warm scents of baked bread, pastries, and hot coffee coming from the cafés along the street. The trees were changing colors, and flowers still bloomed in the windowsills of the shops.

The tram arrived, but no sign of Sonja yet. As Luisa climbed onto the tram, Sonja came hurrying up.

Out of breath, Sonja sat next to Luisa, touching up her hair that was falling from its pins. "I slept through my alarm." Sonja took out a compact and lipstick from her handbag.

Luisa watched her friend touch up her makeup, and nostalgia pinched her heart. She'd miss this. Having a friend to share the day-to-day experiences with. Sure, she might develop friendships in West Berlin. Maybe . . .

"I have some bad news," Luisa said. "Well, good and bad. It depends on how you look at it."

Sonja immediately snapped her compact closed and turned to look at Luisa. "What's going on?"

Luisa told Sonja all about her father's new assignment and promotion.

Sonja didn't answer for what seemed a full minute. "I can't believe it. You can't *go*—stay with me. Move in. There's room. We can get another bed into my room, and—"

Luisa grasped Sonja's arm. "I'm going with my father. It's all decided. Plus, my oma will be close by."

"Is she in good health?"

Luisa confirmed with a nod. "But she's not getting any younger." It was as if Luisa was talking herself into it all over again. Maybe things would change. Maybe she *could* live at Sonja's. Maybe Father wouldn't mind . . . No . . . Luisa couldn't leave her father. Not now.

Sonja's blue eyes grew watery, and she moved close and hugged Luisa. "You will come visit, then? Every week?"

Luisa laughed despite her own tears burning her eyes. "Maybe every few months."

"Too long." Sonja only held her tighter. "Once a month. Promise me that, Luisa. I won't be able to bear it if you don't."

Her friend sure knew how to stir up the theatrics. "I will try my best. Once a month."

Sonja grinned. Then she gasped. "What about Bob Inama? Surely you—"

"Hush," Luisa said firmly. "Surely, nothing. We're friends. I told you that from the beginning. And we'll stay friends. Maybe I'll write to him or some-thing." She shrugged, acting out the nonchalance she didn't feel.

The tram rolled to a stop near the hospital, and as they climbed out, another nurse, who apparently Sonja knew, flagged them down. As the two women began to talk, Luisa fell behind them a step. She startled when she heard someone say, "Ms. Voigt."

Luisa turned and saw the one person she had never expected to see again. "Greta?"

Even though she wore sunglasses and a scarf tied about her head, Luisa recognized the woman. Greta brought a finger to her lips, then tilted her head . . . Luisa frowned. Greta was now walking away. Was Luisa supposed to fol-low? She looked over at Sonja, who was nearly to the hospital doors, talking to the other nurse. Then Luisa looked to where Greta had walked down the street.

Since Luisa had caught the tram on time, she had a few minutes before she had to clock in. Pulse surging, she hurried after Greta. Maybe she'd finally get some answers about Mrs. Weber.

Greta stopped beneath a row of sycamore trees. Before speaking, she looked around as if checking for anyone who might be close enough to hear them. "I have something for you," she said in a hushed tone when she seemed satisfied they had enough privacy. "It's from Mrs. Weber."

The way Greta said *Mrs. Weber* made Luisa wonder if that was the wom-an's true name.

Greta pulled out several deutsche marks from her handbag. "She wanted to thank you."

Luisa put her hand up. "I won't take money from Mrs. Weber or whatever her name is."

An unidentifiable emotion flickered in Greta's eyes. "She wants you to have it, Ms. Voigt. She insisted."

"I insist right back," Luisa said. "But I would like to know what's happened to her. Where did she go? The hospital staff wants to question me this morning."

The money was out again in a flash, and Greta added more to it. "How much for your silence?"

Luisa stared, trying to process this new information. Greta was *bribing* her for her silence. "I—I don't need money to keep quiet if that is what you're implying."

Greta's eyes narrowed. "What is your price? You must understand that no one can know anything about the note Mrs. Weber wrote. No one can know about me or about where you came to deliver the note."

"All right . . ." Luisa fell silent as someone passed near them on the sidewalk. When they were alone again, she said, "Mrs. Weber told me she wanted to see her daughter before she had to return to East Germany."

Greta didn't speak for a moment, as if she were trying to make a decision. "Whatever story she told you, forget it. Forget all of it. All you did was rebandage the woman's surgery site. You know nothing else."

Luisa swallowed against the sudden feeling of pebbles in her throat. "All right. I know nothing else."

Greta's eyes had narrowed, but she seemed to be gazing at Luisa with newfound trust. "Very well. And thank you. I can still pay you, but after I leave here, we will have no more contact. So your decision now is your final decision."

It wasn't a hard decision to make, especially after Bob had told her to follow her heart. "When I speak to the hospital staff, I will reveal only how I helped her medically."

Greta gave a satisfied nod. Then in an unexpected gesture, she took Luisa's hand and squeezed. "Thank you for being a champion of those who have been persecuted." And then Greta released Luisa's hand and turned. She slipped into the group of pedestrians waiting at the corner for the light to change.

Luisa hadn't gotten any of her questions answered, and now Greta seemed finished with the whole business. Except Luisa wasn't exactly sure what business it had been. Once Greta had disappeared from sight, Luisa turned and walked back to the hospital. She clocked in, then went about her duties, all the while waiting for the request to meet with the hospital staff.

It wasn't long in coming.

"Ms. Voigt," Mrs. Klein said as Luisa was leaving one patient ward and about to enter another. "Please come with me."

Luisa simply nodded since she already knew why she was being summoned. She walked with Mrs. Klein to an office where two other staff members waited. Luisa was surprised when a police officer walked in a moment later, who introduced himself as Officer Braun. The five of them sat around a table, and Luisa recited everything she could remember about the woman.

Even as she spoke, her pulse pounded in her throat. She wasn't lying, not exactly, but she was withholding potentially valuable information.

"You do understand that Mrs. Weber is now a fugitive from the law and her country?" the police officer asked.

He was a younger man, perhaps in his early thirties, with cropped hair and a precise mustache. Luisa wondered if he knew her father. She committed his name, Braun, to memory.

"I understand that now," Luisa said. "But I have told you about my interactions with Mrs. Weber." *Not everything though,* chanted through her mind.

Officer Braun studied her face in a disconcerting way, watching her for a moment before asking the next question. "Did you notice anything suspicious about Mrs. Weber? What was her emotional state?"

Luisa hoped that her expression wouldn't give her away. "She seemed grateful for someone to talk to."

Officer Braun gazed at her for another long moment, then said, "That will be all. If there is anything else you remember, anything at all, please alert Mrs. Klein immediately."

"I will." Luisa felt as if she'd been dunked into a cool river after a hot day in the sun.

After she was mercifully excused, for the rest of the day Luisa found that her nerves had been jangled. Every sharp sound made her flinch, and by the end of her shift, she had an intense headache.

Sonja wasn't at the tram stop, so maybe she was working late or had gotten off early. It was just as well because the moment the tram turned the corner and was within sight, Luisa decided she needed to run an errand before returning home.

From memory, Luisa made her way through the neighborhoods she'd walked through the day before. This time, though, she didn't have a blue envelope with her. This time, Luisa was going to get answers. She wouldn't leave until she did.

Arriving on the familiar street, she slowed her step as doubts set in. Whatever Greta and Mrs. Weber were involved in was clearly not legal. The offered bribe and her interrogation with the police officer had made that more than clear.

Luisa found the house easily, and she opened the gate and walked up the path. This time she didn't hesitate before knocking firmly on the door. No one answered, and she couldn't detect any sound coming from within. Luisa knocked again.

Still no answer.

Then she noticed that the drapes in the front room weren't closed all the way. With a quick look around, Luisa determined no one in the neighborhood was paying attention to her. So she stepped close to the window, cupped her hands over her eyes and peered inside.

It was hard to understand what she was seeing at first. The place was entirely empty. Not a chair, or a table, or a lamp. Did anyone live here at all?

What had Greta been doing here? Luisa had seen her just that morning. Was it possible to move so quickly?

Luisa stepped off the porch, more mysteries piling on top of each other in her mind. Whatever answers she'd thought she might find were completely swept away now.

CHAPTER TEN

- *"The decentralization, demilitarization, denazification and democratization of Germany*

- *The division of Germany and Berlin, and Austria and Vienna into the four occupations zones outlined at Yalta*

- *Prosecution of Nazi war criminals*

- *Return of all Nazi annexations to their pre-war borders*

- *Shifting Germany's eastern border west to reduce its size, and expulsion of German populations living outside this new border in Czechoslovakia, Poland and Hungary*

- *Transformation of Germany's pre-war heavy-industry economy (which had been extremely important for the Nazi military build-up) into a combination of agriculture and light domestic industry*

- *Recognition of the Soviet-controlled Polish government*

- *Announcement of the Potsdam Declaration by Truman, Churchill and Chinese leader Chiang Kai-sheck outlining the terms of surrender for Japan: to surrender or face 'prompt and utter destruction.'"*

—Agreements Made in the Potsdam Conference among the Superpowers, July 17–August 2, 1945

HANAU, WEST GERMANY
NOVEMBER 1960

"Fire, one," the command came, and Bob fired the semiautomatic M1 rifle.

Each bullet hit the target on the firing range. But before Bob could think of it as a job well done, he'd already loaded the rifle again with a new clip and taken position, ready for the command.

"Fire, two."

Aim. Fire. Bull's-eye.

The training had lasted all afternoon, and Bob had stayed completely focused. But on the way back to the barracks, he finally let his mind shift to the church social that night. A choir group was performing, and there would be food. Bob knew he'd enjoy both, but his thoughts strayed to a particular young woman. Luisa hadn't been at church last week, and it wasn't like he could ask one of the German church members about her. He hadn't seen Sonja either. Perhaps Luisa was on vacation. Or maybe she'd had to work last Sunday.

Bob was curious about what had happened at Luisa's meeting with her boss—had they ever found that woman who'd disappeared from the hospital?

"You're quiet," Murdock said, as they cleaned up the barracks before the dinner hour.

"He's always quiet," Jones called out with a laugh from where he scrubbed the doorframe.

Murdock slung an arm about Bob's shoulders. "What's troubling you? You were hitting those targets like there was an East German holding them."

Bob tamped down the irritation that prickled his neck. His friends were teasing, and it would only bring unwanted attention if he said anything. The East German soldiers were doing their jobs, like everyone else, so it bothered him that some US soldiers thought that an East German soldier was a personal enemy. But not everyone saw it that way, so he usually kept silent on the matter.

"Long week, I guess," he said.

"Everything all right back home?" Murdock asked, his tone serious for once. Mail had arrived yesterday, and both Bob and Murdock had received letters from home.

"Everything's fine."

The good thing about Murdock was that he knew when to back off. He dropped his arm from Bob's shoulder. "You still going to that church choir tonight?"

"I am."

"You couldn't pay me to go to that thing," Jones quipped.

Murdock chuckled. "A little culture never hurt anyone." He winked at Bob.

By the time he and Murdock boarded the train to Frankfurt that evening, Bob was feeling edgy again. He wasn't sure if he was anticipating seeing Luisa, or if he was worried that she'd be a no-show. Just like she had been last Sunday.

The closer they got to Frankfurt, the more he worried. It was like his subconscious was trying to tell him something, but he didn't know what. Murdock was busy talking to a group of Germans across the aisle.

"It's our stop," Murdock said, pulling Bob out of his scattered thoughts.

They walked the rest of the way to the church building and ended up being nearly thirty minutes early for the choir performance. Which meant that Bob spent most of the time keeping an eye on the door and the new arrivals. None of them were Luisa.

When Sonja walked in, relief pushed through Bob. She was with her brother—at least that's what he assumed, since the pair looked like siblings. But how could Bob manage to interrupt their conversation and ask about Luisa without being too . . . obvious?

Forgetting he was trying to be subtle, he left Murdock where they'd taken their seats and approached Sonja. After a quick greeting, Bob said in his best German, "Is Luisa coming tonight?" He tried for casual, but Sonja was way too astute to not read into it.

A pretty smile bloomed on her face. "She got stalled in a conversation as we were coming into the building."

Bob couldn't help his own smile growing on his face. "Great."

Sonja headed past him and into the social hall. Bob stayed near the door, wondering what to do. Should he wait here? Go back and sit down? If he did that, there was no telling if Luisa would sit by him, and then he'd have to wait until after the choir sang to speak to her.

So he moved into the main hallway and waited there. He nodded to a couple of latecomers. And still he waited. When the program started, Bob was torn between continuing to wait or returning to his seat.

Then the outer door opened, and Luisa walked in with another woman. They were talking, but Luisa's eyes caught his immediately. Bob shoved his hands into his pockets and wondered what excuse he could come up with about standing outside in the hall while the program was already underway.

And now Luisa's attention was back on the woman. "It's so nice to catch up with you, Maria," Luisa said. "I'll see you after the concert."

Maria bobbed her head, took one look at Bob standing there awkwardly, then ducked into the social hall.

"Hello, Bob," Luisa said. "Are you leaving or something?"

Bob cleared his throat. "Not exactly. I was . . . well, I was looking for you."

A pretty red stole over her cheeks. "You were? And why is that?"

Was she trying to make things complicated on purpose? The music rose in crescendo, and when it quieted, they were both still standing in the hallway.

"I'm teasing, Bob," Luisa said. "I'm glad you waited for me. Do you want to sit together?"

"That would be fine."

Luisa smiled, and he smiled. But before they went inside, he said, "How did your meeting go?"

Her brows pinched together. "Oh, that. Well . . ."

She paused so long that Bob wondered if she didn't want him to know. "You don't have to tell me," he started to say.

"No, it's complicated, and I still don't understand all that went on." Her gaze held Bob's. "Maybe you can make sense of it."

So Luisa told him about her boss, Mrs. Klein, and the meeting they'd had with a police officer. Luisa had told them about treating Mrs. Weber and that her disappearance was a mystery to her too. "At least, at the time of the interview it was."

"What do you mean?" They drifted closer to the outer doors as they talked, away from the choir program.

"Greta approached me at the tram stop near the hospital the morning after Mrs. Weber disappeared, and she offered me money for my silence," Luisa said. "She said she didn't want anyone to know about the note from Mrs. Weber. I refused the money of course."

Bob listened carefully as Luisa told him how she later went back to Greta's house, only to find it empty.

"She moved?" Bob asked.

"I'm not sure."

"Something's going on," he commented. "Do you think it's illegal?"

"All I know is that Mrs. Weber was desperate, and she was fearful about returning to East Germany." She bit her lip and looked out the window where they stood near the entrance.

"Maybe it was illegal, technically, but maybe you also saved her," Bob said in a quiet voice.

Luisa turned her luminous eyes to meet his gaze. "How so?"

"I don't know how much you want to discuss politics, since I'm American and you're German, but . . . the Soviets have done a number on East Germany."

Luisa didn't argue or seem offended. "I know, and I hate it. Our beautiful country is divided, and the Soviets use our own people against us."

Bob exhaled. The direction of the conversation had taken an unexpected turn. He knew this was a delicate subject—Luisa's own father wasn't too happy with Americans being in Germany. "Maybe your help was somehow a blessing to her."

Luisa clasped her hands in front of her. "I hope so." She offered a fleeting smile that didn't exactly reach her eyes. "I need to tell you something, Bob."

The seriousness of her tone sat like a rock in his stomach.

"What is it?" he asked, even though he wasn't sure he wanted to know if it was some sort of bad news.

"My father got a job promotion," Luisa said in a careful tone. "He's . . . he's been reassigned. To West Berlin."

Bob blinked, trying to comprehend. "A job promotion is always nice."

"Yes, it is," she said, her voice sounding small. "But I'm moving with him. I don't feel like I have a choice since my grandmother lives in East Berlin. She's widowed, and although we've tried to get her to move to Frankfurt for years, she refuses to apply for permission. Says she doesn't want to leave her home. So if I move with my father, I'll get to see Oma more . . ."

Bob did not like that she was moving—but he especially didn't like *where* she was moving. West Berlin was surrounded by eastern territory and Soviet rule. She'd be in the epicenter of tension and conflict. He wanted to warn her, but she certainly already knew of the danger, and it wasn't like he could tell her not to move with her father. This wasn't a time to think about himself and how he would miss their friendship. He'd miss looking forward to seeing her, though. Talking to her. Laughing with her.

"It sounds like an adventure." Bob tried to keep his tone upbeat. "And good for your father *and* your grandmother." His heart was already starting to ache though.

"I agree," she said, although it sounded like she was trying to convince herself.

"Family is the most important thing in life."

"I know." She paused, looking down at her clasped hands, then back up at him.

Bob furrowed his brows. Her eyes began to water, which only made his throat ache.

"It's just that . . . I'll miss you, Bob Inama," she whispered.

The air between them went absolutely still. Even the sounds of the music program had faded.

"I'll miss you too, Luisa," he said. "You've been a good friend."

Her smile was quick, and then she ducked her head and stepped past him. "Let's go listen to the program before Sonja starts to worry about where I am."

Bob walked with her to the door of the social hall, wondering how much time they had until she left Frankfurt and how he would feel when she was gone.

The following week seemed to move at a sloth's pace. Bob was counting down the days and hours until Sunday's meeting. He couldn't remember a time when he'd felt this anxious about seeing a friend.

Sunday finally arrived bright and early, and Bob took the early train. He didn't want to risk the possibility that Luisa would arrive before him and disappear into the chapel. He had plenty of questions for her—how her week went, if she and her father had picked a moving date yet, whether she'd heard anything more about the missing Mrs. Weber, or if Greta had shown up again.

But Luisa wasn't there.

He found himself hovering in the church hallway a few moments after the American meeting started. The German meeting was already well underway.

When Sonja walked in with her brother, Bob felt immediate relief. Perhaps Luisa was with them? Coming up the walk still?

When Sonja saw Bob, she paused, letting her brother pass by.

"Hello, Bob," Sonja said in English. "Good to see you."

"You too," Bob said, smiling at her fractured English. And then at the risk of his face growing hot, he asked, "Is Luisa coming today?"

"Didn't you know?" Sonja said, her eyes widening. "She moved to West Berlin with her father."

Bob's forehead tightened. "I knew she was moving, but I didn't realize it was this soon."

"They needed her father sooner than expected," she said with a shrug. "They decided they could leave without selling their house quite yet."

Bob tried to grapple with the fact that Luisa was gone, truly gone. They hadn't even been able to say goodbye. Well, what had he expected? For her to call up to the barracks? Hop on a train to see him in person?

"I'm sorry, Bob," Sonja said in a softer tone. "I didn't realize she hadn't told you about the date change. Maybe she didn't want . . ."

Sonja's implying that *maybe* Bob had become attached to a woman who wasn't all that interested in him only made things worse.

"Thanks for letting me know," Bob rushed to say. "I know she was looking forward to seeing her grandmother more." Then, as casually as possible, he added, "How does she like it?"

"Well . . ." Sonja pursed her lips. "She called me a couple of days ago. Said she found a new job right away but didn't say much else. She was kind of quiet about it all, but I suppose she'll get used to it."

Music swelled from German voices in the chapel.

"I'll let you go, then," Bob said, taking a step back. "Thanks for letting me know. I hope things will go well for her."

"Me too," Sonja said, her gaze still on him.

He turned and headed into the social hall with the American congregation. He made his way to the last row of chairs and sat down, his ears buzzing and his heart thumping faster than it should. Luisa was gone. That would take some getting used to. Should he have warned her about the dangers she might encounter? Or would that have sounded self-serving on his end? Her family came first, as it should. But even that thought didn't reduce the worry that had taken firm hold of him. He would pray for her safety.

CHAPTER ELEVEN

"From Stettin in the Baltic to Trieste in the Adriatic, an iron curtain has descended across the Continent. Behind that line lie all the capitals of the ancient states of Central and Eastern Europe. Warsaw, Berlin, Prague, Vienna, Budapest, Belgrade, Bucharest and Sofia, all these famous cities and the populations around them lie in the Soviet sphere and are all subject in one form or another, not only to Soviet influence but to a very high and in many cases increasing measure of control fr [from] Moscow."

—Winston Churchill, "Sinews of Peace," March 5, 1946

WEST BERLIN
FEBRUARY 1961

Winter kept a tight grip and didn't want to let go, or at least it seemed like it. Luisa and her father's apartment in Berlin was close to the Soviet sector of the city, where the buildings seemed grayer, the streets barer, and the wind colder. The clouds hung low and seemed almost iridescent with coal dust from heaters burning nonstop. As she walked the streets on the way to the hospital, she was grateful for her winter coat.

Her father had been right. It had been easy to find a job. She'd been hired right after her first interview, and although the pay was less than what she had been earning in Frankfurt, she hoped to at least make a difference. Perhaps her father would change departments again after a year or two? She could only hope. In the couple of months they'd been in Berlin, she'd made it back to Frankfurt once to visit Sonja, and Luisa was already looking forward to her next trip.

Luisa and her father had visited Oma three times now, and each time, she'd brushed off the suggestion of applying for government permission to leave East Berlin. This morning, Luisa had decided to visit Oma alone. Perhaps talking granddaughter to grandmother would be a different dynamic. It wasn't lost on Luisa that Oma saw her father as the man who had taken her daughter away.

A gust of wind had her burrowing her hands into her coat pockets. Her father had chosen an apartment that was a street away from Bernauer Strasse—which bordered East Berlin. The statuesque buildings loomed above her, dark and imposing.

Luisa turned a corner and slowed her step. A group of young men, maybe a couple of years younger than her, were loitering on the side of the street. Going to their jobs? They were passing something between them and snickering.

One of them turned and saw her, so it was too late to cross to the other side of the street without being noticed. There was nothing to be worried about, she told herself. So then why was her pulse jumping? She resumed her speed of walk and kept her eyes averted.

"Hello," one of the men said.

"What's your name?" asked another.

She was closer now, and surely the flush on her cheeks was noticeable.

"That's a nice coat," another of the men said.

Luisa had to hold back from running. It wasn't like she could outrun them anyway. They weren't saying anything cruel. Exhaling, she told herself she would be fine.

One of the men stepped in front of her, so she stepped around him, but he moved again.

"Let me pass," she said in a low voice.

"Where are you from?" he said.

Luisa glanced up at him. He needed a shave, but otherwise, he looked like most men in East Berlin. Dark clothing, face too thin, eyes haunted.

"Leave her be," came a sharp reprimand behind them. An elderly woman emerged from the entryway of the apartment building they were next to. She clutched a threadbare shawl about her bony shoulders.

The man in front of Luisa stepped back. "Sorry, ma'am," he said, although she didn't know if he was speaking to her or to the elderly woman.

Luisa shifted her gaze to the ground and hurried past the men, but when she reached the corner, she heard the woman call after her. Luisa didn't want to stop, but somehow her steps slowed. The men were out of earshot by now and no longer paying her attention. So Luisa turned and headed toward the elderly woman, coming to a stop a few paces from her.

"I have not seen you before," the woman said. "You should not be on this street alone."

"I—we moved here recently," Luisa explained. "I'm working at the hospital as a nurse. But I am going to visit my oma in East Berlin."

The woman narrowed her eyes. "A nurse? What's your name?"

Should she tell this woman her name? Luisa couldn't come up with a good reason not to, especially since this woman had come to her rescue. "Luisa Voigt."

Clutching her shawl tighter against a wind gust, the woman said, "Where did you move from, Luisa Voigt?"

"Frankfurt."

The woman scanned Luisa from head to foot. "This might be West Berlin, but things are not the same. We are in the heart of East Germany still."

Luisa nodded. "Thank you for helping me."

The elderly woman's lips pursed. "Be off with you. If you must cross into East Berlin, always keep your head down. Don't make eye contact. Stay away from the side streets and the Soviet police or the Stasi. Do you understand?"

"I understand," she said in a voice that crackled. "Thank you for helping me."

The woman waved an age-spotted hand. "If you find yourself in trouble again on this street, tell them you are the niece of Mrs. Herrmann." She took a step back, and before the wind could sweep away her words, she said, "I have a lot of nieces in this city."

Luisa wasn't sure if the woman had smiled or not before she disappeared into the apartment building. What a strange occurrence. Luisa had been nearly petrified, and now she didn't know what to think.

She turned toward her path again, and this time, she did as Mrs. Herrmann had advised. After showing her passport to the inner border guard, she headed into East Berlin. Keeping her gaze lowered, she didn't make eye contact with a single soul.

She hurried along the neighborhood street to her oma's. The grayness of the morning hadn't lifted, and it seemed to blend right into the gray buildings and streets. Her grandmother lived in a small house that had seen some damage during the war, like every other place in the neighborhood. It was during the siege on Berlin that her grandfather had been killed. Young boys and older men had been tasked with literally defending their homes. By that time, Uncle Karl, Oma's son, had also been a war casualty in the German army.

Luisa knocked on the door, then waited. Soon she heard Oma's shuffling steps, and the door creaked open. Her grandmother was an older version of Luisa's mother, so it always sent a quick pang through her heart when she first saw Oma. Her fine mahogany hair was threaded with gray now, and her pale green eyes turned up at the corners when she smiled.

"You didn't call," Oma said immediately, but her smile was warm, deepening the wrinkles about her eyes. "Come in, child. It's a cold day."

Luisa smiled at the way Oma called her "child." It had bothered her as a teenager, but now she found it endearing. She stepped into the now-familiar home.

Oma was already bustling toward the small kitchen. Luisa marveled that her grandmother had raised two children in such tight quarters and had done it while keeping everything pristine and in its place.

"I'll make some hot chocolate."

Luisa's mouth almost started watering. "Can I help?"

"No, sit down. It will only take a moment."

Luisa watched as Oma bustled about the kitchen, making hot chocolate by melting a chocolate bar, then stirring it into milk. She added an egg yolk to thicken the drink, then a dash of salt on top.

"Now," Oma said, setting the two steaming cups on the small kitchen table, "have you come here to talk me into leaving my home again?"

Luisa picked up the cup and relished the warmth seeping into her fingers. "Of course. That, and to visit you. How are you doing, Oma?"

Oma took a careful sip of her hot chocolate. "I am fine as always. You and your father worry too much. This is my home, you know. And now you live close by."

"I know." Luisa had heard it more than once. "And I can see that you're fine, but you're family, and we'd like to help you."

Oma stiffened and averted her eyes. Luisa hoped that she hadn't crossed a line.

Then, Oma rose to her feet. "I'd like to show you something since you aren't here with your father. It's time you understand some things."

Luisa's stomach went tight as she watched Oma disappear into the back bedroom. Moments later, she reappeared, carrying a binder. Oma sat down, then turned the binder toward Luisa.

The scrapbook had pictures and newspaper clippings and other memories inside. Oma turned a few pages, then pointed to a picture of Luisa's mother, Uncle Karl, and both of Luisa's grandparents. It looked like the graduation from Gymnasium for her mother.

"This was taken in 1933 and the last time our family was together," Oma said. "Your mother left soon after that, and we didn't see her again. At least for a while. Your opa took it very hard. I did, too, but I also wanted my daughter to be happy." She paused and blinked a few times. "And she *was* happy. Although that knowledge hurt too, with her choosing a different life."

Luisa's throat tightened as she caught a glimpse of her oma's emotions.

"Then she met your father, and . . ." Oma took a determined sip of the hot chocolate. "When she called to say she was engaged to get married, we knew we'd lost her forever. At least it felt that way. That first day was rough, then the entire week. After that, things felt numb. Opa didn't speak of her for a long time. Karl and I would only speak of her when Opa wasn't around. He wouldn't even let us go to the wedding."

Luisa blinked back the threatening tears. The next picture was a wedding picture of her parents that Luisa had always seen in her house. She hadn't even thought to wonder why her grandparents weren't in the picture.

"The day she called to tell me you had been born, everything changed for me," Oma continued. "I had respected my husband's feelings for long enough. We were grandparents, and it was time to end the divide. Besides, she'd been gone for four years, and I couldn't stand another day apart."

Taking a shaky breath, Oma wiped her eyes. "So I told your grandfather that I was taking the train the next morning. This was 1937, and although I hadn't traveled much for years, I was determined to visit my new grandchild."

Luisa smiled, although tears threatened in her eyes too.

"I packed, and about ten minutes after I had arrived at the train station, your grandfather showed up." Oma turned the next scrapbook page. There, in the center of the page was a picture of Oma and Opa—much younger— holding a baby.

Luisa leaned forward. She'd never seen this picture before.

"So, you see," Oma said, "your birth healed our family. Oh, there was still tension because Opa didn't like that his daughter had left in the first place. He thought she should move back with her little family to her hometown. Your father even seemed open to the idea as time went on. But then the war started."

That phrase echoed through Luisa's mind: *Then the war started.*

Oma turned the next page, and what followed was a series of pictures of Luisa at different ages with her grandparents and Uncle Karl. The pictures brought back her early childhood memories. Karl had died the first year of the war, and so she'd been about four years old when she'd last seen him.

In the images of Oma, she saw the likeness to her mother, as well as the happiness on her face. So there had been good times. Joyful times. Luisa was grateful for that. Oma turned another page. This one had a picture of Uncle Karl in his German soldier uniform. He had been in the Wehrmacht—the armed forces established by Adolf Hitler. Karl had been killed in a blitzkrieg campaign in France.

Luisa had been too young to understand her mother's grief. She only knew that her uncle had died and she couldn't have her favorite treats because of rationing. Her little world had been centered on her parents, and since their love never changed, Luisa knew her childhood had been cushioned.

"After learning of Karl's death, there were days I didn't know if I could go on," Oma said in a muted tone. "Opa barely spoke for weeks at a time. We probably should have talked through our feelings more, but we were each processing the loss of our son in our own ways."

Luisa's vision blurred as she gazed at the happy moments that included Karl and Opa.

With shaky hands, Oma closed the scrapbook. Luisa hoped she could see the rest of it, but now wasn't the time to ask.

"So you see, during the war, all I had was Opa," Oma said. "Even in his silence, we were still surviving together. When your mother would call, he would listen in, though say very little. Yet his eyes would always light up when you talked to us. Your little voice put the warmth back into both of our hearts."

Luisa knew what was coming next. It was a story she'd heard from her mother more than once, mostly because Luisa had asked for the details.

"All communication was cut off during the fall of Berlin," Oma said. "We were told all citizens must defend the city. But our soldiers were either gone or dead. That left the old men and young boys to protect the city. I remember finding Opa in the middle of the night cleaning his gun. I was horrified. I don't think either of us slept for days, and if we did, it was in pure delirium."

Luisa could no longer drink the hot chocolate. Her stomach felt like it was anchored to her chair.

"We heard shooting in the neighborhood, and we went to hide," Oma continued in a rasp. "Opa said he was going to unlock the door so the Soviets wouldn't encounter any resistance if they came into the house. We hoped they'd think it was empty and no one was here."

Luisa reached for a tissue and handed it to her grandmother, then took one for herself.

Oma dabbed at her face. "He was too late, or too early; I'm not sure which. They shot him through the front window. I don't even know if they were aware they'd hit someone. The Soviets merely walked past our house, firing into windows. Maybe as a warning, or a challenge. I have no idea."

Luisa shifted her chair closer to her grandmother and slipped an arm around her. "What a terrible thing. I am so sorry."

Oma leaned her head against Luisa's shoulder. "He was trying to keep us safe, you see."

"Yes."

"I think he died in peace. He never wanted the war, and the war took our son away, but being loyal to his country was also important."

Luisa gazed at her grandmother's distressed face. It was so very complicated. The Soviets claimed to have liberated the East Germans from Fascism—into Communism. "Oma, are you staying here to pay penance for the war? For being German?"

Silence.

Luisa reached for her grandmother's hand, and she grasped Luisa's hand so tightly, it was painful. "You don't need to endure Soviet rule as a punishment for a war you didn't start."

"I know I didn't start it," Oma said. "But I am a citizen, and we were all a part of the war. So we are all responsible. The atrocities that were uncovered by the Allies are still hard to comprehend."

Luisa didn't answer for a moment, then she said, "What could you have done differently?"

Oma closed her eyes and exhaled. "I don't know," she whispered, opening her eyes and looking down at her hands. "Helped with the resistance? Been less fearful? Braver?"

"I think you did help," Luisa said. "In your own way. You were a loving mother and grandmother and wife. You survived, Oma. You're still carrying all of your family members in your heart so that they live on. You don't need to punish yourself or pay penance any longer. Apply for permission to emigrate and move in with us."

Oma blinked back tears in her eyes. "You are a dear child," she said. "But leaving this house feels like leaving your grandfather. He died trying to protect me and this home."

CHAPTER TWELVE

"It's them or us. For me, that was the most terrifying thing. That instead of shooting cardboard figures we'd have to shoot our own people. And we knew, just like under Hitler, that if we refused we'd be taken off and shot ourselves."

—GÜNTER BOHNSACK, STASI LIEUTENANT COLONEL, HVA, DIVISION X

EAST BERLIN
FEBRUARY 1961

Oma had turned her down again, but Luisa now understood her grandmother's attachment to the home she'd shared with her husband. And she knew how it felt to move and leave memories behind. Not too long ago, Luisa had done it herself.

What was the solution then? Keep being patient, she supposed.

"Luisa," someone said.

Luisa looked up from where she'd been stocking one of the recently vacated hospital rooms. She hadn't even heard the nurse, Adel, come in. She was a year or two older than Luisa, and she always focused intently on Luisa when she talked. Adel's blue eyes seemed as large as a doe's, and her features just as dainty.

"Can you help out in the maternity ward today? They're short-staffed."

"Yes, of course," Luisa told her. But before she headed down the hallway, Adel stopped her.

"Is everything all right?" Again, those piercing blue eyes.

"Yes, fine," Luisa said.

Adel didn't shift her gaze. "You are worried about something?"

Luisa hid a sigh. "It's my oma. I just visited her in East Berlin." She knew enough not to tell anyone that she was trying to get her grandmother to relocate. Even in West Berlin, there were informers.

"Is she well?"

"She's well," Luisa said. "She lives alone, though, and is getting on in years."

Adel tilted her head, her gaze still watchful. "Well, I'll bet she's grateful you moved so much closer."

"Yes." Luisa turned from the staring woman and this time didn't pause as she hurried down the hall, toward the maternity ward. She'd been to the ward only once since starting this job. Two babies had been born the day before, but she didn't think anyone was currently in labor now.

She paused at the main desk when she entered the wing to find out where she was needed. The nurse at the counter handed her a chart. "Can you check the vitals of Mrs. Keller?"

"Certainly." Easy enough. Luisa took the chart and headed to the woman's room. She found Mrs. Keller turned on her side away from the door, staring at the opposite wall.

"Good morning." Luisa opened the drapes to let in more light. Even though the light was gray, it at least brightened the room a bit.

"You can close them," the young woman said.

Luisa turned in surprise. The patient's name was Mona Keller. Her pale and drawn face, along with her stringy dark hair, made her look like she hadn't slept well in a long time. Well, she had recently delivered a baby, so that was to be expected, right? Luisa didn't have a lot of experience caring for new mothers, but Mrs. Keller seemed despondent. Shouldn't she be happy about the healthy birth of her new baby?

After taking the woman's vitals, Luisa asked, "How is your pain?"

"Does it matter?"

Luisa paused. "You're due soon for more medication, but I need to record how you're feeling right now."

"The pain doesn't signify right now. My husband was imprisoned last week in East Berlin," Mona said. "I don't know when he'll get to see his son now."

Luisa stared at the woman. "I'm so sorry. When will he be released?"

The woman closed her light-brown eyes and exhaled. When she opened her eyes again, they were anguished. "They won't tell me. He's in his final year at the University of Berlin, and he started writing for an underground satirical publication. He and the editor were arrested for illegal distribution, since their publication wasn't authorized. They let the editor go but not him."

The arrest had been reported in the newspaper that morning, which her father had been reading.

"Can your father, or father-in-law, go and speak to the police for you?" Luisa asked.

"There's no one," Mona said in a hushed tone. "Both of our fathers were killed by Soviets in the Berlin invasion. We live with my mother in West Berlin. My mother . . ." Her voice cracked. "She can't receive any more bad news in her life. Only good news. Do you understand?"

Luisa thought about the loss of her mother and the loss of her uncle. "I understand."

"Could you go?" Mona pressed. "You're a pretty young woman, and perhaps the officers will listen to you."

How did Luisa keep getting these types of requests while working as a nurse? First Mrs. Weber, now Mona Keller. Luisa's first instinct was to say no. Maybe she should ask to be reassigned patients. But Mona's brown eyes had filled with tears.

"Please?" Mona said. "He's my son's father. He's . . . all we have."

Luisa's sympathy went out to the woman; it really did. But showing up at the police station in East Berlin with such a request certainly wouldn't put her father in a good light. "What about . . ." She hesitated—maybe she shouldn't offer such a monumental thing. "How about I ask my father? He's the assistant to the police chief here, although I don't know what influence or connections he might have in East Berlin."

Mona's eyes lit up for the first time. "Could you?"

"I can ask him—that's all I can promise," Luisa said. She wanted to help this woman, but she was wary of putting herself in the middle of this predicament. "I'll let you know what he says tomorrow."

Mona reached for Luisa's hand. "Thank you, thank you."

Luisa nodded, her heart tugging again. "Is this your first child?"

Mona seemed to relax at that question. "Yes. We wanted to wait until Hans was graduated, but . . ." Her face flushed pink. "I guess God had other plans."

Luisa squeezed Mona's hand. "I guess so. Get as much rest as you can. I've heard from my friends who are married with children that you need to sleep when you can."

"I will. And thank you again."

When Luisa left Mona's side, she worked the rest of her shift with trepidation. What would her father say? Would he be upset that she was trying to interfere? It was dark by the time she finished her shift, and she avoided the street where she'd run into the gang of men. Instead, she walked the busier streets and didn't encounter any problems.

She tried not to miss Frankfurt and Sonja and their friendship. Luisa would adjust eventually; she had to. She wondered how Bob Inama was doing, and that goofy friend of his—Murdock. Maybe she'd write to Bob. But it was hard to wrap her mind around that since even when they were together, they were separated by their cultures and countries. And now . . . they were separated by kilometers too.

Luisa was relieved when she turned onto the street of her apartment because it tore her thoughts away from her memories of Frankfurt.

Her father should be home very soon; then she could ask him her questions. Luisa unlocked the door, paused to glance at her mother's shoes, then headed into the kitchen. They'd brought her mother's blue dishes and yellow pots and pans, so even in this far-off apartment, it still felt like home. Luisa set about preparing sauerkraut with meat. By the time the apartment was filled with the fragrance of cooking food, Luisa heard the front door open.

She turned with a smile, only to replace it with a frown. "Is something the matter?"

Her father's troubled gaze met hers as he took off his hat then shrugged off his police uniform coat. "Nothing you should be bothered over. Some days in police work are rougher than others."

Well, Luisa knew that of course, but surely her father could talk to her about it? She'd fallen asleep many nights to the murmur of voices from her parents' late-night discussions. Trying not to show how deflated she felt, she moved to the stove and lifted the pan from it. She dished up the sauerkraut with meat, then set the plates on the table along with glasses of juice.

Her father sat down heavily, and she didn't comment on his sigh. When they were both nearly finished eating, her father said, "How was the hospital today?"

Luisa was glad he'd started this thread of conversation first, making it easier on her. She told him about Mona and her husband, who'd been arrested for writing articles for an underground publication.

Lines creased on his forehead. "And he's still in prison?"

"I told Mona I'd try to find out more information about her husband. His name is Hans Keller."

Her father set down his glass after taking another drink. "Absolutely not, Luisa. I don't want you involved with anything that has to do with the Stasi or Soviets."

"Mona is desperate, and she has nowhere else to turn."

Her father stood abruptly. He picked up his plate and glass and carried them to the sink.

Luisa's eyes stung with tears as she watched her father's stiff shoulders while he cleaned the dishes. She picked up her plate and glass, then set them in the sink. She grabbed a dish towel and began to dry. They worked in tense silence. After the dishes were put away, her father leaned against the counter and folded his arms.

"Today we had a call from the East German police," he said in a careful voice. "They asked us to help find someone who'd escaped from their prison. A fugitive."

Luisa's pulse stuttered. Was it Mona's husband?

But her dad shook his head as if he knew what she was about to ask. "It wasn't Hans Keller." Her dad sighed and rubbed his forefingers over his forehead.

"Did you find him?"

Her father's head dropped. "Yes."

Luisa waited for a long moment to see if her father would continue, but when he didn't, she prompted, "What happened?"

After a long breath, he said, "He was at a safe house. Which is no longer a safe house, of course."

"So you arrested him?"

Her father's voice was subdued when he said, "We did."

"What will happen to him now?"

"I don't know," her father said. "But this isn't only a conflict between the West and the East; you must understand that. Berlin is the center of the Cold War—the playing ground of the Allies as they stand off against each other. I'm learning quickly that everyone, on both sides of the border, is always on alert, waiting for something to happen. One heated disagreement could lead to an international incident, or worse . . ."

"Nuclear war."

Her father nodded. "I'll ask the police chief about that woman's husband. But if he doesn't want to inquire, then it will stop there. Understand?"

"I understand."

CHAPTER THIRTEEN

"I traveled by train to Torento, and by bus up to Sanzeno, my grandparents' village. I stayed in my grandfather's cousin David's home. David drove me around the area, where my grandfather, as a young boy, lived, played, and worked. I took about 2,500 slides of Germany and Austria. However, during the Rexburg [Teton] Dam flood, I lost them all."

—Bob Inama

SANZENO, ITALY
FEBRUARY 1961

"Albert?"

Bob turned, surprised at hearing his given name. He'd barely stepped off the bus in the small village of Sanzeno, Italy, home of his grandparents.

"You have arrived," the man continued in accented English. His smile was broad, welcoming.

Bob wasn't sure what he expected his cousin David to look like, but the man instantly reminded Bob of his Grandfather Inama. David was around forty years old, about six feet tall, well built and dark haired. A gold cross gleamed on his necklace. Bob knew that his Italian relatives were devoted Catholics.

Bob hoisted his duffle over his shoulder and strode to his cousin. "Thank you for meeting me."

David pulled Bob into a fierce hug, surprising him some. He'd been granted leave and permission to travel to Italy, and he'd spent weeks planning the route. More than one letter had been exchanged with David.

"Look at you," David said after releasing him, his grin even wider now. He patted Bob's cheeks and said something in Italian. Then he squeezed both of Bob's shoulders. "You are tall."

The English was hard to follow, but Bob caught his cousin's meaning. "You are tall, too."

David laughed good-naturedly. "You tease. Good. Humor is very good, yes?"

Bob hoped he'd caught most of David's words. "Humor is good," he repeated.

"Especially in Germany." The frown that crossed David's face was almost comical, but Bob knew there was deep-seated history between Italians and Germans over the war. Though nearly two decades in the past, it still affected them all.

"Come," David said, slapping Bob on the back. "My wife is waiting. And my parents and children . . . They will ask many questions."

Bob thanked him, and somehow they communicated with a lot of gestures and select English words.

"Hungry?" David asked, patting his stomach.

Bob smiled. "Yes. Hungry."

David chuckled. His laughter was warm and welcoming, and any reservations Bob might have had about staying with his cousin on such a journey now faded. Bob soon learned that during his stay in the village, he'd never go without food or drink. From the moment he stepped inside David's quaint home, Bob was plied with both.

Sure enough, Bob met David's wife, their children, and his parents. His children indeed asked him many questions, what felt like over a hundred. Their English was better than their parents, but the process was still slow going. They asked him everything from "Are you an American cowboy?" to "Are you friends with Elvis Presley?"

David chuckled at every question, and his wife rolled her eyes a time or two but didn't chastise the children. Everyone was eager to try out their English with Bob, and he was just as eager to learn some Italian.

After their meal, Bob walked about the village with David and was introduced to several people. A thrill ran through Bob each time he met someone who remembered one of his grandparents. The conversations, which he could barely follow, were in Italian and some scattered English, but they still managed to communicate with lots of gesturing and smiling.

Bob reported that his grandmother Marie and his grandfather Giuseppe were both doing well on their Rupert, Idaho, farm.

Sanzeno was beautiful and charming, and very small, with a population under one thousand people. With the cobbled roads, the stone village homes, and the statuesque beauty of the Alps, Bob felt like he was walking through a postcard. The colorfully painted homes and archways—yellow, peach, red, blue—with their balconies and *terrazza*, made him wonder how his grandparents had viewed America and its environment when they'd emigrated around 1910.

"I must show you the fishing pond," David told Bob as the sun set over the village. "This is the perfect time to catch something, when the pond is cold and the sun is setting."

Bob didn't mind putting off his sleep a while longer, and he walked with David to a wooded area that sported a pond. A few young men were there, lines cast into the water as they waited for something to bite.

David handed over one of the rods he'd brought, and the two fished until the oranges of the setting sun shifted to violet, then finally to the dark of the deepening night.

"Come, my family will be waiting," David said. "And I'm sure you'll need to get through more questions from my children before they allow you to sleep."

THE SLOW MARCH OF LIGHT

As they walked back to David's home, Bob said, "The village seems untouched by the modern world for the most part. I'm impressed."

David shrugged. "You're right, but most of the children who grow up here end up leaving. They find a job or go to a university. They don't return except for visits because the infrastructure isn't here to make a living."

Bob understood that, but he loved the quiet of the evening, the warm glow of the lights coming from the village homes, and how nature was all around them. This was probably why his grandparents stayed on their farm and never wanted to live in a bigger city. There was something to be said for the quieter life.

Throughout supper, David's children asked Bob more questions. This time about Germany and what it was like to be a soldier. "Do you get to shoot guns?" "Do you fly in a jet?" "Do you like fishing?"

At the last question, Bob smiled. "I love fishing."

Over the next several days, David showed Bob every haunt he could think of where Bob's grandparents had spent time in and around Sanzeno.

David took Bob to visit two couples who had also immigrated to Idaho but had since returned. They were the only ones Bob could have a full conversation with. But everyone was so kind, and Bob felt their hospitality and kindness deep in his own soul.

More than once, they visited the water fountain in the center of the village. The villagers would get their water from that fountain. David, in his broken English, told Bob stories about the history of the village, such as how at the end of WWII, food was so scarce that the people had to cut off bark from trees and boil it for food. And soon after the war, a fire in the village destroyed many of the buildings. That was why some of the architecture was new.

One evening, as they were walking back to David's home, he said, "Your grandfather sent us money. For the church." He waved toward a newly rebuilt church. "He paid for the bells."

Bob followed where his cousin pointed to the belfry. It brought a rush of pride to know this story about his grandfather. A stubborn, but an apparently generous, man.

Over the course of the week and a half, Bob and David had many talks. David told him about how he loved the village, despite how small it was. Bob hiked the surrounding areas, marveling that he was in one of the most beautiful locations on earth—in the heart of the Italian Alps. With David, Bob visited the other small villages close to Sanzeno, and David introduced him to more extended relatives. Bob's only regret was that he didn't speak better Italian.

Near the end of Bob's final day, David took him to the village cemetery. The day was warm for February, and Bob walked among the gravestones. Some of them were so old that they'd cracked and the engraving was nearly illegible. But he stopped in front of his great-grandparents' gravestones. So many years had passed, a full century, yet their blood still continued on. Through his grandfather, then his father, and now Bob.

A cold breeze stirred against Bob's jacket. He raised his camera to take pictures of all the grave markers in the cemetery. Then he walked around the church and took more pictures, both inside and outside. When Bob came outside again, David was still in the cemetery and seemed lost in his own thoughts as he picked his way among the headstones.

The temperature began to drop with the setting sun. Bob turned his face toward the fading glow. The beauty of the Alps rose above and all around him, making him feel like he was cocooned in the middle of a painting. For a moment, he felt the ache his grandparents must have felt when they'd left this majestic paradise for the mines of Wyoming and the rolling farms of Idaho—a wilder, more open country.

Bob raised his camera a final time and snapped a picture of David among the headstones of their ancestors. The temperature continued to fall as Bob remained lost in the thought that his past and his present were colliding on this small plot of land.

When the last of the pale-gold light on the horizon turned violet, David motioned for Bob to join him. It was time for the final dinner in Sanzeno.

The walk back to David's home was solemn. After the meal, Bob walked to the farthest point of the terrace at the back of the house, feeling like he was already missing his cousin's family. Here, he had a good view of the hills and the expanse of the valley. He might never return again to this place, but for a short time, he'd connected to his heritage.

Clasping his hands together, Bob said a prayer of thanks. If it hadn't been for the draft and the subsequent assignment in West Germany, he likely would have never stood on the soil of his ancestors. Standing in this place now, he knew he would never regret getting drafted into the army. Gratitude stirred through him, and he slipped his hands into his pockets as he scanned the surrounding beauty.

Something shifted inside of him, like a greater acceptance of the direction of his life. He was not alone. He'd always known that. God was evident in too many areas of his life. Bob had received too many confirmations to doubt. And here and now, he knew that there was a greater purpose to serving in the army. He might not know all of the reasons, but visiting his grandparents' homeland was certainly one of them.

For a moment, a pang pinched in his chest. He wouldn't be able to tell Luisa about his trip to Italy. She had moved away so quickly, they'd never exchanged addresses, although she could have written him at the army *Kaserne*. Worry niggled his mind as he thought of her living in such a volatile city, surrounded by East German control on all sides. But she was German herself, and her father was *ein Polizist*, so Bob's worries were certainly unfounded. He needed to put thoughts of her in the past.

Three days later, after Bob had arrived back at the barracks in Hanau, West Germany, he was called into Major Taggett's office. On the short walk to the office, a myriad of thoughts ran through Bob's mind. Perhaps the sergeant major wanted to inquire after his trip. Perhaps he was going to receive a rundown of upcoming events at the barracks. Bob hoped he wasn't being summoned for a violation of anything. But nothing he could've done wrong came to mind.

The nameplate of Major Taggett on the office door was like a siren warning. Bob exhaled, telling himself there was nothing to worry about. He knocked on the door, then entered at the invitation.

Major Taggett stood behind his desk, his expression solemn. He was a WWII veteran and as rigid as they came, a straight shooter without any humor to his personality. Not all of the soldiers liked him, but Bob didn't mind his brusque character. In fact, he liked the man and respected his lifelong career in the army. Bob guessed Major Taggett to be in his early forties, and based on his build, he likely would have no trouble entering combat at any moment.

Bob saluted the man, and the first words out of Major Taggett's mouth were "Sit down, Bob."

Why had Major Taggett addressed him by his first name and not his last name or rank? Bob tried not to act bothered as he took a seat, trying to breathe normally and focus on what was about to come next.

Major Taggett tapped a file on his desk, and Bob didn't need to crane his neck to look—something told him that the file contained information about him.

"I have your college transcripts here," Major Taggett said. "You studied prelaw and economics, yes?"

"That's correct, Major Taggett," Bob said.

Major Taggett's gaze was both searching and intense at the same time. "Bob, I would like you to volunteer for something."

Surprise rushed through Bob, and he was relieved not to be in trouble after all. But when he'd received his draft notice, some fellows from his church congregation who'd joined the National Guard had advised him to never volunteer for anything. Bob had sworn he wouldn't, but now the heat in his neck intensified.

"If you give me an order, I'll obey."

The major's brows lifted slightly, and he clasped his hands atop the folder. "Bob, I do have an order for you. We'd like you to register as a student at the University of Berlin and major in economics."

Bob blinked. Of all the scenarios that had gone through his mind, he wouldn't have ever come up with this request.

"We need you to do well enough to become the teacher's assistant to a professor by the name of Schmitt." The major studied Bob closely, but truthfully he didn't know how to react. "Schmitt is an economist who lives in West Berlin but teaches at the University of Berlin in the eastern sector. He's working on a project to help the East German cities get back on their feet. If he brings you on as his teacher's assistant, then you can go on his work trips."

The word *why* was on the tip of Bob's tongue when Major Taggett answered.

"Because of your acumen in both mapping and targeting, and your foundation in the German language, we believe you'll be a good candidate for this undercover mission." The major leaned forward, shifting his elbows onto the desk. "Do you have a girlfriend, Inama?"

Bob was still trying to process the information that he was being assigned to go undercover in East Germany. It took him a moment to wonder what having a girlfriend had to do with this assignment . . . unless the major doubted he'd make it out alive? A cold chill raced across the back of his neck. "No," he said—the word simple but true. Luisa was a friend, and he hadn't had time to date much during his last semesters in college.

"Well, you now have *three* girlfriends," the major announced, irony in his tone. "One in Los Angeles, one in Chicago, and one in New York City." Taggett smiled, a rare thing, and Bob might have smiled back, but he was trying to figure out where all of this was going.

"In East Germany, you're going to plot out the ammunition targets for our country, such as government buildings, freight yards, weapon arsenals, communication towers and centers, and underground bunkers. You're going to write down the longitude and latitude of each target as the address on the envelopes you'll send to your girlfriends." The major flipped open the file on his desk and picked up an envelope on top. He turned it so that Bob could see the face of the envelope. There, scrawled across the front, was what looked to be the numbers of an address.

Bob reached for the envelope and looked at it as Taggett continued. "There is a mail drop outside the university you'll use for your letters."

Nodding, Bob handed the envelope back. He could do this. Could he? Was there any choice? The steel of Taggett's eyes told him no.

"Now, listen carefully, Bob," Taggett said in a lowered tone. "No one will know about this assignment, do you understand? You'll be issued a fake ID with the name of Peter Jones. If you're compromised, or if you're caught, then you will only tell them your fake name. Nothing more. Your unit will be told you're on special assignment at the Seventh Army headquarters in Frankfurt. They know you have a background in prelaw and will assume you're helping on a case. We'll also have someone respond to any letters you receive from your family. Now, and in the future, whatever happens, everything you see and hear while on this assignment is not to be discussed with anyone other than me."

"Yes, sir," Bob said. His voice sounded hoarse.

Major Taggett held Bob's gaze. "Whomever you've trusted in the past, it doesn't matter. Trust no one now. You've been selected because you've excelled in all assignments, and now your country is depending on you in this war. It may not be a war of men in arms, but it is a war all the same. Our country needs to gather intel in order to give us the upper hand should the worst happen."

Bob knew what the worst was. Every minute of every day, one slight, one skirmish, or one shooting could lead to the eruption of a third world war, and this time the superpowers could unleash the monster of all weapons—the nuclear bomb. "Yes, Major Taggett," Bob said again.

Major Taggett wasn't finished. "As far as your parents, any of your friends, or any acquaintances know, you are *not* on this mission. It does not exist. And if the mission doesn't exist, then you cannot fail. There will be no official record of this assignment, so if it fails, you are on your own." He paused, his jaw tight. "Do you understand, Inama?"

CHAPTER FOURTEEN

"[At the close of WWII] the victorious Allies unfurled a map and carved up the city—the houses then lining the south side of Bernauer Strasse wound up in the Soviet sector while the street itself and the sidewalk in front belonged to the French. By this cartographic fiat, some sectors of the population would find themselves economically rejuvenated by the Marshall Plan and reintroduced to bourgeois democratic society, while the rest were stuck with the Soviets."

—MARK EHRMAN, "BORDERS AND BARRIERS"

WEST BERLIN
FEBRUARY 1961

Luisa walked the main roads on her way to the hospital in West Berlin. The late February weather was mild, and the breeze was not as cold or hard as it had been, but instead brought the promise of spring. She looked forward to seeing Mona and telling her that her father had received an answer to the inquiry that morning about her husband. Luisa couldn't wait to share the news.

When she stepped into the shared hospital ward, Mona was out of bed, dressed and holding her baby. A small suitcase perched on the stripped bed beside her. Luisa knew that it wasn't time for Mona to be released after such a difficult birth.

"You're being discharged?" Luisa asked when she reached Mona's side.

The woman's pale complexion and hollows beneath her eyes only confirmed that this was all too soon.

"I've been ordered to East Berlin for questioning," Mona said. "I must report this afternoon, or . . ."

Mona didn't finish, but Luisa could hear the fear and anxiety in every word she spoke. "Is this about your husband?"

With a nod, Mona pursed her lips. "I don't have any inside information. My husband never told me that he wrote articles. I found out after the fact."

Luisa now wondered if her news would make a difference. "My father says that there's only a single charge against him, so he shouldn't be in prison much longer."

"Thank you for asking your father to inquire," Mona said.

Mona wouldn't meet her gaze, making Luisa wonder if she was telling the truth about not knowing about her husband's underground publication. But that was not for Luisa to figure out. "Can you not let them know that you recently gave birth?"

Mona bit her lip and lifted her gaze. "I don't want to delay. I don't want anything to jeopardize his release. Do you . . . do you think you can check on my mother if I don't return soon? My mother's name is Sofia Beck."

How could Luisa say no? "All right, give me her phone number, and I'll check on her. And why don't you call me when you return so I know you're all right?"

Gratitude filled Mona's eyes, and they exchanged phone numbers.

"Remember, though," Mona said, "they might be listening."

Luisa frowned. "What do you mean?"

"With my husband's charges, I'm a person of interest now. The Stasi might be listening in on my phone conversations."

Luisa didn't have anything to hide, but she didn't like the thought of being monitored. Mona wasn't a criminal, and she was pretty sure her husband wasn't either. Luisa rested a hand on Mona's shoulder. "I'll call your mother to check in."

Mona wiped the tears that had fallen on her cheeks. "Thank you."

After Mona left, Luisa felt empty inside for some reason. She went about her duties the rest of the shift, but she had a hard time focusing on her tasks. Her mind kept leaping to worries about Mona and wondering how the interview was going.

The moment Luisa returned home that evening, she called the phone number Mona had given her. The phone rang four times before it was picked up by a woman.

"Hello, it's Luisa Voigt. I'm a nurse at the hospital where Mona delivered her baby. Is this Mrs. Beck?"

The woman exhaled. "Mona told me about you. Is everything all right?" Her voice was reedy and faint.

"I was calling to check with you," Luisa said. "Have you heard from Mona yet?"

"I have," Mrs. Beck said. "She called an hour ago. They are going to . . ." Her words broke apart.

Luisa stiffened and turned toward the kitchen window. She couldn't see much outside with the dark approaching. Only the tops of trees and the violet sky beyond. "What's happened?" she asked.

"They're keeping her longer, and they told me to come and fetch the baby."

Luisa closed her eyes. "Why do they want Mona?"

"I don't know," Mrs. Beck said, her voice breaking again. "I have to get the baby tomorrow. I don't know how I'll manage the baby without Mona."

Luisa opened her eyes as Mrs. Beck talked about her worries, for the baby, for her daughter, and for her son-in-law. So many unknowns. Luisa also worried about the new mother's health. If Mrs. Beck fetched the baby, then Mona wouldn't be able to breastfeed.

"I will come with you," Luisa heard herself offer. She would have to call into work and take the morning off, but Mrs. Beck's frantic tone told Luisa that the woman needed help.

Mrs. Beck exhaled into the phone. "You would do such a thing?" Her tone was already sounding less stressed.

"I can let the hospital know that I'm taking the morning off, and we'll take the bus."

Once they worked out the specifics, Luisa hung up with the woman, feeling the weight of responsibility, but also feeling lighter. She couldn't do much, but she could help Mrs. Beck bring back the baby.

She turned and nearly let out a yell when she saw her father standing there. She hadn't even heard him come in because she'd been so caught up in her plans.

His dark brows were furrowed as he gave her a hard stare. "What's this?"

Luisa swallowed back her nervousness, then explained about Mona and the baby. Her father listened, although she could tell it was hard for him not to interrupt with questions.

"You will not go," he said. "You can't put yourself on the radar of the East German police. They already know there was an inquiry from the West about him. That needs to be enough."

Luisa felt sick thinking about calling Mrs. Beck and telling her no. "I don't even have to go into the police station. I'd be there to just travel with Mona's mother. To help her out with the baby."

Her father's brows were still angry arches when she finished. "It is too dangerous. You get involved in their lives, and you will then be involved. You don't want your name linked to someone in jail, no matter how innocent."

Luisa fisted her hands, trying to contain the disappointment running hot through her. She couldn't defy her father. She understood his logic, but she also believed it was ridiculous that she couldn't accompany Mrs. Beck to fetch her grandson. There was no reason for Mona to be detained anyway. What was happening to her right now? Had she been given a bed? Food?

Her father moved closer and set his hand on her shoulder. Much like she'd touched Mona earlier that day, trying to offer some comfort.

"You have a good heart, Luisa," her father said. "Sometimes you remind me so much of your mother that it's . . . difficult."

"But . . . ?"

"But you're a nurse," he said. "You're already helping people. It's your profession, and your nature as well. If you picked up every broken bird you found, what do you think would eventually happen?"

She thought of her willingness to take the morning off to help Mrs. Beck. "I might not be employed anymore?"

"Exactly." Her father dropped his hand, and his tone turned more serious. "I cannot allow you to go into a dangerous situation. Your mother would never forgive me."

Whenever her father brought her mother into the conversation, she knew that he was speaking out of fear of losing another family member. She couldn't argue against that. Yet, how could she go about a regular day tomorrow and let Mrs. Beck travel to East Berlin alone in such a distressed state?

The phone rang, and both of them flinched.

"You can get that," her father said.

They both knew it would be for her. Likely Sonja, who called every once in a while, or maybe the hospital with a change to her schedule. Perhaps it was even Mrs. Beck. Luisa answered, knowing her father would hear every word spoken.

"Luisa!" Sonja's cheerful tone sailed across the distance. "I'm so glad you answered."

Luisa found herself smiling as she pushed down the emotion from her conversation with her father. She put a hand on the mouthpiece and said, "It's Sonja."

He nodded, then trudged down the hallway to change out of his police uniform.

Luisa moved to the stove and set out a pan to heat up gravy sauce for the leftover roast. "I'm glad you called," she said, hoping that her voice didn't sound shaky.

"Ah, well, I have so much to tell you."

Luisa pulled out potato salad from the icebox as she listened to Sonja talk about her job in Frankfurt. Pushing back the envy, Luisa laughed at some of the silly stories Sonja told of the children who were under her care. "One boy thought he was Superman from a comic book, so he used a sheet for a cape and jumped off his porch steps. Landed wrong and broke his wrist. But he insists it doesn't hurt."

Luisa smiled. "He's a tough guy."

"Speaking of tough guys, Bob Inama asked about you."

"Oh?" Luisa asked as she stirred the gravy. Sonja had told her this a handful of times. She'd thought about writing him at one point . . . well, at several points, but hadn't.

"He went to Italy for a couple of weeks, I guess," Sonja said. "When he was back at church, I told him you're enjoying your job but miss a lot of things about Frankfurt."

"That's true." Luisa shouldn't be having any sort of thoughts about an American soldier. So being in West Berlin was probably a good thing right now.

"Well, tell him I said hello next time you see him," Luisa said. It was the best—no, safest—thing she could say.

"You can tell him yourself," Sonja said. "Come for a visit. Please? You've been gone too long."

Luisa laughed. "You make it sound like years instead of months." She might be teasing, but she'd love to return to Frankfurt.

Sonja joined her laughter. "Oh, I almost forgot why I was calling. A woman came up to me at the bus stop today and told me that she needed to speak to you. She gave me a phone number. I tried to tell her that you no longer lived in Frankfurt, but she disappeared almost as soon as she appeared."

Luisa frowned as she scooped out the potato salad into two bowls. Her mind leaped back to her Frankfurt days. Who might want her to call? Maybe their old neighbor, Mrs. Wagner?

"She said her name was Greta, but she didn't give me a last name."

Luisa's spatula paused over the simmering gravy. "What did you say?"

"Greta," Sonja said. "Do you know her? Who is she? She was pretty but seemed like one of those women who never smile or have any fun. Maybe she's . . ."

Closing her eyes, Luisa tried to soak in the information Sonja had just given her. After all this time, why now? How did the woman know that Luisa was friends with Sonja? And—

"Luisa," Sonja said, her tone sharp. "Are you still there?"

"I'm still here," Luisa said. "Sorry. What were you saying?"

"Can you get a pen and paper and write down the number?" Sonja said. "I don't want Greta tracking me down again. She was kind of intense, if you know what I mean. Maybe she's part Soviet."

Luisa didn't laugh, but she knew what her friend meant. She set down the spatula, then rummaged for a notepad.

"Oh, and this was really strange. She told me as soon as I gave you the phone number, I had to get rid of it on my end." Sonja laughed. "What a strange duck, right?"

Luisa tried to match her friend's light tone. "Right. Now, what's the number?" She jotted down the number, then had to endure Sonja's chatter about her brother and Charlotte, who might be getting engaged soon.

Yes, Luisa was interested, but right now, curiosity had taken over all her thoughts. What did Greta want? Was it about Mrs. Weber? Had the woman been found? Had she returned to East Germany?

The minutes dragged on before Sonja finally hung up, and it was at that moment Luisa realized she'd nearly burned the gravy. She hurried to stir it and added some water. Then she set the table, and as she dished the roast onto the plates, she heard her father's footsteps coming down the hallway. By the time he stepped into the kitchen, she'd composed herself from her frenzied thoughts.

"How is Sonja?" her father asked.

For the next several moments during their meal, they chatted easily. Mostly about Sonja. A little about some of the men her father worked with. Luisa told him about a couple of her patients. It was almost like a normal conversation between father and daughter. Almost.

Almost, because of the dread building in Luisa's chest. Her father was scrutinizing her, assessing, and questioning. Did he not believe that she'd stay out of the situation with Mona? But how could she disappoint Mrs. Beck? And what did Greta want?

Luisa waited a full two hours after her father had retired for the night before stealing back into the kitchen. He was surely sound asleep, and even though it was after midnight, she didn't know when else to call Greta's number. Luisa couldn't sleep anyway. Perhaps no one would answer, or perhaps Greta would be upset over a middle-of-the-night phone call.

Somehow Luisa didn't think so. She bounced a foot as she dialed the number she'd memorized. Although she'd written it down, Luisa had thought better of keeping the scrap of paper and instead had ripped it up and thrown it away.

The phone picked up on the second ring. No one said hello. No one said anything. Not for a full thirty seconds. But for some reason, Luisa remained on the line, not understanding why she did so.

"Call from a secure line."

It was Greta's voice. Luisa knew it by the hairs that had risen on the back of her neck. "How? Where?"

But the line went dead with a soft click.

Luisa wrapped her fingers around the floral pendant at her neck as she sat alone in the dark, silent kitchen. She had even more questions now.

CHAPTER FIFTEEN

"The inner-German border became one of the Cold War Europe's most menacing frontiers—an 858-mile death-strip of barbed wire fences, control points, watchtowers, mines, and later, automatic shooting devices."

—David Clay Large, *Berlin*

WEST BERLIN
FEBRUARY 1961

Luisa made her father's lunch—black bread, meat and cheese, with plenty of mayonnaise—to take with him. She worked carefully, deliberately, to prevent the trembling in her hands from being noticeable. Her father was only a few feet away, drinking his morning herbal tea as he pored over the newspapers.

She needed him not to be late today. She needed him to leave quickly so that she could slip out moments behind him. When her father at last left the apartment, Luisa flew into action. She called the hospital and told them she wouldn't be in that morning and possibly the rest of the day. Then she snatched her coat, pulled her hair into a taut bun, and slipped on her shoes. Next, she pulled out a narrow tin box from beneath her mattress, where she kept her savings. She removed the money she'd need, plus a little extra, then left the apartment, glancing at her mother's heeled shoes as she headed out the door.

Enough time had passed that her father was out of sight, but Luisa's pulse was still drumming from her rushed preparations. Whatever happened, she had to be home before her father arrived that evening. If all went well, she'd be back by lunchtime. Perhaps she could even report to the hospital for a few hours.

But right now, she needed to find a safe phone on the way to the bus station. The morning was still early and brisk. She paused at a public telephone booth, and since no one was inside, she slipped in.

She rubbed her hands together to warm them up, then put in a coin and dialed Greta's number. Two rings, and the call was picked up.

Again, no one spoke on the other end, and neither did Luisa as she waited. Thirty seconds passed, then she heard Greta's voice. "Is this a safe line?"

"It's a public phone box near the bus station." Luisa heard a small exhale from the other end.

"We need your help," Greta said.

"Why me?"

"You're trustworthy." Greta's tone was matter-of-fact. "And your oma is in East Berlin, so you have a perfect excuse to travel back and forth."

How did Greta know about her oma? "My father is *ein Polizist*," Luisa said. "I can't jeopardize his job." She thought she heard a scoff, but it was too faint to decipher. "I don't want to put my oma at risk either."

"We know all about you, ma'am, and your family situation," Greta said. "You have an option here. But you have seen how East Germany is. Think about that. Think about those who are desperate for a new start in life. If you're absolutely sure you don't want to help, then I understand, but you must hang up right now."

Luisa was so stunned, she did nothing. A moment passed, then two, as she searched her mind for a response.

"Will they be like Mrs.—"

"Don't speak her name," Greta cut in. "Not over the phone. Even if you're on a safe line. Your clothing or purse could be bugged. Maybe not now because you're new to our organization, but eventually it will happen."

A tremor snaked its way along Luisa's back, but not because she was afraid. Because she sensed the monumental decision she had to make—right now. Perhaps it was because she was a trained nurse, or perhaps it was because she had seen the neighborhood of her oma. And Luisa's greatest desire was that her oma leave the GDR.

She drew in a steady breath. "Tell me one thing," Luisa said. "How did you know about my oma?"

The pause on the other end of the line was heavy. "One of our agents works with you at the hospital. You'll learn about her soon enough."

Luisa's mind raced. Who had she spoken to about her oma? Adel was the only one she could think of. Was Adel an agent of some sort?

Greta continued as if Luisa's silence was agreement to help. "There's a woman who needs the address of our safe house," Greta said. "I'm going to give you two sets of addresses. Memorize them both. The first one is the safe house in West Berlin. The second is the home of Mrs. Belding in East Berlin. She needs the address before dark. Today."

Luisa's mind was reeling. A safe house? Why would the woman need a safe house? West Germany had a refugee center for those in need. Unless she was a criminal of some sort? Luisa's stomach felt like it had bottomed out. But her thoughts were already pushing forward, and she realized she did want to help. "*Today?* But how? And I thought we weren't giving out names."

"Mrs. Belding is not her real name," Greta said, "but she will know you when you inquire for her. You're not going into work today, correct?"

"Correct." She couldn't take a full breath. How did Greta know this as well? Luisa hadn't even known for sure until this morning. Had the contact at the hospital informed Greta? Luisa noticed a man approaching the phone box. Her time was limited now.

"Find a way to reach that address and deliver your message," Greta said in a soft voice. "A woman's safety depends on it. Do not bring attention to yourself. You will be unobtrusive in all things. Do you understand?"

"Yes," Luisa said.

"Another contact will be in touch with you for other assignments."

"Not you?"

The man outside the phone box tucked his newspaper under his arm, giving up all pretense of being patient.

"I may not speak to you again," Greta said. "The contact at the hospital will take it from here. Do you have any questions?"

Luisa had plenty of questions, but Greta probably wouldn't answer any of them. "I should go," she said. "There is a man waiting for the phone."

"What does he look like?" Greta was quick to ask.

"Hat, dark jacket, a couple inches taller than me. Is he my contact?"

"Remember details," Greta said. "Always remember the details of anyone you encounter. If you are stopped in East Berlin, tell them you're visiting your oma or running an errand for her. My final parting advice is that next time, disconnect the call before someone has a chance to observe you for too long. Find another place to call, and always call on safe lines."

"All right." Luisa's breathing tensed as Greta gave her two addresses—neither of which she recognized or knew how to locate. But both of which she memorized. Before Luisa could ask for any further instruction, the line clicked off. Greta had hung up.

Luisa's hands were shaking again as she hung up the phone. She opened the booth door and stepped out into the sharp wind. She nodded to the man without making eye contact. But as Luisa walked away from him and toward the bus station, she clocked in his description. Sandy hair. Thin mustache. Pinched eyes. Nicotine-stained fingers.

Nerves were still doing a number on Luisa's stomach as she reached the bus station. Mrs. Beck was already there, and despite the phone call with Greta and her upcoming task, Luisa was relieved to see the woman.

Mrs. Beck looked like a former, or older, version of Mona. Dark hair, deep-set eyes. The deep wrinkles of a life lived too hard.

"You are Ms. Voigt?" she asked.

"Yes. Mrs. Beck?"

Mrs. Beck grasped Luisa's hand and squeezed. "Thank you for coming with me. You are a dear young woman."

Luisa tried to smile, but it wouldn't come. "I hope that your daughter and son-in-law will be released soon."

"God willing," Mrs. Beck said.

They headed for the ticket office, and Luisa bought a map as well. The bus ride into East Berlin wouldn't take long, but it would be nice to be out of the cold.

On the bus, she felt self-conscious as she looked up the address she needed in comparison to the police station. Since her conversation with Greta, Luisa was looking at everyone differently. She made quick mental notes of those near them on the bus. Was she being watched? Were *they* being watched?

She turned her attention to her map, and after memorizing the directions, she tucked the map into her purse. She didn't want to look like a tourist once they were in East Berlin.

When they arrived at their bus stop, the cold wind greeted them the moment they exited, and Mrs. Beck burrowed her hands into her pockets. The passengers from the bus dispersed quickly, and soon it felt like she and Mrs. Beck were the only ones cutting through the wind. Overhead, clouds moved across the sky, darkening. It was going to rain any moment, and Luisa wondered how they'd keep the baby dry until they returned to the bus station.

Somber gray buildings towered along the next street they turned on. They looked like they hadn't been repaired from the bomb damage of WWII, and perhaps they hadn't. The pockmarked façade spoke of bullets from guns and heavier machinery. Even if the wind hadn't been so cold, Luisa would have shivered anyway.

"There it is." Mrs. Beck motioned toward a stately government building bedecked with red Soviet flags.

Luisa scanned the pillars and the windows. Nerves burned in her chest. *Small. Stay small,* she told herself. When they reached the steps leading up to the doors, Luisa said, "I'll meet you at the bus station."

Mrs. Beck turned with a troubled gaze. "You're not coming in? But—"

Luisa touched the woman's arm. "It's better that they don't question both of us or separate us. I have something to do that will take only a moment, then I'll meet you at the bus. All right?"

Mrs. Beck looked like she wanted to protest, but Luisa had already dropped her hand and stepped away. She turned and walked, not looking back, not wanting to see Mrs. Beck's pleading gaze.

Luisa turned the corner, then the next, reading the names of the street signs as she went. Otherwise, she kept her head down and walked at a pace that was neither too fast nor too slow. But she watched everything and everyone. She knew there were Stasi about—the East German secret police. They wouldn't have on any sort of uniform if they were undercover. There were also the regular East German police in their drab gray uniforms, and the Soviet police in their darker gray uniforms, with red on the shoulder tabs and collar decals.

She didn't want to be stopped or questioned.

When she reached the street with the name she'd memorized, Luisa was both relieved and jumpy. She'd come this far. Now all she had to do was knock on the right door. Without slowing her pace, trying to hide the fact that this was her first time in the neighborhood, she reached the apartment building. It rose five floors, and some of the windows had been blacked out. Left over from the war? Or was this a practice still for privacy?

The street was empty of pedestrians, yet Luisa felt far from alone. She couldn't quite explain it, but she felt like she was being watched by more than one pair of eyes. Walking into the apartment building, she headed to the second floor, her shoes echoing on the cement steps. It was then she realized she hadn't thought up a reason for visiting "Mrs. Belding" if she should be stopped and questioned.

Thankfully, no one was in the corridor. She knocked tentatively on the door and waited as she pressed two fingers against the floral pendant hidden beneath her coat. She could hear shuffling beyond the door, and she wondered if she should knock again or keep waiting.

Then the door swung open.

It was a girl. A young woman of maybe sixteen or seventeen.

Luisa tightened her hold on her purse. "May I speak to Mrs. Belding?"

The teenager's gaze flicked behind her, then she stepped into the hallway and pulled the door closed with a quiet click. She put her finger to her lips, then motioned for Luisa to follow her. Luisa followed her to the stairwell.

"I am Mrs. Belding," the young woman said.

Luisa's mouth felt drier than sandpaper. Was this teenager really in need of a safe house? "Are you sure?"

The teen scanned Luisa from head to foot. "You have a message from Greta?"

Relief jolted through Luisa. This was the right place and the right person. "Yes." She released a slow breath. Then she quoted the address she'd been told.

Satisfaction gleamed in the young woman's eyes. "You should leave a different way than you came. They're watching all comings and goings of this building." She lowered her voice to a whisper. "Not all Stasi wear uniforms, you know."

Luisa nodded numbly. "How should I leave? There was only one way in."

"Go to the basement, then you'll find another set of steps that will take you out to an alley in the rear," the young woman said.

"All right."

"Thank you." Then she waved Luisa off. "Go now."

So Luisa left. She hurried down the stairs and kept going until she was underground. The dank cold nearly cut to her bones, so she was relieved when she stepped into the alley. The place was dead quiet, and that didn't settle right with her either.

Luisa walked briskly back to the bus station.

As people ebbed around her, getting on and off busses, the minutes ticked by. Mrs. Beck should be back soon. Luisa hoped, at least. Another hour passed, then another. Luisa was now starting to worry that she'd have to leave East Berlin without Mrs. Beck.

Luisa pressed her fingers against the pendant at her breastbone as she searched through the incoming passengers. Then there she was. Luisa's chest burned with relief when she saw Mrs. Beck come into view, cradling a bundled infant against her chest.

Luisa's exhale was audible as she strode forward. When Mrs. Beck's gaze found hers, the relief on the older woman's face was evident.

"Thank goodness you're still here," Mrs. Beck said, her face aglow with relief. "I didn't know if you'd wait."

"I'm relieved to see you," Luisa said. "Now, your arms must be aching. Let me hold the baby."

Mrs. Beck hesitated only a moment, then she handed over the precious cargo.

Luisa smiled down at the sleeping child. It was impossible not to. He had a full head of fuzzy blond hair, and his pale eyelashes were long and silky. "What's his name?"

"Hans. After his father."

"Hello, Hans," Luisa crooned, quite forgetting that she was in the middle of an East Berlin bus station.

Mrs. Beck was all business. "Let's get our tickets and get out of here as soon as possible."

As they headed toward the ticket booth, Luisa asked about Mona.

Mrs. Beck's reply was barely above a whisper. "They won't tell me anything. They said I should have her lawyer keep me apprised. But everyone knows—" She looked about them, then lowered her voice even more. "The attorneys here simply work for the government. The *Volkspolizei*, the attorneys, the military—they are all controlled by the same leadership."

Someone from behind bumped into them, and Luisa tightened her hold on little Hans. "We'll talk about it later," Luisa said.

Mrs. Beck's mouth formed a rigid line.

Tickets in hand, they boarded the bus. Luisa had never felt so much relief in her life as she did when the bus started moving forward and they were once again inside West Berlin.

Mrs. Beck reached over and grasped her hand. "Thank you for coming with me."

Luisa only nodded because her throat had gone taut. She hadn't done much, but she had been an emotional support. And in this case, that was enough. Still, she hoped that the baby's parents would soon be released and the family reunited.

She knew all about broken families.

CHAPTER SIXTEEN

"We concluded that our biggest threat would be the Stasi and the ordinary police, because they were so effective. We did not believe that elite military forces would be used to target us but that all of us were well known, and that the Stasi and the police, the Volkspolizei, would be looking for us."

—Colonel Darrell Katz,
US 10th Special Forces Group (Airborne), Bad Toelz, Germany

WEST BERLIN
MARCH 1961

"You'll study the language for one month," Major Taggett had told Bob. He'd arrived in West Berlin after riding through East German territory on a night train. The train had wound 110 miles through East Germany in the dark of night, but that hadn't mattered. The windows were painted so no one could see outside. With all of the inspection stops in East Germany, including Erfurt, Leipzig, and Dessau, the trip lasted about six hours. The train commander and military police made a visual inspection at the random stops, while the Soviet soldiers paced the length of the train. The Soviets would randomly go through people's IDs and ask questions. Mostly harassing. Bob watched more than one passenger ordered off the train.

It was a good moment when Bob climbed off the train in the early morning, after gathering his single bag. He headed out of the train station, safe at last in West Berlin, his fake ID securely tucked away. The afternoon sun was weak, and the wind had a cold bite to it. No matter.

"Grow your hair out," Taggett's final instructions had been. "Look German, act German, speak German. The more German you appear, the less you'll be questioned. Be punctual always."

How did one *act* German? How did one become another person entirely? Peter. He was simply Peter Jones now, an American college student here to attend a German university. No rank, no title. Bob was wearing civilian clothing, nothing to stand out. Gray slacks, tan shirt, and a dark-gray overcoat. It felt odd not to be in uniform or fatigues. After being in the US Army for over a year, he'd become accustomed to it.

Conversation buzzed behind him as an older couple walked out of the station not too long after him. Bob slowed his step and tried to catch their rapid German, but he comprehended only about fifty percent of what they said. Did Berliners have a slightly different accent? He needed to work on that. And that was his first task in West Berlin. Before attending Professor Schmitt's economics class, Bob was going to be living in a German home to study the language for a month.

It wasn't lost on Bob that Luisa Voigt was somewhere in West Berlin too, but he wasn't here as an American soldier. All former relations were officially cut off until this assignment was completed.

Bob had long since memorized the location of the house he'd be living in for the next month. He'd been told that a German couple—husband and wife—lived there, and his days would be spent immersed in the language. The couple had no idea about his spy work. They were simply being paid to help a university student get a better grasp of the language. They knew he was American, but they must never find out his true purpose.

Bob walked along the streets he'd memorized the locations of. He wasn't in a hurry, so he took his time sightseeing along the way. He passed apartment buildings four or five stories high with plaster exteriors and exposed beams.

The parks were mostly dormant since it was winter, as were the garden plots in front of the houses.

Soon the cold deepened, and Bob increased his pace. The afternoon sun was dim and did little to warm the cold March air. In his carefully packed briefcase, Bob carried paper, envelopes, and classified maps—which he'd study at night after his German lessons.

After about twenty minutes, he arrived in a modest neighborhood, one that felt new and fresh and restored. Fifteen years had passed since the war, and the West Berliners had worked hard with the Allies to rebuild. Bob turned up a path leading to a one-story house with a small winter yard and a picket fence. It was obvious the landscape was well taken care of.

Striding up to the front door, Bob set his traveling bag on the porch and knocked. The door opened, and a petite, dark-haired woman stood on the other side. Behind her was a taller man, whom Bob assumed was her husband. Both wore glasses, and Mr. Neumann's hair was more gray than brown.

"Mr. and Mrs. Neumann?"

"Sprechen si bitte Deutsch," the woman said.

She wanted him to speak only German? Bob nodded in agreement, then said, "Mein name ist Peter Jones."

Mrs. Neumann smiled and stepped aside, while her husband motioned for Bob to come inside. "Komm herein."

Bob picked up his traveling bag, and gripping his briefcase with his other hand, he walked into the Neumann home. The colors of the walls, floors, and furniture were mostly neutral, pale yellows and taupe, but the place felt welcoming. Warm. It had been a long time since Bob had been inside another person's home, and he felt an immediate sense of ease. Pictures on the walls of fields and flowers made the place homey, and he could smell baked bread.

"Come this way," Mr. Neumann said in German. "I'll show you to your living quarters, then we will eat."

Bob followed the man down the hallway and into a nearly empty room. A bed sat pushed up against the far wall, and a side table and single chair were the only other furniture. Mr. Neumann showed him the narrow closet, where Bob set his belongings for the time being. Next, he was shown where the bathroom was down the hall, and another room—which contained a bookcase, a desk, and several chairs.

"Hier ist das Klassenzimmer."

Bob understood clearly enough—the room was intended for his German lessons.

"You must use your time wisely," Mr. Neumann continued, his blue eyes focused on Bob. "Do you understand?"

"Ich verstehe," Bob said. *I understand*.

"Your evenings will be free after lessons, but I advise you to review the day's learning," Mrs. Neumann said.

"I will."

"Eight hours a day may not be enough to achieve fluency." Mr. Neumann moved toward the door. "Thankfully you have a good foundation already. Although your accent needs work." His smile was brief.

"Vielen Dank," Bob said.

"You're welcome," Mr. Neumann said. "Remember, we're here to push you and make you better. The results are up to you."

Bob nodded, then Mr. Neumann led him down the hallway and into the kitchen. The table was set for dinner, and Mrs. Neumann served knödeln, a potato dumpling.

Bob hadn't realized how hungry he was, or perhaps it was because he'd missed homemade food so much, but he had trouble pacing himself and eating politely. After he was finished, Mrs. Neumann brought out berliners.

"These are my husband's favorite," she said, giving him a quick smile.

Bob bit into the jelly-filled, donut-like pastry. He decided they could easily become his favorite German treat too. Mrs. Neumann's cooking was better than any German café, restaurant, or army cafeteria by a longshot.

The Neumanns asked him questions about where he was from and why he decided to come to Germany for school. Bob answered what he could, keeping details vague. The words of Major Taggett kept running through Bob's mind—and he knew that the less he told them, the better off they would all be. And the safer the information of his undercover mission would stay.

As the evening marched on, both of the Neumanns said good night to Bob, and he was left to his own devices. He knew it would be a while before his mind shut off enough to sleep. Inside his bedroom, he opened his briefcase and pulled out the map of East Germany, given to him by Major Taggett.

He spread out the map across the surface of the desk in the bedroom. Then he braced his palms on the edge of the desk and began to study. He mouthed the German names of the cities and locations closest to East Berlin. He'd be attending the university there, so it was better to know the streets he'd have to walk, sooner than later. Next, Bob's gaze zeroed in on the blank spaces. Taggett had explained that the East German maps had empty spaces, or sometimes pale orange gaps, that represented Stasi areas. These were the places Bob had to investigate—an orange space was a good indicator of where there would be military buildings, bunkers, shooting ranges, freight yards, or weapon arsenals.

He noted what looked like government buildings that would now be Soviet occupied. Perhaps Taggett and the US Army already knew about those locations, seeing as travel between West Berlin and East Berlin was common. Yet Bob would make note of them anyway.

Bob tapped a finger on an orange space on the map. Since Taggett had told Bob not to show this map to anyone and not to carry it on his person when in East Germany, he assumed that this map was unauthorized for the general public. So it stood to reason that there were things to figure out here. Clues, as it were.

He traced a path from Berlin all the way down to Leipzig, surprised at the number of blank orange spaces. All of those areas were targets of interest now. Somehow, some way, he needed to access them. He hoped that Taggett's plan, of Bob becoming Professor Schmitt's assistant, would work. If not, they'd have to find a new way.

The following morning, Bob was up early thanks to a cheerful bird outside his window. In the near darkness, he shifted the curtain of his single window to see a small yellow bird with a mostly gray head. Its tiny talons clung to the branch of a cherry tree not far from the window. The bird paused in its song, then continued after Bob released the curtain.

Once in the classroom with Mr. and Mrs. Neumann, it was clear to Bob that they were adept teachers and had a ready system in place. Bob's German was mostly book learned, with the addition of common phrases picked up while in Hanau and Frankfurt. But his new German lessons were taking things to a whole new plateau. That, and the knowledge that he'd have to pass himself off as a proficient student.

First and foremost, he needed to excel in a university class that would use only German. And he didn't want to draw attention to himself. Speaking German with an American accent would certainly do that. The morning hours passed swiftly, but after a short break for lunch and more hours studying in the classroom, he felt the beginnings of a headache.

Bob knew a headache would be the least of his problems, so even after his formal instruction was finished for the day, he reviewed his notes throughout the evening in his bedroom. He repeated the words and phrases he'd studied, saying them faster and faster, trying to make them feel natural on his tongue. No easy feat.

Before he went to sleep, he pulled out a couple of letters he'd brought with him—letters from his family. He'd read them before, and he'd clipped off the salutations so that his name wouldn't appear on the letters. He wondered if anyone in his family would notice a difference in his writing when the army wrote back to them on his behalf. The divide between himself and his family felt sharper tonight. He was used to missing them, but now he couldn't even write to them. It was as if something inside of him had been erased.

Bob tucked away the letters, turned out the light in his Berlin bedroom, and closed his eyes. He would get through this, somehow. The army had put their faith and trust in him. Bob fell asleep with repeating prayers in his heart—prayers for his friends, family, and country, all circling each other.

The next morning, after Bob arose to his new alarm clock of the yellow songbird, Mr. and Mrs. Neumann were again relentless in their instruction. After a lunch of schnitzel, a pork steak, along with pasta, Mr. Neumann rose from the table. "Come, we will sit in the front room and have a conversation as one might on a social visit. Remember to pay attention to the way I say the sounds, and then mimic them."

"I will," Bob said in German.

Once in the living room, Mr. Neumann began asking questions, faster than he had before.

Bob tried to keep up and answer the questions—which he knew were simple ones from the lessons of the past two days. Mr. Neumann stopped Bob frequently to correct his words.

"You're getting better," Mr. Neumann said. "But let's try again."

"All right."

"Where are you from?" Mr. Neumann asked in German.

"America," Bob said.

"Where do you live?"

"West Berlin."

"Where are you going?"

"To the University of Berlin," Bob said. "I'm a student." He stumbled on the words, and Neumann made him repeat them.

The questioning continued . . .

Over the next weeks, Bob had a hard time shutting his mind off at night. The days and nights seemed endless as he remained sequestered in the house. The same four walls. The same ceiling. The same routine. The same bird waking him up—or at least he thought it was the same bird.

But the strict routine proved successful, and he was getting better at the language. German verbs and nouns and phrases constantly ran through his mind, keeping him awake into the late hours. Once those thoughts were exhausted, his mind would drift to his family. His parents, his sister, his former life at Utah State. His growing-up days in Idaho. Then he thought of his more recent acquaintances. Komori at Fort Sill. Murdock at Hanau. Jones. And finally Luisa.

She was in the same city, working at a hospital most likely. But which sector? Had she been visiting her grandmother in East Berlin? And where was her father assigned? Bob wondered if he might run into her, by chance, of course. He'd need to be aware because the last thing he could risk was Luisa blowing his cover. Perhaps this was something he should have mentioned to Taggett, but Bob hadn't thought of the risks until now.

Then his mind moved forward to the actual work he'd be doing. Once Bob was stationed in his new apartment, where he'd live alone, he'd begin his new life as a student at the University of Berlin. Soon enough he'd be in Professor Schmitt's class, and Bob would have to prove his merit to the man.

If there was ever a time to pray for his future, it was now.

Mornings always came before dawn, with the melodic birdsong, and he no longer required an alarm. And Bob found more and more things to be grateful for. His trip to his grandparents' Italian village had taught him to find the sliver of light in any dark situation. Right now, he was in a nice home, with good food, and being given a once-in-a-lifetime crash course in German. A language he already loved.

CHAPTER SEVENTEEN

"How did the Stasi persuade people to become informants?

- *Appeals to patriotism*
- *Cash or material reward*
- *Blackmail*
- *Offers of immunity from threatened prosecution*
- *Making the mission sound like an exciting adventure"*

—Max Hertzberg, "Stasi Tactics – Zersetzung"

WEST BERLIN
MARCH 1961

"Can I speak to you, Luisa?"

She turned to see Adel walking toward her in a nurse's uniform. They were both working the day shift, and the ward was quiet at the moment. Luisa hadn't asked Adel if she was the connection to Greta. In fact, over the past few weeks, she hadn't heard from anyone—not Greta, and not any other mysterious contacts.

Adel motioned for Luisa to follow her, so Luisa did, and in a moment, they stood in a storage room that contained hospital supplies.

"Shut the door, please," Adel instructed as if there was nothing unusual about speaking in a storage closet. "Now, I want to tell you that you did an excellent job with your assignment."

Was Adel speaking about Luisa's nursing work at the hospital?

"Mrs. Belding reached the safe house and is now relocated and doing well."

Luisa stared. Her hunch had been right, but hearing the confirmation aloud was an entirely different matter. "Thank you for letting me know. Are you . . . ?"

"Your next contact?" Adel's pretty smile emerged. "I am, and I have another assignment for you if you agree to help."

Luisa waited, but then realized that Adel wanted her to agree before hearing the assignment. "If it's possible for me to help, then I am willing."

"That's excellent," Adel said. "Now, know that we're grateful for your help, and if ever the time comes and you need help with your grandmother, we will do whatever it takes."

Luisa wasn't quite sure what that meant, but she appreciated it all the same. "What will I have to do?"

Adel rested a thin hand on Luisa's shoulder. "Your assignments will come at the park. On the bench closest to the largest tree, you'll find the notice underneath the bench. Make sure no one sees you retrieve it."

"All right." She felt breathless, but she nodded. "What about—?"

"Time's up," Adel said. "Oh, and this is for you." She handed over a square envelope, then left the storage room.

Luisa looked down at the envelope and opened it with trembling fingers. There was no reason to delay. Despite no signature, Luisa knew who it was from—Mona. Several weeks had passed since that day Luisa traveled to the police station with Mona's mother. Weeks of wondering and worrying.

Thank you for all of your help. I was finally released from questioning, and two weeks later, my husband was released as well. He's been expelled from the university and forbidden by the Stasi to cross into East Germany again. But we are grateful because he now

has a job, and I'm able to spend the days with our son. My mother
sends her love. Thank you again.

Luisa didn't know what type of job Mona's husband had found in West
Berlin, but Luisa was happy for the small family. She reread it a second time
then tucked the note into her uniform so she wouldn't lose it. Throughout the
rest of her shift, Luisa was anxious about going to the bench at the park. Was
there an assignment already waiting for her? As soon as her shift was over, she
hurried to the park in the early afternoon light.

The park came into view, and for a brief moment, Luisa soaked in the
early signs of spring. The grass was no longer brown and dead. New green
shoots poked up, making the entire park look different—brighter and more
cheerful. The temperature was still cool, though, and the weather demanded
a coat or cardigan depending on the hour.

She walked quickly to the deserted bench near the designated tree. A
quick glance about told her that no one was close enough to be paying attention to her. Luisa sat on the bench and busied herself with searching through
her purse, as if she were looking for something. She pulled out a small notebook, then dropped it and bent to pick it up. As she straightened, she felt
beneath the edge of the bench, locating a taped envelope. She slid the envelope
into the notebook in one swift motion, so by the time she'd straightened and
turned to her purse, the envelope was out of sight.

Luisa left the park then, and once she reached home, she opened the envelope. It was an assignment.

Luisa examined the student ID card for the Free University of Berlin
with her name on it. Three words were on the card. *Student. Research trip.*
Humanities class. Was this to be her excuse for traveling in East Germany?
Another paper contained an address and a man's name: Uncle Leon Richter.
Not a real name, she was sure, but it would connect her to the right person.

She narrowed her eyes. Her meeting place was an underground bar and
restaurant called Auerbachs Keller. In Leipzig. A city nearly two hundred

kilometers away. This would be an all-day event, depending on how smoothly she could get there and back.

Her explanation for going into East Germany would be a research trip for a humanities class that she wasn't taking. Auerbachs Keller, or Cellar, was famous for its part in Goethe's *Faust*. As a college student at Leipzig University, Goethe would visit the restaurant, and in his literary masterpiece, it is the first place that Mephistopheles takes Faust on their travels. The sculptures depicting *Mephisto and Faust* and *Bewitched Students* sat in front of the restaurant. And inside were the paintings dated to 1625 that had inspired Goethe to begin with. Amid the iconic paintings, Luisa was to meet someone who would give her the next instructions.

Luisa thought of the scenarios she could tell her father. The only one which came to mind was that she had to work a double shift. She only hoped he'd believe her.

She hurried home in the light of the setting sun. She wanted to arrive before her father did so she could make her preparations without him noticing. This meant she had to take the shortcut to their apartment building. Fortunately, there was no sign of loitering men, and she was glad not to be bothered. But there was one woman she recognized, the elderly woman from before—Mrs. Herrmann—who walked slowly along the sidewalk, carrying a large bag that seemed about to topple her over.

Luisa quickened her pace, and when Mrs. Herrmann looked up, Luisa said, "Can I help you carry that?"

Mrs. Herrmann's eyes narrowed briefly, but it was clear she recognized Luisa.

"I haven't seen you for a while."

"I took your advice, and I take the main roads to work now."

Mrs. Herrmann's gaze was piercing. "Except now?"

"Except now," Luisa confirmed. "I was short on time."

The elderly woman tutted. "If you help me, you'll be even more short on time."

"That is fine." She was right, but Luisa still felt compelled to stop and offer help.

The elderly woman shrugged, then handed over her bag. "Follow me. It's not far."

But it was far, at least for an elderly woman and a rather heavy bag. Luisa wanted to ask what was inside, but she didn't know if that would be polite.

Mrs. Herrmann's steps were slow as she went into the apartment building, then started up a narrow flight of steps. She held onto the railing with her knobby hand, and Luisa tried not to give in to the impatience building up inside of her. She'd been the one to offer her help, after all. Would she have offered, though, if she'd known Mrs. Herrmann lived on the second floor? Correction, third floor?

Mrs. Herrmann's breathing had shallowed by the time they reached her apartment door.

Luisa waited as the woman found her key, then opened the door.

"Come inside," Mrs. Herrmann said before Luisa could make her excuses and dash off. "I want to show you something."

Luisa was torn between curiosity and the desire to rush home ahead of the approaching darkness. But her feet kept moving, and she walked into the clean apartment. Everything inside seemed to be at least thirty years old but well cared for. The wood floor was polished to a shine, and the afghan across the back of a small couch was folded neatly.

"Set the bag here," Mrs. Herrmann directed.

Luisa did so, then watched Mrs. Herrmann pull out a large radio that looked more sophisticated than anything Luisa had ever seen.

"This cost a pretty penny, but it will do the job."

"What job?" Luisa couldn't help but ask. She'd never seen one so sleek.

"Why, the job of capturing the news from East Berlin," Mrs. Herrmann said.

Luisa frowned. What could Mrs. Herrmann want with news such as that? East Berlin, and East Germany in general, only broadcast what was approved by the Soviets.

Mrs. Herrmann patted Luisa's arm. "Thank you for your help, young lady. It's nice to know who will be willing to help when the wall goes up."

"What wall?" Luisa said.

Mrs. Herrmann pressed her lips together, then tapped the radio. "Information is power. Information can save lives." She gazed at Luisa, and it was uncanny how the woman seemed to see straight into her soul. "We will be on the front lines soon, and we'll be needed."

Luisa was confused. Was this woman rambling?

But Mrs. Herrmann shuffled to the window. "Our apartment buildings are right on the border of East Berlin, don't you see?"

Luisa joined her at the window. It was true, but what was the woman's point? "Yes, I see," she confirmed. Her heart had started to flutter. Why was she nervous?

"You should go, dear," Mrs. Herrmann said. "You have much to prepare for."

Luisa wanted to question the woman further, but it was true. She did have to prepare. But how did Mrs. Herrmann know that?

Luisa left the apartment and hurried down the flight of stairs. The lighting inside the building was dim since the sun had set. By the time she was outside, she was much later than she wanted to be. Her father might even be home, and Luisa would have missed her chance to call into work and tell them she wouldn't be there tomorrow.

She slowed when she saw a group of men at the corner of the street, the area she had to pass by. Luisa clutched her purse close and continued walking, keeping her gaze straightforward.

"Hey, I remember you," one of the men said as she neared.

She didn't look at him, and she didn't change her pace. She focused on steady breaths, although the hairs on the back of her neck had risen and her heart felt like it was about to fly away.

"Where have you been?" the same man said, and his friends chuckled.

She was past them now by a few steps. So far, so good. But then she heard footfalls behind her. They were following her. She was nearly to her street, and she didn't really want them to see which building she went into, but how far could she really walk?

She stopped abruptly and turned. Folding her arms, she watched the men come to a stop. One was grinning at her. The others were watching her with a feral look that made her stomach churn painfully.

"My aunt, Mrs. Herrmann, doesn't appreciate your interference."

One of the men—the one who'd called out to her—stepped back. "You're Mrs. Herrmann's niece?"

Luisa lifted her chin. "I am. And I'd caution you to use your time more wisely."

The men snickered, but when she turned and left, they didn't follow her. Before turning into her apartment building, she glanced back, and they'd disappeared.

Luisa's time was far gone, and she hurried into her apartment. By some small miracle, her father wasn't home, and she made the call to the hospital to give her excuses. Now that work was taken care of, she went through her purse and collected what she'd need for the long day tomorrow. Then she withdrew money she'd saved. West German money went a lot farther in the east.

She heard her father's footsteps outside the apartment door, and Luisa rushed out of her room and hurried into the kitchen. When her father entered, she was busy cooking sausage and potatoes. The look on his face made her pause in her actions.

"Hard day?" she asked him, hoping she didn't sound nervous.

Without shedding his hat or uniform coat, he sat down at the kitchen table. "We've been bombarded with calls today from the Soviets."

Luisa stilled. Her father hadn't been very forthright about his work when they lived in Frankfurt, but the isolation of West Berlin seemed to make him more talkative.

She gave him her full attention by turning away from the stove. "What are the Soviets asking?"

"They're accusing us of aiding an underground network," her father said. "They think we're harboring criminals and fugitives and helping them with false papers."

Luisa bit her lip. Fugitives from East Berlin had been fleeing to the West for decades, but if they were criminals, then West Berlin was supposed to return them for their sentencing. "I'm sorry. Will they not believe the department?"

Her father looked down at his clasped hands. "The police chief thinks there might be someone in the department who's involved."

She frowned. "Not you . . ."

"Not me." But her father wasn't meeting her gaze.

Luisa didn't know what she'd feel if she found out her father was involved. *She* was involved in activities that he wouldn't like. Yet she couldn't back out. She was in too deep now. But her father . . . He could lose his livelihood. Be imprisoned. And Luisa . . . ? She didn't know what might happen to her.

They ate dinner mostly in silence, and Luisa slept little that night. Her dreams were dark things out of reach, and her thoughts filled with worries when she awakened. But she'd told her father she had the early shift at the hospital, and she rose before dawn and dressed.

The sun was starting to rise by the time Luisa stepped out of the apartment, passing by her mother's slippers by the door. Luisa had dressed carefully, not wanting to draw attention but also wanting to look professional. At the train station, she looked up the route for Leipzig, which was about 190 kilometers away. It would take a couple of hours with stops included.

Luisa gazed out the windows as the train left Berlin and headed toward Leipzig. She couldn't help but notice the bullet-riddled buildings they passed. East Germany hadn't done much cleanup after the war in general—it seemed they took pride in their war-torn landscape. Red Soviet flags and the yellow, black, and red East German flags hung from every important government and business building.

Once the train neared Leipzig, East German guards walked up the aisles, asking for IDs. The questioning was standard, but Luisa was nervous all the same. She felt relieved to walk out of the train station after nothing more than a few questions of where she was from and why was she in Leipzig.

Luisa headed toward Leipzig University and Auerbachs. Leipzig was the third largest industrial city in East Germany, yet the place was subdued. The green trees heavy with buds smelled heavenly. Whatever dreariness surrounded her in the form of stone and metal, the trees had brought spring anyway.

She walked past a large building that was under construction. On the side of another building were huge posters of the Soviet leaders. A man on a bicycle whizzed past her, his gaze focused forward. Everyone on the streets walked with a brisk purpose, their eyes forward or down. No one was chatting or socializing.

Luisa continued her own brisk pace to Grimmaische Street. She saw the sculptures right away and paused to read the stone inscription beneath the two men: "Szene in Auerbachs-Keller Aus Goethes Faust Mephisto verzaubert die Studenten." *The scene in Auerbachs-Keller from Goethe's* Faust. *Mephisto enchants the students.*

Luisa knew something about the story of Faust. It was a play based on the German legend about a scholar. The scholar had a successful career but was unsatisfied with life, so he makes a deal with the devil and exchanges his immortal soul for unlimited knowledge.

She checked her watch and saw that it was only a few minutes before she was to meet Uncle Leon. She had no idea what he looked like, so he would have to find her.

Luisa's skin tingled with nerves as she entered the restaurant. "I'm meeting someone," she told the hostess, then hovered near the back door. Keeping her eyes on the surrounding décor of arched ceilings, wood-paneled pillars, and the parquet floor, she didn't turn her head as people came and went.

"Miss Voigt," someone said next to her.

She turned to see an older man, perhaps her father's age. His face was narrow, his shoulders slim, and his eyes alert.

"Uncle?" she said.

His thin mouth curved for a moment, then straightened. "Our table is this way."

As he led her through the restaurant, she realized he'd already been seated and waiting. He indicated for her to sit, then settled on the other side.

"How was your journey, niece?" he asked as a waiter approached.

"It was fine," she said, glancing at the waiter.

"We'll take two orders of spaetzle and two beers," Uncle Leon said without waiting for her to peruse the menu.

"I'll have juice," Luisa was quick to say. It seemed this was all business, even the ordering of food.

"I hope you're hungry," Leon said as the waiter walked away. "The food is very good here."

Then, without waiting for her to answer, he pulled out a slim, wrapped box in blue paper from his briefcase. "Happy birthday," he said, handing it over to her.

She looked at the wrapped gift and tried not to look confused. "Thank you."

Leon glanced in the direction the waiter had gone, then lowered his voice. "You have passed the first test by coming to Leipzig. Now, inside this box is a purse with a false compartment. Inside the compartment are passport photos of three East Germans. You will take them to your contact, and she will put the photos into borrowed West German passports from those willing to give them up for a few weeks. Then I need those passports returned to me."

Luisa blinked. "And I am to bring them to you?"

Uncle Leon smiled. "I would love to see my niece again."

The waiter was back.

"Of course," Luisa said with a smile of her own.

"Next time you come, you'll have to see the Zoological Garden," Leon said as the waiter set down their drinks. "The acacia trees are about ready to bloom. They smell like heaven."

The waiter moved off, and it took a moment for Leon's gaze to settle fully on her. "If you have qualms, then this is not the task for you. Westerners have been arrested for helping with East Germans' escape plans."

Luisa knew what the consequences might be. Her father was already getting a taste of it on the police force. "I will do it."

CHAPTER EIGHTEEN

"It was very important for me to become a TA to Schmitt because Schmitt, for some reason, had permission from the East Germans and Soviets to travel into East Germany (the Soviet sector). Schmitt was an economist, trying to help East German cities get back on their feet. Therefore this provided part of the cover—me, being a college graduate in economics. There were some theories that I was more up to date on than Schmitt, so I could help him out."

—Bob Inama

WEST BERLIN
APRIL 1961

April was a friendlier month in West Berlin than March had been. But Bob would have been happy in any weather since he hadn't stepped outside the home he'd lived in for an entire month. Ironically, he knew he'd miss his time with Mr. and Mrs. Neumann. They'd become friends of sorts—spending all day with a person had that effect. And although the couple had been focused on teaching him German, they'd been kind and accommodating.

With so much German night and day, Bob's thoughts frequently bounced into German from English. More than once in the past week, he'd awakened with German words the first to enter his brain. If it was possible, his English sounded more accented than his German now.

The real test was about to begin.

Following the directions given to him by Major Taggett, Bob headed to his new place—an apartment a couple of miles into West Berlin. His class would start that afternoon at the University of Berlin, which was in the Soviet sector. Bob planned on walking and sightseeing along the way. He hadn't had any communication from Taggett since arriving in Berlin, and although Bob had known that would be the case, it was still an eerie feeling to finally be on his own.

When Bob arrived at the four-story apartment building, he double-checked the address from his memory, then entered the dim interior. Up a flight of stairs, he found his apartment number on the second floor. He pulled out the key that Taggett had sent with him and unlocked the door.

Inside the place were musty, off-white walls and cracked linoleum floors. The studio apartment had no separate rooms, only a single space. There was a bed, a table, two chairs, and an empty bookcase. The kitchen had a few basics, but none of the warmth of Mrs. Neumann's kitchen. Their home had been welcoming, much nicer and more comfortable. But now wasn't the time to worry about niceness or comfort.

With only his briefcase, Bob locked the door behind him and continued to the street level. He walked through the neighborhood, then turned onto a main road that would take him into East Berlin via Checkpoint Charlie—the border crossing the Neumanns had told him about. It was the only place that non-Germans could cross by road or on foot.

Bob and Mr. Neumann had practiced the questions the East German border guards would likely ask, so Bob was prepared technically. But that didn't stop his pulse from rising as if it were trying to reach the trees.

He saw the line of cars, and that alone alerted him that he was near Checkpoint Charlie. Bob joined the queue of people waiting to cross over. It was a short line this time of morning. The queue of people waiting to come into West Berlin was much longer. Bob glanced at a few of them, his gaze momentarily stalling on a young woman with similar hair color to Luisa. It wasn't her, though.

When it was Bob's turn to show his ID, he hoped the guard wouldn't notice the beads of perspiration on his forehead.

"What is your name?" the East German guard asked in German, his thick brows slanted.

"Peter Jones."

The guard was about Bob's age, and his uniform looked a bit worn. Bob knew he was only doing his job, so there was no reason for animosity between them. But the guard was peering at Bob as if they were instant mortal enemies.

"Where are you from?"

"America," Bob replied, following the Neumanns' advice to answer only the questions asked and not to give out additional information.

"Where are you going?"

Bob answered, and what proceeded were nearly the exact questions that the Neumanns had drilled him with. After the guard conferred with another guard, Bob was handed back his ID and waved through.

The guards were now questioning someone else and not paying attention to Bob any longer. But he wasn't fooled—there were plenty of eyes on him. Taggett had told him there were eyes everywhere in Berlin, on both sides of the inner border. Everyone watched everyone else. No one trusted anyone. All were suspicious. Bob's job was to not raise anyone's suspicions or interest. He walked at a steady, brisk pace. Past the gray buildings bedecked with red flags.

Bob took note of the names of the streets he passed, comparing them to the map he'd studied. He recited the names in his mind, wanting to be able to pronounce them right. He was on the right route. As he neared the university, the foot traffic morphed to younger people in their twenties.

Classes must have been in transition because when Bob stepped through the main university doors, people were rushing about, books tucked under their arms or briefcases clutched tight. Bob paused, looking about for signs, interpreting the German words in his mind.

He saw the word *Büro*, which he recognized meant office, and he entered to speak with the registrar about his class. The process went smoothly, and Bob was impressed. Taggett had done his job well, and soon Bob was moving through the students again, textbook in hand. When he entered the classroom, it was about a third full, and he took a seat near the back.

Soon a man walked in who had to be the professor. The man was in his early fifties, wore glasses, and had a stocky build—he was maybe five-six or five-seven. He took off his hat and set it on the empty, sterile-looking desk. His gray hair had been mostly concealed by his hat, and Bob amended his first impression. The professor was at least in his mid- to late fifties.

The students pulled out textbooks from their bags or briefcases, and Professor Schmitt said, "Guten Tag." *Good afternoon.*

After roll call, the students opened their textbooks, and Bob turned to the same page as the young man in front of him. After a quick scan of the subject headings, Bob was relieved to find out he already knew the material. In English, of course. But the textbook had an older copyright, and this class seemed to be a beginning economics class.

Over the next thirty minutes, Bob took notes like everyone else as Professor Schmitt elaborated on the text and gave some examples. Bob was surprised at how easily he followed along, at least a lot more easily than he expected.

"Peter Jones," the professor said. "If the real gross domestic product of our country has increased, but the production of goods has remained the same, then the production of services has . . . what?"

Bob was still recovering from being called upon in class on his first day. Everyone glanced over at him. He cleared his throat and answered, "Then the production of services has increased." He was positive his voice shook, but hopefully no one noticed.

"Very good," the professor said, then turned and wrote something on the board as if he hadn't just upended Bob's world. Everyone was focusing on the lecture. No one was looking at him like he was an interloper. Apparently, he'd passed some test of normalcy.

"Now, we'll have our quiz," Schmitt said.

Several in the class groaned under their breaths.

"If you've caught up on your reading, you will do well on the quiz," he continued as he passed out a round of tests. "You should never fall behind."

Bob looked at the paper in front of him. A quiz on the first day of class? There was no help for it. He read through the first question once, then twice. Thankfully, he knew the answer. And the next. By the time he reached the end of the quiz, he was pretty sure he'd gotten everything correct. He was hopefully well on his way to impressing the professor and becoming his teacher's assistant.

After the quizzes were turned in, Bob remained in the back of the classroom until the last student was gone. He approached Schmitt as he stuffed the quizzes into his briefcase.

"Thank you for the lesson," Bob said in what he hoped was excellent German.

Schmitt paused and eyed him through his glasses. "You are the American?"

"Yes."

Schmitt nodded. "Welcome to Germany, Mr. Jones." Then he clipped his briefcase closed and walked out of the classroom.

Bob waited for a moment. The man was the ticket to Bob's undercover work. Was there anything else he could do to impress him? He opened the textbook and glanced through a few of the chapters. All things he knew, although outdated. In the next class period, he decided, he'd have to interact more. Raise his hand and answer questions. Insert himself. Impress the professor.

When Bob was next in the classroom, he didn't sit at the back but in the second row. And when the professor asked a question, he always raised his hand. Schmitt didn't always call on Bob, but when he did, the professor seemed impressed. It was all that Bob could hope for.

Two weeks later, after taking several quizzes and earning perfect grades so far, Bob stalled again after class. When all of the other students had left, he approached Schmitt.

"Can I speak to you for a moment?" Bob asked. "Do you have time?"

Schmitt hesitated. "I have a moment. But I do have office hours."

"Yes, I know," Bob said. "I wanted to tell you I read about your assignment of helping with the East German city-revitalization plans."

Schmitt seemed to straighten a little. "Yes."

"I wondered if you needed an assistant," Bob continued. "I've studied economics at an American university, and I'd love to see if I could help out with your project."

Schmitt said nothing, but Bob could see the interest in his eyes.

"Thank you for considering," Bob said. "Whatever you decide, I'm enjoying your class." He left then, feeling the gaze of Professor Schmitt long after he'd left the classroom.

A week went by, and another week. Bob continued to excel in all of his assignments and quizzes. More than once, he found Schmitt's gaze on him. Yes, it might be unusual for a German professor to employ an American assistant, but he hadn't said no yet, so Bob took that as a good sign.

The next few weeks passed with Bob being diligent in his studies, aiming for excellent marks. He'd been in the class for several weeks when Schmitt asked him to stay after class one Wednesday. Hope shot straight through Bob, and he approached the professor's desk, hoping this was good news.

"I've decided I'd like you to be my assistant," Schmitt said, a satisfied look on his face.

Bob almost laughed in triumph. *Mission accomplished*. At least this portion. But this was very, very good news.

"Can you drive?" Schmitt asked.

Bob was surprised at the question, but he immediately answered, "Yes."

Schmitt almost smiled, but not quite. "Good. Meet me tomorrow morning. We'll be gone for a couple of days, so bring an overnight bag. I have some presentations to give, and it will be useful to have an assistant with me. You'll need to take notes. Do you think you can take this job?"

"Yes, of course," Bob said. "Thank you, sir." He held out his hand, and Schmitt grasped it.

"Tomorrow, then." Schmitt picked up his briefcase and was out the door before Bob could wrap his mind around what had just happened.

Tomorrow he'd begin the work that he'd spent months preparing for.

CHAPTER NINETEEN

"It is difficult to portray how life was so hard and dreary. The ache to get away from the Stasi secret police snoops, from the grey meat, from the clothes that itched, and the air that stung your eyes was palpable."

—Hans-Peter Spitzner, East German

WEST BERLIN
APRIL 1961

The storage closet smelled of astringent, and Luisa wrinkled her nose as she entered on the heels of Adel. Luisa had been anticipating this meeting ever since she returned yesterday from an assignment. Fortunately, she was on the same shift as Adel again.

"What is it?" Adel asked, turning to face her as she tucked a stray hair beneath her nurse's cap. "This had better be quick. The hospital is busy."

"The contact you sent me to told me to deliver this." Luisa opened the false compartment inside her new purse and handed over the wrapped passport photos.

A line appeared between Adel's brows as she opened the wrapping. She scanned through the three photos quickly, then met Luisa's gaze. "We'll need to request the same lunch break, so we can find matches."

"What do you mean?" Luisa asked.

"We'll go to the Free University and look for the West Germans who resemble these pictures," Adel said. "Ask them if they're willing to give up their passports to help an East German in need. Later they can claim their passports were lost and apply for new ones."

Luisa wasn't sure openly approaching others was a good idea. "What if—"

"What if we meet a West German informer?"

"Yes."

Adel didn't break her gaze. "It's always possible, but it's also a risk we'll have to take." She placed a hand on Luisa's shoulder. "Once we have the altered passports, these East Germans can start a new life. You'll be changing the generations that come after them. Oh, and leave on your nurse's uniform. It's hard to say no to a nurse."

It was not a hard decision, after all. The day was warm when Luisa walked out of the hospital with Adel. Luisa wondered if it was possible to find volunteers in the short amount of time they had for a lunch break. Once they reached the campus, Luisa saw that a lot of students were outside, enjoying the nice weather. Some were studying while sitting on lawns or benches. Others were talking in groups.

Adel handed Luisa one of the passport photos. It was of a young man with reddish brown hair, deep-set eyes, and a crook in his nose. This might be difficult to match. While Luisa was looking around, she saw Adel motion toward her.

"I think I've found a match," Adel said. "See the woman over there in the green skirt?"

Luisa had to agree. The woman in the passport photo was older than the college student, but there was certainly a resemblance. Luisa walked with Adel as she approached the woman.

She was bent over a textbook, intent on reading as the breeze stirred her hair.

"Hello, ma'am. Have you ever been to East Germany?" Adel asked.

The student looked up and surveyed them.

Luisa offered her a friendly smile.

"I have," the student said. "My cousins live there."

"Ah," Adel said. "Then you're familiar with the living conditions."

The student frowned and closed her textbook. "What do you mean?"

Adel held out the picture. "What I mean is that there's a young woman who's in East Germany now. She wants to live a better life, but she can't cross the inner border without approval from the Soviets. She's willing to leave everything behind to start a new life in West Berlin. But she needs your help."

"*My* help?" the student said. "How?"

Luisa was impressed that the student seemed so interested.

"My friend here will tell you." Adel looked over at Luisa with a nod.

Luisa rocked back on her heels. She hadn't expected this. But both women were looking at her now. "We need your passport. We'll put the picture of the East German in place of your picture."

The student narrowed her eyes. "Then she'll be able to cross into West Berlin?"

"Yes," Luisa confirmed. She was almost certain the student was going to turn them down, and they'd watch her walk away.

Instead the student said, "You're going to smuggle my passport into East Berlin?"

Luisa sure hoped this woman wasn't an informer or GDR sympathizer. "Yes."

Adel folded her arms. "What will it be? Will you help an East German in need?"

The student bit her lip, then reached for her schoolbag. She rummaged through it for a moment, then took out a leather case. Inside was her passport.

"Take it," the student said. "Someone helped me out of a tough situation once, so I will return the favor."

Adel readily took the passport.

"And how long should I wait before claiming a lost passport?" the student asked.

"Three weeks," Adel said without hesitation.

"Very well," the student said. Then she gathered her things and walked away. A few feet off, she paused and looked back, a soft smile on her face.

"I don't believe it," Luisa said.

"Most humans are decent," Adel said, "when given a chance. Come on. We have only a short time to find two more people. Any luck with the red-haired man?"

"Not yet," Luisa said, still reeling from the fact that a stranger had handed over her passport. Then she saw him. A red-haired student. He was chatting with two other young men. His nose wasn't broken, but maybe the East German could claim a recent injury?

"There," Luisa said. "I found him."

"Very good." Adel followed Luisa as she approached the three young men.

"Hello," Luisa said. "Can we speak to you for a moment?"

His friends snickered, but the red-head's eyes about popped out. "Is my mother all right? Is she at the hospital?"

Luisa was too stunned to reply at first.

"It's not your mother, or anyone else in your family," Adel said. "It has nothing to do with the hospital."

The color returned to the young man's face, and Adel nudged Luisa.

She began with the same approach Adel had used moments earlier. "Have you ever been to East Germany?" Luisa asked.

"My parents live there." He adjusted the strap of the backpack over his shoulder. "They want me to return after I graduate."

"Oh, will you?" Luisa asked, feeling emboldened from their earlier experience with the other student.

He met Luisa's gaze. "No. Are you taking a survey or something?"

"Not exactly," she said. "We are helping a few East Germans come to the West, like you did." She hoped she wasn't assuming too much.

The student folded his arms. "Tell me more."

She held out the passport photo of the red-headed East German. "This man needs your help."

The student took the picture and examined it. "Do you think you can truly get away with this?"

Luisa really had no answer for that because this was her first assignment with passports.

"We've helped more than ten people so far," Adel announced.

The student's brows lifted. "That's impressive." He handed back the photo, and for a moment Luisa thought they would be turned down.

"I want to help," he said. "Use my passport, and I will help you match others."

Adel's smile was wide as she extended her hand. "I'm Adel, and this is Luisa."

He smiled at her right back. "Jonas."

By the time Luisa and Adel left the university campus, they'd matched all of the passport photos. Luisa felt humbled at the willingness of complete strangers to help others.

"How will it all happen?" Luisa asked.

"You'll see," Adel said, giving her a half smile. "Are you still in?"

"I'm still in."

Those words echoed in her mind a week later when Adel handed her the doctored passports along with a few other items in the storage closet of the hospital.

"What are the Marlboro cigarettes for?" Luisa asked.

"For the East Germans to have on their person in case they're searched," Adel explained. "It will be good for them to have something Western in their possession, as though they really are visitors to the GDR. Uncle Leon will also tell them to remove all labels from their clothing so it doesn't read 'People's Own Manufacture.'"

"So they don't look East German?" Luisa asked.

"Correct," Adel said. "Now hide the passports among the Western groceries you take your grandmother this weekend. Uncle Leon will meet you near the bus station. There's an alley to the east."

Luisa nodded. She slipped the items into the bag she'd brought to the hospital.

"Good luck, my friend."

Luisa met Adel's gaze. They *were* friends, although in the most unlikely circumstances. "What happens if . . ." She couldn't finish, but it was clear that Adel knew what she was asking.

"You would be arrested, Luisa," she said. "From there, I don't know." Her gaze was sharp, almost challenging.

Luisa knew she could back out, but she didn't want to. She'd witnessed strangers agreeing to give up their own passports. "I'll let you know how it goes."

"That's my hope too."

If Luisa could tell Adel how the assignment went, that would mean she'd returned from the GDR unscathed.

To her surprise, Adel pulled her into a quick hug. "Give your oma my best."

"I will."

After her shift, Luisa headed to her apartment, feeling like she was carrying precious cargo, which she was. About two streets from her apartment, she nearly tripped when stepping off the curb. A car slowed on the other side of the street, then stopped. An older man, likely in his fifties, climbed out and another man took his place. A younger man with dark hair, glasses, and eyes that seemed nearly as dark as his hair.

Bob Inama . . .

No, it couldn't be. He wasn't in a US Army uniform. His hair was longer, and he seemed thinner. His gait and the set of his shoulders were familiar; that was all. It was impossible that Bob would be in West Berlin. He was stationed in Hanau. Besides, the car pulling away from the curb had West Berlin license plates, and the older man was as German as they come.

Still, Luisa stared after the car, unable to help herself. And as the car turned the corner up ahead, she thought the passenger looked over at her. It was a fleeting glance, yet confusion raced through her mind. It wasn't him, though. It *couldn't* be him.

She was letting her imagination take over her common sense—what she knew was real. Luisa hurried away, keeping her bag close, and headed toward her apartment once again. Her father was already home, and Luisa hoped there was no reason he'd look inside her bag. He wouldn't, right?

She greeted him, then walked to her bedroom, where she tucked her bag behind her pillow for now. Then she went into the kitchen, where her father was looking in the small box refrigerator. "How does soup and sandwiches sound for dinner?" she asked.

He stepped back as she pulled out the deli meat, cheese, and gherkins. Then he busied himself setting the table, but he seemed preoccupied.

"Are you working this weekend?" she asked.

"Yes." He filled up two glasses with water from the kitchen tap.

"I thought I might visit Oma," Luisa continued. "Is there anything you want me to take to her?"

Her father paused in his step. "Not that I can think of. She always appreciates bananas. And ketchup."

"Right." Luisa smiled. In the GDR they had only one brand of ketchup, and bananas were hard to come by too.

The rest of the evening with her father went smoothly, although Luisa's thoughts kept shifting to the doctored passports she had in her bedroom. She was grateful when her father turned on the radio to the RIAS station because she wouldn't have to come up with conversation.

Her thoughts had already fast-forwarded to the weekend, when she'd be involved in an assignment that could get her arrested.

CHAPTER TWENTY

"I did attend [Schmitt's] presentations because one of my assignments was to take notes and type them and give them to Professor Schmitt. The presentations were very dry. I thought the information was off and outdated. The people who attended were middle-aged and older. There were Communist leaders and some college professors. What resources they had in East Germany came from Russia. By attending those meetings, they could move up in the Communist party."

—Bob Inama

WEST BERLIN
MAY 1961

Bob wasn't sure if he'd slept at all the night before. The bed had felt hard, and his ears had picked up every sound coming from the streets. He should be used to the new place by now, but the anticipation of spending four days with Schmitt and beginning his first plotting assignment had his mind restless.

As the dawn shifted the gray of the apartment walls into a soft yellow, Bob rose to review the maps Taggett had sent with him. Bob didn't know exactly where Schmitt would be taking him today, but Bob wanted to be familiar with the various cities so he could be on the lookout for potential military targets. He planned to ask questions, sure, but he didn't want Schmitt to get suspicious. And he wouldn't be able to take any maps with him.

Bob might've been good at mapping, but keeping the names of the

155

German streets straight tested his abilities. Yet he supposed his mind would adjust with more time and experience. Soon he began his preparations for the trip. It didn't take long. He packed the camera given to him by Taggett so that he could take microfilm photos to send along with the envelopes to his "girl-friends." He packed both the West German and East German mark, although he assumed Schmitt would be paying for most things.

The evening before, Bob had bought a few food supplies, but he was ready so early, he decided to head out to a café for breakfast. He'd be able to return in plenty of time to meet Schmitt.

Dressed in his usual civilian clothing, Bob was ready. He combed through his dark hair that now reached his collar, then put on his glasses. Next, he slipped on a jacket since the day was looking cloudy.

Stepping out onto the street in the early morning, Bob breathed in the fragrant, moist air that felt heavy with pending rain. Berlin was an aromatic city in May, with flowering chestnut trees. Homes and shops had windowsills full of flowers, and the foliage about the neighborhoods was lush green and full. Bob walked a couple of blocks until he reached a café that had a decent line of people.

He got into line and kept his ears tuned to the conversations about him, trying to understand what people were saying. He was pleased that he was able to comprehend most of the phrases. Once it was his turn to order, he bought a chocolate croissant. The young man behind the counter didn't seem to notice Bob's accent.

He sat at a table meant for someone much shorter than him and ate while he watched pedestrians move along the street. The morning felt lively, upbeat, as people hurried to school or work. A tram passed, its exhaust making the air taste acrid. But the day was too nice to be bothered at all.

Once Bob finished his pastry, he still had plenty of time before he had to meet Professor Schmitt. So Bob walked a few neighborhoods, taking in the sight of the gardens and parks. In a world where he wasn't on an undercover assignment, he would have written to his family about the beautiful views and the interesting people and the excellent food. But the narrative had to stay in his head. His family would never know that he'd walked the streets of Berlin. The weight of his thoughts throbbed against his temples, and he tried to draw himself back to the present tasks that loomed.

Yet again, his mind strayed, and he thought of Luisa. His steps slowed as he neared a hospital. He had no idea where she worked exactly, but what if it was this very building? She could be inside working, right now, which meant they were only a couple of hundred yards apart. He knew even if he did see her, he couldn't speak to her. Not like this. Not now. His thoughts turned melancholy, and what should have been a nice walk became a burden on his heart.

It was time to focus on his assignment.

Back at the apartment, he grabbed his traveling bag and went downstairs to wait in the apartment building entrance. He had no idea if the professor would be on time or not, but a few minutes later, a dark sedan slowed, then stopped at the curb in front of the building.

Bob recognized the professor's car. A couple of days ago, they'd driven it to deliver a lecture at a West Berlin university. Bob started toward the car. By the time he reached it, the professor had climbed out.

"She's all yours," he said in German, stripping off his leather driving gloves. "Need these?"

"No, I'll be fine," Bob said. It had been a while since he'd driven a civilian car, and when he slid into the driver's seat, he smiled.

"She's a beauty, isn't she?" the professor said.

"She is," Bob agreed.

Schmitt set his driving gloves on the dash, then fiddled with the radio. Bob recognized it as the Western RIAS radio station. Schmitt kept the volume pretty low, not loud enough to make out what was being said.

As Bob pulled onto the road, Schmitt tapped a cigarette out of a Stuyvesants pack. He lit the thing, then mercifully rolled his window down halfway after taking the first drag.

"Head to Checkpoint Charlie," Schmitt said as they drove, but there wasn't much conversation beyond that. The professor seemed pensive. In class, he had no trouble lecturing, but one-on-one, he wasn't talkative. This suited Bob just fine.

When Checkpoint Charlie came into sight, Bob slowed when he saw the delay. A line of cars had built up.

Schmitt cursed, and even though it was in German, the words jolted through Bob. "This better not take too long," Schmitt said, adding in another curse word for good measure.

When they stopped behind the car in front of them, Schmitt switched off the radio. Their car was about fifth in line, and no one was moving. Bob didn't know if this was typical, but Schmitt seemed agitated and lit another cigarette. The smoke filled the interior of the car before making a weak escape out the window.

"Leave the engine running," Schmitt said. Then he glanced over at Bob, holding out the cigarette pack. "Want one, Jones?"

Bob shook his head, then focused on the activity at the border. Two Soviet tanks were in place, manned with Soviet soldiers, their guns pointed west. Not unusual, right? He hoped not. The East German border guards, with their gray uniforms and rifles in hand, made an imposing picture of power.

"What are they doing?" Bob asked at last.

"Probably arresting someone."

A shiver ran through Bob, like a foreboding sixth sense. But he was safe. He truly was a student at the University of Berlin. And Schmitt was truly his professor. The other parts of his story were murky, but it wasn't like he was bringing classified information across the border, so there was no reason to detain him for going either direction. Schmitt didn't know that Bob was undercover, and the target plotting would all be mailed at the post drop at the university in East Berlin.

Time crawled, and despite Bob's internal pep talk, his palms began to sweat and the collar of his shirt grew damp. The car in front of them inched forward, and Bob stepped on the gas. Sure enough, the car that had been holding up the line was parked to the side and looked abandoned.

"Stop here, and roll down your window," the professor said. "Get your ID ready. They won't bother you much since you're American."

Bob already knew this since he used this checkpoint to get to the university. He rolled down his window as two guards approached the car. Upon seeing both passengers, the guards split, each going to one side of the car. Bob handed over his ID and let the professor do the talking to both men.

The guard on the driver's side looked from the fake ID to Bob. He knew his hair was longer, but everything else was the same.

"What is your name?" the guard asked.

"Peter Jones," he replied.

"Where are you from?"

"America," he said, staying as close to the truth as possible.

"Like I told you, he's my assistant," the professor cut in. "I'm an economist, and I have lectures scheduled. I'm reporting on the economic structure for the cities of East Germany."

The guard handed Bob's ID back to him but kept his sharp gaze on Bob's face.

"Thank you," Bob said.

The guard's brows shifted upward as if he were surprised to be thanked.

"You're cleared," the guard on the professor's side said as he stepped back.

With a nod from Schmitt, Bob pressed on the gas and the car moved forward, but despite the distance growing between the car and the border check, Bob felt like they were still being watched. As he drove, he was surprised at how empty the streets near the border were. There weren't many pedestrians.

"Maybe you should try a cigarette," Schmitt said with a dry chuckle.

"No, thank you, sir." Bob didn't realize how nervous he'd been until he found he was gripping the steering wheel.

At the next traffic light, Bob removed his glasses and cleaned the lenses. Not that the military plastic was blurry or foggy, but it gave him a moment to collect his thoughts.

"We're taking the next street," the professor said as he pulled out a map and glanced at it. "Heading to Potsdam first, then Brandenburg tomorrow."

Bob's mind raced with the locations Schmitt had named. Potsdam was outside of Berlin, maybe twenty miles. In Potsdam, there were Soviet Guard brigades and a cannon artillery brigade. He had to somehow find an excuse to stop and take pictures.

"Have you lived in West Berlin all your life?" Bob ventured.

Schmitt grunted, and for a moment Bob wondered if the professor would answer. After several moments, he said, "I'm originally from Marburg, West Germany. My wife is from there, too. And like most German men, I was in the German army in WWII."

Silence fell between them for a while longer.

Finally, Bob asked, "Did you always want to be a professor?"

"I became a professor to teach German and Soviet literary works so we wouldn't forget our literature. The economics classes happened later." Then abruptly he said, "Take this exit. This is Potsdam."

Bob made the turn. "I brought my camera. Do you mind if I take pictures at some of the landmarks?" He held his breath . . . He wanted pictures of more than landmarks.

"You can take as many pictures as you like," Schmitt said, not even looking at Bob.

Relief pushed through him. Maybe plotting targets wouldn't be so complicated after all.

"Right at the next street," Schmitt said.

Bob slowed and took the turn. He also scanned the buildings to pick out possible locations of interest. Ah. There was what looked like a government building, with its red Soviet flags.

"Left here," Schmitt said.

They were in the heart of the city now. The streets were far less crowded than anything he'd seen in West Berlin, and the colors of the place as a whole seemed drab and plain. Darker clothing and gray buildings seemed to match the sky, creating a monochrome display.

They came to a stoplight, and another car rolled up next to them. A sleek, black sedan.

"Eyes forward," Schmitt said as he quickly slid his map beneath his leg. "It's a Stasi member. You can tell by their uniforms. But of course Americans have nothing to hide, right?"

Bob obeyed, keeping his gaze forward, although from his peripheral vision, he could see the man in the next car over looking at them. Sure enough, the man was wearing the gray uniform of the Stasi, with the gold-and-red shoulder tags.

The Stasi's official name was *Ministerium für Staatsicherheit*, and they were the secret police agency of the GDR, responsible for both foreign espionage and domestic political surveillance. Not people Bob wanted to draw attention from.

As the Stasi car drove in their blind spot for the next couple of miles, Bob second- and triple-guessed his agreement to take on this assignment.

"Left up ahead," Schmitt said.

When the Stasi car continued straight, Bob exhaled with relief. His body felt like jelly, as if it had become part of the driver's seat.

Schmitt lit another cigarette and drew in a deep pull. "There's the Sanssouci Palace," he said. "The summer palace of Frederick the Great, King of Prussia, you know. Surely, you'll want pictures of that. You can walk over after we settle at the inn but be back before my presentation."

"Of course. Thank you."

As they drove past the massive complex with its ornate façade and extensive gardens and fountains, Schmitt added, "Rivals Versailles, no?"

Bob couldn't say. He'd never seen Versailles in person. "It's very extravagant."

Another dry chuckle from Schmitt. "Extravagant, yes." He cursed as if he couldn't stand the display of gaudy wealth from a bygone era.

When they reached the inn, Bob had lunch with the professor, then left him to his second beer. Bob walked quickly, matching the pace of the other pedestrians. Yet he was on a singular errand, looking for military targets. He passed an alley where a man stood, a cigarette smoldering between his fingers. The man looked ordinary—dark hat over brown hair, short-sleeve button-down shirt, a newspaper in his other hand. But he wasn't reading an article. His eyes were on Bob.

Bob tried to not let it bother him. Who knew if the man was Stasi—it wasn't like the undercover members wore uniforms. Besides, Bob was only walking along the street, and there was no crime in that. Still, the back of his neck prickled until he'd turned the corner and was completely out of sight. He took note of the sign on the next street so he wouldn't get lost on the way back.

He took a few photos of the Sanssouci Palace, like any American tourist might do. Before moving on, he looked behind him. No one seemed to be watching him, but the image of the man in the alley wouldn't leave.

On the next street, his steps slowed. He'd recognize the outside of a military yard anywhere. Behind a massive gate was a gray building, studded with red Soviet flags. Guards manned both the gate and the front of the building. Not guards. Soviet soldiers.

Although Bob was on the other side of the street, he could see enough through the gate to know that the place was massive, and behind the building, there were more buildings. And what looked to be a wide field.

He turned the next corner and circled the place, keeping his pace quick. He paused twice, taking pictures, then he wrote down the address of the place so that he could figure out the exact coordinates. He crossed the street when he spotted a gap in the wall. Pausing in front of it, he peered through to see cannon artillery, which only confirmed his suspicions. This was one of the Potsdam's brigade. A viable target. Another couple of pictures and he was on his way back to the inn.

Bob found Schmitt still in the café area, his cheeks ruddy.

"Join me for a drink," Schmitt said, his tone unusually jovial. "Did I tell you about my presentation that I'll be giving tonight?"

"Not yet," Bob replied, his heart still pounding from his mission. Had anyone noticed him? Wouldn't they be after him if they had? He relaxed by small degrees as Schmitt talked about economic recovery. His ideas seemed outdated, but Schmitt didn't seem to be looking for any input, and Bob wasn't sure he wanted to contradict his professor anyway—at least not in this setting.

"We should have a good crowd in Brandenburg," Schmitt said with a chuckle.

Drinking must have put the professor in a very good mood. "That sounds great," Bob said, unsure how he was supposed to respond.

Schmitt rested his elbows on the table. "There will be Communist leaders, of course, and a few college professors."

Bob hid his surprise at the news.

They ordered food, and Schmitt ordered two more beers. He didn't even ask Bob if he wanted one. It seemed the professor had given up on that venture. By the end of the meal, Schmitt had lowered his head and gone still.

"Are you all right?" Bob asked.

Schmitt lifted his head and blinked reddened eyes at Bob. "Why wouldn't I be all right?"

Bob sighed. "Perhaps you need to rest before the lecture tonight."

After a slow nod, he said, "That's a good idea." He lowered his head again.

Bob rose and grasped his arm. "Come on. I'll help you to your room."

Schmitt stood, swaying against Bob. The pair walked to Schmitt's room, and Bob could only hope he'd be back to normal in time for the lecture.

Once he was alone in his hotel room, he began a letter—to one of the girlfriends that Taggett had told him to make up.

> *Dear Lucille,*
>
> *I hope this letter finds you well. Classes at the University of Berlin are both easier and harder than I expected. But I'm enjoying becoming completely immersed in German. The language is intriguing, and I'm glad I made the choice to come over here. It's certainly a different experience than I expected, but I have no complaints. I'm loving the food and the rich history here as well.*
>
> *I miss you though and think of you often.*
>
> *Tell me how you are doing. How is your family? How is your job?*
>
> *Liebe Grüße,*
>
> *Peter*

Then, on the envelope, he wrote the return address as the coordinates that he'd pinpointed. The numbers would make sense only to Major Taggett, and then he'd pass them along through his own channels.

Somehow the professor pulled off the lecture, and the rest of the night was uneventful. The following morning, they were on their way early.

Brandenburg was a city of red-bricked Gothic buildings, including the Brandenburg Cathedral and the medieval St. Paul's Monastery. Bob wished he was only on a sightseeing visit and not focused on looking for military garrisons or weapon arsenals. He had a chance to walk around the city. He took pictures of two locations that he suspected were military holdings of some sort.

That afternoon, Schmitt presented his lecture, while Bob took notes. Two Soviet officials sat on the row directly behind him. He could feel the heat of their gazes on his neck, like needles against his skin, or was he imagining things?

Were they analyzing him? Reading what he was writing? His hand trembled as he took notes. He tried to focus on the lecture but found that his notes were sparse at the end of it. The Soviet officers approached Schmitt after, but Bob couldn't hear anything that was said among the group. He kept his focus on his notes, adding a few things and hoping the Soviets would leave soon. After waiting until the last possible moment to rise from his chair, Bob headed toward the professor.

Schmitt introduced Bob to the Soviet officers. One nodded. The other merely looked at him. Neither made an effort to shake his hand. It was like they saw him as inconsequential, which Bob considered a good thing.

The following morning buzzed with warmth as Bob and Schmitt loaded into the car. It was the hottest morning Bob could remember in Germany. With three targets plotted, he was feeling accomplished about his progress, but they were still in East Germany and at the mercy of the Soviets and the Stasi.

When they reached the Berlin inner border again, two guards approached their car at Checkpoint Charlie, splitting up and flanking both sides of the car, their rifles handy, their gazes perceptive. Bob knew this time he had information on him that could be condemning. Yet he reasoned with himself that he'd taken enough tourist-type photos that if his camera were ever confiscated, the military targets would hardly be noticed among the others. Regardless, he would be relieved when they were across the border.

Bob offered his ID, then answered the few questions. The professor's credentials carried the most weight. Especially since the guard on Bob's side decided to quiz him on the economics class he said he was taking from the professor.

Bob answered good-naturedly in his learned German, trying to tamp down the nerves coiling in his stomach. He was confident in his knowledge, but how would that translate to a border guard who appeared younger than he? The East German was expressionless though, and when he waved them on, Bob felt like he'd won some sort of race.

As Schmitt's car crossed into West Berlin, Bob hadn't realized how on edge he'd been for the past couple of hours. The very air of West Berlin felt lighter, warmer, more fragrant. But how could that be?

"They're getting stricter at the border," Schmitt said. "More picky. I don't like it. Checkpoint Charlie used to be the easiest checkpoint. There are rumors that the GDR will build a permanent wall. Something grander than the barbed wire and wood fences."

Bob glanced over at Schmitt, whose face was set in a grim line. "What type of wall?"

Schmitt took a drag on his freshly lit cigarette and smirked. "Something to keep people separated permanently."

When Bob stopped at their original meeting place, Schmitt hopped out of the car, cigarette in hand.

"Check the car for any bugs," Schmitt said.

So Bob looked beneath the car and along the sides of it for any sort of surveillance equipment but found nothing. When Schmitt met his gaze, Bob shook his head.

The professor gave a single nod, then said, "See you in class, Jones."

CHAPTER TWENTY-ONE

"We are not immune from villains among us. If I knew of any already, they wouldn't live past tomorrow. Short shrift. It's because I'm a humanist, that I am of this view. All this blithering about to execute or not to execute, for the death penalty or against—all rot, comrades. Execute! And, when necessary, without a court judgment."

—Erich Mielke, Head of the East German Ministry for State Security

EAST BERLIN
JUNE 1961

Luisa had delivered twelve passports over the past month. So why was she feeling so much trepidation this morning? Perhaps it was because everything had gone wrong. First of all, her father was coming with her to visit Oma, which would normally be a great thing, except for the fact that she had to make a delivery. She still hadn't figured out how she'd make an excuse to her father to slip into an alley and pass along a package to a stranger.

Well, Uncle Leon wasn't a stranger to her any longer. Yet somehow, Luisa needed to not only avoid arousing suspicion with the Soviets or the Stasi but also evade her police officer father.

"Are you feeling all right, Luisa?" her father asked as they waited in his car at the inner border.

She glanced over at him. "I'm fine," she said. "Just tired." She looked out her window, hoping that her father hadn't seen the lie in her eyes. They'd be over the border soon, and then she had to put her plan into action. It was a feeble action at that.

When they were stopped by the border guards and asked for their IDs and day passes, Luisa was already counting down the minutes until she'd have her errand completed. She eyed the area past the border, into East Berlin. It was now or never.

"Can we stop at the café?" she said as her father started driving again. "I need to use the ladies' room."

Her father frowned. "It's not too far to your grandmother's."

"I know, but I can't wait." When her father slowed, she felt both triumphant and guilty. She climbed out of the car with her purse, which her father didn't comment on. She walked into the café, then looked about for a rear exit. Relieved to see it, she headed toward it. Seconds later, she stood behind the café in an alley.

Turning the corner, she saw Leon standing there. Tall, hat askew, smoking.

He looked over and raised his brows. "I expected you to come from the other way."

She shrugged because she didn't want to explain. He stubbed out his cigarette, and she moved toward him quickly. She handed over the passports from the hidden compartment in her purse as well as a few items from West Berlin that would help the East Germans appear more like the Wessis.

"Any trouble?" Uncle Leon asked.

"I'm with my father," she said, then turned to hurry away.

"Wait," Uncle Leon said.

Luisa hesitated and looked over her shoulder.

"I might have been followed," Uncle Leon said. "Tell your contact that I'll be silent for a few weeks. I need to make sure I'm not drawing any suspicion. Our next meeting will be at a different location."

"All right," Luisa said, but adrenaline was buzzing through her. What did he mean he was being followed?

"Go now," he said. "Be safe and be careful."

"I will," Luisa said. "You, too."

Uncle Leon nodded, then lit another cigarette and leaned against the wall of the alley as if he had no other concerns.

Luisa turned again and hurried back the way she had come. She didn't look back but went into the café through the back door. Certain that a few people were curious about her path, she focused straight ahead.

When she slipped into her father's car, she hid a sigh of relief. Her father pulled away from the curb, and she closed her eyes for a moment, absorbing that she was fine. Everything was fine.

Then her father slammed on the brakes, and her eyes flew open. There was a Soviet car in front of them, and two Soviet police had climbed out.

Luisa's heart hammered as the Soviets grew closer. Their intense gazes swung toward Luisa, and she could practically feel them peering right into her thoughts and reading them.

They walked right toward her father's car, and in seconds, they'd be tapping on the window. What would she say? How would she explain to her father? Would they arrest her on the spot? Her father too?

Luisa's breathing went shallow, and she opened her mouth to warn her father when the two Soviets veered from the car and entered the alley that she'd been in moments before. *Uncle Leon.* Was he still in there? Surely he was. It had been only a short time since she'd left him there.

She was absolutely frozen in place as the men disappeared from sight, and she imagined what Uncle Leon must be thinking. Did he think she'd ratted him out? Turned him in?

Despite not wanting to look curious, Luisa's gaze was glued to the opening in the alley. But her father pulled around the Soviet car before she could see or decipher anything happening in the narrow space. Her stomach felt like someone was sitting on it, and she wasn't sure she'd be able to hang onto her composure much longer.

Were they arresting Leon right now? Had they found the passports on his person already? She rubbed the palms of her clammy hands against her skirt.

"You should lie down when we get to Grandmother's," her father said.

"I'm all right," Luisa said, but the words came out as a squeak. She didn't want to lie down. She didn't want to be in this car, getting farther and farther away from Uncle Leon. Yet, at the same time, she was grateful to be free from whatever had happened to him. It could have been her.

She slumped against the seat, unable to pretend any longer that she was fine, that she was all right. Thoughts of those Soviet police arresting Leon were plaguing her. Her father's hand pressed against her forehead, and she might have appreciated the gesture at another time and in another circumstance. But here, now, she felt wracked with guilt and pain and regret. No, she didn't regret trying to help East Germans escape to a better life, a safer life, but Uncle Leon should have been more careful.

She should have been more careful. But how? She was merely a player in the game, but as soon as that thought entered her mind, she knew it was wrong to not take responsibility. She should have insisted that they meet someplace new each time. Or she should have somehow alerted Leon that her father would be with her, so she couldn't make the delivery that day.

The car slowed, and her father said, "We're here."

She opened her eyes and hated that tears burned in them—she was feeling hysterical. Her father's compassion only made her feel worse and more agitated. He stopped in front of her grandmother's home, then paused before opening his door.

"You'll feel better after you lie down. Come on."

She nodded through blurry eyes and climbed out of the car. Once inside her grandmother's, she greeted Oma, then excused herself to lie down in the second bedroom. But staring at the beige walls didn't help. Not only was she worried about Leon's fate, but she knew that there was a group of East Germans who would soon have their hopes dashed once they learned what happened. In addition, the names of the West Germans would be revealed. The innocent students who'd agreed to help a fellow German in need could be traced.

Luisa wished she could sleep, but she couldn't. Her father's and Oma's voices came down the hallway as soft murmurs. They were probably talking about her, probably concerned about her. But Luisa didn't want any care and compassion. She wanted to do something. Get Leon out of whatever situation he was in. Fix what had been broken.

Yet where could she turn? What could she do? She hadn't prayed much in her life, but right now it felt necessary. Closing her eyes for a few moments, she prayed for a clear mind and direction. She prayed for Leon. And she prayed for those East Germans who would face such disappointment tonight. And finally, she prayed that her grandmother would agree to relocate.

After she finished, there was no use hiding out in the bedroom. She'd visit with her oma and then return home with her father and deliver the news to Adel. Luisa rose from the bed and went into the kitchen, where Oma had set out a lunch of pasta and sausage.

"Feeling better?" Oma asked.

"I am, thank you." She gave her father a grateful smile.

He was watching her carefully, so she needed to act as if she were feeling better and not worry him anymore. It was getting harder and harder to keep things from him.

As they ate with Oma, Luisa tried to stay engaged in the conversation, although it was difficult. Then her father turned their conversation. "Our house should sell soon in Frankfurt," he began. "Would you like to help us look for a new house in West Berlin? One we can all fit in?"

Oma's eyes shifted to her nearly empty plate. "It would be too much. We've already talked about it."

"Yes, but that was weeks ago," her father said. "We've had an offer on our house, and it will probably go through. So now, we will be permanently in West Berlin."

Luisa didn't like the thought of living permanently in West Berlin, but as long as her grandmother was close, she'd make the best of it. She didn't relish the thought of leaving her father anytime soon either.

Oma patted Luisa's hand. "I explained things to Luisa, and she understands why I must stay here. Don't you?"

Luisa's mouth felt dry, and she took a sip of juice. Yes, she understood her grandmother's reluctance, but that didn't mean that Luisa had changed her mind. "You can get a travel pass for a day or two," she told Oma. "Come over and look around with me. Then decide."

"My husband built this house," Oma said. "He died in it. Leaving these walls is like leaving him behind."

Luisa met her father's gaze. She could tell that he'd heard this before too. How did one convince a woman to leave a beloved home she was so attached to?

"We could rent out this home," her father suggested. "So that you will still own it but are simply not living in it."

Oma reached for Luisa's father's hand too until she was grasping both of their hands, creating a triangle among the three of them. "Not now. I can't."

He squeezed Oma's hand. "We understand, but we will also keep pestering you."

Oma's smile was faint, and Luisa wanted to scoop up her grandmother and transport her across the inner border. Away from the place where Soviet police could imprison a person for the smallest offense, where Stasi men and women reported on neighbors and coworkers, and where elderly women felt stuck with no choices.

After visiting Oma, Luisa and her father loaded into the car. The day had advanced enough that the sun had nearly reached the horizon. They were still hours from curfew, and Luisa's father drove carefully, obeying all speed laws.

As they neared the border crossing, Luisa gazed at the buildings they drove by. Once again she thought of Leon. She fought back tears and swallowed down the painful burning in her throat. Soon enough, she'd be able to report to Adel. Until then, she'd have to hold everything inside.

Her attention was caught by two men in a car, passing by them, going the opposite direction. The dark-haired man wearing glasses reminded her of Bob Inama. She was certainly imagining things. American soldiers didn't wear regular clothes or drive civilian West German cars in East Germany. The man next to him though was the same man she'd seen in West Berlin weeks ago.

Had she imagined Bob back then, or was she imagining that it was him now? She turned in her seat to watch the car pass, but it was already too late to catch a better glimpse. Besides, what would her father think if she told him she thought she saw an American soldier she'd been friends with in Frankfurt?

It couldn't be Bob, and that was that.

The border crossing went smoothly, and once they reached their apartment, Luisa had already come up with an idea. She wanted to talk with Adel right away. It was still an hour before sundown, and a walk would do her good.

"Do you mind if I go to the hospital? I want to check in on one of my patients," Luisa said as they walked up to the apartment.

"Are you feeling better?"

"I am," Luisa said, biting back the lie on her tongue. "I think a walk will help even more."

Her father nodded in that absent way of his, and she knew his thoughts were already elsewhere. So moments later, she slipped out of the apartment and headed straight to the hospital. By now, she knew Adel's schedule as well as she knew her own.

The moment she reached the hospital, she sought out Adel. By the look on her face at seeing Luisa unexpectedly, it was clear that Adel knew something was going on. Without a word, the two women headed to the hallway with the storage closet. Luisa entered first then turned as Adel stepped inside. "What happened?" Adel asked in a clipped tone.

Luisa told her everything.

"You are sure those Soviets were after Leon?"

"He warned me in the alley," Luisa said. "And then as we were driving away, I knew he couldn't have had enough time to leave without me seeing him. So the Soviet police must have found him in the alley."

Adel closed her eyes for a moment. When she opened them again, she said, "Maybe there was another way out? Maybe he followed you into the café and waited or hid there until the Soviets left."

Luisa hadn't thought about that, but now she hoped it was true. Perhaps Leon hadn't been arrested after all. Perhaps all of those passports were on their way to their new owners.

"How do we find out?" Luisa asked, hoping that everything would be fine after all.

"I know someone who can make a call to the East German police and find out if he was arrested."

"You know his real name then?" Luisa asked.

"I do," Adel said. Suddenly, Luisa wanted to ask what his real name was. Maybe her father could find out . . . No. It was better to let Adel handle it. This, Luisa knew.

"Let me know as soon as you can," Luisa said.

"Of course." Adel grasped Luisa's hand. "We have to stay positive. If he's been arrested, then we'll continue to move forward. Leon would want it that way."

Luisa nodded, although her heart was sinking.

She walked home slowly, and only while eating dinner with her father did she attempt any levity. Every moment that passed on the clock brought her a moment closer to discovering the worst had happened. And still the phone didn't ring.

Finally, her father turned in for the night, and Luisa sat in the quiet, dark kitchen, her fingers wrapped around her floral pendant. When would Adel find out? When would she call?

Luisa was absolutely convinced she wouldn't be able to sleep until she knew. She rested her arms on the kitchen table and laid her head upon them. When the phone rang, Luisa was jarred awake. She didn't even know what time it was, but she reached for the phone and picked it up before it could ring a second time.

"Hello?" she whispered into the phone.

"Luisa?"

"Yes. What did you find out?"

Adel released an audible breath. "You were right."

Luisa closed her eyes as her emotions collided and tumbled against each other. If she was right, then that meant Leon had been arrested. The Soviet police she'd seen were the same ones who'd caught him. And that also meant she'd been moments away from being caught herself.

"Can we do anything?" she continued to whisper.

"As of now, we do nothing," Adel said. "We stop the passport ring. They might already know our names. So you and I will lie low. We're nurses right now, nothing more."

Luisa's nod was slow as if she was weighed down by a heavy anchor. "What do you think will happen to him?" *Him* being Leon.

"I've heard everything from six months to two years in prison," Adel said. "We won't find out until he's sentenced."

"And what about the East Germans?"

"They'll know something is up when Leon doesn't show," she said. "And I don't think it will be long before the Stasi match the photos to the correct names. They'll also put in a request for the West Germans who offered their passports to be charged—but that probably won't go anywhere."

"Was it something I did?" Luisa asked.

Adel didn't even hesitate. "Of course not. You couldn't have known you almost walked into a trap. The Stasi have many informers, and they might have suspected for a while but only now did something. Or they might have been tipped off earlier today."

Luisa winced. "I hate to think of Leon in prison. And I hate to think of those people who just had their hopes dashed. Is there nothing that can be done for them?"

"There's always hope, Luisa," Adel said in a soothing tone. "Don't forget. This door might have closed for now, but we'll find another one to open soon."

"I'll help however I can." Even though Luisa had had the scare of her life today, she didn't want to turn her back or shy away from another assignment. The danger was real, yes, but Leon was an example of a man who was willing to risk it all to give other people—strangers even—a new start in life.

"Thank you, Luisa," Adel said. "You're a gem and a blessing to our organization."

Now wasn't the time to feel any satisfaction or pride. The only thing she felt was a desire to find a way around all the restrictions and laws and rules to help her fellow human beings in need.

CHAPTER TWENTY-TWO

"The government of the States of the Warsaw Pact appeal to the parliament and government of the GDR and suggest that they ensure that the subversion against the countries of the Socialist Bloc is effectively barred and a reliable guard is set up around the whole area of Berlin."

—East German Radio Announcement, 1:11 a.m., Sunday, August 13, 1961

EAST BERLIN
AUGUST 1961

Dear Gwen,

I hope Los Angeles is treating you well. I'll start a new semester of classes soon at the University of Berlin, and I'm looking forward to it. This is a beautiful city, and the summer has been hot, but I've grown used to the heat. My German is coming along very well, and soon, I'll have an accent when I speak English.

I miss you greatly, and I think of you whenever I eat in a café. I know you would find them charming. Tell me all your news. I'm looking forward to your next letter.

Much love,

Peter

Bob reread the letter, then, satisfied, he sealed the envelope. Gwen wasn't real, of course, and perhaps Major Taggett would enjoy reading the letter. He carefully wrote the coordinates of a plotted target as the return address on the envelope. Writing the letter made Bob wonder how his family was doing. They were getting replies from a stand-in acting on Bob's behalf, but did they suspect anything? And what if they sent important news that he wouldn't hear about?

Bob knew that ignorance on his family's part was best. Like Taggett had told him, no one could know his mission. And truthfully he didn't want his parents to worry about his safety or to know that he was in danger every time he crossed into East Germany. But that didn't stop his thoughts about his family and the fact that there was no way to contact them while he was on this assignment.

"Coffee or tea?" the waitress asked, hovering over his café table where he'd been writing the letter.

He glanced up. "Juice is fine, and I'll have the sandwich. Plus two eclairs, wrapped up."

She nodded and didn't offer so much as a smile. It was the way of life in East Germany, it seemed. Few smiles, little laughter, heavy hearts.

Bob looked about the café. One thing he'd noticed in West and East Berlin alike is that the people were creatures of habit. Over the weeks and months, he'd haunted a few of the same places and he'd begun to recognize the usual patrons. These people sat in the same places at the same time of day.

This particular café was in the center of East Berlin and close to a neighborhood of houses. No one spoke to him, although he always felt that he was being observed. Bob knew that many East Germans worked for the Stasi, and even more were informers. It probably accounted for the grim faces, the careful conversations, the avoidance of strangers. Everyone was watching everyone. If only they knew he wasn't a student at all. Not that anyone had asked.

Last night, Schmitt had given a lecture in East Berlin and then proceeded to drink himself into a stupor at the hotel restaurant. This morning, or perhaps this afternoon—when Schmitt roused—they'd be going to Schönefeld for another lecture. But right now, Bob figured he had at least two hours before he needed to worry about returning to the hotel and checking in on the professor.

The waitress returned, bringing his breakfast.

"Thank you. This looks great."

She didn't answer, but nodded and set off to help someone else.

Bob ate the sandwich quickly, his mind settling on the direction he wanted to go. Since East Berlin was a more populated city, he knew that Stasi were all around him. Perhaps the man at the next table, or even the waitress who'd feigned little interest in her job. He'd have to be careful here, more so than in the outlying cities he'd visited with his professor.

He'd be looking for anything military that could be a useful target, especially in areas that appeared as blank spaces on his map. When Bob finished his meal, he paid in D-marks, or West German money, which he knew was always appreciated, and put the bag of eclairs into his briefcase. Something for Schmitt later.

Then Bob set off on foot. He headed toward a section he knew from studying the Berlin maps. The blank orange space started only a few streets away, and if Bob hadn't been on an errand, he might have appreciated the tidy yards of the homes he passed.

He turned onto a street that looked like it was full of warehouses. This was the orange rectangle on the map. He scanned the gray buildings, noted the red Soviet flags hanging from one of them, and decided that there was something here.

Bob looked about for guards and, not seeing any, determined they must be within the grounds. Next, he scanned both areas of the street, checking for pedestrians who seemed more interested in him than heading to their destination. An older woman laden with a couple of wrapped packages sidestepped him. Her eyes seemed to bore into him for a few moments, but then she continued on. He watched her retreat, unable to explain why he felt like he should run after her and explain that he was just a university student.

When she turned the corner, she glanced back, and Bob's pulse stuttered.

What if she was an informer and what if she was about to report him to the police? Another quick glance along the street told Bob he'd better hurry before others began to wonder about him. He reached into his pocket and pulled out his camera to take microfilm photos. He snapped a few photos, then hid the camera again.

He memorized the coordinates to write down later. These buildings were certainly government buildings of some sort—maybe weapon arsenals? Things had gone quiet though, and for the moment, there were no pedestrians on the street. Was this fortune or something to worry over? Or maybe the streets were always emptier on a weekend morning. Bob continued walking, then paused and quickly took more photographs. When he reached the end of the orange space, according to the map, he was in a commercial district with shops.

Relief jutted through him, and he slowed his step to take in the sights of the small shops, including a bakery. Then he heard a woman say, "Bob?"

He knew that voice, but he wasn't sure he believed it. Turning, he saw the woman he least expected to see. *Luisa.*

She wore a pale-blue blouse and navy skirt. Her honey-blond hair was drawn up into a rather severe ponytail, but that only brought more attention to her face and gray-blue eyes.

"Bob?" she said again. Her voice was quiet, questioning, as if she were doubting that it was him.

And how he wished that were true. She knew his true identity as an American soldier, and East Germany was not the place he wanted that revealed.

He didn't want to attract any attention from those on the sidewalk, yet there was really nowhere for him to hide from her view without making it obvious he was dodging her.

Painfully, he ignored her and continued walking at his normal pace until he came to a narrow alley between shops. He stepped into the cool shadows and waited. Would she follow? Would she think she had the wrong person and pass by?

Luisa arrived a moment later, her brow furrowed, her lips pressed tight. "Bob," she said again. "Is that truly you? I thought I saw you, but I wasn't sure—"

He grasped her arm and drew her deeper into the alley. They were alone, save a scrounging cat that looked like it was one step away from skin and bones.

"I can't be seen speaking to you," Bob said in German.

Luisa's gray-blue eyes widened as she studied him. "What's wrong? Do you have a girlfriend or something?"

"No," Bob said quickly. "Not a girlfriend. I can't explain what's going on, Luisa. But if you see me again, please don't speak to me. We shouldn't even be in this alley now."

He looked down the length of the alley. No one had spotted them. No one was watching. Yet. It wasn't easy to shove her away like this. But he had no choice.

"Your German is very good now," she said, so quietly he almost didn't catch her words.

Bob nodded. He didn't want to explain or say more than he had to.

"And I saw you driving with another man in a West German car. Then before that . . . in West Berlin—getting into a car with that same man. Why are you in East Berlin, Bob? Are you in trouble?"

"Not exactly." He looked away again, searching the alley, as if the cement would give him the easy answer. "But that could change at any moment of any day."

Luisa exhaled, and in that exhale, he knew she was holding back questions. But she seemed reconciled to his flimsy explanation. Perhaps it was being the daughter of a police officer that gave her such patience.

"Luisa," he continued quietly, holding her gaze. "I'd hate any harm to come to you. Please understand that I wish I could tell you more. But I can't. As far as either of us are concerned, you don't know me. You've never seen me before, and you would never recognize me on the street, no matter where that happens to be."

She blinked rapidly as if she were trying to hold back tears. That didn't ease the lump building in Bob's throat.

"You speak German very well," she said at last. "And you look . . . different. Your hair is longer, and you aren't in uniform. I almost thought I was seeing things . . . but then I *knew* it was you. My instincts told me it was you, even if I knew that logically it didn't make sense."

Bob gave a brief nod. His chest rippled with emotion that he couldn't express, not here, not ever. This might be the last time he ever saw Luisa. Even when in Frankfurt, their friendship was precarious and fleeting. Here . . . it was impossible.

"Bob, I'm worried about you—"

"Don't worry." He took a step back. "I am well. But I need you . . ."

"You need me to stay silent." Her smile was sad as she fidgeted with her purse. "I understand too well about silence. Living in West Berlin has taught me that. I'm here to visit my oma, and if there was any way I could convince her to come to the West, I would."

"She doesn't want to leave?" Bob asked.

"No."

Their gazes connected, and it was like their thoughts were the same. Who would *choose* to remain in East Germany?

"You don't need to worry, Bob," Luisa said. "I would never tell anyone that I saw you or who you really are."

Bob blinked against the burning in his eyes. "Thank you. That means a lot to me," he said in a rasp. "I wish things could be different right now."

Luisa's smile was fleeting. "In a world where you're not an American soldier and I'm not a German nurse?"

He nodded, remembering her father's aversion to American soldiers. But that wasn't the only impossibility between them.

She touched his arm, a fleeting movement, like the wing of a bird. "But we don't live in that world, do we?" A pause stretched between them. "Take care of yourself, Bob."

"Take care of yourself too, and please stay safe. I'll keep you in my prayers, Luisa." Silence stood between them like a foreboding sentinel. At last, Bob motioned toward the street. "You should leave first. I'll wait a few minutes before exiting."

Luisa's gaze clung to his for another long moment. Perhaps she wanted to say more, but there was really nothing more to say because none of this was in his control. He was on assignment, and that was his entire world right now.

"Goodbye, then," she said, stepping close.

At first, he thought she might embrace him. But she only squeezed his arm. Light and quick, almost as if she were touching a hot pan. Then she was gone. Out of the alley and out of sight.

If Bob couldn't still feel the pressure of her hand on his arm, he might have thought the past few moments had been a dream. He might have believed he'd conjured her out of the summer air like a heat wave. But Luisa had been absolutely real, which meant that fear thudded through his veins. What if she changed her mind and mentioned something to her father? Or to an acquaintance? Maybe a coworker?

What would she say? That she saw an American soldier skulking around the streets of East Berlin? Eyes and ears were everywhere. It would take only one slipup. Yet . . . he knew she'd never report on him. She wasn't Stasi or anything. West Germans didn't report to the GDR. At least not someone like Luisa.

Or . . . what if her safety was compromised because she spoke to *him*? What if all of his precautions had, in the end, put her in danger?

Bob had to shake her from his thoughts because worrying about any consequences from their brief meeting in the alley would only torture him. His thoughts had already become jumbled, and he needed to think straight, not worry about *what ifs*. He needed to be more careful and vigilant. He needed to make sure he never ran into Luisa again. Yet it was a strange sort of relief to have another person recognize his true self—to confirm in a way that he was still Bob, that he hadn't disappeared from existence after all. On the other hand, seeing Luisa had brought risk. His entire assignment could be at stake now, and if there was one thing he couldn't do, it was let down Taggett or his country. They were depending on him.

Bob waited in the alley a full five minutes, or maybe ten. It took some time for calm to return and for him to rationalize away the encounter with Luisa and tell himself that there would be no future consequences. The look in her eyes had told him she understood. Even though he couldn't answer her questions, she knew he was involved in something that he couldn't share with anyone.

Still, right now, he wanted to track her down. Speak to her privately. Help her understand. Yet that was the very last thing he should do.

Bob left the alley and walked back the way he'd come. He nearly missed a step when he saw Luisa come out of a shop up ahead of him. She carried a small grocery sack. Like a magnet, her gaze turned toward him. He nearly froze on the spot but forced his steps forward. Casually.

Would she speak to him again?

No. She gave the slightest nod, then looked forward. But before she did, he saw it in her eyes—she would keep his secret. She would pretend she'd never seen an American soldier undercover in Berlin.

Bob couldn't explain the relief flowing through him because it contrasted sharply with a feeling of regret—regret that he couldn't explain anything to her, that he'd never be able to.

But it was time to return to the hotel and find out if Schmitt was ready to head to their next destination: Schönefeld. A city east of Berlin.

As he headed toward the hotel, it appeared that more East German police were in the streets than usual. Eyes seemed to follow him, and Bob knew enough to keep his eyes lowered and stay on the opposite side of the street when possible. He didn't see the older woman with the packages again, but he still worried that she'd thought him suspicious.

Turning onto the street where the hotel was located, he slowed his step when he saw several East German police at the entrance. Had something happened? He approached, his fingernails digging into his palms as he tried to curb his anxiety. The police were watching, or surveying, a building across the street.

As Bob passed by them, he kept his expression impassive. Right now they were focused on something else, but there was always a risk that they'd become suspicious of him. Luckily, none of them stopped him to ask for papers. Before he could step through the entrance, a commotion across the street caught his attention. The East German police hurried toward a man who'd been brought out of the building. He was handcuffed and being hauled to a waiting police car.

Bob took a step back, then back again until he was at the hotel entrance. He didn't want to be caught gawking. What had the man's crime been? Bob escaped into the hotel, where he found a grumpy Schmitt waiting for him in the lobby.

"Where have you been?" Schmitt demanded, stubbing out his cigarette in the ashtray next to the chair he was sitting in.

"I grabbed something at a café," Bob said, his voice sounding breathless even though he hadn't been running. He presented the wrapped eclairs to Schmitt.

But instead of the pastries mollifying the professor, Schmitt didn't take his eyes from Bob as he rose to his feet. "You were gone much longer than it takes to purchase food."

Bob's stomach hardened. Schmitt's tone held suspicion. Or was it impatience? "I sat for a while and ate my share."

This explanation was perfectly reasonable and believable, and mostly true. So why was Schmitt still looking at him like he was trying to see right into his thoughts?

"People watching, eh?"

Bob nodded, hoping that would be the end of the conversation.

But Schmitt wasn't letting it go. "We don't have time for that. You know we're on a schedule."

"I'm sorry," Bob said. "It won't happen again."

Finally, Schmitt broke his gaze so he could fish around for another cigarette. They headed out of the side entrance of the hotel to the parking lot. By the time they were seated in the car, Schmitt had taken several drags as if he were in a smoking marathon. Bob told himself to relax and not worry. The police presence had gotten him rattled; that was all. Schmitt's mood didn't have anything to do with Bob.

When they pulled out of the parking lot, Bob discovered that the East German police had made quick work of their arrest and had already left. Bob turned in the same direction where he'd just walked. As they passed the warehouses Bob had photographed earlier, he ventured to ask, "What's this district used for?"

The professor grunted and cast him a side-eyed glance. "Soviet supplies, of course. They like to stockpile." His voice held an edge. "There's supposed to be a political prisoner facility farther inside the compound."

An unexpected shiver traveled along Bob's arms. From Schmitt's words or from his tone of voice? "It must be well hidden."

"Oh, yes," Schmitt agreed, his tone mocking.

Bob tried not to let the possible presence of the prison bother him, tried not to worry about something that wasn't concrete. Yet, when they were past the compound, Bob's anxiety eased. But then they turned onto the street where he'd encountered Luisa, and he found himself looking for her. Was she still shopping? Had she left already? Gone to her grandmother's?

They passed what looked like a grocery mart, where a couple was loading food into a trunk of a car with West Germany license plates. Maybe Bob could find a better subject to talk about. "It looks like those West Berliners are stocking up."

Schmitt scoffed. "They're using the higher value of the West German deutsche mark against the East German mark. So they're buying up supplies here to save money, then taking them back home. Which effectively depletes the reserves here."

Bob was surprised at the revelation. "Because the food is less expensive in East Germany?"

"Yes, but the wages are not as high."

Ah, now Bob understood. He glanced back at the West German couple with new eyes. All around them, East Berlin still displayed the ravages of war, and now that the Communists had taken over the socialist parties, the East German citizens lived under strict order. How must they feel, watching the West Germans taking advantage of them?

"Pull over at that café," Schmitt said. "I need coffee."

And so Bob found himself sitting at a café again that morning. He wasn't too excited to be slowing down their travel—especially since Schmitt had complained they were on a tight schedule. The man was a dichotomy. Bob kept his eyes peeled for any sighting of Luisa. But she was nowhere to be seen, and he couldn't decide if he was disappointed or relieved.

That night, in their hotel in Schönefeld, Bob's sleep was restless. Thoughts of meeting Luisa so unexpectedly, of the increased police presence, of watching the man who was arrested being loaded into a police car—they all combined with the knowledge of the risks he was taking every day. It felt as if he'd barely fallen into a deep sleep when someone pounding on his hotel room door woke him with a start.

"Jones!" Schmitt called through the door. "Get up. We're leaving now!"

Bob scrambled out of bed, half-awake, his mind dull. The light beyond the hotel room curtains was a dismal gray. It was barely dawn, so why was Schmitt in such a hurry? Bob cracked open the door to see Schmitt opening another door across the hallway.

"What's wrong?" Bob said. "Are we changing plans?"

Schmitt turned, and it was then Bob noticed the man's mussed hair and puffy eyes—as if he'd too had trouble sleeping.

"The world changed overnight," Schmitt said, a deep crease in his brow. "The Soviets erected a barbed wire barrier straight through Berlin. We need to get across that border before the riots start and the bullets follow."

CHAPTER TWENTY-THREE

"Troops in East Germany have sealed the border between East and West Berlin, shutting off the escape route for thousands of refugees from the East. Barbed wire fences up to six feet (1.83 metres) high were put up during the night, and Berliners woke this morning to find themselves living in a divided city. Train services between the two sectors of the city have been cut, and all road traffic across the border has been stopped."

—BBC Report, August 13, 1961

WEST BERLIN
AUGUST 1961

A buzzing filled Luisa's dreams until she realized the buzzing was real, and there was a fly somewhere in her bedroom. Still, it took her a moment to wake up from her dreams and adjust to reality. Her dream had been disturbing. She saw Bob on the streets of East Berlin, and every time she tried to wave at him or speak to him, he'd turn away. He kept disappearing in alleyways, into shops, behind buildings. Wherever Luisa turned, she'd see him over and over, only to be evaded once again.

Why had Bob been in East Berlin of all places? Why was he dressed as a civilian? What had happened to him?

Luisa opened her eyes and gazed at the ceiling as her father's voice floated down the hallway. Who was he speaking to? It sounded like a phone call. He was asking questions by the sound of it. And he sounded concerned. Maybe it was Oma?

Luisa scrambled out of bed and drew on her robe even though she didn't need the warmth. She moved down the hallway and hovered there before entering the kitchen. If it was a work call, she probably shouldn't be eavesdropping. But her father abruptly hung up and called, "Luisa!"

"I'm here," she said, stepping into view. "What is it?"

Her father's face was drained of color, and Luisa braced herself for whatever bad news he was about to share. What he said, though, couldn't have surprised her more.

"A wall went up overnight," her father said. "Straight through Berlin, dividing the West from the East. The Soviets have put their foot down. No more illegal crossings or the East Germans will be shot."

Luisa stared. Tried to comprehend.

Her father rubbed a hand over his face. "Both sides are at a standoff, and people are already gathering. Some are panicking and crossing the border. It's only a matter of time before deadly force will be used."

"To keep them from crossing?"

"Yes." He took a breath. "I don't know what this means for Oma." He finally focused on Luisa as if he were remembering something. "Stay away from the wall today, Luisa."

She didn't have a chance to reply because the phone rang again, and her father answered. It sounded like someone from the police department, giving him another update.

A wall.

Was Bob Inama's presence in East Berlin related to the building of the new wall? If so, how? She couldn't wrap her mind around it. She simply had no answers.

But she couldn't sit in her apartment all morning, until her afternoon shift, while the entire city was in turmoil. She had to forget Bob for now. Whatever he was involved with was his business, not hers. She might not even see him again. Pulse thrumming, she moved about the kitchen, making a quick breakfast of yogurt and muesli. Her father ate quickly, then left the apartment without so much as a backward glance. His mind was already at the border.

Luisa turned on the RIAS radio station. She listened for a few moments, her heart sinking with each word. It was true; it was all true. She shifted to the BBC News.

"Berliners woke to a divided city this morning," a newscaster said. "The troops in East Germany have sealed the border between East and West Berlin. This has effectively shut off the escape route for thousands of refugees from the East."

Luisa sat at the kitchen table, her head in her hands, as the announcer continued. "The barbed wire fences put up overnight are nearly two meters high. In addition, train services between the two sectors of the city have been cut. All road traffic across the border has also been stopped. Konrad Adenauer, West German chancellor, says, 'They are and remain our German brothers and sisters.' Protestors are gathering now at the West Berlin side of the wall—"

Luisa turned off the radio and hurried to her bedroom. She dressed in a few minutes flat. Then she hurried out of the apartment, not stopping to change out her mother's slippers to heeled shoes. Her father had forgotten. She didn't have a plan, but she knew which direction she wanted to go. Two streets over, she saw it. She had to slow her steps to take in the unbelievable sight.

Dozens of West Berliners were milling about near the barbed wire that stretched over almost everyone's heads. She continued walking, heading toward the throng of people. Several of them were chanting in unison, complaining about the wall.

Luisa was so focused on her destination that she almost didn't hear someone calling her name.

"Luisa! Luisa!"

She turned to see Adel coming through the crowd, waving frantically.

"I thought that was you," Adel said, reaching Luisa's side. She grasped Luisa's arm as the crowd surged about them. "They're trampling the barbed wire past here. Want to come?"

"I—" Luisa nearly stumbled as someone bumped into her from behind. "All right." Her mind was a whir, and she wondered if this crowd of West Berliners could really change anything.

"Come on," Adel said. With Adel still holding onto Luisa's arm, the pair made it out of the thick of the crowd, then hurried to where the barbed wire was being trampled.

East Germans, most of them around her age, were flowing into West Germany. Most of them carried nothing. A few carried a bag or two. Then, as Luisa watched, East German soldiers rushed forward, bayonets driving back the West Germans who were helping with the crossing.

Then another group of soldiers turned their rifles on the remaining East Germans and ordered them to return to their neighborhoods. The West German protestors began shouting, but they were no match for bayonets.

"We have to do something," Adel said. "We can't let this happen."

"What?" Luisa said, sidestepping someone who bumped into her. People surged around her, raging and chanting, yet the barbed wire still divided the city. "What can we do?"

She could see right into the eyes of the East Germans forced away from the wall. She could see the desperation and despair in their gazes. The inner border had been a divider before, but this new wall was a different matter altogether.

"I have an idea," Luisa said. "Come with me."

"What is it?" Adel asked.

But Luisa was already threading through the crowd, and Adel hurried to keep up. Luisa didn't stop until she reached Mrs. Herrmann's building.

"Who lives here?" Adel asked as Luisa headed into the building.

"A woman who might be able to give us an idea of how to help."

Adel continued up the stairs with Luisa.

Luisa knocked on Mrs. Herrmann's door, hoping it wasn't too early, but surely the woman had heard the news. She had a modern radio, and she had seemed to know that a wall had been in the planning stages.

Footsteps approached the door, and it opened, revealing Mrs. Herrmann's lined face. Her eyes landed on Luisa, then immediately cut to Adel. "Who's this?"

"Adel works with me at the hospital," Luisa said. "We'd like to speak to you."

"Come in, then." Mrs. Herrmann locked the door behind them, then eyed both of the women as they stood in her front room.

"How did you know the wall would be built?" Luisa asked.

Again Mrs. Herrmann looked at Adel as if wondering if she could be trusted.

"I've worked at the hospital for five years," Adel said. "During that time, I've worked for an underground organization that altered passports and then smuggled them into East Germany. You can trust me with any information."

Mrs. Herrmann didn't look surprised. "I've heard of such organizations that create forged passports. How is it going?"

Adel bit her lip. "Our main contact in East Germany was arrested a few weeks ago."

Again, Mrs. Herrmann didn't seem surprised. "The GDR is overwhelmed, but they've become smarter in their methods. Building a wall is that next step. Now they can fully perpetuate their agenda in the East with less interference from the West."

"We need to find a way to stop this," Luisa said.

"No one can stop this."

Hearing it from Mrs. Herrmann felt like a slap. "There must be something we can do," Luisa said. "How can the Soviets divide us even more against our own people?"

"They want control and order," Mrs. Herrmann said. "East Germans have been leaving in droves. The GDR is putting a stop to that now."

Luisa's shoulders hunched. She knew all of this, but she didn't want it to affect her own family. Would she be able to cross and visit Oma?

"I am sorry to deliver bad news, but the wall will only be fortified." Mrs. Herrmann glanced at her radio, as if it had already given her future knowledge. "The wall will become a death zone for anyone trying to escape."

Luisa braced herself against the front door. "What can we do? Anything?"

"Come, sit down," Mrs. Herrmann said. "I'll get you ladies a drink."

At the table, with a glass of water in hand, Luisa said, "Maybe the other governments will rise up and protest. No one can think this is fair."

But Mrs. Herrmann shook her head. "There have been many walls separating lands throughout history. You need to understand what is at stake. WWII was devastating, but WWIII would end civilization."

"So you don't think the other governments will give the Soviets an ultimatum?"

Mrs. Herrmann took a swallow of her water. "I don't."

"What if . . . what if someone is killed while crossing?" Luisa asked.

No one spoke for a moment. It was like a cold wind had swept through the apartment.

Mrs. Herrmann set her hands on the table. "There are still many options to help, even with a more secure border."

"How?" Adel was quick to say.

Mrs. Herrmann looked from Adel to Luisa, then said, "Tunneling."

Luisa gazed at the older woman. "Beneath the wall? But . . ." She looked at Adel, who seemed equally surprised.

"Beneath the wall," Mrs. Herrmann said. "There is an organization that has already begun the process. But what I need to know is if both of you are willing to help."

Luisa bit the inside of her cheek. She had so many questions, but for now, she only nodded. Adel nodded as well.

"Well, then, come back in a week, and I will give you the next instructions," Mrs. Herrmann said. "By then we should have a better sense of the type of barriers we'll have to push through." Her gaze focused on Luisa. "Your apartment building is a prime location."

"What do you mean?" Luisa asked.

"Being so close to the border, it would be an ideal place for a tunnel to connect to East Germany."

The very thought made Luisa both proud and nervous at the same time. "I can help," she said, because she could. Even if it was inside her own building, and her father was only steps away. Adel also agreed to do whatever was needed.

When Luisa and Adel left the woman's apartment, they hurried back toward the wall. The number of protesters seemed to have doubled. A group had gathered below an East Berlin apartment building that butted up against the barbed wire. Luisa froze when she saw a woman climb out of a second-story apartment window and balance on the sill. Below her, West Berliners were encouraging her to jump, telling her they'd catch her.

"What's she doing?" Luisa said, bringing a hand to her mouth.

Adel gripped her hand. "She's going to jump, and there are more behind her."

Luisa gasped as the woman jumped, and members of the crowd broke her fall. Then the wave of people divided as someone ran up with a large blanket. The next person who jumped, a man in his thirties, headed for the blanket.

"The world has gone mad," Luisa said, but she understood the desperation. What would she have done if she'd found herself on the East side when the wall went up?

"And it's not even lunchtime yet," Adel mused.

Luisa didn't really want to see any more people jump. She didn't think she'd ever get the image out of her brain. But then things seemed to escalate, and protestors backed away from the wall as a line of armed guards moved closer to the barbed wire separation.

Two people jumped at the same time from the apartment window, and the West Berliners weren't ready for both.

"Oh no," Adel gasped.

"Let's go." Luisa headed into the crowd, toward the location where one of the jumpers had landed. Surely the young man's fall had been broken somewhat, but she was equally sure he'd been injured.

Adel stayed right behind her, as Luisa pushed her way through people. "I'm a nurse!" she cried. "Make way so I can help!"

The way cleared enough for Luisa to spot the fallen man. She knelt by his side, scanning for injury. "I'm a nurse, sir," she said quickly. "Can you tell me what hurts?"

His dark hair was disheveled, and his brown eyes blinked up at Luisa. It was good that he was focusing on her. For a moment, his brown eyes reminded her of Bob's, but she brushed that thought away.

"My ankle," he said with a wince.

Adel knelt close to his foot and gingerly pressed against his ankle.

The man groaned, and Luisa said, "We'll get you some help. Did you hit your head or anything else?"

"I don't think so," he said.

"Do you think you can sit up?"

"I'll try." And in a moment, he was sitting. Someone offered him water, and two others said they'd drive him to the hospital.

When the young man was taken care of, Luisa hoisted Adel to her feet. "We should probably report to work early."

Adel brushed off her hands. "Let's go."

CHAPTER TWENTY-FOUR

"Behind the line of soldiers and along the face of the Brandenburg Gate, crews of workers were unrolling wide, six-foot-high rolls of barbed wire. Following them were men with long steel rods, which they thrust under the strands of wire and twisted the strands into a tangle. As the crews rolling out the wire moved on, fresh teams with more rolls of wire took their place, followed by more men with iron bars who twisted the tangle higher."

—John Wilkes, US Airman

WEST BERLIN
SEPTEMBER 1961

The ringing phone echoed through the quiet apartment, jolting Luisa awake. She'd only lain down for a moment, but it seemed she'd fallen into a disjointed sleep. "What time is it?" she asked as she scrambled off her bed. Was her father home from work yet? The orange slanting light in the kitchen told her that the sun was setting, which meant her father was likely finishing up his shift and would be home within an hour.

She picked up the phone on the second ring, cutting the shrill in half, and its tinny echo still pinged in her ears when she brought the earpiece to her ear.

Luisa said nothing. Only listened. After about twenty seconds, with no noise from the other end of the phone, she heard the click of someone hanging up. It was her signal.

Pulse skipping, she slipped on her shoes, then left the apartment. Quickly, she locked the door and headed down the steps to the ground-level floor. She stopped before a plain door that looked like all of the other doors in the building. After glancing at both ends of the corridor to verify she was alone, she unlocked the door.

She shut the door, turned the lock, then turned on the light. The glow was dim since the lampshade was a deep blue. The windows were also covered with heavy drapes so that at night, no light could be seen coming from inside.

Upon first glance, it looked like a regular apartment. Standard furniture. A landscape picture on the wall. Even the bedroom was nothing remarkable. Unless one knew where to look. This place had been prepared over the past several weeks, put into service by Mrs. Herrmann's contacts. Luisa didn't know who the head of the organization was, but she and Adel were given instructions through Mrs. Herrmann.

The sound of a ringing phone jolted the silence, although it was much fainter than the one in her apartment. Luisa hurried to the bedroom and picked up the phone, her only light the faint glow coming from the living room lamp.

No one spoke into the phone and neither did Luisa. She knew to wait though, and after about twenty seconds, the instructions came. The voice was Mrs. Herrmann's.

"Her name is Erika, and she'll be arriving tonight," Mrs. Herrmann said. "She may have a child with her."

A child? That would complicate things. Children weren't quiet. "How old?" Luisa asked. It might be too much information to expect over the phone.

"Six," Mrs. Herrmann replied.

"What time?" Luisa had to plan and somehow not let her father find out.

"Late." Mrs. Herrmann hesitated. "After midnight."

That was good, in Luisa's opinion. Her father would certainly be turned in for the night, and Luisa could get the small family settled and then get some sleep for herself. Luisa had no role in moving any of the escapees to the next location. She had to make sure they arrived and were accommodated. Then she'd set up the signal—an empty flower vase in the window—to let the next contact know that the evacuees had arrived.

The first time she'd done this task, she'd marveled at how the next day, the man who'd come through the underground network had completely disappeared. It had been Luisa's job to make sure no evidence of him had been left. He'd done a good job for the most part, but Luisa had later found traces of whiskers in the bathroom sink. So she'd cleaned that out and thrown away the razor he'd used.

Adel helped in the operation by purchasing the food or any items needed in the apartment. She then handed them over to Luisa, who had to make sure she dropped off the purchased items before going up to her own apartment.

Now she headed to the front room, turned off the light, and left the apartment. She'd return as soon as she could be sure her father was asleep. The time of the refugees' arrival was never exact, and Luisa would have to be in the apartment to unlock the trapdoor in the floor.

Luisa was nearly finished preparing dinner when she heard her father come into their apartment. He looked happier than he normally did, and that brought immense relief to her. He wouldn't be up late stewing over something.

"How was your day?" she asked as she set plates on the table.

Her father crossed to the cupboards and took down the glasses. He was helping her set the table instead of collapsing with distress or exhaustion into a chair. This was a very good sign.

"We had a young man wanted for petty theft turn himself in today," her father said, filling up each of the glasses with condensed juice. Then he added carbonated water. "The police chief is giving me the credit since my investigation put pressure on those he knew. I guess word got back to him that we were nipping at his trail, and he knew he couldn't keep hiding."

"Nice work," Luisa said. "If someone turns themselves in, do they get a lighter sentence?"

"It can happen," her father said. "Not a guarantee, but it does show remorse in the criminal's behalf, and a judge likes to see that."

Luisa nodded. She used hot pads to carry over a steaming pot of stew she'd made with *brötchen* to go with it.

Her father took his seat at the table. "How did it go for you today?"

Luisa's mind immediately flashed to how she'd been checking out the downstairs apartment less than an hour ago. She rerouted her thoughts to her job. "No major emergencies today," she said with a smile. "We had it easy, I guess."

"Oh, I almost forgot." Her father reached into his shirt pocket and withdrew a folded piece of paper. "This came to my office address." He set the paper on the table. It looked like some sort of an official letter.

"The house has sold," her father said. "We can finally begin looking for a house. Three bedrooms. There will be plenty of room for Oma now."

Yes, they needed to find a permanent place to live. And yes, they needed a room for Oma. But how could she leave her mission to aid East Germans? It had just gone into operation. Surely, they could find someone else. But . . . Luisa took a steady breath as she dished up the stew, hoping her father wouldn't notice the slight tremble to her hands.

As they ate, her father told another story about something at the station, but Luisa's mind had already shifted to what her new reality might be. She knew she was treading on thin ice already where her father was concerned. How would it look if she told him she didn't want to move—at least not yet?

Luisa remained on edge as the evening proceeded. Her father was unusually talkative and open tonight, which only made her feel guilty that she was doing things she knew he wouldn't approve of. But she no longer had a choice. In the beginning, sure, but now that she'd seen some of these people in desperate need of help, it was impossible to say no.

Her father insisted on cleaning up after dinner, and that only gave Luisa more time to second-guess herself. So to distract herself, she called Sonja to get updated on everything in Frankfurt. The big news was that her brother was engaged to be married. Sure, Luisa was happy for him, but she found her mind straying as Sonja talked about all the small details that were going into planning the event.

"You should come out for the wedding," Sonja said. "I can't remember what you look like."

This caught Luisa's attention and made her laugh. It really was good to talk to Sonja, and it brought back the things that Luisa missed about Frankfurt. By the time they'd hung up, the apartment was quiet. Had her father already gone to bed? Luisa left the phone in its place in the kitchen, then headed to her bedroom. The light coming from the partially opened door of her father's bedroom told her he was reading.

She paused outside his door. "Good night, Father," she called through the door.

"Good night."

Since Luisa had taken a short nap, staying up until midnight or even later wouldn't be a problem. She listened in the darkness of her room, waiting for her father to go to sleep. She knew the sounds of his preparations, and sure enough, he rose from his bed with a telltale creak. His footsteps moved to the bathroom, then a few moments later back to his bedroom. Another creak of the bed.

All was silent.

Luisa waited a good thirty minutes, then she crept out of bed. She didn't want to put on her shoes until she left the apartment. They'd create too loud of a footfall. Opening the door to her bedroom, she hesitated, first listening, then looking toward her father's bedroom door. As usual, he slept with the door ajar. When her mother had been alive, they'd always kept it closed, but since her death, it was as if her father wanted to be on alert. Which was usually fine, but not tonight.

Luisa stood in the doorway of her bedroom for several more moments, listening for any sounds. She exhaled slowly, carefully, then continued down the hallway. The path was a straight shot, and there was nothing to navigate around. She reached the front door. Her mother's slippers were in their usual place. Luisa waited another heartbeat, then turned the doorknob and slipped out, shutting the door quietly behind her. She locked the door, then found her way to the lower level in the dimness. She hadn't dared bring a flashlight and risk someone else in the building noticing her.

Once she was inside the lower-level apartment, she leaned against the door for a moment to steady her breathing. She'd made it. She was fine.

Now, to wait for Erika. Luisa turned on the lamp and moved to the back bedroom, where the entrance to the underground tunnel was located.

She scooted the bed to the side, then pulled up the rug on the floor. Under that was a metal hatch, locked from this side. Luisa used her second key to unlock it, then she lifted the hatch. Cool, stale air wafted out, and she wrinkled her nose. A shiver ran through her as she peered through the deep darkness into nothing. She couldn't see where the tunnel went, although she knew it headed east. She didn't even know where it started.

Luisa left the trapdoor open, then sat on the edge of the bed. There was really nothing to do except wait. She knew very well that it could be hours before anyone arrived. As she waited, she thought of her oma. Luisa and her father had been to see her only once since the wall went up. It was much more complicated to get a day pass now because the GDR's paperwork had increased.

Her father had pleaded with Oma to put in a request to leave the GDR. And instead of saying no outright, Oma had gone quiet for several moments. Then she'd said she'd think about it. That alone had given Luisa more hope than ever.

To her surprise, only fifteen or twenty minutes had passed when she heard a faint scraping coming from below the floorboards.

Immediately on alert, Luisa left her spot and crouched near the opening. The shuffling grew closer, and Luisa's pulse jumped.

Breathing. She could hear the person breathing, so the woman must be close. When a shape separated from the darkness, Luisa strained to make out any features. It was a woman, all right, with pale-blond hair pulled back into a ponytail. A child clutched her hand, and on her back was a small backpack.

"Erika?" Luisa whispered.

From what little light came in from the hallway, Luisa could see relief in Erika's eyes.

"I'm here to help you," Luisa said.

The woman straightened from her crouch. "This lady will help us," she told her daughter.

The child's eyes were luminous in the dim light.

"Can you take my hand?" Luisa asked.

The girl looked at her mother.

"Go on."

Then the child grasped Luisa's hand. Her fingers were cold and damp. Luisa drew the child up the rest of the way, then she stretched out her hand to help Erika out as well.

Luisa then crouched before the girl. "Are you thirsty or hungry?"

She shook her head and leaned against her mother.

"I have a nice bed here if you're tired," Luisa said.

The girl looked at her mother again, who nodded. Luisa helped the child settle on the bed, then turned to Erika.

The woman had her hands clasped to her chest. "Thank you," she whispered. Her face was streaked with tears, and her clothing was wrinkled and dirty. But she was smiling.

"What about you?" Luisa said "Let's get you something to drink. And soon, you will be relocated to another place."

"Tonight?" Erika asked, her wide, brown eyes on Luisa.

"Tonight."

Erika leaned over her daughter and kissed her forehead. When she straightened, she said, "Yes, I could use a drink."

"Come. She'll be fine here until you return."

After Luisa locked the trapdoor and put the rug back down, she led Erika out into the kitchen. The woman perched on the edge of one of the chairs, reminding Luisa of a small bird. After fixing tea that was only as warm as hot tap water, Luisa sat across from the woman.

"I'm sorry," Erika said.

Luisa frowned. "For what?"

"For coming early," Erika said. "I panicked, I guess. I mean, my husband—"

Luisa held up her hand. "You don't have to tell me anything. I'm only here to help you, so don't feel obligated to explain."

Erika lowered her eyes and wrapped her fingers about the tea mug. She sipped at the tea, closing her eyes as if she were relishing the taste.

The minutes slipped by, and when Erika spoke next, her tone was mournful. "My husband died in jail," she said. "They wouldn't tell me what happened. Well, they did, but I didn't believe them. I went to the office to ask for reports. I knew they were laughing at me, and I could only imagine what they were saying behind my back."

"I'm sorry about your husband."

Erika bit her trembling lip. "Me too." She lowered her gaze. "My in-laws watched everything I did. We were living with them because my own parents are gone, and my husband couldn't find a job. He was blacklisted, we think. So I went job hunting, and I was turned down after every interview."

"Blacklisted?" Luisa asked.

"Yes." Erika looked up, her eyes wide. "He was fired after one of his co-workers used supplies from his office to create leaflets complaining about the government. My husband was told that he should have noticed and turned in the coworker. I think they saw him as an accomplice, so somehow he was blacklisted from employment."

Luisa folded her hands atop the table.

"We went to the Employment Office one day to get more leads for positions, and he said he needed a job because he was unemployed."

"Did they help him?"

"Oh, they helped him, all right," Erika said. "They first got upset that he used the word *unemployed* because they claim there is no unemployment in the GDR. They told him he was 'seeking work.'"

"Same thing?"

"Same thing. It had been a hard week, a hard month really, and my husband got into an argument with the office worker. The next thing we knew, he was arrested."

It was a lot to take in. Luisa didn't know how long ago this had all happened, but Erika was clearly struggling. Luisa placed a hand over the woman's hand. "I'm sorry."

Her voice cracked. "They wouldn't even let me visit him. They wouldn't tell me anything about how he was doing. When I dropped things off, I don't think they got to him. Then they contacted his parents to let them know he'd died in jail." She took a shaky breath, then continued, "When I overheard my in-laws whispering about how they were reporting my comings and goings to the Stasi, I realized they were informers. What if they turned in their own son?"

It was hard to believe they could be so cruel to their son, but Erika's tears testified otherwise.

"I knew I had to get out then," Erika said, lifting her chin. "They'd never let their granddaughter go willingly, so I had to escape without their knowledge. Or I know they would have tracked me down."

Luisa squeezed her hand. "Well, you did escape. And you'll be able to build a new life, free from people who have no qualms about informing on family members."

With her other hand, Erika swiped a tear. "A new start. That's what I needed. Except I'm without my husband."

The woman's grief was almost palpable, and Luisa wished there was more she could do. "You'll always have a part of him in your daughter, and he'll always be in your heart."

Erika leaned forward and hugged Luisa. She was surprised, but grateful she'd offered some comfort, although she truly had no idea what Erika's future would hold.

CHAPTER TWENTY-FIVE

"On October 27, 1961, combat-ready American and Soviet tanks faced off in Berlin at the U.S. Army's Checkpoint Charlie. Tensions between the United States and the Soviet Union over access to the outpost city of Berlin and its Soviet-controlled eastern sector had increased to the point of direct military confrontation.... The American leadership ... were determined not to recognize the East German border guards as having any authority in Berlin. Repeated Soviet-instigated efforts to restrict access by American personnel to the Soviet sector continued, substantially increasing tensions in Berlin.... With the attention of the world fixed on Berlin, American and Soviet tanks, barely one hundred yards apart, faced each other for more than 24 hours with their main guns trained on each other. At the same time, American military and diplomatic personnel with military police escorts continued to move through the checkpoint, exercising their rights to travel into the Soviet sector. On the morning of the 28th Soviet tanks withdrew. Shortly afterwards, the U.S. armor pulled back. The stand-off at Checkpoint Charlie was over."

—Thomas L. Hendrix, US Army Heritage and Education Center

LEIPZIG, EAST GERMANY
NOVEMBER 1961

"Turn on the next road," Professor Schmitt said, directing Bob to the hotel they'd be staying at in the East German city of Leipzig, about 120 miles south of Berlin.

Another gray street, another row of gray buildings. The biting cold almost deterred Bob from his plan to walk around Leipzig. Still, Bob hoped to get some spare time to scout out the city and find something worth sending to Major Taggett.

In addition to the cold, the day was gray. And having to cross the newly reinforced Checkpoint Charlie into East Germany hadn't improved Schmitt's mood. Bob exhaled in frustration. Crossing the border took more and more time lately. Since the Berlin Wall had been built, tensions had only risen between East and West Berliners. And a couple of weeks ago, on October 22, E. Allan Lightner, US senior diplomat in West Berlin, was stopped by East German border guards, who demanded to see Lightner's passport. He insisted that only Soviets had that right. Lightner was turned away from the checkpoint by the East Germans.

In retaliation, General Lucius Clay ordered US military police in jeeps to escort the next American diplomat entering East Berlin. The result? A standoff on October 27, with American M48 tanks revving their engines, facing the East Berlin border, and an equal number of T55 Soviet tanks facing the Americans—guns trained on each other.

For sixteen hours, no one on either side had let down their guard.

The raised tensions mimicked the German lives that had been so drastically changed. The barbed wire wall had been erected overnight on August 13 and ran some eighty-seven miles straight through the city of Berlin. Since then, other fortifications had been erected—cement walls, more guard towers, and armed border guards.

And the stories of those trying to escape to West Berlin made Bob shudder. Like the woman, Ida Siekmann, whose apartment building was right on the border of the new wall. The entrance to her building had been blocked off by the East German police. But while her apartment building was technically in East Berlin, the street and sidewalk around the building were in West Berlin. So she'd tried to escape by jumping out her window. She died on the way to the hospital.

Bob wondered if these stories made it into the GDR news.

Everywhere they traveled now in East Germany felt oppressive. More so than it already had. It was as if a candle that had already been burning low had been snuffed out completely. No one made eye contact; instead, people went about their business with their heads down.

"This city is in economic shambles," Schmitt muttered. "They've lost half of the population."

Bob's gaze cut to the buildings they were passing—apartment complexes built in the Renaissance style with Gothic embellishments.

"Empty," Schmitt said, as if answering Bob's unspoken question. "Massive factories, apartment buildings, villas . . . thousands of buildings are simply empty."

Bob felt somber as they drove through the quiet streets to the hotel. He spotted only a few pedestrians, who glanced at their car, then quickly looked away. Bob parked at the hotel, then gauging Schmitt's mood, he said, "I'd like to see the sights and take some pictures."

"Go ahead, although there's not much to see." Schmitt opened the car door to climb out. "I'm going to review my lecture notes, so be back in an hour. We're meeting the city planner for dinner beforehand."

"Of course." When Schmitt wasn't irritable, Bob sometimes worried more. The man had been asking him more personal questions lately, as if he were digging for information. Bob had made a point of telling Schmitt only what he'd already told him.

But right now, he'd focus on getting pictures while there was still daylight. Then he'd return to the hotel in time for the dinner. Bob had trained himself to listen carefully to dinner conversations without appearing to pay much attention. Once in a while, he would hear a nugget of valuable information he could share with Taggett in one of his letters.

After checking into the hotel, Bob set out on foot to explore, tugging his coat closer to his body. He couldn't go too far, and in the morning, he hoped to make another trek. Most likely Schmitt would follow his pattern of sleeping in.

Leipzig had once been a stately, beautiful city, and there were still traces of that beauty around, showing through the gray of winter. But Schmitt was right—the place felt like a ghost town more than anything. History was in the making here. Bob could feel it. He tried to imagine what this city would look like in the summer, when everything was brighter—the trees greener, the sky bluer, and the dormant bushes flowering and fragrant.

Bob turned on the streets he'd memorized from his maps, but he adjusted his route any time he saw an East German policeman. He could be stopped and asked to show his ID at any moment. What if they searched his person and found his camera? He'd explain he was an American student, but if they felt anything was suspicious, he could be taken in for questioning.

And of course there was always the Stasi. Regular men and women who would inform on anything they thought out of place. Bob paused at a shop, pretending to be reading a flyer on the window as a police officer walked past him. He stayed in one place for several moments, taking in the other pedestrians and trying to figure out if any of them were watching him. When things seemed to be clear, he walked to the next blackout district. It didn't take him long to locate what he was looking for. Another military target—a freight yard.

A man and woman were walking up ahead. Otherwise, the street was quiet. Bob waited a few moments. Then he took a handful of pictures, walked several yards, then took another two. He already knew the coordinates, and now that he'd verified them, he'd add them to the envelope that contained a letter written to Ruth—his pretend girlfriend in Chicago. She'd be delighted to hear from him again.

The hour was up all too soon, and Bob headed back to the hotel, walking briskly as the cold seeped through every article of clothing he wore. No pedestrian he passed met his gaze. No one had a friendly look or smile to offer. The chill sliding along his neck was from more than the cold weather. Every person he passed could be watching him or decide to follow him. He paused at one corner and looked behind him. No one had their eyes on him. But the sense of unease continued.

When he entered the hotel, he was relieved to be inside again. He waited another ten minutes in the lobby, thawing out, before Schmitt appeared.

"It's close enough to walk," Schmitt said, not breaking his stride as he headed to the hotel entrance.

Bob buttoned up his coat again, then walked with Schmitt to a restaurant about half a mile away. Bob stayed silent throughout these dinners for the most part. Once in a while, he was pulled into conversation, but that didn't last very long.

This dinner, however, proved to be different.

They met with the city planner of Leipzig and his assistant—Wagner and Roth. Wagner greeted them both, then he and Schmitt dove into a deep conversation, covering most of what Schmitt would be talking about in his presentation. But Roth seemed to have a keen interest in Bob, so much so that Bob began to feel uncomfortable.

"What do you think about East Germany, Mr. Jones?" Roth said, his skinny mustache twitching.

"It's beautiful," Bob answered in German. *Beautiful and desolate.*

"And you enjoy your studies?" Roth continued.

"Of course. Economics has always interested me."

"But why East Germany?" Roth asked. "Why did you leave America to come here?"

Bob hoped his answers would be good enough. "So I can study economic recovery firsthand. It's one thing to read a textbook, but another to see economics in action."

Roth narrowed his eyes. "Where did you learn your German? It's quite good."

"I studied in Idaho." He left it there, hoping that Roth would lose interest soon. He didn't.

"*Idaho*? I've never heard of the place. Where is it?"

"In the northwestern part of the United States," Bob said. "My teacher was fluent."

"Hmm." Roth took a swallow of his beer. "Was he German? East German or West German?"

Bob suppressed a sigh. "I didn't ask."

Roth tsked, then dug into his meal for a moment. "What are your plans after school? Will you stay in Germany? Or return to this Idaho?"

"I haven't decided yet," Bob said. "Perhaps the professor will have a rec- ommendation for me."

The conversation finally faded, and Roth tuned into what his boss was discussing with Schmitt. But throughout the rest of the meal, Bob felt like he was standing in the middle of a courtroom, and Roth was the sole juror.

Why Bob felt that way, he couldn't exactly explain. Roth's questions had been conversational, right? Perhaps he was a curious sort of character. Bob lis- tened carefully to the others speaking, cataloging any information he should pass on. The meal ended, and Bob and Schmitt walked back to the hotel to get their car. They then pulled up behind Wagner and Roth's car and began to follow them. They drove through an industrial area of Leipzig, then stopped in front of a three-story building adorned in red Soviet flags.

Bob turned off the engine as Schmitt finished his current cigarette. They climbed out of the car, and Bob took in the surrounding sights. Across the street was what looked like a communications tower. For air traffic? He wished he could walk around the tower and see what was behind the tall fence.

Glancing over at Schmitt, Bob saw the man bend to fix something with his pant leg. Bob slipped his hand into the interior pocket of his jacket and quickly brought out his camera. This site might warrant another letter to one of his three girlfriends. He gave a little cough as he snapped a picture of the tower, hoping the cough would conceal the click of the camera.

Bob slipped the camera back into his pocket and turned.

211

Schmitt's gaze was on him.

"R-ready?" Bob fumbled to say.

Schmitt hesitated, as if he were about to say something, but then seemed to change his mind. The professor turned, his back stiff, and headed toward the steps leading up to the building, where Wagner and Roth waited, involved in their own conversation.

It was several seconds before Bob could force his feet to move. Had Schmitt seen him take the picture of the tower? Should Bob try to explain his reasoning for taking such a photo? He followed the professor, ignoring the increased thumping of his pulse. Schmitt would have said something if he was suspicious, right? He wasn't one to let something go. Right?

Bob caught up with the men as they reached the building entrance. They headed into the meeting room, and no one asked him why he'd taken a picture. No one was staring at him with suspicious gazes. Inside the meeting room, about a dozen others had gathered—likely city officials from around Leipzig. Bob committed the names to memory—he'd write them down later.

The professor began the lecture as usual, by giving a lengthy description of his credentials and background. Then he started into the subject of economic recovery and the ideas he had for Leipzig.

Bob wasn't necessarily tired, but staying focused was hard, especially when he'd heard this lecture multiple times. He took notes diligently, though. When Schmitt was finished, Bob continued to wait while a few people spoke to the professor.

As they drove back to the hotel, Schmitt said, "You have the rest of the night off. Not much light to take pictures though."

Bob told himself not to be so sensitive to Schmitt's words, but his tone had been ironic . . . almost mocking.

Regardless, Bob had a job to do. He couldn't worry about things that might not be real. Heading outside, he found that Schmitt was right. The winter gloom had grown heavier, and it would soon be completely dark. He walked around for a good while but found nothing else to photograph.

The following morning, Bob was surprised to see Schmitt already in the lobby when he came in search of breakfast. Did they have an early appointment Bob didn't know about? Was he about to be berated for being late?

"Pack up, Jones," Schmitt said in a clipped tone. "We're leaving now."

Bob didn't ask questions because it was clear Schmitt wasn't in a good mood today. Heading back to his room, Bob took a few moments he probably didn't have to say a quick prayer. Bob prayed for his family, his friends, and his country, then finally for patience with Schmitt's sour mood. Bob had already packed, so he only had to gather his bag and head back to Schmitt.

Outside, winter clouds had gathered, and the morning air was crisp and cold. Bob cracked his window partway as they headed out of Leipzig, giving him a little relief from Schmitt's cigarette smoke. But it wasn't long before Bob rolled the window up again because of the temperature. "Do you have any more meetings today?"

"No. Head for Checkpoint Charlie."

Outside of Leipzig, the clouds continued to stack, and it seemed there might be either rain or snow on the way. They'd been driving only a short time before Bob had to slow down. There seemed to be a blockade up ahead.

The cars in front of them slowed down as well, and soon they were in a queue, waiting to be allowed through the blockade. Bob wondered about the number of Soviet tanks—not a completely unusual sight but one that always got his heart pumping faster. Was there some sort of drill today or a government official traveling on this part of the road?

The East German guards milled about in front of the Soviet tanks, their PPSh-41 rifles in hand, their gazes sharp.

Bob glanced over at Schmitt to see if he had any explanations, but he merely took another drag on his cigarette and kept his gaze straight ahead.

When it was Bob's turn to pull forward, one of the guards raised his hand for them to stop. Which Bob did. Two guards approached Bob's side. This felt a little unusual since they usually split up and headed for opposite sides of the car to question both passengers.

Bob rolled down his window and was about to hand over his ID, when one of the guards said, "Steig aus dem Auto." *Step out of the car.*

Bob swallowed back the nerves climbing his throat and opened the car door, then climbed out. "My ID is here." He showed the paper with his picture and the name of Peter Jones.

The guard didn't even look at it, but glanced over at Schmitt, who had climbed out as well. Bob hoped the professor would straighten all of this out soon. But Schmitt had entered a conversation with another guard, their tones rapid and quiet.

Then Bob heard Schmitt say, "Er ist ein amerikanischer Soldat."

He's an American soldier.

Bob's entire body froze. Schmitt knew . . . *knew* that Bob was with the US Army. *How?*

The guard closest to Bob yanked his arms behind him and snapped on handcuffs before Bob could so much as take a breath.

"Don't move," the second guard said, raising his rifle.

Bob stared at the barrel of the rifle. "What's going on?" Bob's wrists were already smarting from the tight handcuffs. Maybe this was all a mistake. Maybe the professor was talking about something else—and not the fact that Bob was with the US Army. He wanted to turn and seek out the professor, but the rifle forced him to remain still. Regardless, Bob said, "Professor Schmitt?"

The rifle inched higher. "Don't speak."

Then the professor stepped up next to the guard, and Bob caught a full view of the man—his expression hard, his eyes even harder.

Bob hadn't misunderstood. Somehow, Schmitt had found him out.

Then the world went black as the first guard blindfolded Bob, and his stomach plummeted as if he'd fallen into a vast cavern.

"Move," one of the guards said, a hand clamped around his arm as he shoved Bob into walking forward.

Unable to see the ground, Bob nearly stumbled. Where were they taking him? Was this how they questioned people at a blockade? Handcuffed and blindfolded?

Then, finally, the professor spoke. But the words were like a bucket of ice water. "Auf Wiedersehen, dummkopf."

Goodbye, idiot.

Bob knew then, without a doubt, that Schmitt had planned this. He'd alerted the Soviets, and this blockade was not for a government official. It was for *him*. Somehow, Schmitt had figured out what Bob had been doing.

Bob breathed in, breathed out. Nothing about this situation would have a positive outcome. He had no doubt about that.

"Bend," one of the guards said in German, and Bob ducked his head.

He was pushed into some sort of vehicle—a truck, he guessed. As the vehicle rumbled to life, Bob thought of the pictures on his camera right now. The camera was still in Schmitt's car. And the notepaper and envelopes were in his briefcase. One letter was written but not addressed yet. What would happen when Schmitt turned over Bob's belongings?

The truck began to move, and Bob couldn't guess which direction they were heading. East or north? South? Any direction but west, he guessed.

Taggett's words spun in Bob's mind: *If you're compromised, or if you're caught, then you will tell them only your fake name. Nothing more . . . There will be no official record of this assignment, so if it fails, you are on your own.*

Bob was on his own. No one was coming to get him out of whatever prison they took him to. Would it be a prison? Or would he be executed before that? Or even worse, tortured? Torture would happen. He knew it. A soldier had never been imprisoned by a rival without facing violent interrogation. This time, Bob's number had been called.

He closed his eyes as the truck continued on for what seemed like hours. And it might have been, but he had no way to track the time. The East German guards spoke from time to time but never directly to Bob. And the rumble of the truck prevented him from comprehending much. Either that, or his mind was in shock.

He wondered what Taggett would think. When would he realize that Bob had been arrested? What about his parents and sister? They would have no idea. For all they knew, Bob was still at the army barracks in Hanau, going through training and eating three meals a day. Would they find out? Would anyone?

The truck slowed, then gained speed again. Bob's stomach pinched with hunger—another sign of how long they'd been driving. They could be in Poland by now for all he knew. His wrists felt like they were on fire, and his limbs had grown heavy with a deep ache from having his arms behind his back. The truck slowed, then sped up again, then turned.

Bob swayed with the movements, nausea beginning to rise. It was agitation. Fear of the unknown. Basic training in the army had taught him to push past the physical pain, time and time again, to keep going. To rise above hunger and fatigue and ignore discomforts. But his mind was bordering on panic, expanding with larger fears by the moment. He had to pull back, stay logical, and keep alert.

He was a US soldier. He knew and understood pain and discomfort. He'd accepted this assignment. He'd never been forced. Yet . . . if he had known what he knew now—that Schmitt would turn him in . . . How had he not seen this coming? What had been his mistake?

The truck jolted to a stop, and the engine shut off. There was no silence, though. The East German guards were already commanding him to move, and Bob did. He climbed out of the truck, his legs feeling like water, his feet half numb.

His shoes hit gravel, and he nearly slipped. The guard holding onto his upper arm thankfully kept a steel grip, so Bob was able to keep his balance. Being outside, although still blindfolded and handcuffed, was a relief. What little light came through his blindfold was cut off shortly when they stepped inside a building.

Bob's footsteps slapped against hard rock as he was led along what he guessed was a corridor, then down a set of stairs. Without his sight, he became more aware of the sounds and smells. Damp. Cold. Musty. Stale. Then he heard footsteps stopping and a door being opened. Heavy and thick, by the sound of it.

Bob was shoved into the even darker space. Mercifully, his blindfold and handcuffs were removed. They took off his shoes and socks, removed his shoelaces, then set his shoes on the ground. At least he could keep those. Before his vision could adjust to his new surroundings, the door shut, leaving him in near total darkness.

It took a few moments for him to realize there was faint light coming in through a cell window, high above his head. Fifteen feet from the ground, if he had to guess. He could just make out a portion of the gray sky. Cutting across it in a horizontal slash ran a line of barbed wire. Fitting that his only view of the outside world was marred by the reminder that he was on the wrong side of that fence. Slowly, he turned and assessed the bleak room.

The room was about ten feet by twelve feet. And the only items in the room were a bed, a chair, and a bucket. A rope extended from the bucket to the ceiling above, and Bob realized this was his latrine. He could almost taste the sour staleness of the air, and he rotated toward the door. Sure enough, the door was heavy—iron, to be exact.

He stepped forward and ran his fingers along the door, knowing there was no way to open it from the inside. The feel of the door sent a shiver through him, landing in his stomach, twisting into a spiral. He leaned his forehead against the cold door and closed his eyes. This barrier represented his loss of freedom. *Why*, he wanted to ask God. Either that or *Help me. Save me.*

Instead, he whispered a prayer for his family, his friends, and his country. And finally, he prayed for himself. *Sustain me. Protect me. Teach me what I need to know. Bless the other prisoners in this place.*

The air around him seemed to grow colder by the minute, and Bob suspected it was because his adrenaline had worn off. His hands were trembling by the time he ended his prayer and opened his eyes. But he'd spoken to God. He'd stated his desires, and surely God would hear him. His prayers had often been answered, when studying for tests in college, when traveling to his grandfather's hometown, when learning better German, and when working to become Professor Schmitt's teacher's assistant so that he could fulfill his army assignment.

Bob's gaze tracked the length of the door. At the bottom was a slot, and he crouched so he could push his hand through. Perhaps this was where they'd give him food. Rationed food, most likely.

He straightened again. He was absolutely alone, and he wasn't sure at first if that was a good thing or a bad thing. Another prisoner would be someone to talk to, sure, but other complications could arise. He decided it was good to be alone.

Bob crossed to the other side of the small room and placed his hand on the stone wall below the window. Even if he were able to climb up and reach it, the window wouldn't allow a small child through, let alone a broad-shouldered man like Bob. Besides, what else was beyond that window besides a barbed wire fence? Attack dogs? Guard towers? Soldiers with guns?

He wondered who else might have stood in this very spot, looking toward the window, feeling helpless. But there were no traces of whoever might have stayed here before. Had it been an American? A German? The small room had a forlorn quality to it, as if the dank dimness was a place of loss.

Bob sank onto the edge of the cot. It was so hard, it might as well have been the cement floor. Removing his glasses, he rubbed his eyes. He tried to think why Schmitt decided to rat on him. What had Schmitt seen, heard, or suspected? Maybe it was all a strange fluke, and Bob would be questioned and released. He'd been so careful, and he didn't see how anyone would have gotten ahold of his letters.

Before he could piece anything together, the metal door swung open. Two guards entered, and he was hoisted up from the bed before he could gain his own footing. They handcuffed him, then steered him out of the cell. Their grips on his upper arms were like steel vises.

"Where are we going?" Bob asked in German. "Where are you taking me?"

Neither guard answered, and as they led him down the hallway, then up the stairs he'd come down a short time ago, Bob sensed what was coming. Perhaps it was his mind preparing his body.

They reached a door, and one of the guards opened it. Bob was led into a room with only a chair in the middle of the floor. He was shoved into the chair, then his ankles and forearms were secured with shackles. Bob's stomach hollowed out as fear tripled his heart rate. Yet this was no surprise. He was a prisoner. Of the enemy.

Two military officers walked in. Soviets. Dark uniforms with red shoulder tabs. The older one with wire-gray hair wore glasses. The other had a square jaw and a prominent dimple in his chin. Both of them stood in front of Bob, while one of the earlier guards shone a bright light into his face.

Bob squinted against the hot glow, unable to make out anyone's expressions.

"What is your name, and what is your business in East Germany?" one of the Soviet officers asked in rough English.

"My name is Peter Jones," he said in English.

"What is your business in East Germany?" the Soviet officer repeated, taking off his glasses and handing them to the other officer.

"My name is Peter Jones," he repeated.

The first blow struck him across the face.

CHAPTER TWENTY-SIX

"Most of the time they offered me hard bread. Occasionally we had a stew-type dish. I did have water in a container in my room. Sometimes they served mush. I was given meals twice a day. I had no latrine. Instead I had a bucket with a rope on it hanging from the floor above. They pulled it up and emptied it about once a week. While in prison, I was always handcuffed and escorted by armed guards. In the [interrogation] room I sat in a chair with my ankles and forearms secured with shackles."

—Bob Inama

EAST GERMAN PRISON
DECEMBER 1961

When Bob opened his swollen eyes, his face was pressed against the scratchy fabric of his cot in the small prison cell. It was an improvement. Usually he woke up on the cold floor. The winter cold made the cell feel like he was living in a deep freeze. His head throbbed, and his shoulders felt raw and sore. And his nose was surely broken. He wondered if it would ever truly heal. Pain spread to his back, culminating into a dull numbness that he knew, by experience, would sharpen once he moved.

It was often like this after a beating. Bob should know. He'd lost count of them by now and guessed he'd been in this prison for weeks. Close to four, maybe. Was it December now? Bob rolled over onto his side and stifled a groan. He must have passed out again, and the guards had carried him down the stairs.

At least they were getting a workout. And at least the beatings were shorter. Predictable even. He wondered if the officers were tired of hearing the same reply over and over.

My name is Peter Jones.

My name is Peter Jones.

My name is Peter Jones.

That is, if he answered at all. Staying silent usually guaranteed a fiercer beating, which meant it was over with more quickly.

Today, he'd told the Soviet officer with the glasses that he had a nice right hook.

The second officer smirked, then the first officer delivered that right hook a second time.

Bob stared up at the ceiling. Based on the patch of orange light shining through the cell window onto the opposite wall, it was nearly sunset. Another day survived. Another beating endured. Another night of quiet.

He heard the sound of approaching footsteps long before he should have. It was like that with isolation. His hearing had somehow amplified, and he could probably out-smell a rodent. The heightened sense of smell wasn't exactly a gift, though, given that the latrine bucket in his cell was emptied only once a week.

It seemed stew was the meal of the day, if he could trust his nose, and he hoped it would have a bit of meat in it. Meals came twice a day. Usually, he got only hard bread, and once in a while, mush. He heard the footsteps halt outside the metal door, then the scrape of a bowl sliding across the cement through the opening. The guard's hand flashed in and out of view, and Bob recognized the ring on the guard's hand—a flat, broad gold ring. Bob guessed it to be either a wedding ring or a family ring of some sort.

Bob didn't move yet; he'd wait until the dizziness passed. But he called out anyway. "Thank you, Adolf."

Adolf wasn't really the guard's name, but it seemed to fit regardless. An inside joke for Bob, but "Adolf" hadn't complained. In fact, Adolf hadn't ever spoken to him. None of the guards said anything to him. Still, he felt Adolf was somehow more personable, more approachable.

The footsteps moved away, and the silence returned. Well, it was never completely silent. There was always some sort of sound to identify. A scrape of another door opening. Shuffling on the stairs beyond the cell. A thunderstorm outside. Voices, both German and Soviet.

Bob knew there were other prisoners also in the basement, even though he'd never seen any of them. He'd heard them, the faint sounds of voices. Sometimes crying. Sometimes singing. The singing was nice. More than once, he'd hummed along. That was when grief wasn't pressing down on him like an ocean undercurrent, threatening to drown him. The days he could hum were the good days.

Once, Bob had lain on the ground in front of the metal door to look out the slat. The corridor had been dim, and he stiffened when he heard approaching footsteps. Those footsteps continued walking past Bob's cell, went another eight steps, then stopped. A door scraped open, and Bob had closed his eyes when he heard another poor soul taken up the stairs, likely to the interrogation room.

"Get up," Bob whispered to himself. "Eat. Keep your strength."

Now he moved slowly off the cot, careful to maintain his equilibrium. His head started to pound, but not as intensely as it had in the past. It seemed that day's beating had been concentrated on his upper body.

Gingerly, Bob took the few steps to the door. By the time he had bent and picked up the bowl of stew, he was out of breath. Sitting on the only chair in the cell, he drank down the stew. No meat today. He let the food settle and relished feeling full, or nearly full, for a short time. He'd lost weight already, certainly the weight he'd put on while eating in cafés with Schmitt. But he didn't want to lose muscle mass. So every morning, he did a workout regimen, no matter how sore he was from the beating the day before.

He set the bowl halfway through the opening at the bottom of the door so Adolf would know he was finished. Then he climbed back onto the cot. The orange glow from the window had faded to gray, and the cell grew darker by the moment. But he didn't sleep yet. Not until he heard Adolf's footsteps again.

"Thank you, Adolf," Bob called out in a rasp.

There was no reply, but Bob knew Adolf had heard him. It was enough to know. It had to be enough. He had little else to hold onto.

Memories of his family, of his army unit, of his friends all competed for space as he willed his body to relax and ignore the pulsing pain. Sometimes he even thought of Luisa. How confident he'd been that day he saw her in East Berlin—telling her to pretend she didn't know him. As if he were protected in every other way from being discovered. In the end, he was discovered anyway.

Something scuttled close by. Probably a rat. Not close enough to bother moving. The creature wouldn't find any crumbs here anyway.

Bob's thoughts shifted again. How long would he remain here? Would he even make it out alive? These questions plagued him so much that Bob had to find a way to shut them out. There was nothing he could do to ensure his release. Literally nothing. Betraying his country had never been an option. So he would endure. Come what may.

As his thoughts mellowed enough for him to sleep, he thought of his blessings. He hadn't been executed. His parents, mercifully, weren't worried and feeling helpless about him. No one had linked him to Luisa, so she was safe. Sleep came, but it was fraught with anxious dreams. Yet each time Bob awoke, he couldn't think of what he'd been dreaming about.

Voices sounded, urgent and shouting.

With a grimace, Bob sat up in bed. It was sometime in the middle of the night, and the cell was nearly pitch black. And even colder. But something had changed. There was a new energy in the air, and Bob couldn't quite define it.

A commotion in the corridor outside his cell drew his attention.

"Hello?" he called. "What's going on?"

No one answered, but there was certainly someone walking along the corridor. Perhaps it was another prisoner.

Bob couldn't fall back asleep for a long time, and it felt like he'd barely closed down his mind when he was awakened again. The darkness of the cell had eased to violet, telling him that dawn had arrived.

Adolf hovered over him, holding handcuffs. The guard was younger than Bob by a few years, maybe twenty-one or even twenty? He was around six feet, nearly the same height as Bob. He was a good-looking man by any account, and Bob imagined that if Adolf had been one of his army comrades, Murdock would have teased him about his lady friends. Bob was broader than Adolf, but that mattered little when Adolf had the gun and handcuffs.

Bob struggled to his feet and extended his arms for the handcuffs. He knew what was coming. Another interrogation. Bob couldn't hide the wince as he was handcuffed. They headed toward the corridor. Everything still throbbed and ached. They reached the stairs, and in the dim lighting, Adolf looked heavy-hearted to be dragging Bob back to the interrogation room.

As they neared the top of the stairs, Bob heard a conversation coming from the interrogation room. The two officers were speaking to each other. Talking about what sounded like a news story of an East German trying to escape into West Berlin.

"He swam across the Teltow Canal," the officer with the glasses said.

"But how?" the second officer asked. "The water is bitter cold."

Bob knew that the Teltow Canal separated the East German region of Brandenburg from West Berlin.

"I don't know," the first officer said. "It took him four hours, and then he returned to East Germany to load some friends in the trunk of his car."

"And the border guards never caught it?"

"Not this time," the first officer said. "But they won't make the same mistake twice. All of the car trunks will now be checked."

The other officer chuckled.

For a moment, Bob thought how insane it was that there had to be a wall to keep people on one side of the country when their fellow Germans were on the other side. Hadn't the Cold War already destroyed enough?

They were nearly to the interrogation room now, and Bob's insides had tied themselves into a knot. Another beating was sure to follow another round of questions. There was only one thing he could do and that was pray. *Please, God, sustain me through another interrogation.* Somehow praying made him feel less alone, less like a man hidden deep in an East German prison with no identity.

As Bob entered the room with Adolf, the other two officers turned. All Bob saw was their pallid faces, their bland eyes, and their smirks.

Bob didn't need to be asked to sit down. He knew the routine. Shackles. Questions. Beating. Blackout.

"Tell me, soldier," the first officer said, taking off his glasses. "Why were you taking pictures in our East German cities?"

Bob didn't answer, and it was as if no one expected him to because after only the barest of hesitations, the first officer swung his fist. Bob's head snapped to the side. The sharp taste of blood in his mouth was a familiar occurrence now.

"You might as well tell us your real name," the officer ground out. "We know you're with the US Army. We know your ID is fake. If we don't know your name, then no one else will. And you'll never get out of here."

Bob had thought about this. Maybe what he said next was because he'd endured dozens of beatings, and because he knew that the only way out would be if either the Cold War ended or someone in the army cared enough to track him down.

"My name is Bob Inama," he rasped.

The surprised looks on the officers' faces were clear.

"My name is Bob Inama," he said, his voice gaining strength. "My rank is Specialist Fourth Class. My ID is 10423570."

The beating was lighter that day, and he didn't pass out this time. But he didn't exactly consider that a good thing. Perhaps the officers wanted to get back to their conversation about the daring East German escapes, or perhaps they were rewarding him for giving them information at last, even though it was only about himself. Bob rose from the interrogation chair, his face much worse for the wear, his head throbbing both inside and out. Before he left the room, he paused and turned back to the officers. "Thank you."

The first officer frowned, and the second officer looked like he'd bitten into a lemon.

"Thank you for what?" the first officer said.

"For doing well at your job," Bob said.

The second officer scoffed. "For beating you?"

"Yes." Bob headed out of the room, handcuffed once again. Adolf at his side. When Bob swayed a bit at the top of the stairs, Adolf gripped his upper arm and steadied him as they descended.

"Thank you," Bob said.

Adolf didn't respond but continued walking with Bob, supporting him. Bob's weary gaze shifted to the walls along the stairwell. Wall after wall in this prison.

At the cell door, Adolf pushed it open, and Bob paused before stepping inside. "Thank you for helping me back to my cell."

For a moment, Bob thought Adolf might speak. But the moment passed, and Bob shuffled inside. His cot was sounding half decent right now.

Sleep would not come, and Bob thought of the plight of East Germans and how the wall separated them from their own people. He wondered how Luisa endured the separation from her grandmother. He had no idea, but it gave him something else to add to his prayers. This was one thing he could do in prison. Pray for himself, for others, for his country, for the world, and for peace.

But was prayer enough? Was praying the only thing Bob could do? Yes, he was confined to a cell day after day, but there had to be something. He could forgive, he thought. Forgive Schmitt for turning him in. But Bob wasn't ready to do that yet. On his two-year mission as a young man, he'd learned the value of fasting along with prayer. Many religions practiced fasting—to draw closer to God and to supplicate Him for desired blessings.

If there was ever a time Bob needed blessings, this was it. So he decided he would fast. And maybe the forgiveness would come later.

The following day was free of a beating, which only meant that the next one would be more intense. Perhaps the officers were so caught up in the news about people attempting to escape across the Berlin Wall that they had quite forgotten their prisoners. Bob needn't have hoped.

The reprieve from the interrogations and beatings ended soon enough. But a bright spot grew on the horizon of his endless days. Adolf had started to speak to him. His English was poor, so their conversations were mostly in German.

"Are you ill?" Adolf said through the steel door one morning when Bob told him he wasn't eating.

"I'm fasting," Bob said.

"You're fasting . . . like a Muslim?"

"Yes, it's something I do in my church to draw closer to God," Bob explained.

Adolf didn't say anything for a moment, but he also didn't step away from the door. The bowl of stew—this one with meat in it—was still poking halfway through the slot at the bottom of the door.

"We fast to know what God wants of us. We also fast for the desires of our hearts," Bob said. "The righteous desires, that is."

Another pause, and then Adolf removed the bowl.

Bob thought he'd known deprivation after being in this ten-by-twelve cell for a month, but as he gave up all sustenance for the day, his hunger took on a new dimension. Yet that evening he received another blessing—Adolf didn't come to collect him for interrogation.

CHAPTER TWENTY-SEVEN

"Stasi File Authority—Project Group Reconstruction
Time Required for the Reconstruction:

1 worker reconstructs on average 10 pages per day

40 workers reconstruct on average 400 pages per day

40 workers reconstruct on average in a year
of 250 working days 100,000 pages

There are, on average, 2,500 pages in one sack

100,000 pages amounts to 40 sacks per year

In all, at the Stasi File Authority there are 15,000 stacks

This means that to reconstruct everything
it would take 40 workers 375 years"

—Herr Raillard, Director of the
Stasi File Authority Office, Nuremberg

WEST BERLIN
DECEMBER 1961

Last week, Luisa had helped a man named Elias come through the trap-door. Tonight, it had been Nina—a woman in her fifties.

"You will be contacted very soon," Luisa assured the woman bundled in a new, thick coat to fight off the December freeze. "Before dawn. The signal is three soft raps on the door, a pause, followed by two more."

Nina nodded and smoothed back her gray-streaked hair with trembling hands. Luisa almost hated to leave the woman alone. Her dark eyes were wide with anticipation, or maybe fear. Still, Luisa was impressed at the woman's gumption and resolve.

Luisa set a sandwich in front of the woman, courtesy of Adel's earlier shopping.

"Thank you," Nina said. "You are an angel."

Luisa only smiled, then slipped out into the dark corridor. She quietly walked up the stairs to her own apartment. After unlocking the door, she moved inside as silently as possible. She paused in the dim hallway before entering her bedroom. Was her father's door open a little wider than when she'd left?

She wasn't sure, but all seemed quiet from his room. He must still be sleeping. Her breathing took ages to even out, even after she'd been in bed for a while. It was after midnight, so she'd get a decent rest if only she could turn off her thoughts.

Morning came quickly, with the pale glow of the winter sun. Luisa rose from bed and beat her father to the kitchen by only a few moments.

"Good morning," he said as he entered.

Luisa greeted him as well. Did her smile seem forced? Her voice too high-pitched? She fixed a breakfast of bread with meat and cheese and mayo, while her father seemed absorbed in his newspaper and said nothing else.

There. Nothing was wrong. He wasn't usually talkative in the morning. Luisa had to remind herself of that more than once. Yet her pulse drummed with guilt, although she knew she was doing the right thing by helping the East Germans. But if her father found out . . . or some other authority, would her father's job be at risk?

When the phone rang, Luisa nearly jumped. She glanced over at her father, but he didn't seem to be on alert. "I'll get it," she said as casually as she could manage. When she answered, there was no sound. No words. "I guess it's a wrong number, or it was disconnected."

Setting down the phone, Luisa tried to steady her breathing. The caller would know she was not alone. Which meant that she had to retrieve the message another way—by visiting Mrs. Herrmann.

Luisa hurried through her preparations quicker than usual so that she was the first to leave the apartment. "Have a good day, Father," she called to him.

"When is your shift over, Luisa?"

She paused with her hand on the front doorknob. Her mind was racing unnecessarily. Why couldn't she think straight? "I'll be home before dinner." She hoped that would be the case. Who knew what Mrs. Herrmann was asking for?

Her father simply nodded, and Luisa made her escape.

As she hurried out onto the street, she had to stop herself from looking at the first-level apartment where the tunnel was. She couldn't be sure that her father wasn't watching for her out the window. Luisa kept her gaze forward and headed in her usual direction to the hospital. When she was well out of sight of her father's potential view, Luisa changed directions.

When she arrived at Mrs. Herrmann's apartment, Luisa was out of breath, mostly with anticipation. Right after the first knock, the woman answered, stepped back to usher Luisa inside, then shut and locked the door.

"Thank you for coming." Mrs. Herrmann turned toward her. "I need you to go into East Germany."

Luisa felt like icy water had been dumped over her head. With the Berlin Wall now fortified and heavily guarded, it was one thing to travel with her father and visit Oma, but a request from Mrs. Herrmann could mean only one thing—this was an assignment. And there was even more danger of being caught.

"Come into the kitchen." Mrs. Herrmann led the way. Once in the kitchen, she opened a lower cupboard and pulled out a box. She set the box on the counter, then opened up a false bottom.

When she lifted out a long, thin piece of metal, Luisa frowned. "What's that?"

"Radio transmitters," Mrs. Herrmann said. "They need to be delivered to East Berlin."

Luisa had no words. If she was caught, there was no way she'd be able to explain away carrying multiple transmitters. It was one thing to help with the tunnels on the West Berlin side of the wall, and before the wall, to help with the passports. But with the wall up, and people being shot for trying to escape, the stakes were higher.

Mrs. Herrmann didn't seem to notice Luisa's hesitation as she moved to the kitchen counter, where a chocolate frosted cake was displayed. "It's your grandmother's birthday," Mrs. Herrmann announced, "and you're taking her a birthday cake."

Luisa wiped her suddenly damp palms over her skirt. Her grandmother's birthday was not for another month. "All right."

After wrapping a hand towel around the transmitters, Mrs. Herrmann set the bundle back into the false bottom. Then she set the cake on top and added the box lid. "There. The border guards will look into the box and see the delicious cake. Your only challenge will be to stop them from swiping at the frosting."

Luisa smiled to cover her nervousness, although her pulse tapped double-time.

"Now," Mrs. Herrmann continued. "Remember this address to a bakery. And once you get there, tell the woman at the front counter that you want her to decorate your cake. She goes by Mrs. Lange."

Luisa listened carefully and committed the address to memory. She wondered if Mrs. Herrmann was ever fearful. The woman was years older, yet she seemed to jump in with both feet on every issue.

"Are you originally from West Berlin?" Luisa asked.

The woman smiled, her eyes crinkling even more at the corners. "I am now, and that is enough. You see, someone helped me find a home here many years ago, and now, I help others."

"Where are you from, then?"

Her smile turned downward. "Perhaps someday I'll tell you, Ms. Voigt, but right now, the delivery window is growing smaller. Please make haste without making haste. Do you understand?"

Luisa's mind was whirring by the time she left Mrs. Herrmann's apartment. What other underground operations was this woman involved in? After obtaining a day pass, Luisa walked briskly to the checkpoint, holding the box close. Surely she'd cross the border just fine—if Mrs. Herrmann thought she could do it, then Luisa could do it.

The pedestrian queue going into East Germany was only a few people deep. Somehow, Luisa got through with only a check of her passport and a couple of questions. The guard did look inside the cake box, but he didn't swipe at the frosting.

As she walked away from the checkpoint, she tried not to stare at the East Germans in line, hoping to cross. Plenty of them were being turned away. Luisa's sympathy went out to them. Only a few quick glances told her how desperate they were becoming. She'd heard the reports on the radio about daring escapes, which only led to stricter controls for everyone.

The December cold seemed to ignore the fact that Luisa was wearing a warm coat. She turned onto the street leading to her grandmother's neighborhood. The address Luisa had been given by Mrs. Herrmann was a small bakery. Once Luisa reached it, she hesitated. The bakery looked almost empty, and there was no bread displayed in the modest window.

Was this the right place?

She opened the door and headed inside. A woman with a worn face was scrubbing down the main counter. She looked up as Luisa entered, and her brows pinched.

"We are out of most things," the woman said.

"Are you Mrs. Lange?"

The woman's brow lines deepened.

"I'd like to show you the cake I brought for my oma," Luisa said, crossing to the counter and setting down the box. "Do you think you can decorate it? Add some lettering and a few flowers?"

The woman's gaze fell, and she set down her rag. "I can do that." Then she reached for the box and lifted out the cake. "How about I get you a new box? This one has a tear on the side."

This must be part of the plan. "Of course."

Mrs. Lange smiled and set the old box below the counter, then lifted up another box. She then proceeded to decorate the cake, her thick fingers deftly adding delicate flowers. Once the cake was decorated, the woman set it carefully into the new box, then handed it over to Luisa.

"How much do I owe you?"

Mrs. Lange raised her hand. "No charge. Tell your oma happy birthday." She looked pointedly at the box, then back to Luisa.

Was the baker trying to send her a message or something? "I will, thank you," Luisa said.

At Mrs. Lange's firm nod, Luisa headed out of the shop feeling like she was carrying a precious treasure. What sort of message had the baker added? The cold neighborhood streets held no answer, and Luisa had no choice but to continue to her grandmother's home.

The house looked quiet—which was hard to explain—but that's what Luisa sensed. Was Oma not home? Luisa's mind raced, thinking of where her grandmother might be. Shopping or at a friend's for a visit?

Luisa knocked on the door and was surprised at how quickly it opened.

Her grandmother's eyes were wide. "Come in," she whispered. "I wasn't expecting you."

"I thought I'd surprise you." Luisa stepped in out of the cold.

The cozy warmth of the house was missing. And then Luisa realized that Oma was wearing her coat and a scarf. "Are you leaving somewhere?"

"No," her grandmother said in a clipped tone. "What have you there?"

"It's an early birthday treat." Luisa walked through the living room, wondering why things were so dark. The gray day outside only made the interior dimmer. Why hadn't Oma turned on a light or two?

Oma joined her in the kitchen, her gaze focused on the bakery box. Luisa lifted the lid, and there was the beautifully decorated cake. Mrs. Lange had slipped a piece of paper inside as well. Luisa knew immediately this was a message for Mrs. Herrmann. Luisa reached in and plucked the paper, as if it was no big deal it was there. She tucked it into her coat pocket.

"What do you think?" Luisa said, because Oma was staring at the cake as if she'd never seen one before. "Chocolate. Your favorite."

Instead of smiling and thanking her, or even giving her a hug and a kiss, Oma's eyes filled with tears.

"Oma?" Luisa asked. "What's wrong?"

Her grandmother dabbed at her eyes, then gave Luisa a warning look and shook her head. "The cake is beautiful, dear. But you didn't need to trouble yourself. We have plenty of sweets in East Berlin."

Luisa frowned. Oma's words sounded stilted and falsely cheerful.

"Of course you do," Luisa said. "But this is a gift."

"I'll be sure to share it with my neighbors so it doesn't go to waste," Oma continued. "But in the future, know that I have everything I need. You shouldn't bring things from the West."

Luisa gave a slow nod. "All right."

Her grandmother's expression seemed to be a mixture of panic and desperation, even though a smile stretched across her face.

An involuntary shiver spread through Luisa—mostly from the cold, but also from worry. "Is your furnace broken, Oma?"

"Oh, no," she said, her tone still bright. "We're conserving a little energy in the neighborhood today. It saves money and conserves energy for other things."

Luisa was stunned. The entire neighborhood was suffering on this cold December day?

"Now, if you can stay for a few minutes," Oma continued, "we can listen to a radio program. I have fresh batteries in the radio."

The last thing Luisa wanted to do was listen to any type of GDR broadcast, but she didn't dare leave so soon either. She had to find out what was going on with her grandmother.

Without waiting for an answer, Oma crossed to the radio and switched it on. The short transmitter reminded Luisa of the longer ones she'd delivered to the bakery. Again, curiosity shot through her about the note sequestered in her pocket.

The radio crackled on, and the announcer's voice was reciting factory production numbers throughout East Germany.

Her grandmother latched onto Luisa's arm and guided her into the living room. The volume level of the radio easily filled the small house. Then Oma pulled Luisa close enough to whisper in her ear. "The Stasi have my house bugged," she said in a hushed tone. "When I came home from shopping yesterday, I saw two of them leaving. They walked right in and went through my things. I have no doubt that they can now listen to everything that goes on. And last night, all of the power went out in the neighborhood." Her voice was trembling with emotion, but Oma held back the tears.

"Why?" Luisa asked. "Why would the Stasi be spying on you?"

Oma looked away for a moment, but her grip tightened on Luisa's arm. "I put in a request to leave the GDR a few days ago. Ironically, putting in an application to leave puts all applicants under scrutiny because the GDR is suspicious of why you don't want to live here anymore. But I'm ready to come west. I will say my goodbyes to my memories and my home. But the application was denied." She lifted her chin and met Luisa's gaze.

The radio program blared from the kitchen, but Luisa had heard every word spoken by Oma and the many words not spoken. "They turned you down?"

Her grandmother nodded. "And then the Stasi showed up."

Luisa's knees felt like water. What did the GDR want with an elderly woman who lived alone? But then Luisa thought of the woman in the bakery who seemed to be only a handful of years younger than Oma. Perhaps the elderly weren't so easily dismissed when it came to secrets.

"I can get you out," Luisa said in a fierce whisper. "I know an organization that can help."

Her grandmother's eyes rounded with fear. "No," she replied. "I could never risk such a thing. This will . . . pass . . . And if not, I can endure one more thing." But the tremble in Oma's voice told Luisa otherwise.

"Oma," Luisa said. "I will find a way. Say your goodbyes because when I come again, you won't have any extra time."

Her grandmother's gaze clung to Luisa's. "What are you in the middle of?"

Luisa released a sigh. "Don't worry. We are very careful."

Oma's eyes slipped shut. "I can't have you in danger—not on my behalf."

Bending, Luisa kissed her grandmother's papery cheek. Her skin was too cold to the touch. What kind of government would allow an elderly woman to freeze in her own home? "Don't worry about me, Oma. Have faith, and all will be well."

CHAPTER TWENTY-EIGHT

"The interrogation of Miriam Weber, aged sixteen, took place every night for ten nights for the six hours between 10 pm and 4 am. Lights went out in the cell at 8 pm, and she slept for two hours before being taken to the interrogation room. She was returned to her cell two hours before the lights went on again at 6 am. She was not permitted to sleep during the day. A guard watched through the peephole and banged on the door if she nodded off."

—ANNA FUNDER, *STASILAND*

EAST GERMAN PRISON
DECEMBER 1961

"I'm fasting today," Bob told Adolf as the bowl half-filled with mush appeared beneath his door.

"It's Thursday," came Adolf's quiet reply.

Bob smiled even though Adolf couldn't see him. He loved that Adolf now spoke to him from time to time. Sometimes, he refused to speak—and that's when Bob guessed there were other guards about. But other times, like now, Adolf spoke hesitantly.

"When I fast, good things happen. So fasting more will only bring more good things." He could almost hear Adolf thinking.

"You're in prison," Adolf said at last. His voice was muffled, but Bob's hearing seemed amplified, so he understood each word. "What's good about that?"

Bob waited a moment before answering. "I've found a friend. Not much else can replace that in life."

Adolf didn't answer, but Bob knew he'd heard and understood. The bowl disappeared from sight, and soon, Adolf's footsteps retreated.

Bob closed his eyes. He didn't have to look down to see how thin he'd become. Fasting had only exacerbated that. Yet there had been blessings he couldn't deny. First, someone to talk to—Adolf—who'd become an unlikely friend. Perhaps it was only one-sided, but Bob wasn't bothered by the possibility.

And he had plenty of time to reflect and to pray. When else in his life would he ever have so much time for introspection? His body felt strong even though he was sure he had never been in poorer shape. Yet, day after day, he was able to rise, eat, endure interrogations and beatings, and watch the patch of sunset fade on the cell wall . . . testifying that there was still a world out there. Still a world he could look forward to seeing someday. Life was waiting for him.

When he had first arrived in this East German prison, Bob had wondered if each day would be his last. He no longer wondered that, and the dark thoughts no longer plagued him. He'd been digging deep into his soul and thinking about Schmitt a lot. How the man had his own fears, his own challenges. In Schmitt's mind, he'd been a patriot to his country, which put him on the opposite side of Bob.

What would Bob have done in Schmitt's shoes? Bob would never know. He had tricked Schmitt into trusting him, so who was the villain here? The more that Bob put himself in Schmitt's position, the more compassion Bob had. And forgiveness now ebbed over him. His religion taught him that he was required to forgive others. Forgiveness eased burdens, released pain. And even in this confined cell, the peace that forgiveness brought was sweet indeed.

Now when he awakened each morning, he was eager to learn something new about himself, dwell on a long-forgotten memory, and dream of what his future might be beyond these stone walls.

The following week, Bob knew that one of the days was Christmas—he guessed either Tuesday or Wednesday. The calendar was a jumble in his mind most days. He had nothing to give and nothing to receive, except for the chance of reflecting on the birth of the Savior and the unconditional love He brought into a world of fear and uncertainty. It was something that warmed Bob with gratitude in this bitter-cold prison cell.

The sound of footsteps alerted Bob to Adolf bringing his meal. The bowl slid beneath the door was a welcome sight. Something warmer than the air. As usual, Bob paced himself while he ate the thin stew. He was so hungry, but he didn't want to make himself sick by eating too fast. He would have thought that after months of eating only two scant meals a day, his body would be used to the lack of food. But it never seemed to be enough.

When Bob finished, he realized that the guard's footsteps outside his cell hadn't retreated. Something was going on. Something unusual. "Is there news today?" Bob called. He often asked this, but Adolf rarely gave him news from the outside world. "Or maybe dessert for Christmas Day?"

Again, no response.

Adolf didn't answer, so Bob soon gave up. When he slid the empty bowl under the door, Adolf took it, then opened the door. It seemed that Adolf had let him eat before another interrogation.

"Come out," Adolf said in a harsher voice than Bob had heard from the man.

Bob stepped into the corridor, limping from his most recent beating, not to mention the fact that his feet were nearly numb from the biting cold of the cell. December wasn't a friendly month in an East German prison. As it was, he was resigned to his fate that day. Surely another interrogation and beating. He stopped abruptly when he saw two other men in the corridor—prisoners, by the looks of them. Their clothing was as foul and ragged as Bob's own. He looked from one face to the other, curious about these prisoners he'd never seen before but had likely heard through the cement walls.

Their features were blunt, their beards grown out and scraggly, their tangled hair falling to their shoulders. Bob supposed he looked just as rough around the edges. No shower, no shaving, no cleanup for months would do that to a man.

But it was the eyes of the other prisoners that Bob most related to. Haunted. Dark. Despondent. Bob felt like he was seeing his own reflection, as if he were looking in a mirror.

The other prisoners studied Bob as well. What did they think of *him*? He wasn't sure which nationality they were, but he guessed they weren't American. Beyond them stood another set of East German guards. A guard for each man, it seemed. As they were all led up the stairs and past the interrogation room, Bob was more confused than ever. Maybe they were being released? His adrenaline began to slowly climb.

Then Adolf opened a door leading outside, and Bob stepped into the chilly, fresh air for the first time since his arrest. The frigid air was like a slap to his senses. His cell might be cold, but outside was like an icebox.

Adolf and the other East German guards brought the prisoners to a stop in a courtyard. A line of poles had been buried in the frozen ground, extending over six feet above the earthen floor. All around, the courtyard was walled in by a gray stone wall. This was not an exercise yard.

It was a firing range.

Bob's shoulders tensed as his stomach seemed to flip upside down. Despite the winter temperature, his forehead dampened with sweat. The bitter cold would soon cease to be an issue.

Another guard stood at the ready, his 9mm semiautomatic pistol unholstered.

Each of the prisoners was led to a pole, Bob to the third one, but before he was tied to it, Adolf grabbed Bob's upper arm and pulled him toward the first pole. He heard the shuffling of feet as one of the other prisoners was moved to the pole where he'd been. Adolf kept his gaze lowered, his jaw clenched. He did not make eye contact, and Bob didn't know if that made things even worse. He was pushed against the first pole, and the cold metal dug into his spine. Then his hands were tied behind him. One of the other East German soldiers put hoods over their faces.

Bob's last image before he died would be the gray walls of a prison. Now the darkness was complete.

This was it. The end.

Bob blew out a slow breath. He believed in heaven. He knew about crossing to the other side, where loved ones would be waiting to greet him.

Right now, Bob should be grieving in his final moments on earth. But he was mostly wondering about how much it might hurt. Would it hurt more than his daily beatings?

Of course it was going to hurt. It was going to kill him.

Now that they had his real name, at least someone would find out about his death . . . eventually. Bob thought of his parents and his sister. How do you say goodbye to your family when you are thousands of miles away? The tears pricking his eyes were more for them rather than himself. To his family, learning of his death would be a shock. Would they even know anything beyond that he had died?

I'm sorry, Mother, he mouthed, staring into the dark void of the hood over his head. If only he could explain to her. Tell her how sorry he was that somehow he'd been caught. He thought of his Grandfather Inama. Would the man ever see the pictures Bob had taken in the Italian village? Would his parents and sister discover the pictures if the US Army mailed Bob's effects back home?

Footsteps shuffled in front of him. Which one of the guards stood before him now? Adolf? Bob hated to think it was Adolf who'd have to shoot him. Even if Adolf might never admit it, they had a rapport and a friendship of sorts.

Another scuffle of footsteps, followed by the cock of three pistols, told

Bob that the guards were in position, ready to shoot. Bob was shaking—from cold, from fear—it all seemed the same.

Would it be his grandfather Peter Johnson who greeted Bob on the other side? He'd been close to his maternal grandfather. Yes . . . Bob decided. Grandfather Johnson would be there. Waiting for Bob.

Time slowed. As his sluggish heart rate counted down the seconds to the firing of the guns, he thought of how Grandfather Johnson had been a man of faith and deeply devoted to serving others. To the core, he was down-to-earth, a farmer, a businessman, and a mayor.

Bob almost smiled at the memory of how his grandfather used to try to talk Bob into trading pocketknives with him. Grandfather would show only the top of the knife, and when they traded, Bob always got a knife with a dull blade. At his grandfather's funeral, Bob had put a pocketknife in his casket—

The guns fired.

Bob waited. To feel the pain. For his knees to buckle, his body to go slack. But he was still standing straight. In fact, nothing had changed. There wasn't even any pain. Maybe his death had been so instantaneous that he'd skipped all of that.

Death wasn't that bad after all. But where was Grandfather Johnson? Maybe it took a while for someone to take him into the next world.

Then the hood was pulled off of Bob's head, and he realized two things instantaneously. First, he was still alive. And second, he *hadn't* been shot. His mind took another few seconds to process that the other two prisoners were dead.

Bullets through their foreheads. Bodies slumped forward. Their breathing stilled.

Bob wanted to look away from the dead men, but his gaze wouldn't shift. He stared at them numbly, and only then did his knees feel like they were about to cave in. His stomach roiled, and he might have sunk to the ground right there in the dirt, but Adolf was at his side, holding him up.

Together, they walked back to the prison cell in the basement.

Bob's mind moved from one place to another, disjointed, trying to understand what had happened. Somehow he was able to walk, even though his body was strangely numb. Those two prisoners had been alive one moment, then gone the next. They would never see their families again. They would never walk out of this prison. They would never hope, feel, smile, laugh, cry, or dream again. Their voices had been forever silenced.

Yet, Bob was alive. Why had *he* been spared? Why had the other two prisoners been shot?

Why? Why? Why?

But the words wouldn't form; they remained stuck in his throat.

And Adolf didn't volunteer any information. As usual.

When Adolf opened the prison cell door, Bob walked inside, his thoughts completely scattered. What had just happened, and how was he back inside his cell now?

He turned as Adolf pulled the door closed. "Thank you, my friend." His voice came out a hoarse whisper, and he didn't know if Adolf heard him.

When Adolf's footsteps had long since receded, Bob crossed to his cot and sank down. His hands trembled, and his eyes burned with hot tears. He raised a hand to wipe away the falling tears, but it was no use. He was too shaky. So he hung his head, and as the tears dripped one by one down his cheeks, Bob knew without a doubt that somehow, Adolf had saved his life that day.

"I have never had such a friend," Bob whispered to himself. "Who would have thought I'd find him in an East German prison?" He closed his eyes and began to pray. *Thank you, God, for sparing me once again. I don't know what I have done to be worthy of this grace.*

When Bob finished his prayer, he lay down on his cot. The tears leaking from his eyes were hot and fast. What had Adolf sacrificed to move Bob to a different post? How many prisoners had endured what those two men had? How many more would be killed in the future?

For once he didn't mind the cold night. It would only get colder as the days and nights passed, but his life had been spared. Both gratitude and humility flooded him. He was alive, and that was no small thing.

He closed his eyes, hoping for a scrap of sleep. Even a few hours would be nice. He was exhausted with the relief of surviving a firing squad, yet he couldn't get the faces of those slain prisoners out of his mind. Not as they were in death—their heads bent, their limbs slack. But in life. How his and their gazes had connected in those few moments in the corridor. How each man had a name, a life, and a family.

Had their lives been taken in order to spare his? Had Bob survived at the cost of someone else's death? The idea was somehow more painful than when he thought he was going to die. For some reason, Bob was alive, and those two men were gone—men who'd paid the ultimate price for whatever had brought them to prison in the first place. He didn't even know where they were from, and he wished he knew something about them. Anything. So at the very least, he could honor their memories.

Not surprisingly, sleep didn't come. The day passed in a long, slow march of light across the cell wall high above his head. He knew the patch of light by sight, and he knew when it reached a certain crack in the wall, Adolf would bring him dinner.

Sure enough, as the patch of light inched into place, footsteps grew near. Bob rose from his bed and moved to the door. His legs acted as if they were surprised to be in use.

Bob felt lightheaded as he leaned against the door while waiting for Adolf. When the bowl appeared beneath the door, Bob said, "What happened this morning, Adolf? Did you know that I'd be safe when you moved me to the first pole?"

Adolf didn't answer, but he also didn't move away.

"Whatever you did, Adolf, thank you," Bob said.

Another pause. Still Adolf didn't answer.

Perhaps Bob would never know for sure, and perhaps Adolf would never admit to anything, but the fact was, Bob was still alive. "Did you know their names?" Bob asked. "Those other prisoners?"

A heartbeat. Then two. "Yes," Adolf said.

"Can you tell me their names?" Bob asked, wondering if he was asking too many questions. The last thing he wanted was for Adolf to stop speaking to him completely.

"Why do you want to know their names?"

Bob closed his eyes and pressed his forehead against the metal door. "So I can pray for their families."

Silence from the other side of the door, then Adolf said, "I don't know how you do it." His words were muted, but Bob made them out with no problem.

"Do what?"

"You are grateful," Adolf continued. "Every day, you are grateful."

"I am grateful to live life one more day," Bob said. "That is true. But I also believe that if I'm ever released, I'll look back and know that I've grown more here than I could have in any other situation."

"What about your family?" Adolf asked. "Do you pray for them?"

"Certainly," Bob said. He didn't mind that his food was untouched at his feet. This conversation felt more important. "I pray for my family daily. I pray for my country. And I pray for peace between our people."

A sound came from Adolf—a scoff?

"And Adolf," Bob added. "I pray for you, too."

Voices came from somewhere in the corridor, and Adolf moved away quickly, without any sort of reply.

Bob bent and picked up the bowl of food. Then he moved to the lone chair in the cell and sat down to eat his supper. Another meal. Another night approaching. Another endless space of time with little to fill it. Except . . . think of things to be grateful for. The cell was dry . . . one thing to be grateful for.

There was meat in the stew tonight. Another thing to be grateful for.

He ate slowly, savoring the food. He wished he had a toothbrush, a comb, a shower . . . anything to feel human again. But he was alive. And two men who'd stood by him in the same courtyard that morning weren't.

When Adolf's footsteps approached again, Bob had the bowl beneath the door. Instead of simply picking up the bowl, Adolf unlocked the cell. The expression in his eyes told Bob that he was leaving the cell.

Sure enough, Adolf handcuffed him, then escorted him up the stairs and into the interrogation room, where two military officers waited with their batons and bright light.

Bob was strapped to the interrogation chair, and the questions began.

"My name is Bob Inama.

"My rank is Specialist Fourth Class.

"My ID is 10423570."

CHAPTER TWENTY-NINE

"My flat was the only one in the block with a working bathroom. Needless to say, that did not stop the Stasi from bugging it. In fact, I was later told by an ex-Stasi operative in the 1990s that the flat had fourteen listening devices placed in the bedroom alone, as well as my phone being tapped. Two doors down from my corridor was a Stasi-owned room, which was the 'listening center' for the whole building—I never knew."

—MARK WOOD, *REUTERS*

WEST BERLIN
JANUARY 1962

Christmas had come and gone, but Luisa had found little joy in the season, even though she'd done her best to be cheerful at the hospital and around her father. Right now, the interior of the hospital felt drab with the Christmas decorations removed and the dull winter sky the only thing to see out the windows.

Hospital staff buzzed about the hallways, and Luisa nodded greetings, but her thoughts were far away. She clung fiercely to the hope that through faith in God, she'd see a miracle. For she needed one now. On the day she'd found out her sweet grandmother was being watched by the Stasi, Luisa had headed directly to Mrs. Herrmann's after crossing the border.

Luisa was ready to start digging a new tunnel if necessary, but Mrs.

Herrmann had told her to be patient. One tunnel had recently been discovered by the Soviets, so the underground operations were keeping quiet for a couple of weeks.

But Luisa was done with waiting. Every hour and every day that Oma lived in continued fear tore at Luisa's heart little by little. Any day now, she expected she'd be called upon to help with another tunnel rescue. Their tunnel was still safe as far as Luisa knew, but everyone was being more vigilant. She knew her father was worried about Oma as well. But his worry didn't seem to extend to breaking the law.

"Anything?" Adel asked, approaching Luisa as she studied a chart without reading a word.

Luisa looked up. Her friend's dainty features wore a frown. Adel hadn't been happy with all the waiting either. "Nothing. I have to get her out. It's been weeks."

Adel didn't need to ask to know that Luisa was referring to her oma. "Do you want me to come with you to Mrs. Herrmann's after shift?"

"Can you?"

Adel nodded and squeezed Luisa's hand before moving down the hallway. Luisa watched her go, grateful for a friend. She only hoped that whatever plan they came up with wouldn't backfire. The last person she wanted harmed was Oma.

Less than an hour later, Luisa and Adel were hurrying through the January wind that had intensified, drawing in a smattering of dark clouds. In contrast to her grandmother's cold, drafty home, Mrs. Herrmann's apartment was filled with warmth and the scent of baked goods.

The older woman didn't seem surprised at their arrival.

"Tell us the tunnel is open again," Luisa said right away, not wanting to waste a moment.

Mrs. Herrmann set a hand on her hip. "We are sending someone through tomorrow night, and if that's successful, we'll consider your grandmother next."

Luisa didn't know whether to be relieved or more worried now. This was really going to happen.

"Luisa," Mrs. Herrmann said, "are you sure your grandmother will be up for it? We worry about the older citizens."

Luisa wanted to say yes with surety, but in truth, she didn't know how her grandmother would react. "I will take her through the tunnel myself."

Mrs. Herrmann's brows slanted. "Are you sure? It's a great risk."

"A huge risk," Adel added. "If you're caught . . ."

Luisa didn't need her friend to finish the sentence. "I need to make sure my grandmother gets through that tunnel."

Mrs. Herrmann sighed. "All right. I will contact you as soon as things are settled. At that time, I'll give you the address of the entrance location."

Luisa looked at Adel, who nodded. "I'll be at the exit, waiting for you both. Don't worry. You can do this."

Luisa trusted both Adel and Mrs. Herrmann. She had to. This was the only way.

When the signal came two days later, Luisa stayed awake until long after her father had fallen asleep. She then crept downstairs to the ground-level apartment, where she helped a man in his forties out of the trapdoor. He was dirty and perspiring and looked as if he'd seen a ghost.

Luisa's heart lurched as she wondered how Oma would fare crawling through a tunnel for such a long distance. As Luisa aided the man, she had to stop herself from asking him a dozen questions. Perhaps it would be better if she didn't know all of the details.

After the rescue, Luisa felt like she was walking on eggshells in everything she did. She was hyperaware of what her father said and did. She found herself gazing at the phone, wondering when it would ring with the signal. Sonja had called once, but Luisa had barely paid attention to what she said.

Luisa continued to wait. She continued to hope. And she had started to pray more. Bob had told her in that alley that he'd keep her in his prayers. She wanted to do the same for him and others in her life.

Three days later, Luisa answered the phone after dinner. Her father was in the living room, reading the paper while the radio sounded in the background—another East German escape had been botched.

"Hello?" Luisa said into the receiver. There was no answer. She waited a couple of heartbeats. "Hello?" The silence made the back of her neck prickle. She hung up.

Thankfully, her father didn't ask who'd called. He seemed caught up in whatever newspaper story he was reading.

Was this call for her grandmother? Was the plan already being put into action? Or was a different person coming through the tunnel tonight? She'd never been so impatient for her father to turn in for the night. She had to literally clench her fists in bed so that she didn't leave prematurely. "Patience," she whispered to herself over and over.

Once in the downstairs apartment, Luisa phoned Mrs. Herrmann, who answered on the first ring.

"Tomorrow night you will bring your grandmother to the bakery in East Berlin," Mrs. Herrmann said. "She will enter the tunnel there."

Mrs. Herrmann continued with her instructions. The information came like water from a firehose, but Luisa logged in every detail. She had a lot of questions, but she knew she wouldn't be able to ask them. The less she knew about the technicalities of the operation and who else was involved, the better.

When she hung up, Luisa sat in the dark basement apartment for a few moments. Tomorrow. Tomorrow, her grandmother would be making an escape. Now, all Luisa had to do was convince her.

The following morning over breakfast, Luisa told her father, "I'm going to visit Oma after my shift. She requested a few items on my last visit there."

As predicted her father's brow furrowed as he looked up from his newspaper. "Tonight?"

"Yes." Luisa tried to sound nonchalant despite her skipping pulse.

"Maybe I can change my shift," her father said.

"It's all right," Luisa said. "I won't be too late." She held her breath, waiting.

Her father nodded and returned to his newspaper.

Was that it? Luisa felt as if she'd won some sort of unexpected award. The first hurdle had been cleared.

The rest of the day, Luisa's mind turned over one scenario after another. Luisa somehow being detained at the border. Her grandmother refusing to leave. The Stasi waiting in the neighborhood. Her grandmother panicking in the tunnel. And those were only a few of the ways things could go wrong.

The moment her shift ended, Luisa said goodbye to Adel, who'd be getting off later before heading to the basement apartment. Luisa changed into her civilian clothing, then began to walk to the border crossing, keeping her coat snug about her. She had a bag slung over her shoulder with some herbs and teas that she could explain were for her grandmother's arthritis.

A couple of the border guards were familiar to her, although usually she was crossing the other way this time of the evening. But it proved to be to her advantage. She told the guards she was attending a music performance. After checking her ID, they waved her through.

Now if only her grandmother would agree to the plan. Luisa hurried along the cold streets and shivered in the even colder air. By the time she arrived at her grandmother's neighborhood, it was nearly dark. She was relieved to see a light on in the house—this meant her grandmother had heat as well.

Knocking on the door would be a surprise, she knew, and she wondered for a moment if Oma would answer. Of course she would. Everyone in East Germany was afraid to go against any authority. And to her grandmother, she could very well be an official or *ein Polizist*.

When the door cracked open, sure enough, Oma's eyes were as wide as saucers. "Luisa, what are you doing here?"

Oma opened the door wider, and Luisa stepped into the warmth. At last, her toes would thaw out. "I've brought you some of those herbs to help your arthritis."

Her grandmother's eyes narrowed. Yes, she'd requested them, but for Luisa to show up after dark was another matter.

Luisa gave a small shake of her head, trying to convey to her grandmother that she needed to go along with this. She had to be subtle in case any Stasi were listening in on their conversation.

"Well, that's very kind of you," Oma said, seeming to understand. "Come into the kitchen. I've been listening to the radio." She turned it up a notch, then walked with Luisa back to the middle of the living room. The farthest spot, Luisa guessed, from any possible listening devices.

Luisa took her grandmother's hands in hers. "Oma, I have found a way to get you out of the city. But we need to leave tonight."

Her grandmother went very still, although surprise sparked in her gaze.

"I've been helping with some rescues," Luisa continued, her voice a whisper. "We have a tunneling system."

"Luisa," Oma said with a gasp. "Those tunnels have been found out, and those people put into prison."

Luisa squeezed her oma's hand. "Our tunnel is secure. It begins not far from here and ends close to where I live." She hesitated giving the exact specifics. Just in case . . .

Her grandmother closed her eyes. "I can't let you risk this. I'm too old to climb through a tunnel."

"It takes only two hours," Luisa said. "Think of the many hard things you've done in your life. You can do two hours."

Oma released Luisa's hands and moved to the couch, where she sank onto a cushion.

Luisa didn't follow but remained standing. She took it as a good sign that her grandmother hadn't shooed her out. She seemed to be thinking about it—weighing the pros and cons.

Oma leaned forward and buried her face in her hands. Still Luisa waited, although she felt like sitting next to her grandmother and comforting her. And talking her into taking the chance. It was a risk—they both knew it.

The moments ticked by, and the radio blared a program neither of them were listening to. Luisa prayed—no, pleaded—in her heart, as she clasped her floral pendant close. She had faith in the tunnel. She'd witnessed its success.

When her grandmother finally lifted her head, tears were in her eyes.

Luisa's heart seemed to freeze. Oma was going to say no.

Her grandmother rose to her feet, then walked to where Luisa stood in the middle of the room. Grasping her hands, Oma leaned close. "What do I need to bring?"

Luisa pulled her grandmother into a close hug. She wanted to cry, or laugh, or both. When she released Oma, they were both crying.

"Only what you can carry in your purse," Luisa whispered. "In case we're stopped."

Oma nodded, then headed down the hallway.

Luisa went into the kitchen and got a drink of water. Suddenly, she felt parched and weak. She wondered what it would be like to be told you were leaving your home forever and all you could take were a few items that could be tucked away in a purse.

When her grandmother emerged, she gave a firm, resolute nod. Then she held her hand out to Luisa. Leaving the radio on, the two stepped outside. Oma locked the door to the home she'd lived in for decades, built by her own husband, and headed into the darkened night.

It wasn't a long walk to the bakery, but every step felt like ten steps. The closer they grew to the bakery, the more Luisa started to second-guess herself. Up until this moment, she'd been of one mind—to get her grandmother out. But now, as they turned onto the street with the bakery, Luisa felt like she was going to throw up. Was this feeling a warning? Did her subconscious know something was afoot? But Luisa couldn't very well cancel the entire plan based on a feeling, could she? She glanced over at Oma, who was staring ahead, her gaze resolute. If she was all right, then Luisa was all right.

The bakery was dark, and Luisa walked around the small building and knocked three times on the back door. After several heartbeats, the door opened. The woman who had received the radio transmitters greeted them.

"Come in, quickly," Mrs. Lange whispered.

Luisa and Oma followed her inside. The darkness of the bakery was deeper than the night outside, where at least there had been moonlight and streetlamps. Taking careful, slow steps, they followed Mrs. Lange down the steps into the basement. Scents of mustiness and damp earth surrounded them.

Once they reached the bottom of the stairs, Mrs. Lange turned on a flashlight. It illuminated a storage room, lined with shelves. They were mostly empty though. The baker shone the light on the far wall.

"There, behind that propped wood," she said in a hushed tone, "is where the tunnel begins."

Three knocks sounded from above. Then a dull thud.

No one moved. "Is there another person going through tonight?" Mrs. Lange asked.

"I don't know," Luisa said.

Oma's eyes shifted from Luisa to the baker, and everyone knew what she was thinking.

"They know the signal," Mrs. Lange said, taking her flashlight with her. "I'll be back."

Luisa wanted to tell the woman no. Maybe this was why she'd felt so worried on the walk over. Maybe they'd been followed by the Stasi.

She and Oma listened as Mrs. Lange's footsteps moved across the upper floor. They heard the door open, then footsteps shuffle in.

"Luisa?" a voice said from the stairwell.

It was a man's voice—her *father's*.

Luisa couldn't move, couldn't even think. But her grandmother was shuffling toward the stairs in the dark.

"What are you doing here?" Oma asked.

Footsteps descended on the stairs, and then a flashlight blinked on. The room was still largely shadowed in darkness, but it was definitely her father, dressed in civilian clothing. "I followed you." He looked from Oma to Luisa. "Please tell me this isn't what I think it is."

Mrs. Lange came down the stairs after him, her own flashlight on. "If there is a problem, you all need to leave," she said.

Her father didn't seem to be listening to the baker. "Luisa?"

Luisa gripped her hands together. When had she started shaking? Her stomach felt like it had been turned inside out. She could see the hurt and betrayal in her father's gaze. "We're getting Oma out. We're going through the tunnel."

"And you've agreed to this mad plan?" her father said, his gaze cutting to Oma.

"Do you have a better one?" she said in a clear, confident voice.

Her father seemed taken aback, and he frowned. "I don't have a better plan to help you escape illegally. I thought you were going to reapply for permission to leave."

"My house has already been bugged by the Stasi," she said. "There will be no end."

No one spoke for a moment, and Luisa could almost see her father's mind work as he argued with himself.

Mrs. Lange finally said, "You must decide this moment and not delay another second."

Above their heads, something thumped. Hard. A man called out, "Kommt raus!" *Come out!*

More thumps, a crash. Multiple male voices.

"It's the Stasi," Mrs. Lange hissed, switching off her flashlight.

Luisa's father's light went off too. "Get into the tunnel," he said in a whisper as another thump sounded from above. "Both of you."

Luisa's heart felt like it was being squeezed with a steel vise. "We should all go."

"They already know I'm here," her father said. "I think I was being

255

watched by a man across the street as I entered the building. They may have been staking out this place."

Another thump. Muffled voices.

"I will stay," Mrs. Lange said. "You all go. They will find only an old woman—East German—who is gathering baking supplies."

"No," her father said. "They know I'm here. We can only hope they didn't see the others. If they don't find me, they'll search this cellar and find the tunnel. Then we'll all be arrested. I will come up with an excuse why I am—"

He didn't finish because the door to the top of the stairs opened.

Luisa felt her father pushing her toward the tunnel. She had no time to think, no time to consider. She grabbed Oma's hand and moved the last few feet to where the boards were propped up. Mrs. Lange lifted them, then handed over her flashlight. "Godspeed."

Luisa crouched and felt her way into the tunnel. "Hold onto my shirt," she whispered to Oma.

Luisa didn't dare turn on the light for a while. Moving forward on her hands and knees, with her grandmother close behind, Luisa could hear the words coming from the storage room.

At least two Stasi officials were speaking to her father. Their voices were raised, although her father's remained calm. She couldn't make out the baker's higher pitched tone at all.

"I'm here on an inspection," her father insisted. "I'm opening a bakery, and I've come to find out the best operations."

Luisa had crawled maybe twenty steps when she heard words that tore at her heart.

"Du bist verhaftet."

You're under arrest.

CHAPTER THIRTY

"Like at most totalitarian prisons, you were reduced to only a number. I was '50-2/49-2.' I shared a cell for a while with an actual agent who was German and had worked for American military intelligence. The prison cells underneath the original redbrick prison were called 'the Submarine' because they were in the basement. Most of them had no access to daylight, and neither was there a toilet, and it was very embarrassing if you had to relieve yourself, with everyone watching and listening, and the smell was terrible."

—Wolfgang Göbel, Inmate at Stasi-Run Prison in Hohenschönhausen

EAST GERMAN PRISON
JANUARY 1962

"My grandfather died when I was in college," Bob said in German as he leaned against the metal door of the prison cell. The stone floor was a stinging cold with the deep January winter that had taken a viselike hold over East Germany. Bob had his knees pulled up to his chest, arms wrapped around his legs in an effort to create some sort of warmth. "My mother's father. We were close growing up. He used to buy and sell farms. Made them productive, then sold them at a profit. He also loved sports and the rodeo."

Adolf was listening on the other side of the door. In fact, Adolf had asked him about his grandparents. Every week or so, Adolf seemed to have a lull in his prison duties, and the two men talked of things in the past. They talked of anything but the bleak present. Adolf had never told Bob his real name, and Bob never asked. But Bob considered his friendship with the guard official now, and no one could ever tell him different.

"My father's father immigrated from Italy," Bob said in German, "and he's one resilient and stubborn man. He's worked hard all of his life. He built a new life in America with his two bare hands, first in mining, and then in farming. His work ethic is a matter of great pride to him."

"You are like him," Adolf said, his voice a dull echo through the door.

Bob frowned. "I don't think so."

A quiet chuckle sounded from Adolf's side of the door. "Perhaps it's hard to see yourself in another person, but the way you describe him reminds me of you."

Bob thought about this. He'd often struggled with how Grandfather Inama had kept Bob and his sister at arm's length. Just because there were religious differences between the families didn't mean they couldn't have a good relationship.

"You are quiet for once," Adolf commented through the door.

Bob smiled to himself. "You got me thinking, I guess."

Another chuckle sounded from Adolf.

"Tell me of your family," Bob said. "Are you married? Where are your parents and grandparents from? Are you native to Germany?"

"A lot of questions," Adolf said.

"I've had a lot of time to think of them," Bob said in a quiet voice.

Adolf didn't reply to that, and Bob wondered after a few moments if the conversation was finished for the day.

Then Adolf said, "I'm not married, but there is a woman I'm interested in."

"Ah." Bob immediately wanted to ask more about the woman, but he wondered if that would cross another line. Adolf was younger than Bob by a few years at least, yet he'd wondered if the gold ring on his finger was a wedding band.

"I was about ten years old when the Soviets arrested my father for speaking out at a town hall meeting," Adolf said. "In 1949, the GDR was formed as a satellite state of the USSR, and everything was nationalized. Anyone who vocally disagreed with the new government was suspicious. Many were arrested."

Bob straightened from his sitting position, listening carefully.

"The new regime didn't want the teachers who'd educated according to the Nazi regime. They wanted new teachers who would teach the socialist agenda. It needed to start with the children."

This made sense—though a terrible sense, Bob thought.

"My father founded the Liberal Democrats branch in our town, then ran for mayor," Adolf said. "He won the election, but in a town hall meeting, he questioned why so many of the men in his village had been arrested and sent to Soviet labor camps."

"Liberal Democrat?" Bob asked. He'd never heard of the political party.

"Oh, there were supposedly different political parties, such as the center-right Christian Democrats, the Liberal Democrats, and the Communists, but in truth, everyone was strongly encouraged to join the Communist Party. The Communists won every election."

Bob shook his head as he watched the patch of light moving across the cell wall. The day was advancing, but he wanted to know more. "What happened after your father's arrest?"

"He was sentenced to five years in a prisoner-of-war camp," Adolf said. "The Soviets reused some of the Nazi concentration camps such as Buchenwald and Sachsenhausen."

Bob was stunned. This was not something he remembered learning in a history class.

"My father was in prison for only a couple of months though," Adolf continued, "and he was told that if he quit the Liberal Democrats and joined the Socialist Unity Party, then he'd be released."

"What did he do?" Bob asked, feeling as if he were sitting on pins and needles.

"He switched parties and came home," Adolf said matter-of-factly.

"Just like that?" Bob asked.

"Just like that," Adolf echoed. "In school, I was taught the doctrine of communism, and I was required to join the *Pioniere*. The Communists founded this organization to teach us to love Marx and our country." Adolf went quiet for a moment, then he said, "All over our school were posters that said *Stop the American Beetle*."

"Who's the American beetle?"

"President Truman," Adolf said. "The poster shows a child holding a magnifying glass and examining a beetle on the ground. The beetle had the face of your president, and its jacket was the colors of the American flag. We all knew—and we were all taught—that America was our number-one enemy."

Was Adolf telling Bob all of this because he still believed the propaganda or because he didn't? It was disheartening to think of a people going from living under a Nazi regime to the communism of the USSR. There were guilty German citizens, certainly, but what about the children, innocent in their youth? And those who didn't agree with the Nazi ideology?

"I'm sorry," Bob said, and he was. "I hope you know that—"

"Sometimes I don't know what to believe," Adolf interrupted. "You are a good man, Bob. I know that at least. And for now, that's enough."

Bob's throat tightened as emotion pushed its way through. "You're a good man too, Adolf."

The guard's laugh was soft. "See what I mean?"

Bob found himself smiling again, but it was bittersweet. "So we have a wall that separates Berlin. Is it effective?"

Adolf scoffed. "We only get GDR news, so I don't know much beyond that. But the wall has been fortified, and there are watchtowers along with armed guards."

"I guess I'll put my escape plans on hold."

"You do that," Adolf said. "I haven't seen it, but I hear the border is pretty hard to sneak through. Mines, dogs, guns pointed at your chest . . ."

A chill tickled Bob's spine. "I'm definitely better off in here, then."

"The food is great."

It was probably the first time Bob had heard Adolf joke about anything. "I couldn't agree more," Bob said. "Although I do miss the schnitzel and brot."

"Ah, you have good taste."

Bob was about to reply when his attuned ears picked up the sound of someone coming down the stairs at the end of the corridor. Adolf moved away, and the conversation was over.

Bob was left to think on all that Adolf had said, of growing up under a regime in which children were taught from young ages that their government was a hero and that everyone else was an enemy. He sat on the cot and pulled his body in close so he could keep all of his body heat to himself. The air was cold enough for it to snow inside the cell, and Bob probably wouldn't mind a little white beauty against the dull-gray stone. It would be a nice change in his day-to-day surroundings.

It was cold enough to shiver, but Bob almost didn't feel the cold anymore, unless he was sitting or lying on the floor. Maybe his body had acclimatized, but if he thought hard enough, he could actually consider the cold his friend. He didn't sweat, although he made himself finish the water from his water container each time it was filled, and things like spiders were in hibernation.

When Adolf's footsteps shuffled back about an hour later, and he unlocked the door, Bob knew the guard wasn't there to continue their conversation. The winter light had nearly faded from the cell, which meant the dinner hour was soon approaching. But it seemed Bob would be skipping dinner if tonight's interrogation ended in another beating—which it always did. Bob only hoped that the aftermath was not too rough.

He rose from the cot, was handcuffed, and resolutely joined Adolf on the walk through the corridor. Over the past months, he'd heard other prisoners traversing the same hallways, and he wondered about them sometimes. Why were they here? Where were they from? What questions did they not answer?

Bob's thighs ached as he climbed the steps. The two Soviet officers were waiting yet again. The first officer had already removed his glasses. Bob was shackled by his forearms and ankles to the chair in the room. Then the Soviets began to ask questions, and Bob gave them his usual answers.

"My name is Bob Inama.

"My rank is Specialist Fourth Class.

"My ID is 10423570."

He didn't pass out this time, and the officers didn't seem as intent on punishing him as usual. When they finished, Adolf came inside the room and unshackled his arms and ankles, then helped him stand.

"Thank you," Bob said as he rose to his feet. "You are excellent at your job."

He'd thanked them enough that there was no longer any surprise in their gazes.

CHAPTER THIRTY-ONE

"In June 1962, NBC News struck a deal . . . to finance the entire escape tunnel, paying 50,000 Deutschmarks—or roughly $150,000 today—for exclusive film rights of the dig. The cloak-and-dagger project was steeped in secrecy. . . . By late September 1962, the leaking tunnel was ready for its first escapees. After passing coded messages to the East over NBC News' short-range radios, the first fugitives were brought down into the tunnel. . . . The story was told in NBC News' documentary 'The Tunnel,' which was meant to air on Oct. 31, 1962 but was held after NBC came under pressure from the State Department not to exacerbate tensions after the Cuban missile crisis."

—"Tunnel 29: How NBC News Funded Big Breach of Berlin Wall"

BELOW EAST AND WEST BERLIN
JANUARY 1962

"I can't do this," Oma said, her voice dull and rough.

Luisa turned her head, keeping the flashlight pointed at the floor of the tunnel. They'd been crawling for at least an hour, but it felt like days. Her hands were sore, scraped, and filthy. Her knees were bruised. She could only imagine how her elderly grandmother felt.

"We're halfway through," Luisa said. "Going back will take just as long as going forward."

Oma's usual bun had tumbled out, and her gray-streaked hair fell along her face in haggard strands. "The distance either way doesn't matter. I can't do this."

Even though everything in Luisa wanted to simply drag her grandmother along, she turned enough to sit with her back against the tunnel wall. She drew her knees to her chest, then glanced over at her grandmother. "Let's rest for a little bit. We're not in a hurry any longer."

Oma shifted until she was sitting too. This was a good sign, Luisa decided. Her grandmother's breathing evened out, and Luisa reached for her hand. She hated that Oma's hand was cold and trembling.

"What do you think happened to your father?" Oma asked, voicing the worry that had been plaguing Luisa the entire time in the tunnel.

"I think the Stasi will call the West Berlin police," Luisa said. "They'll clear him and let him go." At least that's what she hoped. They *had* to let him go. If they didn't . . . She couldn't let herself think about that right now. Not when they had several feet of dirt above them.

"I don't know about that," Oma said, but she didn't continue her train of thought.

The well-being of Luisa's father was their biggest fear right now. That and getting through this tunnel. Luisa wished she had water or some type of food. Anything. She wasn't sure if she was lightheaded because of the exertion or the limited oxygen. Probably both.

"We should keep moving," Luisa said. "It's not going to get easier, but if we are moving, then at least we are progressing."

Her grandmother met Luisa's gaze. Despite the half shadows, Luisa saw the resolve on her grandmother's face and knew she was not a woman to give up easily. Even when she wanted to. "You're right," Oma said. "There's no turning back. Who's to say what is waiting for us back there."

Luisa smiled, even though she could have as easily cried with relief. And fatigue. "Let's say a prayer."

The two women bowed their heads, and Luisa prayed aloud, for them, for her father, for their country. When she finished, her grandmother said, "Thank you, dear."

Luisa once again rotated to her sore knees. The pain couldn't be helped though. The tunnel was too low to walk, and they had to keep moving forward.

The flashlight illuminated only a portion of the way ahead, and the darkness seemed to chase after them. Luisa had a new appreciation for those who built this tunnel—the hours and weeks it must have taken. And she was now benefitting from their hard work.

When the ground began to slope upward, she wanted to cry with relief. Her throat was drier than the dirt they crawled in, and her head was throbbing with pressure. Not to mention the stinging in her hands and knees. All that didn't matter right now though. Her grandmother was still with her, and that was the most important thing.

Pebbles skittered down as they crawled upward. "Are you all right?" Luisa said. "I don't want anything to hit you."

"I'm fine," Oma said, her voice strained.

The tunnel opened up. The shored-up ceiling was now high enough to stand, and Luisa rose to her feet. Every joint ached and burned at the changed movement. It felt like blood was rushing to her head, and Luisa braced a hand against the tunnel wall for a moment. Earth crumbled away, and she dropped her hand. "How are you doing?" she asked Oma, turning and extending her hand.

Her grandmother moved closer with a shuffling step, and Luisa helped her stand.

"Are we almost there?" Oma asked.

"Almost," Luisa said with a smile.

Her grandmother smiled back, her face dirty, her hair scraggly, but it was the most beautiful smile Luisa had ever seen.

Her energy renewed, she walked the last few feet to the exit of the tunnel—the closed trapdoor. They'd made it; they'd truly made it. Luisa knocked on the door, and moments later, Adel lifted it open.

Seeing her friend's smiling face pulled all the emotion that Luisa had been holding back during the tunneling.

"Welcome to the West," Adel said.

Luisa barely held in a sob as she grasped Adel's strong, clean hand and climbed out of the tunnel. Then they both turned and hoisted Oma out as well.

"Hello, I'm Adel," she told Oma. "You must be Luisa's grandmother. It's wonderful to meet you at last."

"Thank you for helping us," Oma said, sounding uneven and tired.

"Come," Adel said. "There's a bathroom you can wash up in, and then I'll heat some soup for you."

As Adel led Oma out of the bedroom and toward the bathroom, Luisa closed the trapdoor, then replaced the rug. She was exhausted and lightheaded and needed water and nourishment, but she needed a moment to herself, too. She was no longer in the confines of the underground tunnel, but she still felt like the weight of the earth was suspended above her.

"Father," she whispered into the dimness. "Where are you? What happened? Why did you take the fall for me?"

She knew that answer, but thinking about it would send her into a curled-up ball that she didn't think she'd be able to escape. Right now, she needed to check on her grandmother and make sure she was taken care of.

Luisa left the bedroom and walked into the kitchen, where she drank a glass of water. Then she changed places with Oma in the bathroom. The interior light was dim, but she was able to make out her face, streaked with dirt and tears. She used the brush on the bathroom counter to comb out her tangles. She'd have to wash her hair later. Then she turned on the water and scrubbed at her face and arms and hands.

By the time she joined Adel and Oma in the kitchen, the soup was heated, and Luisa had to stop herself from gulping it down. Her body still trembled, even though the apartment was cozy and warm. The cold seemed much deeper than could be thawed out.

"Now, tell me," Adel said. "Did you have any trouble entering the tunnel?" The lightness of her tone told Luisa that Oma hadn't said a word about the Stasi bursting into the bakery.

"My father followed us," Luisa said.

Adel leaned forward, her brows pulling together. "What? How? I thought—"

"He must have decided to visit Oma too." Luisa glanced at her grandmother. "He came into the bakery, where the tunnel starts in the basement, asking what was going on. And moments later, the Stasi raided the place."

Adel covered her mouth with a hand. "Oh no," she breathed. "Did he not make it into the tunnel?"

"He never tried." Luisa's chest hitched. "He sent us through, then remained behind. He pretended that he was investigating her shop. But I heard the words from the Stasi—my father was arrested."

Adel shook her head as if she had no words. Neither did Luisa. Every woman in the room knew the best- and worst-case scenarios. And the best case was highly unlikely.

"We need to find out what happened to him," Adel said. "Wait here. I will make some calls. See if anyone has heard anything." She left the kitchen, and a few moments later, her murmured voice could be heard as she spoke into the phone in the bedroom. When she returned, she paused in the entryway. "No one knows anything yet, but they will call your apartment as soon as they do. Or maybe he'll show up there."

Maybe . . . Could Luisa even allow herself to hope for such a thing?

"How far to your apartment?" Oma asked.

Luisa looked over at her. Now that the ordeal was over, her grandmother seemed a hollow shell of her usual self. "Upstairs."

Her grandmother looked stunned. "So close? And you've been helping rescue others? How did your father not know?"

Luisa blinked back the threatening tears. "I was always very careful." She bit her lip. "If only he hadn't followed me tonight."

Adel rested a hand on Luisa's shoulder. "Come on. I'll stay with the both of you while we wait for news. You could both use a little sleep. If a phone call comes in, I'll wake you up immediately."

Less than thirty minutes later, Luisa and Adel were holding vigil on the couch in Luisa's apartment. Her grandmother was sleeping in Luisa's bed. And every sound or movement from the street had Luisa wondering, hoping, expecting.

But her father didn't come.

Adel had been too optimistic that Luisa had any chance of falling asleep. Her gaze kept moving to the front door where her mother's heeled shoes sat. Her father hadn't switched them out for slippers yet. And now he couldn't.

Luisa rose to her feet and paced the apartment. At one point, she walked into her father's bedroom and flipped on the light. It was tidy like usual. His bed pristinely made. Not a wrinkle in sight. There was a Bible on the bedside table. Luisa turned away and turned off the light before the tears began.

Then she hovered in the doorway of her own bedroom, where her grandmother was sleeping. Oma's soft, even breathing comforted Luisa. For so many months, years really, she and her father had wanted Oma to live with them. And now, here she was. But it came at a cost greater than Luisa could have ever imagined.

A piece of paper on her bedside table caught her gaze. She hadn't noticed it before, and she hadn't left it there. Quietly, she crossed to the bedside table and picked up the paper. It was a folded note.

She moved into the hallway and flipped on the light. Her father's handwriting was plain, and his message clear.

Dear Luisa,

When I returned home tonight, the phone rang, and there was no one on the other end. I hung up after a moment, but then

I started thinking about the other times when we've had such calls to our home. It's happened more than once, and I've never told you.

A few nights ago, I awoke in the middle of the night with a sense of emptiness. That used to happen frequently after your mother died. But somehow, this was different. I went to check on you and found the bed empty. I searched about the apartment, but you were nowhere to be found. I prepared to leave and look around outside, and I was even about to call another officer to help me search. I imagined the worst.

Then the front door opened. I moved into the kitchen corner so you wouldn't see me. An intruder wouldn't have a key, so I knew it would be you. I decided not to say a word about it to you. I wanted you to confess whatever you were doing. Perhaps you had a boyfriend. Perhaps you had a habit of late-night walks I didn't know about.

I couldn't think anything more than the most innocent of pursuits. But then, as I was in the kitchen, looking out the window onto the darkened street, wondering what my daughter had truly been up to, I saw someone else exit the building. Two people, in fact. It was clear that one person was not in good shape. She appeared weak and perhaps ill. And since I'd heard no footsteps on the stairs or above us, I knew it had to be from the basement apartment. A place where no one has lived for months. Or so I thought.

I'm not proud that I picked the lock to the basement apartment. It was empty but had clearly been recently occupied. I found a bottle of lotion in the bathroom. The lotion was the same brand you buy. But why would you go to the basement apartment? I couldn't imagine.

Until I found the door to the tunnel.

Dear Luisa, you are a noble and honorable woman. A daughter I have always been proud of. I don't know if I should be raging or grateful for a daughter who would involve herself in an underground organization.

The reason for this letter is that if I am correct, you've gone to put a rescue plan into action for Oma. I don't blame you, but I also can't let you risk so much. You're young and have an entire life ahead of you. If it's the last thing I do, as your father, I will ensure that you have that life you deserve.

If things do not go as planned, I wanted you to know that you are the light in my life, and you have brought me my happiness.

Love,

Father

Adel appeared around the corner. "What is it?"

Luisa wiped at the tears streaking down her face. "My father knew—he guessed mostly, but he knew enough. He came after me, knowing that I was walking into danger." She took a stuttering breath. "Here, read it."

Adel read through the letter, and when she finished, her own eyes were watery. "Oh, Luisa, I'm so sorry. But we don't know what might have happened tonight if he hadn't shown up before the Stasi. You and your grandmother might have been arrested instead."

"I wish it would have been me," Luisa said. "He could have taken Oma through the tunnel."

Before Adel could respond, a knock sounded at the front door.

Luisa nearly jumped out of her skin. "Papa!" She raced to the door, but when she flung it open, it wasn't her father. "Mrs. Herrmann?"

The woman's lined face was grave as she stepped into the apartment. "I have news."

Luisa's heart forgot to beat.

"Your father was arrested, along with the baker," Mrs. Herrmann said. "Your father was questioned thoroughly at the Stasi office throughout the night. His story never changed. He insisted that he was there to do an inspection since he wants to start his own bakery in West Berlin."

"Will they believe him and let him go?"

"I wish I had better news," Mrs. Herrmann said. "They eventually found the tunnel, so they know both he and the baker were lying."

"But my father wasn't involved in any of that. I was," Luisa said, her voice cracking. "It was *me*. All me. I should be the one in the Stasi office."

Mrs. Herrmann grasped Luisa's hands. "He is protecting you, yes, but there would be no sense in you turning yourself in. He's already been sentenced and likely transported."

"Transported?"

"To prison."

Luisa stared at Mrs. Herrmann. "How long?"

"Five years," Mrs. Herrmann said. "I'm very sorry, my dear."

Luisa's eyes slid shut again, guilt washing over her. She had to find something good in all of this, something to hold onto. At least her oma was with her now. That was something to be grateful for.

CHAPTER THIRTY-TWO

"The West bought the freedom of nearly 34,000 of these 'enemies of socialism'—the East German terminology for the inmates. Only the first busload of 1963 was paid in cash—following which there was a barter transaction: people in exchange for goods. Depending on what the shortage-plagued East German economy needed, West Germany supplied food or petroleum. Diamonds also found their way from West to East."

—Marcel Fürstenau, "Putting a Price on Freedom"

EAST GERMAN PRISON
APRIL 1962

Bob had been shivering all night, although the winter of East Germany had softened well into spring. Perhaps he was becoming ill? Morning had come and gone with the scant meal of hard bread, and Bob had climbed back onto the cot and fallen asleep again.

He dreamed that he heard birdsong like he had at the Neumanns' home in West Berlin. But he wasn't in a comfortable home and didn't have a day of studying German stretching out before him.

The birdsong paused, then started again. Maybe this wasn't a dream. He opened his eyes and pushed up on his elbows to get a better view of the high window. The blue of the sky was cut as usual by the silver barbed wire. But today he had a visitor.

Bob blinked, then blinked again. Climbing off the cot, he backed up against the door so he could have a better view. If he hadn't been standing on the cold floor, he would have believed he was still dreaming.

A small yellow songbird had its talons curled around the barbed wire. The incongruence of a bird, which was free to fly away at any moment, resting on a prison fence outside a cold, gray cell room made Bob's eyes sting.

He didn't move, didn't make a sound, so as not to startle the creature. Its head was gray, its breast yellow, its feathers downy.

When the bird's song stopped, Bob could still hear every note in his head. He held as still as possible as the tears spilled onto his cheeks. He knew it wasn't the same songbird that had woken him every morning in West Berlin. But the presence of this bird told him that there was still a world outside. There was still life, there was still beauty, and there was still hope.

Bob didn't know how long he stood pressed against the prison door, but when the bird flew away, the pain and cold of his joints eased for a short time. He settled onto the cot again, his chest expanded, his heart full of gratitude.

The light shifted again in the cell, and he looked over at the window. Clouds were filtering in, lighter gray than winter clouds, but gray nevertheless. A slow sigh moved through him, and his gaze landed on the patch of light on the cell wall across from the window. The light was nearly as gray as the wall itself. Maybe a rainstorm was on its way. Bob didn't mind thunder or rain. It made for a nice change.

Summer was around the corner, and the days would be longer, the nights shorter. The cell warmer. And perhaps the bird would return tomorrow with its song.

When he heard the footsteps of an approaching guard, he assumed it was Adolf. Bob remained on his cot. It wasn't mealtime, so Adolf would be coming to Bob's cell for only one reason. The interrogation and beatings would be the same; they always were, so he might as well stay on the cot until the very last moment.

He heard the familiar clang of the cell unlocking. Then the door opened.

Bob waited another few seconds to open his eyes, and when he did, Adolf was standing next to his cot.

"You are to shower right now," Adolf said, his voice strangely distant, "and we have clean clothing for you."

Bob decided he was dreaming and closed his eyes again.

"Come on. Get up," Adolf said, his tone gentle. "Bring your glasses."

Bob opened his eyes. Adolf was really standing there. This was no dream. Bob moved to a sitting position, his aching limbs protesting. But a shower was worth moving for. Bob wondered if the water would be cold or warm, but he didn't care. The last time he'd showered was the morning in Leipzig before Schmitt had turned him in. Five months? No, six months ago.

Bob retrieved his glasses, which he rarely wore, from the lone chair. Then Adolf led him up the same stairs that led to the interrogation room, but they passed by that room and turned down another hallway. Bob didn't understand why he was being given the privilege of taking a shower. Had Adolf somehow gotten him this favor? Or was it standard for prisoners to shower every six months? Maybe he was going to be interrogated by a higher-up official, and they didn't want him smelling like a stray dog.

The bathroom he was led into was small and smelled of mildew. But Bob wasn't complaining. He took a shower, using the rough-edged soap provided. The flow of water was weak, but it still felt like a hard pummel on his aching limbs, littered with bruises. No one told him to hurry, yet Bob didn't stall. When he stepped out, there was a towel and a pile of folded clothing on the counter.

With trembling hands, Bob dressed. The clothes were musty, but to him they smelled as if they had been cleaned with the purest detergent. Before buttoning the pale-blue shirt, he pulled the collar closed and inhaled. Tears burned in the corners of his eyes. These clothes would make his prison cell more bearable. Then he pulled on the provided socks and slipped his feet into his old shoes. Bob paused a long moment. Surely Adolf was waiting on the other side of the door, but for this space of time, Bob felt renewed. Weak and hungry, sure, but renewed and not defeated.

Before exiting the bathroom, he paused by the sink and looked into the mirror. The image looking back at him was a different Bob. The face was gaunt, the eyes dark hollows, the beard and hair wild. But he knew he was still in there—someplace deep within, but still there.

He could do this. Face the cell once again. He'd showered, was wearing clean clothing, and he hadn't been beaten today. It was a good day.

Sure enough, Adolf was waiting outside of the bathroom, along with two other East German guards. Perhaps Bob had counted his blessings too soon and he'd be interrogated after all.

"Turn around," Adolf said.

Bob turned around, his weary heart rate kicking up a notch. A blindfold was placed over his eyes, and his wrists were handcuffed behind his back.

With the other guards present, Bob didn't question Adolf. It might sound too presumptuous, too familiar, and the last thing Bob wanted to do was get his friend in trouble.

The guards led him out of the building, and the brisk spring wind immediately worked itself through Bob's clean clothing. He smelled earth and grass, and he inhaled deeply while he could. Although the fresh air was divine, panic started to build in his chest. Were they taking him to the courtyard again? Would he be shot to death this time?

But they continued walking, well past where the courtyard would have been, and Bob was ushered into the back of a vehicle—a car, he guessed. It was much quieter than a truck. The upholstered seat was a welcome change from the prison cot and hard chair.

Adolf sat next to him in the back seat. Bob knew that much at least. But they weren't alone, and Bob didn't dare say a word to Adolf around the other guards. They must be taking him to a new location. Maybe a Soviet labor camp? Bob would miss Adolf once he was in his new place.

As time passed on the drive, Bob had no way of knowing which direction they were driving. He didn't know the starting point to begin with. An hour passed at least, maybe two hours, maybe longer.

When the car stopped, Bob followed the order to step out of the car, and then one of the guards removed his blindfold and handcuffs. Blinking in the winter light, Bob looked around at a broad field with a grouping of budding trees in the distance. The road they were on was merely a country lane. Where was the prison, and why had they removed the blindfold?

Then Bob noticed another vehicle on that road, parked as though waiting. He recognized the large red cross on the side of the truck. *A US Army ambulance.*

"Walk to that truck," one of the guards said.

Bob stared at the guard, not comprehending.

"Go, now," the guard ordered.

Bob moved forward, nearly stumbling on his unsteady feet. Then he paused and looked over at Adolf.

Adolf lifted his chin, as if to say, *Go now, while you have the chance*. His expression was set in stone, but his eyes were murky with emotion.

Bob couldn't leave. Not yet. He took the few steps toward Adolf until he was close enough to whisper, "Thank you. I love you, my brother."

Adolf's eyes filled with tears, but he said nothing. Only nodded, jaw set.

It was time. Bob had been given another chance at life, and he was going to take it.

He strode toward the US Army ambulance, unsure how he suddenly had the strength of a healthy man.

Two men separated from the ambulance, but they weren't dressed as US soldiers or medics. They were in plain clothing, and then Bob knew. This was a prisoner exchange. Two of them for one of him.

Bob continued walking right past them, and he didn't slow down until he reached the back of the ambulance.

Two US Army medics were waiting for him, and they both helped him inside. It was then that his legs nearly gave out. Everything inside him felt like it was crashing, and he could barely comprehend that he'd been released.

Free.

He was free.

He would see his family again.

He would see his country again.

He would live.

His eyes closed against the tears, but they kept coming.

One of the medics stayed close, sitting next to him. "Can you tell us what happened?"

Bob didn't move. "My rank is Specialist Fourth Class. My ID is 10423570."

The questions stopped, but he knew he'd have to answer them sometime. He wondered if Taggett had negotiated his release. Or had the GDR decided they were done with him and contacted the US Army?

Bob cut his gaze to the window, and the bleak landscape rolled by. *It's over*, he told himself. *It's finally over.* He marveled that on his last day in prison, he'd seen a small songbird and envied its freedom. And now . . . Bob too was free.

The ambulance slowed at a checkpoint, and Bob leaned closer to the window to look out. He didn't recognize the checkpoint, but so many things had changed during the months he'd been in prison. The Berlin Wall, which had been erected a couple of months before his arrest, resembled a military fortress now. The cement walls were topped with barbed wire, and watchtowers grew up from the ground like rockets.

"Some reinforcements have been made since you last saw the wall," one of the medics, who'd introduced himself as Patrick, said. "Eleven feet high. Eighty-seven miles long. Neighborhoods have been demolished to create a wide berth that can be guarded. Death strips, they call them."

It was hard to comprehend. But as the ambulance slowed and was cleared through the checkpoint, he gazed in awe at the reinforcements to the wall. This was no temporary solution. It was here to stay.

"I always breathe easier when we get to the west side," Patrick continued. "Everyone is on pins and needles every moment of the day."

"Have there been many . . . escapees?"

"All the time," Patrick said. "Most are captured and arrested. Others have been killed. But we've heard rumors of underground organizations that are creative in getting people out."

Bob thought about this. No matter the restrictions and confines that a government might put upon its people, the human spirit still rallied.

"Ironically, two days after the wall went up, a nineteen-year-old East German border guard escaped. Did you hear that story before you were arrested?"

Had he? Bob honestly couldn't remember.

Patrick drummed his fingers. "Conrad Schumann. It seems he didn't want the wall up either. Heard the concrete walls were going up, and he decided to bail first. Back then the wall was barbed wire, so he just leaped over it."

Bob said nothing as the ambulance drove farther into the west side.

"See the smooth pipe at the top?" Patrick asked.

Bob nodded.

"Most sections have the pipe, and that guard tower is one of about 260," Patrick said, his voice filled with awe. "The area's got embedded flares, trip wires, trained guard dogs, and five-inch spikes designed to dissuade anyone from jumping off the wall."

Bob didn't turn his head to look back at the checkpoint. He'd be happy to never see it again, and he wondered what he might remember of this day. Everything felt like a blur, and time didn't have much meaning. "How did they get away with it for so long?"

"You mean, why does the US do nothing about the wall?" Patrick chuckled, but there was no humor in it. "I don't think anyone wants a nuclear war to start, not really. So the question becomes, how much will each side put up with? How many infractions among the Allies can be kept to a low simmer?"

"Because one nuclear missile would change everything," Bob said.

"Exactly."

Bob had been in prison for six months, separated from a world of conflict, and now that he was out again, he was returning to the same world. Nothing had improved in the Cold War. If anything, the situation was only worse. "Where are we going?" Bob asked, his voice sounding faint, even to his ears.

"We're flying you out to the hospital, my friend," Patrick said. "Frankfurt."

"All right," Bob said. Frankfurt would be nice. He'd be able to shave, shower every day, eat something besides dried bread, mush, and weak stew. He never thought he'd look forward to hospital food. He tried to keep his eyes open, to see what he recognized of West Berlin from his time there. But nothing seemed familiar. Had he forgotten? He searched his mind for memories of street names and café names, but he couldn't pull them up.

Bob's eyes slid shut as the rumble of the ambulance lulled him into a half-awake state.

"We're getting out and loading you onto the plane," someone said after a few minutes.

Bob opened his eyes to see Patrick. The medic . . . right. Bob had been released from prison today, and now he was in an ambulance.

Somehow he was able to step out of the ambulance and walk to a waiting cargo plane. Bob was sure he had a lot of questions, but right now, he couldn't remember them. He was warm, he was free, and he wanted to sleep.

CHAPTER THIRTY-THREE

"A prisoner swap was negotiated in which Washington would free convicted Soviet agent Colonel Rudolph Abel in exchange for [Francis Gary] Powers. Abel's 30-year sentence was commuted by Attorney General Robert Kennedy to enable the trade. At 8:52 a.m. on February 10, 1962, Powers walked across the Glienicke Brücke from Potsdam toward West Berlin in a carefully orchestrated handover; Abel crossed in the opposite direction. While the deal was expected to ease tensions between the Americans and Soviets, the Cuban missile crisis soon erased the memory of the diplomatic overture and brought the two superpowers to the brink of nuclear conflict."

—"Prisoner Exchanges across the
Bridge of Spies, from Powers to Shcharansky"

US ARMY GENERAL HOSPITAL
FRANKFURT, WEST GERMANY
APRIL 1962

Bob gazed at the clock on the other side of the hospital room wall. He didn't know if it helped to know the time at every moment or to let the time pass in a blur like it had in prison. But everything here operated like clockwork. Something he had to get used to again. There were so many things to adjust to that Bob decided to focus on only the present hour. Once that passed, he could focus on the next hour. One hour, one day, at a time.

Another change was that Bob wasn't alone. It seemed he was never alone. There was always someone coming into his room to check on him, to change something, or to ask him a question. Fortunately, these were questions he could answer. From time to time he had a roommate, but no one seemed to have the longevity that he had in this place.

He hadn't known a soul when he arrived. No one from the barracks had come to see him. Taggett had called him once. It was strange to hear his voice, and Taggett didn't ask Bob anything about his prison time.

"I'm looking forward to seeing you when you recover," Taggett had said. "We'll talk things through when you return, but for now, you only need to focus on healing."

Which was what Bob was trying to do. Today, the doctor was going to come and do another assessment to evaluate his progress. Bob was looking forward to it, but he was also worried about the next steps and what they might mean.

Even though he was safe and recovering in the hospital, he had no idea how to approach whatever came next. Back at the barracks, he'd be thrown into the regular life of a US Army soldier. Yet so much had changed for Bob. How long would it take before he was back to his regular self? Was that even possible?

Bob rose from his bed and reached for the glass of water on the bedside table. After taking a few careful swallows, he stood, putting weight on his feet. As usual, it took a moment for the lightheadedness to pass. But once it did, he could walk fine, although he tired easily. It seemed he'd had more endurance in prison, but here, in the hospital, he was more than willing to take it easy whenever possible.

The physical therapist ran him through paces twice a day, but Bob liked to do extra work, which amounted to walking about his room a few times. Bob headed toward the window. Below him, the roads intersected and people went about their business. It was a bright spring morning, and the green of the trees reminded him of his old college campus in early summer. The brilliant green contrasted against the blue sky and scattered, billowy clouds. It was all as pretty as a painting.

He recalled the small window in his prison cell that let in a fragment of light. That window had been his clock, his calendar, and at times, an affirmation that there was still a world outside his four walls. And now that he was in that world, it was brighter and louder and busier than he remembered.

In truth, he didn't mind being alone in this hospital room. He didn't have to explain to anyone why he was in this place. Taggett had told him not to say anything about his prison experience or spy work to any of the other patients. That was an easy enough request to fulfill. He wasn't ready to talk about it to anyone other than Taggett anyway.

Bob stood at the window for a long moment, gazing over the people of West Germany, thinking about how their lives starkly contrasted with the East Germans'. Here, there was life, color, laughter, new opportunities, and hope. In East Germany, he'd observed only oppression, quiet, and fear.

It was how the prison guard Adolf was raised, and likely the other guards. Even the military officers who interrogated him and beat him almost daily. They were products of an occupied country and an oppressive government.

Bob released a sigh and leaned his head against the pane of glass. His eyes slipped shut as he recalled the conversations he'd had with Adolf. Bob missed the man, and he wondered how he was doing now. Was he still working in the same prison? Was he in charge of Bob's replacement? Would he ever propose to the woman he'd told Bob about?

The door opened to his hospital room, and Bob turned. Three people walked in. Bob recognized the doctor and one of his regular nurses, but he didn't know the third person—a middle-aged man with spectacles and flyaway hair.

"Good morning, Bob," Dr. Stoddard said, his red hair slicked into place as usual. He motioned for Bob to take a seat or return to the hospital bed.

Bob elected to sit on the hospital bed and leave more room for the others to sit down.

Dr. Stoddard pulled over a chair and sat close to Bob. The nurse and the other man took chairs on the opposite side.

"This is Dr. Greer," Stoddard said. "And you know Nurse Bevin."

"Hello, Bob," Nurse Bevin said. She was only a few years older than Bob, but her hair already had lines of gray. Her eyes were kind and her voice soft, something that Bob was grateful for after his months in prison.

"Hello," Bob greeted the nurse, then he extended his hand to Dr. Greer. The man's handshake was firm and brief.

"Now, Dr. Greer is here to talk to you about the rest of your recovery," Dr. Stoddard said. "I've updated him on your physical condition as well as the notes I've taken during our conversations."

Bob frowned. He hadn't realized his conversations with the doctor would go into any sort of report. But he didn't mind. Everyone in the hospital had one goal in mind—to get him well.

"Dr. Greer wants to ask you questions that have to do with your psychological recovery," Stoddard continued. "If you'd like privacy, then Nurse Bevin and I can leave."

Bob looked at each of them. He had known them for only a couple of weeks—as a patient—but he knew that Taggett trusted them. So Bob trusted them. "You're welcome to stay," Bob said. "Thank you for asking though."

Stoddard nodded, and Bevin smiled.

Bob turned to Dr. Greer.

The man folded his hands and gave a faint smile. "We'd like to run a series of psychological tests over the next few days, and I'd also like to meet with you often to discuss how some things might be different as you go forward."

"Like what things?" Bob asked.

Dr. Greer seemed to hesitate, but when Dr. Stoddard gave an almost imperceptible nod, Greer continued. "I understand that before you were drafted into the army, you were finishing up your prelaw and economics degree at a university in Utah."

"Yes," Bob said, wondering why the conversation was going in this direction. He thought that the doctors might suggest he take some sort of clerical job in the army until he had his full physical strength back.

"What are your plans after the army?" Dr. Greer asked.

An even stranger question. "I was accepted to law school at George Washington University before I was drafted, so I'll apply there again."

Dr. Greer took off his spectacles and rubbed them on the sleeve of his shirt. Then he slipped them back on and peered at Bob. "Here's the thing, Mr. Inama. I've looked at your x-rays and examination reports. The many beatings you endured not only wore you down physically, but mentally as well."

This was perfectly logical, Bob thought, but every day he was getting better and better. "I understand that." Suddenly he was feeling exhausted, but he didn't want his fatigue to show. "I'm not in a hurry. Maybe I once was, but getting drafted taught me to be a lot more patient." He smiled. No one smiled back.

"Mr. Inama," Dr. Greer started again, "you reported that you'd pass out after many of your beatings, and many times you woke up on the floor of your cell, not even remembering how you got there."

Bob dipped his chin. He felt like he'd swallowed a rock.

"I'm sorry to deliver this news to you," Dr. Greer said, his voice slowing and growing quieter. But Bob could hear every syllable. "You will never be able to keep up in a rigorous academic environment, which means that you will never practice law."

The room went silent after that. Even the ticking clock on the opposite wall seemed to pause.

"You've had multiple concussions," Dr. Greer said in the dead silence. "Research has shown that numerous concussions lead to future complications."

Bob's eyes stung. When he'd been drafted, he'd gone through a period of shock and denial, but then he'd decided he could live with delaying his career. Yet if what this doctor was saying was true, there would be no career—at least not in law or anything that would require a rigorous schedule and an even more rigorous aptitude. Bob wanted to argue. Or even tell the doctor he was wrong. If Bob could survive in an East German prison for six long months, he could survive in a classroom.

But Bob didn't argue because he *knew*.

Even in prison he knew. Perhaps it was when he'd been there a month, or two months, and he'd already been beaten beyond conscious thought several times . . . But right now, right here, Bob didn't doubt the doctor.

It hurt to hear it confirmed and spoken aloud.

"I'm sorry, Mr. Inama," Dr. Greer said. "I truly am."

And Bob believed him. He might not know this doctor well, but he was a man of sympathy, which was something Bob appreciated. Tears filled his eyes, unbidden, but he wasn't embarrassed. No one looked away.

Nurse Bevin rose to move close, and she grasped his hand. "Bob, you are blessed to be alive. Hold onto that. It's the most important thing right now."

He gripped her hand tightly, holding on for as long as she'd let him. He was almost twenty-seven years old and had just been told that his life would be very, very small after Germany.

Dr. Stoddard rose and clasped a hand on his shoulder.

Here Bob was, in a hospital room thousands of miles away from his home and family, yet these people knew his heart. And they were there for him when it was broken, and they would help him put it back together.

Bob wasn't sure how the rest of the conversation went between him and the doctors and nurse. Sympathies and real concern were expressed, as were offers to do whatever they could to help him recover. Bob appreciated their gestures of goodwill, but he also suspected that once he left the hospital, the support surrounding him would diminish.

Finally, he was left alone again. He didn't know what to think, what to feel. He did know it was his job to work hard through the recovery process and find an alternate way to live a full life. To find new dreams and new hopes.

Right now, though, in this hospital room—which was quiet now that everyone had left—he'd allow himself a night to grieve.

And then tomorrow, he'd get back to work.

"Bob?" Nurse Bevin bustled in. "You've a visitor."

Bob was sure he looked as surprised as the nurse did delivering this news. Had Taggett come after all? Or maybe one of the men in his unit, like Murdock? It would be nice to see his friend, even if Bob couldn't exactly tell him what had happened or where he'd been for the past six months.

"Who is it?" Bob blurted out. He needn't have asked. Any visitor was welcome.

"She said her name is Ms. Voigt," Bevin said, her gaze steady on him, as if waiting for his reaction.

Bob tried not to react, but that was impossible. He was not expecting this . . . not in a hundred years. Maybe he'd fallen asleep and he was dreaming Nurse Bevin's announcement.

But no, the next moment Luisa Voigt walked into his hospital room.

She was the same, just as he remembered—her gray-blue eyes, the honey blond of her hair, her intuitive gaze, the way she seemed to see more than what he showed on the surface. She was all of this—a familiar friend, yet a stranger too.

It had been six months since he'd last seen her. Things had changed.

The fullness of her face had thinned, and instead of a friendly gleam in her eyes, they were shadowed. Even though her smile was bright as she greeted him, he heard the tremble in her voice as she took a step toward the bed.

"Bob, is that really you?"

CHAPTER THIRTY-FOUR

"There are many people in the world who really don't understand, or say they don't, what is the great issue between the free world and the Communist world. Let them come to Berlin. There are some who say that communism is the wave of the future. Let them come to Berlin. And there are some who say in Europe and elsewhere we can work with the Communists. Let them come to Berlin. And there are even a few who say that it is true that communism is an evil system, but it permits us to make economic progress. Lass' sie nach Berlin kommen. Let them come to Berlin."

—John F. Kennedy, Remarks at the
Rudolph Wilde Platz, West Berlin, June 26, 1963

US ARMY GENERAL HOSPITAL
FRANKFURT, WEST GERMANY
APRIL 1962

The nurse who'd led Luisa through the maze of hallways gave her a brief smile as she left the hospital room. Luisa returned it, hoping her smile appeared genuine, but it was hard to hide her nerves. And misgivings.

Bob looked surprised to see Luisa, but she hoped he wasn't disappointed.

The moment she'd heard from Sonja that Bob Inama was back in Frankfurt, Luisa knew she had to see him. Since she'd last spoken to him that day in East Berlin, she'd been curious about what he'd been doing there. And why he couldn't talk to her. And why he wasn't in uniform. She'd wondered if he'd deserted the army, but it seemed he hadn't. Not if he was here, being taken care of by the army.

Sonja hadn't known why Bob was in the hospital, and Luisa worried that she might miss him in the time it took her to arrange work off and travel to Frankfurt. But no, here he was, sitting up in a rumpled bed. No cast or bandaging in sight. But there were changes—definitely changes. In fact, Luisa didn't know if she'd recognize him if she passed him on the streets of Frankfurt.

He was probably thirty pounds thinner, and his brown eyes seemed nearly black in contrast to the paleness of his face. Bob also seemed older. Not in age, but in experience. And something told Luisa that the experiences hadn't been easy. Yet the kindness in his eyes overrode the new depths that were there.

"Luisa," Bob said, his gaze locked onto hers as if he was looking at an apparition. "You're in Frankfurt? How did you . . ."

His voice trailed off as she took a few tentative steps toward him. Even his voice had changed. It was deeper, raspier, as if he'd recovered from a coughing fit. But Bob seemed to be breathing fine. Yet there was something she couldn't put her finger on. Why was he here?

"Sonja told me that she'd heard you were here," Luisa said, keeping her tone light, unaffected. "You know how hospital gossip can be."

Bob's brow dipped as if he didn't know what she was referring to or he didn't remember Sonja.

"You remember Sonja, right?" Luisa continued. "We graduated from nursing school together."

"I remember Sonja," Bob said, although his words came slower than Luisa remembered.

It wasn't that she couldn't understand everything he said; she did, but his German was very careful. Very precise. Wherever he'd been, and whatever he'd been doing, he'd improved his German even more.

"So." Luisa inhaled, steadying the tremble in her voice. "How are you, Bob? I feel lucky to have made it here before you were discharged."

The statement was leading, but Bob didn't seem to pick up on it, or perhaps he didn't want to explain things. Her visit was a surprise, after all. It wasn't like they'd been writing letters or keeping in contact. So much could change in six months; it had for her.

"I am . . ." Bob started, then paused.

Luisa remained standing, waiting, her purse clutched in front of her. The sounds of the hospital corridor seemed too quiet.

Then Bob looked away.

Luisa tried to remember if there had ever been another moment when Bob Inama had looked away from her. No, this was the first. She didn't know why her throat suddenly constricted and she felt like crying. Nothing had really been said between them today, save for a greeting and a few unanswered questions. Yet the crooked angle of his once broad shoulders, the carved hollows beneath his cheeks, the way his hands trembled ever so slightly . . . Luisa had seen enough of fear and terror and trauma in her work with the escape tunnels, and suddenly she realized . . .

"Oh, Bob." In a moment, she was at his side. Her purse dropped to the ground as she reached out and grasped his hand. "What happened to you? What have you lived through?"

Bob still didn't look at her. And she would have wondered if he'd heard her at all, but his fingers tightened around hers.

Perhaps right now wasn't the time to ask questions. Perhaps right now, all he needed was someone to sit beside him. Perhaps right now, he needed a friend who would hold his hand.

So, that's what Luisa did. She sat in the chair by his bedside for the next hour. He said nothing. She asked no questions. But their hands remained linked.

When the nurse returned to the room, it seemed that whatever fragile peace had existed between Luisa and Bob was stretched thin. Luisa released Bob's hand and rose to her feet.

"I should go now," she said.

Bob's eyes met hers then, and in his gaze she saw gratitude and acknowledgment. It was all she could hope for. He'd appreciated her visit. She hadn't made a mistake.

The nurse bustled about, fastening a blood pressure cuff on Bob's upper arm. As the nurse pumped up the cuff, Luisa gathered her purse and moved toward the door. She should leave—right now—so that he could rest and be taken care of.

But she paused in the doorway and looked back at Bob. Physically, he seemed to be a shadow of his former self, but his soul seemed to fill the whole room. His compassion and humility could never be snuffed out, no matter what he'd gone through.

"Would you mind if I visited tomorrow?" Luisa asked in a tentative voice.

A ghost of a smile flitted across his face so fast that Luisa almost missed it.

Her spirits soared. "All right, then. See you tomorrow."

When he nodded, Luisa wanted to grin, or even laugh. But she schooled herself. She headed out of the hospital, her step lighter than it had been in a long time. Bob had gone through something very difficult, that she was sure of, yet there he was, recovering and fighting for his well-being. Even in his broken state, he was an inspiration to her.

She didn't want to return to Sonja's home yet. Luisa needed time to think, to absorb her scattered thoughts, to center herself. So she headed to a café. The spring breeze was brisk, rattling the new leaves of the overhead trees. But the air felt crisp, fresh, and energetic somehow. At the café, she ordered herbal tea, then sat by one of the tall windows so she could gaze out and people watch.

She knew that not a single person passing along in the street had been left untouched by the Cold War. Whether it was a family divided, the loss of a loved one, violated human rights, or facing unexpected fears, everyone had been impacted.

Luisa took a sip of her tea. She thought of her father and his prison sentence, and the weight that had momentarily lifted from her heart began to descend again. Slowly, but surely. The guilt over what had happened was an old friend, and one that Luisa knew would never leave until her father was released. Until he was safe. But even then, so much had been lost.

Blinking against the stinging in her eyes, Luisa took another sip of the warm, fruity tea. The aromatic taste was soothing and maybe even indulgent. She was in Frankfurt, in the section of the country where she had rights and privileges as a West German citizen. Yet why should she be free when her father was not?

Her thoughts turned to Bob again. What had *he* endured? What was he enduring now?

Before Luisa could stop them, tears coursed down her cheeks. This would not do. Not in a public café. She wiped her tears with a napkin then crumpled it up. Leaving the café, she finally headed toward Sonja's house. Luisa skipped the tram and walked. Perhaps the longer journey would be enough time to settle her heart and dry her tears.

There were things to be happy about and grateful for, she told herself. Her grandmother was alive and in good health. They were together every day, which was a gift. Her father was alive, and God willing, one day he'd be released. And she'd found Bob again.

Luisa's heart slowly twisted. She'd been drawn to Bob from the first moments they'd met at that church social. He'd always been the quiet sort, but one-on-one, his intelligence and good humor was a beacon of light. Seeing him in that hospital room, his body a shell of its former strength, and his dark eyes like a well of hidden pain, made her realize that she truly cared about his future. Even if she couldn't be a part of it.

The tears started again. In a better world, a more peaceful world, where former allies didn't have their thumbs hovering over the red buttons of a nuclear catastrophe, perhaps there would be a place for a German nurse and an American soldier to move their friendship beyond prejudices, cultural mores, and family doubts. But the world had not reached that stage. Not yet.

When Luisa stepped into Sonja's home, her tears had dried. Life was what it was, and she was learning to be grateful for every aspect of it.

"How did it go?" Sonja asked, coming out of the kitchen. Her smile was as bright as her blond curls, and Luisa knew half of that had to do with Sonja's new beau. Luisa wouldn't be surprised if the couple became engaged soon.

Luisa pushed down the twinge of envy as she followed her friend into the warm kitchen that smelled of bubbling roast and baking bread. "He didn't say much, but he was glad to see me."

Sonja's smile widened. "Of course he was. Now tell me everything he did say, even though it wasn't much."

Luisa hid a sigh. She wasn't going to get out of this conversation. Sonja knew her too well for Luisa to try and hide anything. "Well . . ." Her voice caught.

Sonja rested a hand on Luisa's shoulder. "Oh no, what happened? Is he seriously ill? Injured?"

Luisa opened her mouth, but the words wouldn't come.

Sonja frowned. "Sit down. Tell me."

So, Luisa did. There wasn't a lot to tell really, just what her observations had been.

Sonja's expression remained stoic, and after Luisa finished, Sonja said, "You're doing the right thing. Being there for him. If he wants to talk, he'll talk. If not, then you can be assured that he feels your sympathy."

Luisa hated that she was crying again. "It breaks my heart to think that he's been through something awful. What if . . . what if my father is also enduring hell?"

Sonja didn't try to sugarcoat. She simply said, "Sometimes we can only have faith. We can only pray in our helplessness. And as we share our burdens with others, we can make it through together."

Grasping Sonja's hand, Luisa held firm. Sonja was right. But it still didn't make it easier.

"I'm going to visit him tomorrow," Luisa said.

"Good," Sonja said, equally softly. "He will appreciate that."

"There's no future for us, though. No matter how much I like him or how much you think we should be together."

Sonja's laugh was quiet, somber. "That's all right, too. Good friendships are rare in life. Cherish it while you can."

Never had more accurate words been spoken: *while you can*. One day, Bob would return to America. Without her.

Somehow, Luisa made it through the rest of the day, interacting with Sonja's family without bursting into tears. Somehow, she slept through the night. And somehow, the following morning, her step was light as she walked back to the hospital.

A different nurse was in attendance, and she asked for Luisa's relationship to Bob Inama.

"We are friends," Luisa said. "We've known each other a long time." As if that would make her case stronger.

The nurse's cheeks dimpled, but not with a smile—more like a frown. Still, she motioned for Luisa to head on down the corridor to make her visit.

Luisa walked with her gaze forward. Memories of her mother at the hospital were hard to push back as she passed the various rooms with convalescing patients. The sharp smell of disinfectant stung her senses. She didn't know why this felt so different than working at the hospital for her job. She was a nurse, after all. But maybe it was *why* she was here. To visit a patient.

Luisa slowed when she approached Bob's hospital room. The door was open a few inches, and through the crack she could see that he wasn't in the rumpled bed. She knocked lightly on the door as she pushed it open a few more inches.

Bob was standing at the window, and he turned as the door swung wider. She'd nearly forgotten how tall he was. Yesterday in his hospital bed, he'd seemed less imposing and statuesque. But now, she could see that he hadn't lost any of his presence. When he entered a room, there'd always been a quiet confidence about him—something that had drawn her to him.

"Hello," she said, knowing her voice sounded tentative. "I hope you don't mind me visiting."

Bob turned the rest of the way and faced her. His pajama pants and loose top hung from his tall frame. He had more lines about his face than when she'd seen him six or seven months ago. The deep violet beneath his eyes and hollows below his cheeks proved that he wasn't yet fully healthy. She had so many questions, but she also didn't want to bring up any painful topics.

"I don't mind." Bob motioned toward one of the chairs in the room. "Have a seat."

Immediately she sensed that today was a better day for him. Part of that might be because she hadn't shown up out of the blue. He knew she was in Frankfurt, and yesterday the ice had been broken.

Bob sat in a chair across from her, instead of taking to his bed. "It's good to see you, Luisa."

The phrase was a small thing, but it meant so much to hear it. It was so . . . *Bob*. It told her that he was still there. Whatever had happened, he was still the same on the inside. She blinked against the threatening emotion in her eyes and smiled. "It's good to see you, too, Bob."

"Now," he said with a tender smile. "Tell me what you have been doing the past six months and why you are back in Frankfurt."

CHAPTER THIRTY-FIVE

"Good evening, my fellow citizens: This Government, as promised, has maintained the closest surveillance of the Soviet military buildup on the island of Cuba. Within the past week, unmistakable evidence has established the fact that a series of offensive missile sites is now in preparation on that imprisoned island. The purpose of these bases can be none other than to provide a nuclear strike capability against the Western Hemisphere. . . . The characteristics of these new missile sites indicate two distinct types of installations. Several of them include medium range ballistic missiles, capable of carrying a nuclear warhead for a distance of more than 1,000 nautical miles. Each of these missiles, in short, is capable of striking Washington, D. C., the Panama Canal, Cape Canaveral, Mexico City, or any other city in the southeastern part of the United States, in Central America, or in the Caribbean area."

—JOHN F. KENNEDY, "RADIO AND TELEVISION
REPORT TO THE AMERICAN PEOPLE ON THE
SOVIET ARMS BUILDUP IN CUBA," OCTOBER 22, 1962

US ARMY GENERAL HOSPITAL
FRANKFURT, WEST GERMANY
MAY 1962

Luisa was like a ray of sunshine breaking into the cloudy hospital days. When she visited, which was almost every day, Bob found himself smiling for at least an hour after she left. He knew what the nurses were whispering and speculating about in the hallway outside his room. But he didn't care.

On one of her visits, Luisa had told him that when she'd heard about him being in the hospital, she had asked for some time off to come to Frankfurt. Bob was deeply touched, to say the least. He wasn't sure he'd ever had a friend who was as compassionate as Luisa. Her heart was purer than gold.

They'd talked for over an hour every day. Bob didn't ask how long she'd be staying in Frankfurt, and she didn't tell him. Perhaps it was easier to not speak of the inevitable—the goodbye between them. Luisa had told him how her grandmother was stubborn and had refused to leave her home in East Berlin. When Bob had asked her about her father, she'd only smiled and said, "Oh, you know him."

He wasn't sure what she meant by that, but her gaze had lowered, and she fiddled with the floral pendant about her neck. Bob guessed she didn't want to speak about her father. Was it because she knew he'd be bothered by Luisa visiting Bob? Did her father know the true reason she was in Frankfurt? Again, there were just some things he didn't ask her.

He couldn't say if there was a future between him and Luisa. There were too many variables right now. But that didn't stop his hope from growing a little more each day. He hadn't even realized that seed was still there until she walked into his hospital room that first day, bringing with her the warmth that he hadn't realized was missing.

The door opened to his room, and he turned from his usual place at the window, anticipating Luisa's visit.

But it was Nurse Bevin, with Dr. Stoddard and Dr. Greer.

Bob hid a frown. Had he forgotten about an assessment? He didn't think so. Dr. Greer may have told him he no longer had the aptitude to endure a rigorous law school, but Bob wouldn't have forgotten something as simple as a meeting.

"Good morning, Bob," Nurse Bevin said with a smile. "We hope we're not interrupting something."

Bob chuckled, although it didn't settle the nerves coiling inside. It was their long-standing joke. Bob could always be interrupted.

Dr. Stoddard and Dr. Greer were all smiles, too.

That's when Bob grew suspicious. What was this about? Did he have a visitor from the army barracks or something? Major Taggett? Murdock? No, it wouldn't be Murdock. Taggett had said that no one in his unit would know anything about his assignment, so allowing a hospital visit wouldn't be smart.

"Well, Bob," Dr. Stoddard said. He took a stance in the middle of the room, his eyes practically glowing. "We have good news for you."

Bob's mind filled with new possibilities. Maybe Dr. Greer's earlier assessment had changed and Bob could go to law school after all. Bob's gaze cut to Dr. Greer—who was looking as proud as a new father with his just-born baby.

"You have been cleared to return to Hanau," Dr. Stoddard said. "Major Taggett is coming to pick you up himself. He'll be here in, oh . . ." He glanced at the wall at the ticking clock that had counted every second for the past thirty-two days. "Three hours."

Three hours. He was leaving so soon? He knew he'd be leaving sometime, but this was not enough notice . . . to say goodbye . . .

Dr. Stoddard continued speaking about discharge orders, but Bob was thinking about Luisa. Would she come in time? Would she come at all today? He knew she was staying at her friend Sonja's house. Why hadn't he thought to get the phone number there?

Next, Dr. Greer issued some instructions.

Bob nodded in agreement, although he felt disappointed that Dr. Greer didn't stray from his advice of backing away from a law degree.

By the time the medical staff left Bob's hospital room, his forehead felt rigid with pressure, and it was as if all of his energy had left with the nurse and doctors. Bob crossed to the bed that had pretty much become a second home over the past month. He sat on the edge, and through bleary eyes, he watched the afternoon sun's rays slant against the adjacent wall. He was ready—the doctors had proclaimed him ready. He *needed* to be ready. To move on. To begin his life again.

But would Luisa come?

Bob paced the room.

He sat on the bed.

He paced again.

Nurse Bevin showed up with a stack of clothing. A US Army uniform. He really was leaving the hospital. He dressed slowly after the nurse left, and as he pulled on each item of clothing, it felt like he was taking one more step toward the next phase of his life.

After he dressed, he paced again. Then he paused at the window, looking down on the people crossing the road, walking on the sidewalk, and going about their business of the day. Was Luisa among them? He searched for her honey-blond hair, or anything that might be familiar. But he didn't see her.

Then he heard footsteps approach his hospital door. Maybe before his prison experience, he wouldn't have been able to pick out the differences among people's footsteps. But he'd known Adolf's. And he knew Luisa's.

He turned as she pushed open the door. Her smile was so familiar, so bright, that it almost hurt Bob to gaze at her. Would he ever see her again after he left today? It was a question that only she could answer.

"Bob, you look like you're going somewhere," she said, her tone sunny, but a small frown tugged at the edges of her mouth. Her gaze flitted over his uniform. "Are you . . . ?"

She didn't finish, but he knew her question. "I'm being discharged in a couple of hours," he said. "I'm glad you came before I left." He drew in a breath, steadying his own emotions because Luisa wasn't hiding her dismay. "I didn't want to leave without saying goodbye."

She bit her lip. Then in a careful voice, she said, "That's wonderful that you're healed up now."

He'd never told her about prison. He never told her about the beatings. He never told her about Adolf. Bob wasn't sure if he could ever talk about his experiences—beyond reporting them to Major Taggett, that was. But in this moment, he knew he didn't need to explain, or give any details. He knew that she'd guessed. How could she not? Luisa—his intelligent, bright, and lovely friend.

"I'm all healed up," Bob echoed, not fooling either of them.

They stood for a moment, facing each other. Not speaking. It reminded Bob of that final moment in the alleyway in East Berlin when he told her she couldn't act as if she knew him. She'd not asked for an explanation; she'd not complained. It was a strength of hers, he realized. An intuition he believed not many people had.

"That's wonderful, Bob," she said, breaking the stillness between them at last. "I'm so happy for you."

His throat cinched painfully, so he nodded.

"We should write to each other this time," she said, with a high, nervous laugh. "We've lost touch plenty of times. And with you returning to Hanau and me to West Berlin, who knows when we'll see each other again?"

"West Berlin?" Bob's voice had roughened. "You're going back?" He felt like a cad immediately. Of course she was going back. Her father and her grandmother were in Berlin.

But Luisa wasn't looking at him now. In fact, she'd lowered her head, and unmistakable tears slid down her cheeks. Was she . . . hoping for something else? Something more between them?

"Luisa," Bob said in a gentle tone. "If there was any way I thought you might consider . . . a change . . ."

Her chin lifted, and she looked him square in the eyes. "Don't say it, Bob," she whispered. "It will only make this harder."

Bob understood. Completely. Mostly. Had she never considered it? Would it be so far-fetched?

"I need to tell you something so that you understand," she said.

He frowned. "You don't owe me any explanation."

She held up her hand. "I need to explain. I can't have you thinking . . ."

Her voice cracked. After a quick glance at the hospital room door, which was still ajar, she looked at Bob. "It's my father."

Yes, Bob knew this was part of it—a good part of it.

"But it's not what you think," Luisa said. "Remember when I told you about Mrs. Weber last year? How she disappeared from the hospital where I was working?"

Last year felt like a lifetime ago, but he did remember the story about Mrs. Weber. "I remember."

"That was only the beginning," Luisa said. "I didn't know it at the time, but I was already being watched, assessed."

"What do you mean?" Bob asked.

When Luisa spoke again, a story unraveled in front of him, astonishing him to his very core. She'd joined an underground organization in West Berlin to deliver messages about safe houses, then she'd risked her own life and safety to help East Germans secure fake passports.

He didn't need to ask what her father had thought of it all because it was clear from her expression that she hadn't told him. Then she told him about the building of the Berlin Wall and how she couldn't stand seeing the division. Families and countrymen had been cruelly divided, unfairly separated.

When Luisa told him about helping with tunnel rescues in the same apartment building she lived in, Bob was stunned.

"My grandmother finally consented to leave East Berlin," Luisa said, pacing as she spoke. "But her request for permission to leave only alerted the Stasi. They bugged her house. They made an elderly woman feel like a criminal. So I . . ."

Bob's pulse sprinted as he waited for her next words.

She stopped pacing. "I convinced her to come through the tunnel with me. I went into East Berlin and took her to the location. But . . . my father suspected and followed me. I had no idea until he arrived at the bakery too."

Bob didn't move. Didn't speak. He couldn't.

"The Stasi had been staking the place out, and they raided the bakery, nearly catching all of us." Luisa closed her eyes as if she were reliving the memory. "My father and the bakery owner took the fall. They sent me and Oma through the tunnel. We escaped, and they didn't." Luisa opened her eyes and focused her watery gaze on Bob. "My father was arrested and sentenced to five years in prison," she whispered. "Because of me."

Bob heard the fear in her words, and saw the grief in her eyes and the weight of guilt on her shoulders.

"My grandmother and I are still living in West Berlin," she said, her voice scratchy, "waiting for my father's release. I can't leave while he's in prison. Don't you see? I could never leave Germany. I could never make any promises for the future either."

The pain Bob felt in his chest was enough to fell a grown man. But it wasn't his pain right now that needed alleviating. It was Luisa's.

Brushing at the tears on his cheeks, Bob said, "You're doing the right thing, Luisa. And you need to know that your father's arrest is not your fault. Please don't blame yourself."

Luisa's face crumpled then, and Bob stepped forward, pulling her into his arms. He didn't know how long they stood there, together, in an embrace. She had made her decision, and he knew it was the right one. No matter how painful it was for either of them.

"I will pray for him," Bob said. "It might sound like a small thing, but he can still find comfort in terrible circumstances."

Luisa nodded against his chest. "Thank you," she whispered. "Your prayers will mean a lot to both my father and me." She didn't release him, didn't move, and when her shoulders had stopped shaking and her body had stopped trembling, she said, "Will you write to me?"

"Of course," he murmured. "But what happens when you get a sweetheart and marry? Should I still write?"

She uttered a soft, shaky laugh. "A Christmas card would be fine."

Fair enough.

When she stepped out of his arms, he felt like he'd lived an entire lifetime in her embrace, only to return to the cold reality that once she walked out of the room, he'd never see her again.

Luisa, brave and lovely, lifted her tear-stained face to meet his gaze. "It's been an honor knowing you, Bob Inama."

"It's been an honor knowing you, too, Luisa Voigt," he whispered because he didn't trust his voice. "You are the bravest soul I know."

She smiled through her tears. "*You* are the bravest I know, so I guess we are equal." Then she stepped close again, raised up on her toes, and kissed him on the cheek. "Goodbye, Bob."

She moved swiftly to the door then, and after a final look at him, she disappeared from the hospital room.

He was suddenly out of breath, out of strength, and he sat on the bed for several moments, soaking it all in. It was as if part of Bob's heart had been carved out. It would take a while to heal, that he knew. He still had to sort out all that Luisa had told him about working for the underground. While he was in prison, surviving day by day, hour by hour, she was taking risks she didn't have to. Because of her heart, and her love, and her integrity. If Bob grew to be a little more like her, he'd be pleased.

Somehow the time passed, and when the afternoon had advanced to a dull-orange sky, he heard a tap on his hospital room door.

"Inama," Major Taggett boomed.

Bob rose to his feet and saluted the major.

Taggett gave him a hard look up and down, then he smiled and extended his hand. "Well done, Specialist Fourth Class," Taggett said. "I'd like to personally thank you for your service. You've done your country proud."

"Thank you, sir," Bob said.

"Now," Taggett said. "Do you have your things?"

Bob followed the major's gaze about the room. "I don't have any things."

"That's right . . . well, let's get a move on." Taggett strode to the door but paused before opening it. "I don't have to tell you that you aren't free to speak about your assignment, right?"

"Right."

"Only a very few know about it, and we need to keep it that way."

"Yes, Major Taggett."

Taggett paused again. "Oh, and by the way, Professor Schmitt died in a car accident."

Bob searched the major's gaze. The man's expression gave nothing away, but his eyes had hardened. That was when Bob knew that there had been no such "accident." Schmitt had met his fate at the hands of someone in the US Army. Bob supposed he should be glad, but he wasn't. Wasting another life didn't provide any healing. Bob had already forgiven the man, and now . . . the cycle of tragedy had continued.

"Let's go." Taggett pulled the door open and ushered Bob through.

As Bob walked out of the hospital, the fresh spring air swamped his senses. He had much to be grateful for. Much to reflect on. Many things to miss—dearly. Leaving the hospital and leaving Frankfurt meant he was leaving part of his heart behind. And it might take a lifetime to understand why he'd gone through what he'd experienced, but for now, he would put the past behind him, and live in the present.

The future would take care of itself.

CHAPTER THIRTY-SIX

"Come what may, and love it."

—Joseph B. Wirthlin

RICKS COLLEGE
REXBURG, IDAHO
DECEMBER 1975

"Merry Christmas, Professor Inama."

Bob looked up from the stack of final exams he was grading as the last student filed out of the classroom at Ricks College. "Merry Christmas," Bob said with a smile.

Josh was always the last to leave the classroom, and sometimes Bob forgot he was still there. Once Bob had started grading the papers for his political science class, he'd become caught up in the subject matter.

With Josh gone, the classroom was empty of students, and that signified the start of Christmas break. Bob supposed he could grade the final exams at home, but for a moment, he relished the quiet of the empty classroom. Quiet spaces and moments were hard to come by in his busy life. A busy life he loved, full of teaching at a small college in Idaho—a job he never expected to stick with. He also had a busy family life—his wife, Diane, had brought four children to the marriage, and now they had a daughter of their own.

Bob had never known he could love so fiercely and deeply until he met

Diane. After returning from West Germany thirteen years before, he hadn't expected to have a regular life. His goals and dreams of who he wanted to be before he was drafted had been left in the dust. He'd finished his master's degree at Utah State, although he hadn't known where to go from there. Then he received a phone call from Dr. Hugh Bennion, from Ricks College. Dr. Bennion came to visit Bob at Utah State and offered him a teaching job.

Bob's first instinct was to dismiss it. He had no plans to be a professor. What could he teach anyone? But he'd agreed to one year, and then that one-year agreement had turned into a career, and he'd never looked back. Especially after he met Diane. It was then he realized his past experiences had prepared him for the compassion they'd both bring to the marriage.

"Don't work all night," a friendly voice said from the classroom door.

Bob looked over to see one of his colleagues, wearing his signature V-neck sweater. This one in navy. "I won't if you won't."

The older man chuckled, and after they wished each other a happy holiday, Bob finally rose from his desk. He was still a relatively young man in his early forties, yet the aches from his imprisonment in East Germany had never fully gone away. Still, he couldn't complain.

He'd been blessed. Working at a small-town college kept his world concentric—exactly how he liked it. His colleagues were men and women of faith and compassion, which was another comfort to him. There were few people he trusted with personal things, and in this environment it was easier to trust.

Bob headed down the hallway to his office in the Political Science Department. Most of the lights had been turned off, and it appeared as if the department secretary had already left. Bob found a few letters on his desk that he'd take home and look through later. But first, he gathered the various Christmas cards that had arrived over the past couple of weeks. He'd take those home too. Diane would enjoy reading them.

He'd shared with her some of his experiences in Germany soon after they were engaged. She'd listened, asked a few questions, but had sensed he had said his piece. And he had. It was best to move on from such things. His parents and sister still didn't know about his prison time, and he never planned to tell them.

But there were good memories of Germany as well. Proof of that was in three of the Christmas cards. Bob sat at his desk and read through them a second time, a smile growing on his face.

> Inama,
>
> Hope you're enjoying that Idaho winter. You know you're welcome in Oklahoma anytime. The wife and I have a guest room and your kids will love the pond out back. But you've heard all that before. Come for your next summer break. We're adding a new member of the family in March. Darci is over the moon, although she says that I have to put off getting that dog I've wanted. We'll see.
>
> Merry Christmas to you and your family.
>
> Murdock

The memories of Murdock were unstoppable, and maybe Bob would take him up on that offer. Murdock had stayed in the army and now worked at Fort Sill. He'd had an honorable and distinguished career, and Bob couldn't be happier for him.

The next card had a picture of Tom Komori, his wife, and their son and daughter. Komori's son was an exact replica of Tom. Komori had scrawled a brief note on the back:

> Inama,
>
> Best holiday wishes to you and your family. Hope to hear from you soon.
>
> Komori

The next card gave Bob another set of memories.

Dear Bob,

    It's hard to believe another Christmas season is upon us. The twins have been counting down the days since October. Stephen is doing well with his dentistry practice now that he's on his own. It took a few months to build up clients, but he's enjoyed the independence.

    Father either putters around the garden or writes one of his histories. I think he's on his fourth volume by now. As for me, I've started back at the hospital part-time. I've enjoyed the time there but also want to be home with the boys when I'm needed.

    I wish you and Diane the very best this holiday brings.

        Tschüss,

        Luisa Voigt Sommer

Bob sat for a long moment in the silent office as gratitude filled him. He couldn't ask for anything more. His friends from his past in Germany were living happy and full lives. His own family was thriving. His gaze shifted to one of the framed pictures on his desk, of him and his Grandfather Inama.

Upon returning from Germany, Bob had taken the time to travel to his grandparents' home. There, Bob put on a slideshow of the pictures he'd taken in Sanzeno, Italy. Bob talked about the relatives he'd met and the good wishes they'd sent.

For a long time after the final picture was shown, his grandfather had remained silent. Then he'd risen to his feet and crossed to Bob. Pulling him into his arms, his grandfather had tenderly thanked him. Bob had never been embraced by his grandfather until that day. And even now, remembering it, tears filled his eyes.

Bob dragged in a shaky breath. Grandfather Inama had been gone for seven years now, only a year after his grandmother. With her passing, Grandfather Inama had lost his interest in life. It was as if without her, he didn't want to continue. If Bob hadn't been drafted, if he hadn't been assigned

307

to West Germany, then he would have never visited Sanzeno. And he never would have been able to strengthen that bond with his grandfather. A moment he cherished.

Bob straightened a few things on his desk, then rose and picked up the stack of new mail. He paused and flipped through a few of the letters and cards. Most of them appeared to be Christmas cards from former students. Some from colleagues at the college. He stopped on an envelope that looked a bit worn at the edges, as if it was an older letter or one that had traveled a great distance.

He soon realized it was the latter. There was no return address on the interior envelope, but the postal stamps were postmarked from East Germany.

For a moment, Bob stared. Then blinked.

East Germany.

How? Why?

His breath went shallow as he opened the envelope, careful not to rip anything unnecessarily. Inside was a single sheet of paper. The writing was in German, the words angled and sharp, and it was addressed to him.

The note was short, but when Bob read the words, he had to sit down in his chair.

> Bob Inama,
>
> I don't know if this letter will reach you, but I thought I'd write to let you know that I have never forgotten you, or the man you were. My family and I have joined your church, and once a month I fast for you. I often tell my children about your extraordinary faith and endless gratitude. You have my friendship for eternity.
>
> Adolf

Bob reread the letter a second time, the words swimming now through his blurred vision. He might never know Adolf's real name, but it didn't matter. The guard who had been silent for most of the six months of prison had been like a brother. Somehow, he'd been Bob's strength during the darkest time of his life.

Bob closed his eyes as warmth unfurled from his chest and spread through the rest of his body. He never thought he'd find complete closure for what he experienced in prison. He never thought he'd be grateful for the months of beatings and starvation. He never thought he'd ever have any desire to experience anything like that again. But now he did know.

He knew he'd do it all over again, if only for Adolf.

Because now Bob realized why he'd been arrested and why he'd suffered those months and why his life plans were ripped away from him. It was for his brother, Adolf. For Adolf's wife and children. Everything Bob had gone through had had a higher purpose. Every bit had been worth it.

Bob opened his eyes and turned over the envelope. There was no return address. No way to contact Adolf. No way to know his real name or location. That didn't change the fact that Bob considered Adolf his brother. They would meet one day, he knew. Maybe not in this life, but someday.

It was a while before Bob had collected his emotions enough to finish gathering his things. As he walked through the empty halls of the college building, he wondered about Adolf and his life. How long had he worked in that prison? Was he still a prison guard? The Cold War was far from over. The Berlin Wall still stood. The US Army was still stationed in West Germany. Bob might never have answers about Adolf, but he could still pray for the man.

Stepping outside, Bob walked through the empty parking lot as the gray Idaho sky released flakes of snow. The snow was soft and light at first, but by the time he reached his car, he knew he'd need to turn on the windshield wipers. The cold had no effect on the warmth emanating from his heart. His heart was full, overfilled, bursting.

He couldn't wait to show the letter to Diane.

As he drove through the streets of Rexburg, the snowflakes continued falling, reminding him of the day that he drove from Idaho to Logan to find a draft letter from the US Army in his stack of mail.

It had been sixteen years since that moment, almost to the day.

Bob could have never predicted the journey that was in store for him, but looking back, he saw the Lord's hand in every detail. Every frustrating, painful, bewildering, and joyful detail. By the time Bob pulled into the driveway of his home, new tears had started. He turned off the engine and gazed for a moment at the house before him. Holiday lights twinkled along the roof's edge, and the Christmas tree with its homemade ornaments could be seen through the living room window.

He could very well imagine the warm welcome and sweet aromas that would greet him the moment he walked inside.

Home. He was home. This was where he belonged. He gathered up his things and climbed out of the car. Then he headed across the driveway, holding the manila envelope with Adolf's letter close to his chest, over his heart.

"We made it through, Adolf," Bob whispered to the swirling snow. "We made it through." Perhaps somewhere out there, Adolf was looking at the same sky. And perhaps it was snowing in East Germany too. A smile played on Bob's face as he reached for the front doorknob and turned it, stepping forward into the rest of his life.

AFTERWORD

In September 2020, I had the privilege of meeting Bob and his wife, Diane, in their Idaho home. I'm not sure who was more grateful to meet the other person. They had already read the manuscript draft and said that I had captured Bob's personality throughout the story. I felt humbled to hear that, and I can only attribute it to our constant communications from April through July of the same year.

The question arises after reading a book such as this: what is fact and what is fiction? The story line that is exclusive to Bob runs very close to his experiences. I compiled about forty pages of interview notes with Bob, which I stuck to in every instance possible. From the first scene, where Bob is driving his Ford Fairlane, then arrives home to find a draft letter, to the final scene where Bob receives a letter from "Adolf"—they are all Bob's experiences.

Bob Inama, 1960

Throughout this book, Bob Inama's story is complemented by the character of Luisa Voigt, who is a fictional character based on a real acquaintance of Bob's in Frankfurt. Their earlier scenes follow the experiences Bob shared, but her character then deviates once her father is reassigned to West Berlin.

From that point on, Luisa's character journey is completely fictitious, although her experiences helping with the underground rescues are based on those of real-life West Germans who aided their fellow countrymen in the East.

Bob and his wife had compiled a short personal history that I also found useful in the beginning in visualizing how I should approach the scope of the novel. Since a historical novel isn't a memoir or a biography, the timeline is condensed. So with careful consideration, I had to decide where in Bob's life to start the novel and where to place the final scene.

During Bob's service in West Germany, the world was in turmoil, and much of the political strife centered around the actions of the United States and the Soviet Union—the superpowers of the world, who had nuclear technology at their fingertips. I spent weeks reading and studying the Cold War era, from beginning to end, in order to understand the scope and precariousness of Bob's undercover work.

The news that Bob received while recovering at the hospital in Frankfurt was devastating. His severe and continuous beatings had caused enough brain damage to reroute his plans of becoming a government lawyer. Bob found that teaching at a quiet college in a small town, surrounded by family, was his ideal career path.

Because of the nature of the Cold War and how long it lasted, Bob never shared his undercover mission or prison experiences with his parents, his grandparents, or his sister. He told his wife, Diane, some of the basics, but it wasn't until his daughter was going through a difficult trial that Bob decided to share the details of his experiences. He thought he could help his daughter if she knew how much he understood and could relate to emotional pain and turmoil.

When Bob shared with me the mercies that "Adolf" extended to him, I could feel Bob's love and reverence in his tone of voice. With tears in his eyes, even after all these years, this eighty-five-year-old man's voice broke as he explained how he'd thanked Adolf and told him that he loved him. The letter that Bob received from Adolf didn't survive the Teton Dam flood of 1976. Neither did Bob's thousands of pictures he'd taken throughout Europe. But the memories did survive.

Bob may never learn Adolf's real name. They may never meet in this life. Yet Bob Inama's story has certainly changed my life, and it has been an honor to share it with you.

DISCUSSION QUESTIONS

1. When Bob first received the draft letter to join the US Army, he was disappointed to have to reroute his life's plans. Have you experienced such a setback that wasn't of your own making?

2. Once Bob was at Fort Sill, hidden talents began to shine, which would become very valuable later in his undercover assignment. Bob definitely had hard days, but he seemed to make the best out of whatever situation he was put in. Why can this be so difficult to do?

3. While at Fort Sill, Bob became close friends with a Japanese-American soldier. WWII was nearly two decades in the past, yet Bob witnessed continued prejudice toward his friend. Why does it take so long for society to move forward from a painful past?

4. Being assigned to West Germany was another big change in Bob's life. Yet he also saw the blessing in the opportunity to travel around Europe and learn more about his Italian grandparents' heritage and homeland. Have you ever had the opportunity to travel to the land of your ancestors? How has your heritage affected your life?

5. From the beginning of their friendship, Luisa told Bob that her father didn't like American soldiers. Do you think that was a general statement or her father warning her against getting involved with one of them? Why?

6. When Bob was given his undercover assignment, another soldier was

given the duty to respond to letters from his family as if Bob were writing them. Do you think your family would notice something was different if you were in this situation?

7. Why do you think Bob accepted his undercover assignment so readily? What would you have done in his shoes?

8. Bob's grasp of the German language became very important when he went undercover. Not only would he be in physical danger if he was caught in his assignment, but he also had to navigate his way through a foreign country while speaking German. Would needing to learn a foreign language so quickly intimidate you?

9. Even though Bob's personality and character were quite different from that of Professor Schmitt's, Bob stayed amenable in order to keep his cover intact. Have you ever been in a situation where you've had to work hard to get along with someone you didn't connect with?

10. Bob faced many challenges; one of the greatest was being isolated from his loved ones, including his fellow countrymen. What beliefs did Bob draw on to make it through this dark period? What beliefs sustain you through challenging times?

CHAPTER NOTES

CHAPTER ONE

Epigraph: Anonymous (text) and William Bradbury (music), "We Are All Enlisted," *The New Golden Chain* (New York: Biglow & Main Co., 1866).

Bob Inama was drafted at the end of 1959. It was never a question whether he would go if drafted, but it was still something he had to wrap his mind around. Twelve years earlier, in 1947, President Harry S. Truman recommended to Congress that the 1940 Selective Training and Service Act expire. This meant that the military forces would be populated by voluntary enlistments. But when the level of military forces fell below the necessary numbers in 1948, President Truman reinstated the draft to aid in the Cold War. Men between the ages of 19 and 26 were then drafted for twelve months of active service.

Another change came in 1950 with the Korean War, and the draft expanded to men between the ages of 18.5 and 35, for terms of *two* years. In 1951, the Universal Military Training and Service Act was passed, and men between the ages of 18 and 26 were required to register. In 1952, Congress passed the Reserve Forces Act, which required every man who was drafted or enlisted to an eight-year commitment. Following a term of active duty, the soldier was put on reserve and could be called to active duty for war or emergency. Bob Inama was drafted during this time. (For a complete conscription timeline, see "Timeline of Conscription (Mandatory Military Enlistment) in

317

the U.S.," Newshour Extra, PBS, https://www.pbs.org/newshour/extra/app/uploads/2014/03/Timeline-of-of-conscription.pdf.)

CHAPTER TWO

Epigraph: Title 10, US Code; Act of May 5, 1960, replacing the wording first adopted in 1789, with amendment effective October 5, 1962, https://www.army.mil/values/oath.html.

On May 1, 1960, an American U-2 spy plane was shot down. The pilot, Francis Gary Powers, was flying over Soviet airspace on a mission from Pakistan to Norway. US President Eisenhower refused to apologize to Soviet Leader Khrushchev and refused to agree to stay out of Soviet airspace. This fallout between the two nations ended up halting the Paris Summit. Powers was convicted as a spy and sentenced to three years in prison and seven years of hard labor. However, in 1962, Powers was traded for the Soviet spy Rudolf Abel (see "U-2 Overflights and the Capture of Francis Gary Powers, 1960," Office of the Historian, Foreign Service Institute, United States Department of State, https://history.state.gov/milestones/1953-1960/u2-incident).

Later in May 1960, Eisenhower signed the Civil Rights Act of 1960 into law. The act expanded the enforcement powers of the previous 1957 act and strengthened voting rights by creating criminal penalties for anyone who tried to prevent people from voting. Included in the 1960 version was the authorization of court-appointed referees to help African Americans register and vote.

It was during this time of legislation that Bob Inama arrived at Fort Sill in Oklahoma. He reported to the US Army Field "Artillery Center of the World," where he was trained at the artillery fire direction center. In the previous months, at basic training at Fort Ord in California, Bob had become an expert with the M1 rifle, the carbine pistol, and the 50-caliber machine gun. At Fort Sill, Bob continued to hone his skills in reading topographical maps, coordinating targets, and plotting ranges. A video tour of Fort Sill during the

1950s can be seen on YouTube: "Fort Sill, Oklahoma in 1950s" (video), posted February 11, 2012, https://www.youtube.com/watch?v=Vm0S4QvvxE0.

Bob's friend Tom Komori is based on a real person, but his name has been changed. When they went to a restaurant in Lawton, Oklahoma, Bob saw firsthand how poorly his Japanese-American friend was treated. In Bob's own words, "We just walked in, when someone came up to us with a sewer mouth like I had never heard. He told my friend to get out. I was very upset for my friend to think that someone would speak to an American soldier in such a manner. I never went back to Lawton, Oklahoma again."

Today, on display at Fort Sill is "Atomic Annie"—an 85-ton, 84-foot long, 280mm motorized gun. This nuclear gun was created over a period of eight years, and on May 25, 1953, at 8:30 a.m., it was fired at the test site of the Nevada Proving Grounds. Three thousand military spectators, positioned five thousand yards away, watched as an atomic-artillery round detonated 524 feet aboveground. This might have been a milestone in military history—in nine seconds, a single shell had the potential to wipe out an entire enemy division. After the successful detonation of Atomic Annie, twenty more atomic 280mm cannons were produced, but none of them were ever fired (see "History of the Atomic Cannon," The Atomic Cannon, https://theatomiccannon.com/history).

Major Nelson is based on a real person, but his name has been changed. Bob remembered him as being about thirty years old, tall, and well built, with a heavy Southern accent. Major Nelson was well trained, and his priority was making sure his soldiers were prepared for whatever might come.

CHAPTER THREE

Epigraph: "U-2 Spy Incident," History, November 9, 2009, www.history.com/topics/cold-war/u2-spy-incident.

In August 1960, Bob Inama reported to the headquarters of the Seventy-Fifth Field Artillery of the Seventh Army in Hanau, Germany. Here, he continued his training, not knowing of the changes to come. Bob already had a foundation in the German language from his college days, and he was able to absorb the language more in Hanau since he was immersed in it on a daily basis.

Luisa Voigt is based on a friend of Bob's in Frankfurt. For the purposes of the story, Luisa is a fictitious name, as is her character development. Bob shared this: "I met a girl at a church [social in Frankfurt]. The German people met in the chapel, while the English speaking members met in the cultural hall. I saw her at church, but her father disliked American soldiers. I spent time with her at church and church socials."

CHAPTER FOUR

Epigraph: Patrick Wick, US Army Captain and Field Artillery Battery Commander, West Germany, 1970–1973 and 1977–1980, interview by Heather B. Moore, May 5, 2020.

Although WWII had been over for a decade when Bob Inama arrived, Frankfurt and the surrounding German cities were still undergoing renovations and being rebuilt after the devastating destruction from Allied bombings.

Luisa Voigt mentions a few historical attractions for Bob Inama to visit, including the PalmenGarten, which is a botanical garden over one hundred years old. Another historical survivor of the war is Haus Wertheim (Wertheim House). In fact, it was built during the Renaissance and survived both world wars. The Justinuskirche (Saint Justin's Church) is another survivor and at 1,200 years old is one of the oldest churches in Germany. The IG Farben Haus in Frankfurt was once Europe's largest office building and headquarters to the chemical company that supplied the deadly agent used in Auschwitz's gas chambers. After WWII, the building was used by the US government.

Casualties of WWII included one of the major opera houses in the world, Alte Oper. Originally constructed in 1880, it survived WWI with only minimal damage, but WWII turned it into rubble (see Mairi Beautyman, "The 10 Most Beautiful Buildings in Frankfurt," March 25, 2018, TimeOut, https://www.timeout.com/frankfurt/things-to-do/most-beautiful-buildings-in-frankfurt).

CHAPTER FIVE

Epigraph: "The Warsaw Pact Is Formed," History.com, November 13, 2009, www.history.com/this-day-in-history/the-warsaw-pact-is-formed.

Signed in Warsaw, Poland, on May 14, 1955, the Warsaw Pact was a treaty among the Soviet Union, Albania, Poland, Romania, East Germany, Hungary, Bulgaria, and Czechoslovakia. These Warsaw Pact members pledged to defend each other if one of them was attacked by an outside force. A unified military command was also established under Marshal Ivan S. Konev of the Soviet Union. The Warsaw Pact was formed in direct correlation to the decision made by NATO on May 9, 1955, to include West Germany as a member and to allow them to remilitarize (see "The Warsaw Pact Is Formed" 2009).

The man who Luisa's father worked for was a historical figure. Johannes Richard Reinhold Stumm was a German lawyer, and from 1948 to 1962, he headed the West Berlin police as police chief. During his term of office, the Berlin Airlift; the East German uprising of June 17, 1953; the Cuban Missile Crisis; and the building of the Berlin Wall in 1961 all took place.

CHAPTER SIX

Epigraph: The Marshall Plan, available on the George C. Marshall Foundation website, www.marshallfoundation.org/marshall/the-marshall-plan/.

Bob Inama arrived in a Europe that had undergone economic change, technological development, and infrastructure revitalization since the devastating effects of WWII, thanks in part to the Marshall Plan.

Led by Secretary of State George Marshall, the US State Department crafted the Marshall Plan, known officially as the European Recovery Program. The program was developed to bring relief to war-torn Europe, which was suffering from destroyed industrial centers, demolished agricultural production, and ruined transportation infrastructure. The United States was the only significant world power that wasn't in shambles, so it was up to them to help.

Sixteen nations, including Germany, were integrated into the program and received assistance through the Economic Cooperation Administration (ECA) of the United States. Thirteen billion dollars in aid, including shipments of fuel, food, staples, and machinery, were all sent to these European nations. "Marshall was convinced the key to restoration of political stability lay in the revitalization of national economies. Further he saw political stability in Western Europe as a key to blunting the advances of communism in that region" ("History of the Marshall Plan," The George C. Marshall Foundation, www.marshallfoundation.org/marshall/the-marshall-plan /history-marshall-plan/).

This plan, first introduced on June 5, 1947, helped grow the European economies, led to the formation of the North Atlantic Alliance, and was a precursor to the European Union.

CHAPTER SEVEN

Epigraph: Karl Marx and Frederick Engels, *Manifesto of the Communist Party*, February 1848, in *Marx/Engels Selected Works*, vol. 1 (Moscow: Progress Publishers, Moscow, 1969), 26–27, available at https://www.marxists .org/archive/marx/works/download/pdf/Manifesto.pdf.

West Germans and East Germans were treated very differently when crossing the East German border or the inner border between East and West

Berlin. Even before the Berlin Wall was constructed, the sector border was monitored, and East Germans were required to apply to the Ministry of Health for permission each time they wanted medical treatment in the West. There are countless stories of individuals and families who were denied medical care that was more advanced in the West or who were separated from family in ill health. This was the case with a woman named Frau Paul, whose critically ill infant son was transferred to the Westend Hospital in the western sector of Berlin. She and her husband were not allowed to visit him. "My husband and I decided to attempt illegally to leave the territory of the GDR," she stated. "I am not your classic resistance fighter. I was not even part of the opposition" (Funder 2002, 308).

CHAPTER EIGHT

Epigraph: George Orwell, "You and the Atom Bomb," *Tribune*, October 19, 1945, available at https://www.orwellfoundation.com/the-orwell -foundation/orwell/essays-and-other-works/you-and-the-atom-bomb/.

Bob Inama wasn't close with his Grandfather Inama, so Bob saw serving in Europe as an opportunity to strengthen this relationship. When he was given a two-week leave after about six months in Frankfurt, Bob planned a trip to Italy to visit Grandfather Inama's home village. "My grandfather immigrated to America around 1910. My Grandfather Inama was about 6-feet tall and of slender build. He wore a thick moustache. He was a hard worker all of his life. When my father and I went up to visit him, he always spoke Italian, which always made me feel left out of the conversation."

CHAPTER NINE

Epigraph: "False Claim: Nikita Khrushchev 1959 Quote to the United Nations General Assembly," *Reuters*, May 11, 2020, www.reuters.com/article/ uk-factcheck-khrushchev-1959-quote/false-claim-nikita-khrushchev-1959- quote-to-the-united-nations-general-assembly-idUSKBN22N25D.

When Luisa gets the news that her father is transferring to West Berlin, which is in the heart of East Germany, they both know their lives will drastically change. Following WWII, West Berlin was reduced to a city sectioned by the three Allied countries of France, Britain, and the United States. West Berlin was also completely surrounded by East Germany territory, which was Soviet-occupied and controlled (see "What Was the Berlin Wall and How Did It Fall?" Imperial War Museums, https://www.iwm.org.uk/history /what-was-the-berlin-wall-and-how-did-it-fall).

When Luisa is confronted by Greta and offered money for her silence, Luisa begins to step into the world of underground organizations that developed among West Germans who were dedicated to helping their fellow East Germans escape a controlled, miserable existence.

CHAPTER TEN

Epigraph: "The End of WWII and the Division of Europe," Center for European Studies, University of North Carolina at Chapel Hill, europe.unc .edu/the-end-of-wwii-and-the-division-of-europe/.

Bob Inama's dedication and skills stood out among his fellow servicemen. He worked hard to excel in the tasks he was given, and his careful attention to detail caught the attention of his superiors. Bob also had a knack for making the best of whatever situation he found himself in. He enjoyed his days at the army barracks in Hanau. A typical day consisted of eight hours of training, but unlike his other assigned bases, Bob was allowed to take leaves in Germany. He mostly walked or took trains when he traveled, and he was able to visit other countries such as Italy, France, the Netherlands, and Belgium. Bob recalled, "I loved everything about Germany. I loved the food, especially Wiener schnitzel. I loved the beauty of the countryside. I loved the beautiful alpine forests and the flowers plants. I loved the people, even the East German soldiers, who were only doing what they were told. I loved the beautiful old architecture. I loved the music."

CHAPTER ELEVEN

Epigraph: Winston Churchill, "Sinews of Peace" ("Iron Curtain Speech"), March 5, 1946, available at the National Archives, www.nationalarchives .gov.uk/education/resources/cold-war-on-file/iron-curtain-speech/.

Moving to West Berlin enabled Luisa to visit her grandmother. Even before the Berlin Wall was built, it would have been difficult for Oma to cross the inner border. And though the East Berliners were facing many difficulties, they were still tied to their homes and memories.

The city of Berlin became the final battleground of the defending Third Reich as the Allied forces forced their way into Adolf Hitler's final stronghold. Berlin was left in ruins by the time Germany officially surrendered on May 7, 1945. "RAF and US Airforce bombers had laid waste to more than 70 percent of the housing within a five-mile radius of its center" (MacGregor 2019, 9). In the days leading up to the fall of Berlin, German citizens had been ordered to grab their guns and head into their neighborhood streets. These citizens were boys too young to be conscripted into the military, and men too old to pass a physical acumen test. These young boys and elderly were now literally defending their homes. The Allies continued moving in with their armies, their tanks, and their guns, fighting street by street until they captured Reichstag, the heart of the Nazi regime.

Once victory was declared, the two million Berlin citizens were left to live in prefabricated shelters, and their once-beautiful city was divided into four sectors of occupation, each by a different Allied victor (see MacGregor 2019, 9).

CHAPTER TWELVE

Epigraph: Anna Funder, *Stasiland: Stories from Behind the Berlin Wall* (New York: HarperCollins Publishers, 2002), 239.

As Luisa Voigt sympathizes with West Berliners who have fled the East, she soon learns that things are complicated, and she might be in danger if she continues to help. Luisa's character reflects the myriad of West Berliners who risked their own reputations and safety in order to help their fellow citizens.

Everyone was being watched and controlled in East Berlin, and the GDR kept tabs on any ties to West Berliners. The GDR frequently searched homes and assigned informants to those they wanted to monitor. East Germany was called "the most perfected surveillance state of all time. . . . The Stasi (short for *Staatssicherheit*) had 97,000 employees—more than enough to oversee a country of seventeen million people. But it also had over 173,000 informers among the population" (Funder 2002, 57).

Underground publications such as *Eulenspiegel* were distributed secretly. Distribution was, of course, illegal. Some East Germans also wrote and published, sending their manuscripts to West Germany (see Funder 2002, 34). In East Germany, no one could print a brochure or anything else without permission. The Stasi became adept at tracing print material to individual typewriters (see Funder 2002, 173).

CHAPTER THIRTEEN

Epigraph: Bob Inama, interview by Heather B. Moore, April 20, 2020.

While in Europe, Bob Inama took about 2,500 photos of his travels. He looked forward to visiting his grandparent's home village. Bob recalled, "The things that I remember about Sanzeno are that it was right in the heart of the Alps. It was breathtakingly beautiful. In the center of the village there was a water fountain where people came to get their water. At the end of WWII, food was so scarce that the people were cutting the bark off trees and boiling it for food. There was a fire in the village after WWII that destroyed many of the buildings, so most of the architecture was not very old. My Grandfather Inama donated money to the Catholic Church to put bells in the belfry of the newly rebuilt church. There were two couples who had immigrated to Idaho, but later returned to Sanzeno. A few of the people who could speak broken English were very helpful to me. It was frustrating when I could not speak Italian and they couldn't speak English. David spoke very little English, but we still managed to communicate. They were most kind and hospitable. The things that impressed me most was the kindness of the people and beauty of the area."

When Bob returned from his two-week leave, his sergeant major told him that Major Taggett wanted to speak to him immediately. Bob recalled, "Major Taggett was an uncle of a good friend of mine, whom I had met at Utah State. I reported in, and he said, 'Sit down, Bob.' He called me by my first name, and I should have known then that I was going to be in trouble, because you are always called by your last name or rank."

CHAPTER FOURTEEN

Epigraph: Mark Ehrman, "Borders and Barriers," *The Virginia Quarterly Review*, April 1, 2007, available at www.questia.com/read/1P3-1256577881 /borders-and-barriers.

Luisa's father was a member of the *polizei* of West Germany. During the Nazi regime, the state and city police forces were controlled by the *Ordnungspolizei*, but that changed after WWII. The West German sectors were occupied by Allied forces, and military police were in charge of security. But with so many refugees, and with postwar hunger and poverty so prevalent as East Germans fled to West Germany, it became apparent that the military needed help at a local level. The Western Allies organized civilian police forces called the *Landespolizei*. On the Eastern side, East Germany created their own unified national force, called the *Volkspolizei* (see "Landespolizei," Wikipedia, https://en.wikipedia.org/wiki/Landespolizei).

CHAPTER FIFTEEN

Epigraph: David Clay Large, *Berlin: David Clay Large* (New York: Basic Books, 2000), 425, as cited in *The Berlin Wall: The History and Legacy of the World's Most Notorious Wall*, Charles River Editors, 2015.

As Luisa gets deeper into helping East Germans, she enters a world where the Stasi are watching everyone, listening to everything, and keeping files. Journalist Mark Wood, who operated in East Berlin during this period, said, "My flat was the only one on the block with a working bathroom. Needless to say, that did not stop the Stasi from bugging it. In fact, I was later told by an ex-Stasi operative in the 1990s that the flat had fourteen listening devices placed in the bedroom alone, as well as my phone being tapped. Two doors down my corridor was a Stasi-owned room, which was a 'listening center' for the whole building" (MacGregor 2019, 123).

The East Germans didn't know how much they were spied on by the Soviets and GDR until after the Berlin Wall came down and Stasi files were recovered. During the Cold War, millions of files were assembled, unbeknownst to East German citizens. Once the Berlin Wall fell in 1989, the Stasi rushed to destroy the records, shredding, then tearing by hand. A group of citizens stormed the building in the Lichtenberg locality of Berlin and seized the remaining documents (see "Stasi Files: German Plan to Transfer Files Sparks Concern," BBC News, September 27, 2019, https://www.bbc.com/news/world-europe-49847900).

Today, former East Germans can access their records and discover who had informed on them and what was documented by requesting to view their file from the federal commissioner at the Stasi Unterlagen Archiv (see "Access to Records," Federal Commissioner for the Records of the State Security Service of the Former German Democratic Republic, Stasi Unterlagen Archiv, https://www.bstu.de/en/access-to-records/).

CHAPTER SIXTEEN

Epigraph: Ian K. MacGregor, *Checkpoint Charlie: The Cold War, the Berlin Wall, and the Most Dangerous Place on Earth* (New York: Scribner, 2019), 115.

During the Cold War, in order to travel from West Germany to Berlin, train passengers had to show their IDs to Soviet officials. The trains traveling through East Germany were controlled by the Soviets, and the windows were painted over so the passengers couldn't see outside. The US Army was given permission to man one of the train lines, from Marienborn into Berlin, although the line belonged to the Soviets. The military used the track to transport personnel from the US, Britain, and France into West Berlin. As long as all passengers were documented with military ID cards or passports and "official Russian-translated 'flag orders,'" they would be left alone by the Soviet police. This did not always go smoothly, though, and sometimes the Soviet officials would try to board the trains and demand to check passengers. The United States refused to allow that and began to add military police to the train crews (see "Night Train to Berlin," Voices under Berlin: The Tale of a Monterey Mary, http://www.voicesunderberlin.com/BerlinTravel /NightTraintoBerlin.html).

CHAPTER SEVENTEEN

Epigraph: Max Hertzberg. "Stasi Tactics – Zersetzung," Max Hertzberg, November 22, 2016, www.maxhertzberg.co.uk/background/politics/stasi -tactics/.

Auerbachs Keller (or Cellar) is a historical icon in Leipzig, Germany. Built in the sixteenth century, the location earned a worldwide reputation because Goethe used it in his renowned play *Faust*. Johann Wolfgang von Goethe is considered one of the greatest literary figures of Germany, and he used to visit Auerbachs Keller from 1765 to 1768, when he was a student at Leipzig University.

When Bob Inama or Luisa Voigt traveled into East Germany, they found that the West German currency, the deutsche mark, had more purchasing power than the East German ostmark. In reality supplies in East Germany were limited and the pricing was controlled. For example, there was only one brand of ketchup in East Germany (Funder 2002, 268). The costs of goods might have been the same on both sides of the border, but the availability and variety of goods was significantly reduced in East Germany (see Thayer Watkins, "Currency Conversion for the Germanies with Unification," San José State University, https://www.sjsu.edu/faculty/watkins/germancurrency.htm).

Not only were Bob and Luisa on their own missions but they also had to avoid the Stasi's interest at all costs. The Stasi had various signals to communicate with other informers: "1. Watch Out! Subject is coming (touch nose with handkerchief). 2. Subject is moving on, going further, or overtaking (stroke hair with hand, or raise hat briefly). 3. Subject standing still (lay one hand against back, or on the stomach). 4. Observing Agent wishes to terminate observation because cover threatened (bend and retie shoelaces). 5. Subject returning (both hands against back or stomach). 6. Observing Agent wishes to speak with Team Leader or other Observing Agents (take out briefcase or equivalent and examine contents)" (Funder 2002, 6).

CHAPTER EIGHTEEN

Epigraph: Bob Inama, interview by Heather B. Moore, May 21, 2020.

Bob Inama began working and traveling with Professor Schmitt during the same time classes were in session. Bob recalled, "Classes were continuing to be held, so we usually left on Thursday and returned on Sunday. After the classes were completed, we would go during the week for several days at a time. He would schedule conferences to discuss the economic recovery, so we went to the places those conferences were held."

CHAPTER NINETEEN

Epigraph: Ian K. MacGregor, *Checkpoint Charlie: The Cold War, the Berlin Wall, and the Most Dangerous Place on Earth* (New York: Scribner, 2019), 165.

One of the inspirations for Luisa Voigt's actions in helping East Berliners came from Michael Hinze's experiences. In 1961, a West German named Michael Hinze worked with other college students to help get East Germans out of East Berlin. The plan was straightforward, and Hinze approached West Germans and asked for their passports. "We had no trouble getting hold of the papers," Hinze said. "People were more than willing to help others get out of there" (Funder 2002, 209). Hinze matched up ages, eye colors, and height to those they were going to help. "The passport holder would send off to the East Berlin authorities for a transit visa. At the same time, passport-sized photographs of the East Germans were conveyed across the border into West Berlin. When the passports came back to their owners with the visa stamped into them, the students took them to a graphic artist who inserted the photograph of the person trying to escape. The complete passports were then smuggled back to the East Germans wanting to leave" (Funder 2002, 209–10).

Hinze wrapped passports in newspaper and put them in the air vents of his car. He'd travel on a day pass into East Berlin, where he'd then deliver the passports along with other necessities that would make it seem like the East German was truly West German, such as Western brand toothpaste and cigarettes. Hinze also told them to remove the clothing labels that said, "People's Own Manufacture" (Funder 2002, 210).

CHAPTER TWENTY

Epigraph: Bob Inama, interview by Heather B. Moore, June 5, 2020.

Any map Bob Inama or anyone in the US Army would have secured wouldn't have had any military holdings or buildings on it. Author Anna Funder said, "I have a 1986 map of Potsdam in which the areas where there were Stasi buildings—anything from bunkers to multi-storey edifices to shooting ranges—are left blank. On another, a 1984 map of East Berlin, entire city blocks and streets in Stasi areas are simply not represented: they are pale orange gaps in the map" (Funder 2002, 196).

As Bob was plotting targets to send back to the US Army, they were being added to the Strategic Air Command (SAC) list. In 2015, the US Cold War nuclear target lists were declassified for the first time. "According to [the] 1956 Plan, H-Bombs were to be used against priority 'Air Power' targets in the Soviet Union, China, and Eastern Europe. Major cities in Soviet Bloc, including East Berlin, were high priorities in 'Systematic Destruction' for Atomic Bombings" ("U.S. Cold War Nuclear Target Lists Declassified for the First Time," The National Security Archive, The George Washington University, updated April 16, 2016, https://nsarchive2.gwu.edu/nukevault/ebb538-Cold-War-Nuclear-Target-List-Declassified-First-Ever/).

The SAC did stipulate that only lower-yield atomic bombs would be used against Eastern Europe. Several of the Soviet target sites were not far from Berlin, such as Briesen, Gross Dolln, Oraienberg, Werneuchen, and Welzlow. A nuclear bomb at any of these locations would have put Berlin in radiation danger (see "U.S. Cold War Nuclear Target Lists Declassified for the First Time" 2016).

CHAPTER TWENTY-ONE

Epigraph: Anna Funder, *Stasiland: Stories from Behind the Berlin Wall* (New York: HarperCollins Publishers, 2002), 57.

West Germans were not exempt from the reach of the GDR laws. West Germans who were caught helping East Germans escape were arrested and made to serve their time in an Eastern prison. Such was the case in an incident involving East German Wener Coch, who had been given a Western passport. The day he arrived at the railway station, he received a signal from one of the Western students—but this signal was to not get on the train. So Coch went home and later found out that the Western student had been arrested and sentenced to two years in prison (Funder 2002, 211).

Another East German couple was arrested, along with three Western students, and held at the Hohenschönhausen prison for five months before they went to trial. When the time for the trial came, they were all transported to

Rostock on the Baltic Sea, far away from Western media. The prosecutor's statement read: "The accused maintains connections with members of a West Berlin people smuggling and terrorist organisation which lures people out of the GDR" (Funder 2002, 223).

Many organizations in West Berlin aided East Germans who wished to escape into the West. In fact, most of the West Germans who spent time in Eastern prisons were accused of helping with escape operations. Some people turned helping East Germans escape into a lucrative business. Westerners would charge thousands of dollars per person, then arrange to break the escapee out of East Germany, by boat, in auto trunks, or by air (see Craig R. Whitney, "A Daring 'Underground' System Aids East Germans in Fleeing to the West," *New York Times*, August 20, 1975, https://www.nytimes.com/1975/08/20/archives/a-daring-underground-system-aids-east-germans-in-fleeing-to-the.html).

In some cases, the West purchased freedom for either East Germans or West Germans held in prison. In one couple's case, they were not released to the West but "dumped on the street in East Berlin with no papers. . . . Of the estimated 34,000 people bought free between 1963 and 1989 there are at this stage only nine documented cases of such cruelty, where the west paid hard currency and the east did not deliver the people whose freedom had been purchased" (Funder 2002, 229).

CHAPTER TWENTY-TWO

Epigraph: Ian K. MacGregor, *Checkpoint Charlie: The Cold War, the Berlin Wall, and the Most Dangerous Place on Earth* (New York: Scribner, 2019), 31–32.

Plans to build the Berlin Wall began around November 1958 (see *The Berlin Wall* 2015, 30). By early August 1961, rumors were already strong about materials being stockpiled "at various locations near or along the sector and zonal borders" (MacGregor 2019, 28). Adolf Knackstedt worked undercover for the US Army, and he observed, "Much of this materiel consisted of barbed wire and concrete poles. No one seemed to know the purpose of this. All this information was immediately reported through intelligence channels to our command, but it seemed as if no one was concerned or cared about these strange happenings along the 'Iron Curtain'" (MacGregor 2019, 28).

CHAPTER TWENTY-THREE

Epigraph: "1961: Berliners Wake to Divided City," August 13, 1961, On This Day, BBC, news.bbc.co.uk/onthisday/hi/dates/stories/august/13/newsid_3054000/3054060.stm.

On August 13, 1961, Berliners woke to a divided city. The inner border had already existed between West and East Berlin, but now it was fortified with six-foot-high barbed wire fences that had been erected overnight. In addition, train service between the two sectors was stopped, and road traffic across the border halted. Protesters on the West Berlin side gathered at the border, and in one area, they trampled the barbed wire. The protestors were immediately confronted by East German guards with bayonets. The guards didn't have orders to shoot, but that would change in the days to come.

During the week leading up to the early Berlin Wall, nearly 12,500 East Germans had fled. The GDR's actions were to stop people from leaving. Now, the tide was stemmed, but it was not cut off. East Germans would still find ways to escape. They just had a new wall to contend with (see "1961: Berliners Wake to Divided City").

CHAPTER TWENTY-FOUR

Epigraph: Ian K. MacGregor, *Checkpoint Charlie: The Cold War, the Berlin Wall, and the Most Dangerous Place on Earth* (New York: Scribner, 2019), 44.

Applying to leave East Germany was no easy task. It wasn't unheard of for the GDR to grant people the right to leave, but the "Stasi put all applicants under extreme scrutiny" (Funder 2002, 36). Although it was perfectly legal to apply to leave, the Stasi could view the application as a "statement of why you didn't like the GDR. In that case it became a *Hetzschrift* (a smear) or a *Schmäschrift* (a libel) and therefore a criminal offense" (Funder 2002, 36). Both were offenses a person could be arrested for.

Tunnel digging became one of the surer, although dangerous, ways to escape East Berlin. In 1963, a group of college students from West Berlin decided to dig a tunnel underneath the wall. Joachim Neumann spearheaded the digging of more than one tunnel. One tunnel began at a rundown bakery in the West and spanned the length of a football field. This tunnel, known as Tunnel 57, became the most successful escape route during the tenure of the wall.

According to Jessica Camille Aguirre, "Neumann, Kabisch and more than a dozen other men burrowed down 11 meters into the ground from a bakery close to the border, and dug a rectangular opening wide enough for one person to slither through on hands and knees parallel to the ground above. This continued under Bernauer Strasse, under the 12-meter-high wall, under a signal fence that activated an alarm when touched and under the so-called 'Death Strip'—a wide no man's land carpeted by steel spikes and overseen by floodlights and guard towers—until slowly slanting up toward the surface of the earth. The digging took five months, and it was grueling work. The men slept in the abandoned bakery for weeks-long shifts, piling up sacks of dirt in flour sacks and occasionally rinsing off the encrusted mud from their bodies with buckets of water" (Aguirre 2014). The tunnel, luckily, ended up opening into an old outhouse behind an apartment building. In all, fifty-seven people escaped through the tunnel before it was discovered.

CHAPTER TWENTY-FIVE

Epigraph: Thomas L. Hendrix, "Standoff in Berlin, October 1961," US Army, October 22, 2010, www.army.mil/article/46993/standoff_in_berlin_october_1961.

From the moment the Berlin Wall went up, East Germans used desperate measures to escape. The building entrance of Ida Siekmann's apartment was blocked off a few days after the wall went up because the front part of her building was now in East Berlin, even though her actual apartment was in West Berlin. Ida didn't see any other option but to dump her possessions out of her window and jump. West Berliners rushed to her aid, but she died on the way to the hospital. Ida's desperation and panic became a tragic predecessor for many others to come. Between 1961 and 1989, about five thousand East Germans attempted to cross the border. Many were successful, but for others, it was a suicide mission (see Blakemore 2019).

Ida Siekmann's tragic jump from her apartment window wasn't the only dramatic escape into West Berlin. Other border houses and buildings were used as escape routes until the East German guards forced residents out and sealed up the buildings. Two days after the wall was built, an East German border guard named Conrad Schumann leaped over the barbed wire and escaped. Harry Deterling, a train engineer, "stole a steam train and drove it through the last station in East Berlin, bringing twenty-five passengers and prompting big changes to the railroad lines" (Blakemore 2019).

In another incident, an East German soldier, Wolfgang Engles, stole a military tank and drove through the wall. He managed to escape and survive even though he was shot twice. Another desperate attempt was made by Hartmut Richter, who swam four hours to cross the Teltow Canal. Richter returned to East Berlin multiple times to hide friends in the trunk of his car and drive them across the border (see Blakemore 2019).

A couple of months after the wall went up, "East German officials had begun to deny US diplomats the unhindered access to East Berlin that was part of the agreement with Moscow on the postwar occupation of Germany" (see Leslie Colitt, "Berlin Crisis: The Standoff at Checkpoint Charlie," The Guardian, October 24, 2011, https://www.theguardian.com/world/2011 /oct/24/berlin-crisis-standoff-checkpoint-charlie). This didn't go over well with senior US diplomat E. Allan Lightner Jr, who was stopped at the Berlin Wall border on his way to an opera house in East Berlin. When the East Germans asked for his passport, Lightner refused to show it, claiming that they weren't Soviet officials and didn't have the right to check his passport.

Once General Lucius Clay heard of the incident, he ordered US Army military police to accompany the next American diplomat headed to East Berlin. This plan didn't deter the East Germans from asking for passports. So Clay then ordered M48 tanks to the border at Checkpoint Charlie. The Soviets didn't take kindly to the show of aggression, and they sent their own Russian T55 tanks to face the American tanks from the other side. For sixteen hours, from October 27 to 28, in 1961, these US and Soviet tanks faced each other, until Soviet leader Khrushchev agreed to allow military personnel and Allied officials unhindered access into East Berlin (see Colitt 2011).

CHAPTER TWENTY-SIX

Epigraph: Bob Inama, interview by Heather B. Moore, June 17, 2020.

Bob Inama had been careful in his undercover work. Regardless, Professor Schmitt somehow discovered the truth. To this day, Bob doesn't know how. He recalled, "One day we were driving to West Berlin, coming from Leipzig, East Germany, when we ran into a roadblock. It was a Soviet Union and East German roadblock. At first I wasn't really alarmed, but then before I even realized what was happening, I was ordered out of the car, hand-cuffed, and blindfolded. I realized at that moment something had gone terribly wrong. As I was led to another waiting car, Professor Schmitt said in German, 'Goodbye, dummy.' I realized then that Schmitt was a double agent, and that I was in a seriously dangerous situation."

When Bob Inama was imprisoned, he started calling one of the familiar guards "Adolf." Bob recalled, "There was an East German soldier who brought me food every day. He passed it through the narrow slot in the door. He never spoke to me, but each day I recognized his ring. So as a joke, I started calling him Adolf. Adolf was the person who took me up to the interrogation area, and most of the time he would help me back to my cell and put me on my cot." The guard never told Bob his real name.

On the other hand, Bob eventually broke and confessed his real name, rank, and serial number. In Bob's words, "After several beatings, I did reveal my real name along with my rank and serial number, 10423570."

CHAPTER TWENTY-SEVEN

Epigraph: Anna Funder, *Stasiland: Stories from Behind the Berlin Wall* (New York: HarperCollins Publishers, 2002), 268–69.

Money talks in many situations, including in East Germany during the Cold War. East Germans were not opposed to secretly selling people to West Germany for a healthy sum. They called it *haeftlingsfreikauf*. Historian Andreas Apelt said, "Between 1964 and 1989 some 33,755 political prisoners and 250,000 of their relatives were sold to West Germany, for a sum totaling 3.5bn Deutschmarks" (Gavin Haines, "East Germany's Trade in Human Beings," BBC News, November 6, 2014, https://www.bbc.com/news/magazine-29889706). The GDR needed money, and the West was willing to pay to prevent German citizens from being imprisoned. Both sides wanted to keep the trades a secret, "so the operation remained clandestine—people were traded in darkened nooks of the underground railway, the U-Bahn, or sent across the border in buses with revolving license plates. The number plates would switch at the checkpoints, so as not to arouse suspicion on the other side" (Haines 2014).

CHAPTER TWENTY-EIGHT

Epigraph: Anna Funder, *Stasiland: Stories from Behind the Berlin Wall* (New York: HarperCollins Publishers, 2002), 24–25.

Once the Berlin Wall was built, it wasn't long before the number of East German border guards was increased, and they needed to be well-equipped with weapons. "The new wall was guarded by the Grenztruppen, a quasi-military border police force" (Chris Eger, "East v. West during the Cold War: Guns of the Berlin Wall," Guns.com, November 13, 2019, https://www.guns .com/news/2019/11/13/east-v-west-during-the-cold-war-guns-of-the-berlin -wall). Weapons and gear came from surplus Soviet and WWII German army equipment. The PPSh-41 submachine gun was the main weapon, in addition to MPi-K AKM variants, Makarov PMs, and German-made Karabiner S SKS models.

When Bob Inama was in prison, the guards who were part of the firing squad carried Walther P-38 9mm pistols. The P-38 was a popular combat pistol in WWII as well, replacing the earlier Luger. The GDR also installed more than sixty thousand mines along the national border (see Eger 2019).

Bob Inama's camaraderie with his prison guard "Adolf" was certainly a blessing Bob hadn't expected. Bob recalled, "Adolf was forbidden to speak to any of the prisoners. It was against army regulations. He found me on my knees many times. I did speak to him when fasting to let him know I did not want food. Even though we could not speak to one another, we seemed to form some kind of connection or bond." For the purposes of the story, conversations between Bob and Adolf are fictionalized.

CHAPTER TWENTY-NINE

Epigraph: Ian K. MacGregor, *Checkpoint Charlie: The Cold War, the Berlin Wall, and the Most Dangerous Place on Earth* (New York: Scribner, 2019), 122–23, note cited on 316.

In a country where the Stasi collected items from people they were investigating to stash in smell jars, it's no wonder that Luisa Voigt and her father had to be careful. Smell jars were used to hold clothing samples worn close to the skin, often underwear or socks. The jar would be sealed, much like a jam jar, then labeled. The idea was that the Stasi could use trained dogs to track down someone they had stored a scent for (Funder 2002, 8).

CHAPTER THIRTY

Epigraph: Ian K. MacGregor, *Checkpoint Charlie: The Cold War, the Berlin Wall, and the Most Dangerous Place on Earth* (New York: Scribner, 2019), 18–19.

Bob Inama does not know the location of the prison where he spent six months—only that it was in East Germany somewhere. But the Soviets made good use of former prison camps run by the Nazis. Such was the case with Hohenschönhausen, and Nazi concentration camps Sachsenhausen and Buchenwald. Former military espionage prisoner Wolfgang Göbel remembered the bleak prison conditions in Hohenschönhausen, where he was reduced to a number. His cell was in the basement with no access to daylight and no toilet. Communication between prisoners wasn't allowed, and he was subjected to all-night questioning and not allowed to sleep during the day. This sleep deprivation resulted in disorientation and other neurological dysfunctions (see MacGregor 2019, 19).

In 1949, the German Democratic Republic was set up as a satellite state of the USSR. When the Soviets had control over the new GDR, they reconditioned ideologies and values—starting with the children. "Schoolteachers in the eastern regions were immediately dismissed because their job had been to educate children in the values of the Nazi regime. Socialist teachers had to be created" (Funder 2002, 162), and the doctrine of communism was taught.

CHAPTER THIRTY-ONE

· Epigraph: "Tunnel 29: How NBC News Funded Big Breach of Berlin Wall," NBC News, November 7, 2014, www.nbcnews.com/storyline/nbcblk5 /tunnel-29-how-nbc-news-funded-big-breach-berlin-wall-n242006.

Tunneling beneath the Berlin Wall was both risky and time-consuming. Many tunnels were started but not completed since the diggers were caught. In 1962, West German students received funding from American-owned company NBC News to dig a 131-foot tunnel beneath a factory (see Blakemore 2019). "The network agreed to finance the entire escape tunnel, paying 50,000 Deutschmarks—or roughly $150,000 today—for exclusive film rights of the dig" ("Tunnel 29: How NBC News Funded Big Breach of Berlin Wall"). NBC filmed footage of the tunnel and its escapees and planned to broadcast the story, calling it Tunnel 29. In all, fifty-nine East Germans got through before the tunnel was discovered. But the Kennedy administration was against broadcasting the documentary film because of the recent tensions from the Cuban Missile Crisis, as well as the ethics behind the operation and concerns for the safety of the students who built it. The footage that NBC shot in 1962 can be found on YouTube: "The Tunnel (1962) Full Documentary (escape under the Berlin Wall)" (video), posted July 4, 2020, https://www.youtube .com/watch?v=7E3T7eiSBsY.

CHAPTER THIRTY-TWO

Epigraph: Marcel Fürstenau, "Putting a Price on Freedom," DW, November 8, 2012, www.dw.com/en/putting-a-price-on-freedom/a-16159888.

Dr. Wolfgang Vogel was the GDR government lawyer over trading people between East and West Germany. He was in charge of negotiating the prices, which varied, according to the education of the individual. For example, someone with a doctorate would cost more to trade than a tradesperson. "The exception was for clergy—a pastor cost nothing because they were often independent anti-regime thinkers, and it was worth it to the regime to be rid of them" (Funder 2002, 38).

By the time Bob Inama saw the Berlin Wall again, the original stretch of barbed wire and wooden posts had been fortified. By the spring of 1962, buildings and homes had been demolished to create a wide berth around the wall, known as the death strip. In fact, when the line of the wall crossed into a cemetery, the bodies had to be dug up and the gravestones carried away (see Funder 2002, 257). "The wall went right through the centre of town, down Niederkirchnerstrasse through to the Spree River, and along its bank to the Oberbaum Bridge" (Funder 2002, 257). Bob would have seen the new concrete walls, the pipes laid on top to prevent escapees from being able to climb over the wall, and plenty of guard towers.

CHAPTER THIRTY-THREE

Epigraph: "Prisoner Exchanges across the Bridge of Spies, from Powers to Shcharansky," History, updated August 22, 2018, www.history.com/news /prisoner-exchanges-across-the-bridge-of-spies-from-powers-to-shcharansky.

When Bob Inama realized he was being released from prison, there was one thing he'd miss—his friendship with Adolf, a man whose real name Bob didn't even know. Bob recalled, "The questioning and beatings continued, until one morning when Adolf came into my cell and told me to shower and gave me clean clothes to put on. We then walked out to a car. I was ordered to get in along with Adolf. Once again I was blindfolded. We drove for what seemed forever to me. When we stopped, I was ordered out of the car; the blindfold was removed. In the distance, I thought I saw a US Army ambulance. I recognized the large red cross on the side.

"I was then ordered to walk toward the ambulance. For the first time I realized I was going to be released . . . set free. I felt enormous relief and gratitude, after months of not knowing what my fate would be, not knowing if I would ever see my family again, and knowing there was a good possibility that my life would be cut short. I knew I was going home!

"I walked ahead a few steps, stopped and turned toward Adolf. I then walked up close to him so he could hear in my broken German, 'I love you, my brother.'"

CHAPTER THIRTY-FOUR

Epigraph: "Remarks of President John F. Kennedy at the Rudolph Wilde Platz, Berlin, June 26, 1963," John F. Kennedy Presidential Library and Museum, www.jfklibrary.org/archives/other-resources/john-f-kennedy-speeches/berlin-w-germany-rudolph-wilde-platz-19630626.

When Bob Inama learned that he had brain damage, he knew he'd never be able to return to his former life, hopes, and dreams, which he'd held so close in the dismal days of imprisonment. Bob recalled, "Because of brain damage I had suffered during interrogation and beatings during my stay in prison, my dreams and goals of becoming a lawyer were crushed."

CHAPTER THIRTY-FIVE

Epigraph: John F. Kennedy, "Radio and Television Report to the American People on the Soviet Arms Buildup in Cuba," October 22, 1962, Teaching American History, teachingamericanhistory.org/library/document/speech-announcing-the-quarantine-against-cuba/.

When Major Taggett told Bob Inama that Professor Schmitt "had been killed in a car accident," Bob knew what the major meant. A convenient accident was a way to get rid of someone, on both sides of the wall. Herr Christian, a former Stasi member, said that when he failed to report his personal affairs to the Stasi, "I was scared I'd suffer some traffic accident or a mishap at work, or that in some other way a sentence would be carried out" (Funder 2002, 152).

CHAPTER THIRTY-SIX

Epigraph: Joseph B. Wirthlin, "Come What May, and Love It" (general conference address, Salt Lake City, October 2008), https://www.churchof jesuschrist.org/study/general-conference/2008/10/come-what-may-and-love -it?lang=eng.

When Bob Inama returned home to the United States, he was able to spend time with his Grandfather Inama. His grandfather had never been affectionate toward Bob because of a falling out with Bob's dad. Bob showed his grandfather the photos he'd taken of his home village in Italy. Grandfather Inama looked at the pictures for a long time, then with tears in his eyes, he hugged Bob. That was the first time his grandfather had hugged him. Bob recalled, "My Grandfather Inama passed away on October 24, 1968. He was eighty-eight years old. It was just about a year after my grandma died. After she died he had no interest in life. It seemed like he sort of willed himself to die." Unfortunately, the over 2,500 photos that Bob had taken while in Europe, as well as the letter from Adolf, were all destroyed in the Teton Dam flood on June 5, 1976.

Bob Inama reflected on the importance of the quote "Come what may, and love it" to him: "I got this quote from a talk given by Joseph B. Wirthlin several years ago. I was reflecting about my experience and was preparing to share my experience with a youth group. The thought came to me that this quote fit well with my life's experience."

SELECTED BIBLIOGRAPHY

Aguirre, Jessica Camille. "The Story of the Most Successful Tunnel Escape in the History of the Berlin Wall." Smithsonian Magazine, November 7, 2014. https://www.smithsonianmag.com/history/most-successful -tunnel-escape-history-berlin-wall-180953268/.

Baker, Frederick. "The Berlin Wall: Production, Preservation, and Consumption of a 20th-Century Movement," *Antiquity* 67, no. 257 (1993).

The Berlin Wall: The History and Legacy of the World's Most Notorious Wall. Charles River Editors, 2015.

Blakemore, Erin. "All the Ways People Escaped across the Berlin Wall." History, November 8, 2019. https://www.history.com/news/berlin-wall -crossings-east-germany.

Churchill, Winston. "Sinews of Peace" ("Iron Curtain Speech"), March 5, 1946. Available at the National Archives, www.nationalarchives.gov .uk/education/resources/cold-war-on-file/iron-curtain-speech.

Funder, Anna. *Stasiland: Stories from Behind the Berlin Wall.* New York: HarperCollins Publishers, 2002.

History.com editors. "Berlin Wall." History, updated March 31, 2021. https://www.history.com/topics/cold-war/berlin-wall.

Large, David Clay. *Berlin: David Clay Large.* New York: Basic Books, 2000.

MacGregor, Ian K. *Checkpoint Charlie: The Cold War, the Berlin Wall, and the Most Dangerous Place on Earth.* New York: Scribner, 2019.

"U-2 Spy Incident." History, November 9, 2009. www.history.com/topics /cold-war/u2-spy-incident.

"The Warsaw Pact Is Formed." History, November 13, 2009. www.history .com/this-day-in-history/the-warsaw-pact-is-formed.

ACKNOWLEDGMENTS

First and foremost, I'm grateful to Bob Inama. I have written many historical novels, but never one in which the main character of the novel was going to be reading the book. To say I was intimidated is an understatement. But what developed was getting to know a man who I can truthfully say is one of the most Christlike men I've ever met. We developed a trusty method of communication, which consisted of regular emails back and forth in which I'd send a list of questions, and Bob would reply. Bob's wife, Diane, was also a great help if any of the emails went awry, and I'm grateful for her diligence and support.

When I started researching this era, I knew I needed specific advance readers to make sure my research was correct, as well as to help me implement more personal and varied experiences into crafting the story as a whole.

I was blessed to have excellent beta readers, which included author Julie Wright, who is eternally sentenced to reading most of my drafted novels. Patrick Wick answered many questions in advance, and he agreed to read an early version. Patrick served in West Germany in the 1970s on two tours as US Army Captain and Field Artillery Battery Commander, so his comments were invaluable, and I'm grateful for his expertise. Author Donna Weaver also agreed to read the manuscript, and her experience serving in West Germany as US Army Specialist 4, Signal Corps, enriched the story.

My brother Scott Brown spent two years in Germany in the 1980s, and my niece Cassidy Clegg lived in Germany from 2018 to 2019. They were both helpful in detailing locations, food, and the atmosphere of the German cities. Thank you!

I'm very grateful for my agent Ann Leslie Tuttle's support and perceptiveness in editing this story. And many thanks to authors Rebecca Connolly and Jen Geigle Johnson, who were part of the sometimes-daily research efforts as I bounced ideas off them.

I'm blessed with a wonderful team at Shadow Mountain. Chris Schoebinger has spearheaded this project, and as I dove in, I continually marveled at his inspiration that this was a story that needed to be shared with our readers. Thank you to Heidi Gordon and Lisa Mangum for all of their work and support of this project. Thanks as well to Alison Palmer, who was the editor on the book and whose talent transitioned this story from my hands to yours. And many thanks to Senior Sales and Marketing Manager Ilise Levine, and the marketing team of Troy Butcher and Callie Hansen, for their work on my behalf at Shadow Mountain.

Finally, I'm indebted to my family for their continued support. My husband, Chris, and our four children, Kaelin, Kara, Dana, and Rose, as well as my parents, Kent and Gayle Brown, and my father-in-law, Lester Moore. I'm grateful for the journey we're all on together.